Our dad was a larger than life character and a fantastic, happy influence

"Sorry we couldn't get them in print while you were still here!"

Your three boys

About the author

"Allingham" 1936 – 2012

Allingham spent a happy childhood in Halifax the third and youngest child of William, a Welsh born policeman, and Winifred, a local Yorkshire lass.

Apprenticed at 16 to a local iron foundry Allingham's progression to qualified engineer was interrupted by two years of national service, serving as a subaltern in the 1st Guards Brigade. Qualifying as a professional engineer didn't limit his work experiences and over the succeeding decades Allingham travelled to over 65 countries, pursuing careers in public relations, local government, retailing, brewing and innkeeping.

Founding the journal Hong Kong Engineer before his thirtieth birthday and writing all its early leaders demonstrated Allingham's interest in writing, confirmed by a lifetime producing professional technical papers as well as writing, for his own interest, a series of short stories, light verses and other narratives.

In retirement and drawing on a lifetime of rich experience Allingham was at last able to work full time on his final opus: The Grey Haired Knights. This series of four whimsical fantasy novels tells the stories of four 70 year old codgers inspired by the spirit of King Arthur's Merlin to each undertake their own life-affirming Quest.

Published 2017

G2 Entertainment Ltd

ISBN 978-1-782-81-4283

Printed in Europe

The Grey Haired Knights

Four old men, all alike in dignity,
In vile rehab held long incarcerate,
All agree to forget infirmity,
Sense of age, and escape to face their fate.
The four together pledge, as Grey Haired Knights,
To go alone to seek a worthy quest,
A chance for them to put some wrongs to rights,
And then return with stories of their test.
In Avalon, King Arthur restless dreams,
Fearful that his story might be forgot,
He sends Merlin, to make sure the men's schemes
Will add to the legend of Camelot.
What this twelve-line synopsis fails to tell,
My stories of their ventures do full well..

Allingham

Book 1
Arthur's Quest

Prologue

After the Roman Legions left Britain, the dark ages that followed shrouded events from written record. However, during those dark troubled times, the songs and ballads of itinerant minstrels, together with the fireside stories told by father to son, kept alive memories of King Arthur, his Queen Guinevere, the Knights of Camelot's Round Table and the magician Merlin. Later the stories were set down in books as historical fact, romance, poetry, fantasy, stage musicals and film. Thus, for more than a thousand years, the legend has inspired men of all ages.

From the time of the great battle that destroyed Camelot, King Arthur lay wounded in Avalon, restless but immortal, waiting for his time to return and restore good governance to a corrupt world. His dreams of a new age of chivalry, by way of Merlin's magic, sometimes came gently into the hearts and minds of ordinary men.

The four books, 'The Grey Haired Knights', tell how this happened, at the beginning of the twenty-first century, to four men, at or near to life's dread marker of three score years and ten, who put aside their age and infirmities to follow a quest.

Chapter 1

Arthur Thomas, Tristan Edward, Percival St. John Matthews and Geraint Mostyn -Evans, all who were at or about the dread marker of three score years and ten, were easy in each other's company, although they felt incarcerated in the Laurels NHS rehabilitation unit, where bureaucratic incompetence had held them for far too long.

They were not to know then, nor were they ever to know, nor did they ever think to know, that Merlin, the magician at the Court of King Arthur would inspire each one to take on a quest worthy of the legend of the Knights of the Round Table.

Arthur Thomas, the eldest of the four men, left Scagill Grammar School with good O level results, sufficient for the Scagill Building Society to employ him with prospects of a good pension, plus promises of good rates for a mortgage when he needed one.

After he had worked for eighteen months for the building society, he was one of the last to receive his National Service call up papers. They required that he serve two years with an Infantry Regiment.

However, after he completed his basic training, he did little infantry duty. The army had to deal with paper work, not just active service. Consequently, because of his experience with the building society, Arthur served as a pay clerk. Aged almost twenty-one, his obligation to Britain's armed forces complete, he returned to his job with the building society.

Although he had seen no active or overseas service, army life had unsettled him. No longer able to tolerate working mainly with women, and determined to seek a more active life, he packed in his job.

For several years, easily bored, he failed to remain in any job for long. However, just before his thirtieth birthday, as a late entry, he joined the County Police Force. Shortly after, again with a good wage and secure pension, he married Jenny, his long-time sweetheart.

Jenny died, suddenly, childless, only two years after their marriage. Arthur thought he would never find love again. Shocked by his grief, he organised his life as a committed bachelor, rather than a widower.

Arthur was a romantic; romance was in his genes. By his bedside, he kept several books of poetry. Throughout his more than thirty years' service with the force, he had carried, in the breast pocket of his uniform, together with his police notebook, a slim volume by Rupert Brook. Thirty years of uniformed service roughened Arthur's skin; during the same years, it had given the book of poetry a soft patina of age. After he retired, he settled for a quiet life.

Most days he walked alone, far more than he had ever done on the 'beat'. He read a great deal, watched a little television, particularly the early morning programmes, as he preferred to listen to 'Radio Four' until 'Women's Hour' spoilt his morning.

Inspired by oil paintings by masters both old and new, his real love was to paint with oil paints, squeezed from tubes, mixed on his pallet to be applied with brush or pallet knife onto prepared boards.

When not able to paint with oils, he would use a soft pencil or even charcoal to sketch. He dabbled quite successfully with pastel but failed with watercolours.

Some five years after he retired from the police, with the rank of Superintendent, Arthur had a minor but debilitating stroke. His doctor and a stroke-specialist referred him to the Laurels an NHS rehabilitation unit. As expected, Arthur had made a slow full recovery.

Now, that you know enough about Arthur Thomas to make sense of how he coped with the sudden change to his life, I can tell you the story of his quest.

It had been yet another normal day of boredom in the 'Laurels' when Arthur Thomas said, "Oh crumbs! It's Salmon fishcakes again."

The dull old-fashioned expression of disappointment drifted across a round table in a low resigned flat sort of voice that did not have sufficient energy to be cross.

"Course it is you silly old sod, it's Friday, it's always crummy fish cakes on Friday, mostly crumb, some potato, very little fish. At least it has been during the interminable period that this gulag has held me incarcerated. Thursday is macaroni, Wednesday cottage pie, Monday mince, every day same as last week, week after week. It would not do to have variety here, it might over-excite us. This sharp almost estuary voiced rejoinder came from Tristan Edward, a slim, silver grey haired man, still thought to be handsome by ladies of a similar age.

He was one of the four men who sat at a table untidily set for high tea, with thin stainless cutlery, thick white pottery, individual portion paper packets of sugar, bunched together with 'sweetener', in a chipped white pot. Cheap single ply white paper serviettes, a plasticized tablecloth covered with glass, taken together with the lack of a salt pot, confirmed the Laurels institutional nature.

It was the dining room of Scagill Area Health Authority's rehabilitation unit, incorporated for reasons of economy with a geriatric care home.

The room where the men sat had twelve other tables, each occupied by four or six residents, almost all of them women.

13

All were certainly pensioners, some old enough to collect the extra pension that comes with advanced years.

A few men, left to live out their life alone in their own world, sat uncomfortably scattered amongst women residents who were hardly conscious of their presence.

"Roberts' you know, my late husband bought it for me." These petty requests were not real, just a predator's device to get into a one to one situation with any man. It did not matter which of the men a predator approached, it was merely a ruse to make another lady jealous.

Although Arthur Thomas, who was also grey-haired, could have taken exception to the expression 'Silly old Sod', he simply smiled benignly.

To anyone under thirty, Arthur was undoubtedly old, a pensioner for sure. He sat slumped in his chair, wearing a fawn coloured long sleeved knitted woollen cardigan with soft brown leather elbow patches.

He had stuffed both pockets with handkerchiefs, keys, notebook, ballpoint pen, and a small single bladed penknife, all paraphernalia required for his daily needs. A ballpoint pen was essential to arm him for his daily battle with both crosswords in 'The Daily Telegraph' and The Sunday Telegraph'.

He used his penknife to sharpen the soft pencils that he used to draw small still life details and the occasional cartoon of other inmates or members of staff.

The man who had been disparagingly rude to Arthur Thomas was silver-grey-haired Tristan Edward. Tristan had been an established resident in-patient before Arthur arrived. He called the Laurels, 'Ratchet's Retreat', after nurse Ratchet in 'One flew over the Cuckoo's Nest'; it was one of his favourite books.

He would never fail to tell anyone who would listen, that he refused to see the film, even though it starred his favourite actor Jack Nicholson.

"I don't want some two- bit American director to spoil my image of that Indian, or hatchet- faced Ratchet, no sir."

Taking the cure to come off more than one addiction, Tristan occasionally had tantrums. Each week an oxymoron increased his misery. The Laurels kitchen-staff, 'working to rule', or did not work on Sundays. The caring professions left it to low paid hospital porters, encouraged by double time payment, not by altruism, to bring in a mid-day meal in a heated trolley.

They could only do their best to distribute correctly more than fifty pre-ordered individual cardboard boxes amongst the residents, many of whom could not remember yesterday, let alone what they had ordered for today.

Each week a different porter, never seen during the week, dumped a boxed delight in front of each resident, a full twenty minutes before noon.

Tristan, who had never lost his love of good well-prepared food, always complained the loudest. One Sunday morning he made memorable to all residents. His meal hardly touched, he rose from his chair at the round table shared with Arthur, Geraint and Percival.

His gaze swept across twelve other tables that accommodated geriatric feeble frames hardly able to support their heads made light with atrophied minds. He declaimed rather than spoke,

"Which unmitigated two bit run down nationalised airline menu planner, who has obviously never been in a kitchen, inspired this reconstituted reheated pap, tells me that will you. My roast beef is grey. It is thinner, but it tastes the same as the miserable cardboard box in which the equally miserable porter delivered it.

The out of place Yorkshire pudding would not pass muster in Moscow. It was flatter than any blini offered in their gulags. The orange coloured gravy that smothered the plate did not move about, it clung about like a bad smell.

Horseradish was absent without leave. Lumpy mashed potato is a capital offence. In summer, Brussels sprouts are culinary treason."

On another occasion, Tristan behaved no better. Volunteer 'Friends of the Laurels' delivered Sunday Tea; sandwiches, jelly trifle with foamed substitute cream that did not even taste of fresh air, and a piece of fruitcake wrapped in cling film, all boxed in cardboard.

The caterers included in the box a folded moist plastic wrapped paper hand wipe. After the voluntary helpers had collected the cardboard and plastic detritus from the so-called tea, in black bin bags, Tristan had another tantrum.

He raised his voice to draw attention to an opened out hand wipe. "This object is a sham, a deceit, a miserable tissue of lies. It has a label that states it is a lemon scented hygienic hand towel. It is no bigger than a single sheet of army-issue lavatory paper. It smells as if the maker has impregnated it with the same olfactory offence used to scent the blue blocks put into men's urinals in football stadiums, or is it stadia, no matter.

It does not have an odour of fresh citrus lemon, not as we know it. It has the smell of that pernicious weed from Thailand, lemon grass, a stinkweed, more stick than grass. Why can't they use good natural home-grown perfumes? What is wrong with freesia, lavender, briar rose or even fragrant camomile?"

After his outburst, Tristan slumped in his chair, covered his face with a newspaper before he uttered, in a deeply wretched voice, "Dear God, why ever did you give us Sundays?"

The two other long-term residents in rehabilitation were Geraint Mostyn Evans and Percival St. John Matthews. They too each had a full head of grey hair.

Geraint Mostyn Evans found it particularly irksome that the NHS had locked him up with senile people, because he had a head wound that had caused some internal bleeding in addition to massive external bleeding.

16

Most of those responsible for his treatment were more concerned with the injuries inside his head than with the great tear in his scalp, or his fractured pelvis or his broken femur incurred in a spectacular car crash. He did admit, at first, that injuries to his head had upset the link from brain to tongue.

They made it difficult for him to talk. It embarrassed him when he sounded like a drunken Quasimodo having a bad day. For many weeks, the crash injuries had caused him problems with balance.

A minor paralysis also affected his left arm before the problems had slowly righted themselves.

The synaptic connections of his brain found other routes that left him with only a faint lisp and a slight pause in his speech when he had to start words with a hard consonant.

He could not understand why the Laurels managers repeatedly put off, with irrelevant platitudes, his suggestions that he was ready to go home.

Percival St. John Matthews had been a resident of the Laurels rehabilitation unit for eleven weeks, learning to walk again. Eleven weeks when he had come to hate the way his physio would cajole him each day, "Come along Mr. Matthews, step up, step out, Douglas Bader played golf you know, after he had both legs amputated, not just a few toes."

He felt uncertain of his future away from his own home, his refuge. As an archivist and teacher, words were his life. It irritated him that he was captive in what he had once called, "This bowdlerised back water of bad grammar, distressed syntax, poor pronunciation, punctuation and pluralistic pleonasm."

He thought women carers the worst offenders. They ended every sentence with a rising inflection. "Weren't you hungry dearie?" or "You OK luv?' brooking no denial, as they swept past without eye contact.

It grieved Percival when younger assistants would call out, "That's right Percy, you just sit quietly with your book; a nice little read will do you good." "Fowler help me," he would cry out in anguish, not aloud, but to himself, "I have never answered to Percy. I doubt if any of you have ever read a worthwhile book in your life. Mills and Boon, the Daily Mirror or the Sun's TV guide, plus perhaps a weekly bingo card, are your complete canon."

The major problem that affected all four men was that the managers did not run the small rehabilitation unit, as a completely separate entity. They ran it as part of a much bigger geriatric care home.

Overheated, over carpeted, over regulated and overpopulated; it bore down on the well and nearly well in rehabilitation until they felt trapped, institutionalised. The unmistakeable smell of urinary incontinence, combined with the odour of badly cooked food that no amount of air fresheners or Lysol could ever truly mask reinforced the feeling that the Laurels held them' prisoner.

The institutionalised days of all four men had settled even their independent spirits into a routine. Each day started with breakfast served so early that there was no conversation, just newspapers to read.

By nine o'clock, each weekday morning professional staff kept them busy with therapy of one sort or another. After lunch, the main meal of the day, an hour or more therapy followed by cards until tea.

After tea, time spent watching television invoked soporific stupor only broken when they shook themselves alive to go to bed, where sleep was a fitful companion.

Unbeknown to the four men, the fateful change occurred on the Sunday evening that followed Arthur's complaint about Friday's fish cakes.

They were about to start a second rubber of bridge in an anteroom of the Laurels when they were disturbed by an unexpected appearance of what Arthur thought must be a newly admitted geriatric. He was possibly one of the strangest men he had ever seen in all his years as a policeman, during which time he had had to deal with people of types too varied to catalogue.

The stranger stared into the room through the glass in the door; however, he did not attempt to open it. He gave a shy smile that Arthur presumed to be a genuine gesture of recognition when he pointed his thin black walking stick straight at him, while he waved his left hand and slowly nodded his head.

Arthur thought, for a moment, that the old man, apparently satisfied they did not want to be disturbed had somehow faded away, not gone away. Geraint said, "Good God I would not like to have to share a room with whatever that was. He reminded me of the kitchen god figures I saw in restaurants in China. Only a Chinese sage or a Welsh wizard could grow a beard like his."

Tristan said with asperity, "I hope it is a kitchen god, we only seem to have kitchen goddesses here in the UK. Our present lay cook one has no soul. We need a wizard to produce good food from the crap ingredients sent by the NHS central purchasing depot."

The worrier amongst them, Percival, who thought that it might have been rude not to open the door for him, said, "If he is new, perhaps he is lost, poor chap, shall I go to find him Arthur?" Tristan said, "Sit down Percival, he will be alright, I don't think he is so old that he has lost his marbles, his eyes were too bright behind those peculiar glasses."

Boredom had reduced Arthur's mind, from one usually full of ideas, some shrewd, some daft, often romantic, occasionally dire, to an almost blank state. Even his determined attempts to stave off dementia with reading, regular card games and cross-word puzzles did not seem to stop the onset of senility, a state where thoughts are only of what has past, never of what is yet to come. He was therefore confused, when a simple idea came to him, an idea that seemed so important that he had to stop, half way through dealing the cards, to share it with his friends.

Arthur looked carefully, in turn, at his three companions who all looked a bit puzzled, although they did not comment. He spoke slowly, as he gathered his thoughts, "Nah then lads, I don't know where it came from but I have just had an idea. Perhaps the old fellow who peered at us through the door just now made me think that we might all have wasted the last few weeks of our time here.

I know that every day in this dreadful place we are bored stiff, neigh unto rigor mortise. I am sure that you will agree that Sunday is the nadir of our week." Encouraged, as their puzzled look turned to interest, Arthur went on. "Well I don't want to die just yet a while, so perhaps we should not watch television or play cards on Sunday evenings. We could give ourselves hope if we told stories. Scheherazade saved her life by the stories she told for a thousand and one nights.

Well, I hope that we will not need so many stories, or even a fraction of the hundred stories in the ten-day Decameron before we are all discharged from this bleak branch-line siding off life's main line in which we are presently parked."

Tristan interrupted, "Good idea Arthur, I am sure that when we were schoolboys we all read those well fingered rude bits in Chaucer's twenty four Canterbury Tales. They certainly kept the pilgrims entertained."

Arthur resumed, confident that he had their support. He told them that he had noticed the coincidence that they all had given names made famous by the legend of King Arthur's Round Table. He told them that this quirk of their names had given him another idea that he would like them to consider.

Arthur was a bit embarrassed when he suggested that they should form themselves into an informal club, or association, whose name, because of the coincidence of their names, should have a Camelot connection.

He said, "The sole aim of the club will be similar to the British entertainment committees in German prisoner of war camps; to help each of us to survive our incarceration until liberation."

Geraint Mostyn Evans laughed, "We should call ourselves 'The Grey Haired Knights'. If I remember right, in Malory's tales there was a Black Knight, a Red Knight, as well as the weird severed head Green Knight whose challenge Gawain accepted. We already sit together at this round table, although it is a bit small for our purpose, all equally grey and extinguished. However, I fear that we are in need of a little polish if we are to live up to the Arthurian dream."

Tristan said quickly, as he smoothed back his hair with his right hand, "Silver and distinguished, if you don't mind."

Arthur suggested that, as it was his idea, he should take first knock at telling a story. In his magisterial way, he decreed that they would have to draw straws to decide who would take the next turn.

Tristan said, "Well, I'm up for it; it has to be better than the programmes that Sunday TV offers." His life had been virtually TV free, because his work in hotels, bars and cruise ships had meant he was almost constantly on duty.

Percival, fussed as usual. He wondered if it was wise. He asked, "Should we not ask Mr Harris, the Manager."

Very kindly Geraint said, "Shut up mouse, it is a good idea. I have always held that men do not die of heart, liver or kidney failure, it's boredom that makes them drop off this mortal coil." "Well said," replied Arthur. Percival formally seconded Arthur's proposal, even though Arthur had not made one, as such.

Even so, there was a general grunted affirmation. None of the men realised the import of their decision.

"Alright then, cards away, settle down and I will begin," Arthur said. Although he told a story in his well-modulated, easy-going manner, he felt inspired. He had never before been able to command the attention of men with such compelling ease.

He took an incident from his police work when he had been in command of a search, almost a manhunt, when he had found and disarmed a soldier who had gone absent without leave, taking with him a handgun and a grenade. He wove into the story, a foggy wet moorland search, fear, euphoria, comedy and tragedy. The effect on his listeners was profound. They saw Arthur in a new light.

At the dictate of a short straw, each man took his turn to tell a story on the following three Sunday evenings. Each man felt strangely at ease, even inspired as he told his story.

Chapter 2

The June bursting out all over Sunday had made incarceration intolerable to Tristan who had had another of his Sunday tantrums. He had harangued the old ladies at their lunch tables. He called on them to rebel, to throw away the boxed coronation chicken. He declaimed, "It looks and tastes like nothing more than baby puke."

He pleaded for meat, red meat fit for a man to eat. In tones to raise a riot, he railed at them, "Rise up you barmy old bats, put down your knitting, your spectacles, your large print Barbara Cartland novels.

Pick up your pinafores, get yourselves back to the kitchen; stew, bake, broil, fry or preferably grill bloody great steaks, for everyone." Only when he noticed the duty carer enter the dining room, clearly alarmed by his tantrum, did he switch to his well-practiced professional charm.

He changed from a voice that hectored, to his smooth pseudo laidback upper crust accent, "By 'bloody', of course I mean 'rare' ladies." Following this outburst, he collapsed back into his chair, covered his face with a newspaper and groaned, "Oh God, let me free, let me go, let me die. I can't face another bloody Sunday."

Tristan, Percival and Geraint arrived at the anteroom within a minute or two of half past six, eager for Arthur, the retired police superintendent, to tell them another story. It was his turn again, after the stories they had told in turn, decided by the short straw.

They were pleased to see him already seated relaxed, comfortable, in his favoured chair. On this occasion, they could see that he had a notepad on his knee, on which he had prepared notes.

They assumed the notes might be an aid to his story, something he had not needed before. It increased their anticipation of the story that they were sure would break the monotony of a dull day, that only Tristan's tantrum had broken.

After he had asked Geraint to lodge the spare chair against the door, to prevent any interruption, Arthur's relaxed expression changed to one of quiet determination. "Na then lads," he started,

"I am at a bit of a loss. I know that it is again my turn to amuse you with an anecdote or two, but I don't think that I can do it. You all know that the psychoanalysts, the shrinks, brought me here because a bobby found me wandering at night, far from my home. I did not know who or where I was. I was lost to all cognition of normality, of time, or purpose. I had no memory. After Geraint's fantastic account of real life pirates that followed Tristan's tale of London low life villains, and Percival's magical mystery story of Pan Pipes and lost love, I realised that I would have to tell a very good yarn to keep you interested.

Last Sunday, after Geraint's story, I did not go to my cot, as I said I would. I found a quiet corner to think. I picked up this notebook to jot down a few of my better memories that I might embroider to use this evening. It was no use; my mind was as blank as an English hangman's appointments diary. I was concerned that I had had a relapse. I could not remember any story, event or court case of mine, or any tale my colleagues used to tell. I was worried. I felt compelled to do what I had often done after Jenny died, to go for a night walk, a time to think. I thought that if I got back on the beat, as it were, back to the scenes of funny incidents, and the excitement of crimes past, the memories would come back to me.

I waited until all was quiet before I let myself out through the kitchen door. You may remember; it was a warm dry night. I walked the three miles up to the moors at Halter Top, still unable to remember a suitable tale to tell you about what happened, before or during my thirty-five eventful years in the force. There was a near to full moon, the air was clear; no dark shadows to make me nervous, but by God the little chap who seemed to materialise from nowhere made me jump. My memory was still defunct, devoid of fact or fiction. I had always had a good memory for a man's name, face, build, voice or vice. Policemen can always remember a man's criminal proclivity. I could usually get at least three out of five when I was still in the force, always the voice, always the vice, and usually at least one of the others. I did not know the man by any of the five staples of recognition.

This chap knew me, though. 'Escaped have you Arthur?' he said, 'Good idea that.' His voice I should have remembered, it had as many alarm cheeps and squeaks, as a broody grouse under a hovering hawk. His build was so unusually slight, his shoulders so narrow that even in sunlight he would hardly have cast a shadow. Had I met him before, I would have recognised him in the dark at fifty paces. Although he came along with me, in no way could he fall into step. His gait was more of a hop, skip and a jump than my policeman's steady tread. What made it more peculiar, he chose to do it, backwards, to look me in the face. His face was unique, somehow ageless, but at the same time as old as the rocks on Halter Moor. His opaque eyes looked at me over broken rimless bottle thick spectacles held on his beaky nose with tape.

His moustache drooped over his beard that was so white, long and thin I thought it might be the white mist, or that he might be that strange fellow who peered at us through the door to this room, before I started to tell my story, what is it now, four weeks ago?

As we walked, I told him I had come out to clear my head in the cool night air to enable me to remember stories about my past life as a policeman. He gave me a real shock. He challenged me, abruptly, almost angrily.

He said I must stop harping on about events that had passed. He was adamant that as I could not control the past, I should plan what I could do in the future, not fret or brag about what I had or had not done in the past. He raged; he went on vehemently to argue that the past is complete it cannot be altered, even though modern television historians try to impose modern mores and values on past events.

He told me that if I put my mind to it, I could do great things, with the rest of my life. I could become part of a new order, a new age of chivalry, a present Camelot.

I am not sure how it happened; perhaps I lost the path. Whatever I thought I had talked to, or dreamt about, faded into a mist that formed. I do not even know whether the mist was in my mind, or if it was the usual night ground mist of the moor.

Whatever, his disappearance bothered me almost as much as his sudden appearance. Moments later, either he was back, or I was hallucinating. I had four sprigs of white heather in my hand. A voice without a body said, 'Better than rosemary for remembrance'

I don't know why, but whoever or whatever it or he was, the mention of Camelot gave me an idea better than any story I could tell. No Tristan, before you ask, I did not dream it all in my cot. I still have the four white sprigs of heather. Whether I picked them or had them given to me is beyond my recall. When I finally got back to the Laurels, I was cold; my clothes dew damp, my shoes covered in peat from the moorland track. I had to wait behind the manager's garage until the breakfast lady turned in. The kitchen door had locked behind me when I let myself out.

26

Whether it was a manifestation triggered by the many thousand misdirected synapses of my brain, a hallucination, or a dream, my strange companion of the night fixed in my mind an idea I would like you to consider, as I have considered it all week.

I think Tristan's disgraceful behaviour this lunchtime confirmed my decision to leave this place; come what may.

His outburst reminded me of an idea that has been at the back of my mind for a few weeks. Tristan's tantrum, his call for meat, his desperate groan of an unhappy man on the -point of giving up, reminded me of a film I saw, years ago. I can't remember what they called it. I know that it starred Burt Lancaster and that other fellow, the one with the dimple in his chin. Well, after a long time spent in prison for robbery, when the Burt Lancaster character had completed his sentence, the state government had to release him into society.

Because he was old, with no family, or anywhere to go, they put him in an old folk's home; a bit like the geriatric wing here. Despite his age, the man was still a natural born hell raiser. He got all the old folk to riot, to bang on their tables with upturned knives, to shout, 'We want meat, we want meat'. He broke out of the home, teamed up with his old cellmate, the Kirk Douglas character, yes, that was the other one.

They had one hell of an adventure. It rejuvenated them both. If my memory serves me right, they successfully robbed a bank. To make their getaway, they stole a huge steam locomotive that they crashed through the buffers at the end of the railway line, over the Rio-Grande, to freedom in Mexico.

Well, Tristan, I don't think that I can suffer another 'Bloody Sunday' as you called it, not in this place of progressive forgetfulness that fosters slow decline. The mental degeneration caused by incarceration in this so-called rehabilitation clinic cancels out any improvement to our physical health. On balance, I don't think that it is doing us any good. I, therefore, propose that we should follow the example of the two characters in the film by leaving this place. We must break out, escape; flee if we have to. Like those old boys in the film, we could have ourselves an adventure."

"What?" Percival almost trembled, "You mean we should become a gang of desperadoes, I could not take part in such a madcap idea." "No Percival," Arthur replied calmly, "Our adventures need not involve violent or criminal behaviour," "I rather thought each one of us should commit to an adventure of his own. We could meet up again, after a year, to spend a weekend together. We would surely have a few more up to date yarns to tell; who knows, we might set off again to gather up some more tales. As far as I know, none of us has any commitments.

I'm sure that we all have a bit of money from our pensions, plus a bit that we might have put by. We all seem to be fit enough, one way or another. Only the bureaucratic incompetence of the Laurels' management detains us. It is their fear that we might sue them for some spurious reason if they discharge us before they correctly complete all necessary paperwork or fail to record their compliance with approved assessment procedures.

They live in fear of aggressive civil division lawyers who ape their cousins, the attorneys at law, in America who employ scouts to chase Ambulances. Our health does not come into it, only their procedures.

I suggest that we use the week to come to get some cash together, write to our families, what is left of them, to tell them that as the Laurels have discharged us A1 20-20 fit, we have decided to take a long holiday. We can make whatever arrangements we feel necessary before we move out, next Saturday afternoon, in six days' time, to meet up at the Crown Inn in town.

I propose we have a slap up dinner before we set out for a new life, on the Sunday Morning. By the way, it will be the twenty-first day of June, the Summer Solstice, the longest day. Are you up for it?"

There was absolute silence from Arthur's audience of three.

It was as though he had cast a spell on each of them by his audacious proposal. Each man was busy, extrapolating the idea to see how it might fit with the complex ramifications of their personal affairs.

Intrigued by Arthur's idea they tried to foresee all possible consequences.

Arthur let the silence go on. He understood their several disparate reactions. His observation pleased him. He saw brightness return to dulled eyes.

He noticed that they stiffened their backs, broadened their shoulders and held their heads higher.

He recognised their raised pulse rate because it brought colour to their faces. In one brief moment, they had changed from incarcerated neo-zombies, with little hope, to sentient males, men with a future.

"I take it from the change in your demeanour that the idea does not fall on barren ground. Shall I go on?" Arthur asked, delight reflected in his tone of voice.

The idea immediately drew a response from Geraint, the engineer, "Indeed yes, yes indeed. I would like to travel abroad again. Since my accident forced early retirement, I have allowed myself to go stale. This place does accelerate the onset of Alzheimer's. Mind you, with Rolls-Royce not there to pay expenses, travel might be a tad different. No matter, I am sure I can find a way. With the Iron Curtain rolled up and packed away, there are all of the Capitals of the Hapsburg Empire to visit. I have often hankered to have a good look at Turkey, particularly the land beyond Ankara up to Erzurum, towards the border with Iran, Iraq and Armenia.

I want to find out for myself just how European are the people there, not just the politicians. Mind you, I will also miss my quiet life aboard 'Hebden Home', my narrow boat on the cut.

Before I explore the European Capitals or Turkey, I will aim to spend a little quality time in the Mediterranean. I will re-visit Bordighera, where, as a young man, I spent my first holiday abroad. I quite fancy a spell on one of those luxury yachts that never seem to leave the marina in Monte Carlo, Nice or San Marino."

Tristan spoke next, "I shall certainly have a flutter on this one. I fancy a return to the 'Smoke' to see what I can do there. This time, it will be for me, only me, not for a bunch of unknown shareholders who wouldn't know how to box the sheets of a bed corner, silver serve a smoked salmon, fry, poach, coddle, boil or scramble an egg, fillet a fish, or mix a Bloody Mary, a Screwdriver or shake a Martini. No, I've learned my lesson I will be banker or bookmaker, never again the clerk, or the punter."

Arthur turned to look at Percival, the most nervous of the three, who had slumped deep into his chair, the recent colour drained from his cheeks, the spark faded from his eyes. "What's the matter Percival, cat got your tongue?"

"Well no; oh dear, don't you see, I don't know what to say, don't get me wrong, I mean, really, I have always led such a quiet ordered life. It will soon be the annual general meeting of the Antiquarian Society. If I don't go -" Tristan cut in, "Well, if the AGM of that august learned Scagill Society is so crucial to the turn of world events, you have no choice."

Tristan changed from his sarcastic hectoring, to say, quietly, "Come on Percival, Arthur is right; we all have a bit of time left to change this grim existence before our lifeline runs out. Some of our greatest adventurers were antiquarians, Elgin, Burton, Lawrence, not that scruffy D. H. fellow, I mean him of Arabia.

Somewhere in this world, there is a book, some obscure first edition, or manuscript you could discover. Maybe that could be your adventure, your quest. Percival, whose name you carry, was the most saintly of Arthur's Knights of the Round Table. His quest was to seek for the Grail. Perhaps yours lies hidden, waiting for your scholarship to reveal it. Maybe it is in a library in Trincomalee, Timbuktu, or Tibet; who knows?"

Geraint, the Engineer, who also believed Percival to be a doubtful starter, framed a different picture.

"You know Percival, whatever we say about this dreadful rehab place, it is many times better than the geriatric wing. Over there, death is expected. Death boldly walks its corridors; it comes often, usually as a welcome guest, always as a relief to all, to the newly dead, to the bereaved, to the carers. You have already had one serious close encounter with death. That gangrenous part of your foot was already wholly dead. The surgeon cut it away, to give you life. You can already walk pretty well. If you use one of those new battery powered pavement chariots, you will be able to trip around Timbuktu faster than I could follow. Think on these things ye man of much learning but little self-esteem."

Worried about uncertainty Percival wittered, "Really when all is said and done, such a bold new venture is too much for me. Anyway, I will soon be out of here, my physio has said that it will only be a few more weeks. It is all well and good for you three. Oh dear, I don't think I should, do you? Won't we get the manager into trouble?"

Arthur looked thoughtfully at Percival before he said, "Alright Percival, I take it that although you will not come with us, you will not sneak on us, irrespective of any worries that it might cause the management.

I will reserve accommodation at the Crown Inn, here in Scagill, for one night only, ready for us to move out on Sunday morning, to go our separate ways. We must look for more than an adventure. We must seek for a quest, for a quest is a worthy thing. We must endeavour to live honourably, as we seek for a new life. All this has prompted me to further thoughts. When we started to tell our stories four weeks ago, Geraint suggested that we should call ourselves 'The Grey Haired Knights'. It is a good idea, it marks our age, and it fits in well with the point made by whatever it was that challenged me on Halter Moor. We must forget about what we have done in the past and think only about what we can do in the future. I have jotted down, in this notebook here, some ideas about which I would like to have your opinion. I have in mind a sort of code for the Grey Haired Knights to live by when we set out on our quests. I still hope that the 'Once and Future King', whose name I carry, will return to put our country back to rights, however, I fear that I will not live to see it. We should not waste time mourning for the Arthurian legend, or dreaming of a future idyll.

We must determine, from this night forward, to live out our lives in a present Camelot. Malory tells us that Pelinor was King Arthur's favourite knight because he was honourable brave and true. Pelinor spent his life hunting the 'Questing Beast'. As questing Beasts are in short supply these days, we must each seek to find and follow his own quest."

"What are the ideas that you have in that notebook of yours Arthur?" Tristan asked.

Arthur cleared his throat, took up the book, fiddled to find his spectacles before he read in his best parade room command voice. "These are the promises, perhaps I should say vows that I believe we of the order of Grey Haired Knights should keep while on our quests."

He included Percival when he looked at each of the men, in turn, before he went on, "One; we shall put aside the progression of age and ignore infirmity. Two; we shall each go alone to find an honourable cause to champion as a quest. Three; we shall act in accordance with the laws of chivalry, as we know them. Four; we shall stand on our own feet. Sorry, Percival, no offence intended, you know what I mean. Five; we shall not communicate with family or known friends or rely on their support. Six; we shall make new friends, and find new allies if we need help."

Geraint chipped in, "I think you have planned this since you started on your story idea, you sly old police dog. I agree that your ideas are sound. They will force us into new endeavours."

The interruption did not put Arthur off his brief. "Seven; our final promise must be that whatever happens to us during our year long quest, we shall return to the Crown Inn Scagill, at noon on the first Saturday after next year's summer solstice.

The afternoon will provide the opportunity for us to tell new stories about our adventures. After which, we shall retire to freshen up, before we repair to the Crown Inn's restaurant for a right slap up reunion dinner. There is one more thing, I wish each of you to carry one of the sprigs of lucky white heather that I somehow had in my hand when I got back cold and wet from my night walk on Halter Moor.

Keep it safe, as I shall keep mine safe, but from time to time, take it out to look at it. It will remind you of your brother knights and your promise to return."

Chapter 3

Arthur did not tell a story that Sunday night when things changed. Many exaggerations and confessions stimulated their chatter. Only Percival did not join in the ebullient mood, although he interrupted several times with questions. "Where will you stay if you can't go home? If you become ill again, where will you go? How will you get your prescriptions made up?" His friends dismissed his calls for caution out of hand. Years seemed to have slipped off their shoulders. They felt that they already breathed a different cleaner air than the stale overheated incontinent fug of the Laurels, where even on that glorious June day the managers had kept the windows shut.

During the next few days, the three men were busy with telephone calls, they wrote letters; they left the newspapers unread, the crosswords untouched. Tristan did not make any complaints about the food, not even about Tuesday's Turkey Twizzlers. The staff, both professional and domestic, all commented on the mood change with the usual clichés, "My who won the pools then," or equally original, "I see cat has got the cream." The male porter made the more vulgar comment, "What's up with you three, have you pulled."

Each evening, during the week that followed their great decision to leave the rehabilitation unit, Arthur Thomas, Tristan Edward and Geraint Mostyn Evans repaired to the anti-room where the last one in did not lodge the chair against the door.

Each of them hoped that Percival St.John-Matthews would join them. They were so keyed up they behaved like excited children talking about their next holiday. They spoke of their ambitions, of the future, only occasionally of risk, always of the excitement that their reunion would create one year hence, on the first Saturday after the next summer solstice. Who would have travelled furthest, who would be the richer, who the poorer, who would truly deserve the accolade of Grey Haired Knight?

They talked of their present incarceration as though it were a full life sentence. They conspired to leave the Laurels un-noticed, without giving notice, to break out, to emulate prisoners of war escaping from a German stalag. For no real purpose, other than to associate with such films as 'The Great Escape' and 'The Wooden Horse' they arranged to depart at fixed intervals during Saturday afternoon. Geraint agreed to go first, at two o'clock. Tristan, always pedantic, said he would follow 2.30 p.m. Arthur, happy to cap Tristan, declared that he would leave at fifteen hundred hours, Greenwich summer time. Just before their planned time to escape, they each forged a signature in the visitor's book that would imply that a friend or relative had taken them out for the day. If challenged by a member of staff, they would say that the relative was waiting in a car at the end of the drive. Arthur suggested that they should not use the locked front door as their escape route. He suggested that they use the kitchen door because the cooks always left it open during warm weather.

Tristan said, "I will abseil down the wall from my second-floor room on a rope made out of bedsheets." "You'll do no such thing," barked Arthur curtly, we don't want a hue and cry before Sunday." "It was only a dream Arthur old boy, only a dream," Tristan replied sweetly. Also at Arthur's suggestion, they agreed to meet in the bar of the Crown, for pre-dinner drinks, at seven o'clock.

As the day planned for the great escape from the Laurels progressed, although not an actual escape, each man could have simply signed a form to take responsibility for his own discharge, the exhilaration they felt ran close to hysteria. They had each spent many fully protected weeks in the close-closeted world of hospitals, followed by even longer time in the oppressive rehabilitation clinic. Each man knew that during the year ahead, they had chosen to travel alone, exposed to the rough edge of an age with morals and mores of a youth culture, with which they were unfamiliar.

Both Tristan and Geraint, without reference to each other, had tried to persuade Percival to join them and leave the Laurels, pledged a Grey Haired Knight. It was only during the morning of their last day in the Laurels that both men finally accepted his decision to stay.

They had made a positive decision to defy the reality of age, and their present infirmities and they wanted Percival, who they knew as an agreeable soul, to get more out of life than the study of old books.

First to leave, Geraint ignored Arthur's advice. He opted to conceal himself in the loo by the front door. His intention was to demonstrate how lax security was at the Laurels. He got his chance when one of the ladies from the geriatric wing, who suffered from dementia, wandered near to the front door.

She was clearly lost, not just lost in direction or place; she was lost in time, to herself, and to reality. Because she was agitated, she kept the duty carers fully occupied. Geraint had 'Borrowed' a stethoscope from the pocket of a white coat that one of the doctors had left in the staff cloakroom. He knew that a stethoscope was a passport to all corridors in any hospital, clinic or care home.

When visitors rang the front door bell, Tristan slipped out of the loo. After he read a carers name badge, he said, "Don't worry Joan, you look after Vera, I will get the door to let the visitors in."

Like all care homes, the door was alarmed to prevent geriatric residents wandering off. Geraint had long ago learned the sequence of buttons that an authorised person had to press to mute the alarm.

Because for the first time in many weeks he wore a suit, shirt, tie, and the stethoscope, the part-time carers did not recognise him as a patient. He was clean away after he suppressed the alarm, opened the door, admitted the visitors and coolly asked them to sign the visitor's book. Conscious of his newly taken vow of chivalry, he turned back to post the doctor's stethoscope through the letterbox.

His three friends, who watched from the window of the dining room, laughed when they heard, quite distinctly, that he whistled the old Second World War song, Colonel Bogey as he made his escape. It concerned Arthur, instigator of all of that they had agreed to do, that Geraint leaned heavily on his ash stick and struggled with his small case before he reached the taxi he had ordered to meet him at the end of the laurel bush bordered drive.

Tristan was next to go, no dramatics for him, just a quick walk out through the kitchen door. He barked, "Forgot my Hat," to an uninterested kitchen porter. Arthur saw him push an arm into the laurel bushes to haul out a small suitcase that he had hidden the night before. It was a cheap fabric thing with wheels. They did not know that it contained all his material possessions. Arthur noticed how spry he looked; he was amazed at the difference made by a week of anticipation, expectation and hope.

Just before three o'clock Arthur raised a quizzical eyebrow to look at Percival, but pressed no further. After a quick handshake, he followed Tristan's route, through the kitchen. He had caught the mood of the other two escapees, and could not help calling out to the Yorkshire kitchen porter the only German words he had ever known, words he had picked up during the war, in the playground of St Paul's, his junior school. "Ach tung schweinhund - doub ist ein dumpkoff, Ya" Percival, who had heard Arthur's sally said aloud, but very tenderly, "Silly owd sausage." He stood, head bowed, unmoving, for a very long time, until one of the staff roused him. "Are you alright dearie? Why don't you sit with Mrs Wilson? You can have a nice little rest until tea; it's quiet in there without the telly. You'll be alright duck."

It was just before seven in the evening when the three escapees from the Laurels gathered in the bar of the Crown Inn. The last of the three to arrive was Geraint, immaculate in a suit, coordinated shirt and tie the others had not seen before. "Mmm who got you ready," was Tristan's immediate response. "Shut up you tart," Geraint replied urbanely, "Get me a pint will you," As soon as he had the pint in hand he took a great draught that emptied more than half the glass. "I have waited for far too long for that," he said. "Tinned beer is disgusting pasteurised filtered bottled beer is fit for no man. Bottle conditioned real ale is just manageable, but I would kill for two things in life; my morning cup of Yorkshire tea, and an evening pint of well-kept draught real ale, or if it is really spot on, perhaps a shed full."

The headwaiter interrupted, passing leather bound menus to each one in turn. He recited a list of the chef's specials dishes that all three ignored; they were too busy with their plans. Not wanting to intrude, the headwaiter said that he would come back in a few minutes to take their order.

After he had studied the menu closely, Arthur went to speak to him. "Please set our table for four, at the round table I reserved; I expect to be joined by a colleague, quite soon." Geraint and Tristan were intrigued, both said, as one, "Who might that be?" "Never you mind, just you wait and see," was the only response he gave. When the headwaiter returned for their order they were further mystified. After he had ordered for himself, Arthur gave a precise order for a fourth person, "Vegetable soup, breast of chicken in a white wine sauce, no mushrooms mind, followed by the chocolate mousse."

Their conversation attracted a deal of attention from the other people in the bar. It was unusually lively for three grey-haired men each one clearly of pensionable age. When Arthur sensed this, he asked a waiter if they could go through to their table, adding, as the waiter put their glasses of beer on a tray, "Please have a half of beer ready for our colleague who will join us and a further round of pints for the three of us would be welcome."

Before the three men had finished their chosen first course, they heard a slight commotion in the hotel entrance. It was Percival, who struggled with a large old-fashioned leather suitcase. A porter took his case and raglan-sleeved raincoat before the restaurant manager brought him to his place at the round table. A waiter put a lion head bowl of hot soup before him, another followed to place a half pint glass of beer at his right hand.

Tristan and Geraint sat silent, wide-eyed, astonished. Arthur stood to greet Percival. "You are thrice welcome, Sir Percival, Grey Haired Knight. I know that I speak for us all. As we are now complete, we can sup in solid comfort and true companionship at this our Round Table, without the need of a toast to absent friends." "Did he tell you that he would join us?" Tristan asked, looking at Arthur. "No", Percival said, happy to relieve Arthur of the need to answer, "I did not tell him. I did not decide until about an hour ago that I would be part of this wild caper, as I had called it. That predator woman, Mrs Wilson I think they call her, made me decide. You know the one, the very tall woman with starey eyes who can't keep her top plate in place. She asked me to fix her hair drier. I thought I should help, but I felt trapped when I went to her room. When I sat down to check the fuse, she put her hand on my knee. I had a panic attack and fled to the sanctuary of my room. I was desolate. I was alone with you three gone. Odd thing, though, I don't think that I was alone, though perhaps I just imagined it.

You must remember that stranger with the long white beard and the wide brimmed hat, the fellow who looked through the door of the anteroom, on the evening when Arthur proposed that we tell each other stories to stave off the madness that threatened us all. Well, I do not think the story telling has worked. I must be deranged or delusional, if not completely mad. That evening I thought that we were rude not to ask the fellow if he were lost, but I had forgotten all about him. I had not seen him or thought about him since. Somehow, I felt sure that I met him in the corridor outside my room. He looked at me, through those bottle thick glasses; I thought that he smiled when he pointed his stick at me. I remember he pointed it at Arthur in the same odd wavy way. I think that I may have fainted. I don't know if I did faint, because I have never fainted before, but some time must have passed before I opened my eyes again. Whatever he or it was had gone if there had been anything at all. It made me realise that you daft lot probably did have the right idea. To lose a foot I can live with, to lose my mind I could not."

"Well done lad," Arthur said, "I knew you had it in you. I hope that you have brought the sprig of white heather that I gave you, the one I brought down from Halter moor after that cold night when I wandered in both mind and body. It was on that night that I was somehow inspired by the idea that we should live the rest of our lives as part of a new and present Camelot. Keep it safe as a reminder of your friends the Grey Haired Knights and your vow to return for our reunion in a year's time."

"Never mind about next year" wittered Percival, "Where shall I stay tonight, I dare not go home, I am sure the Laurels management will send someone to my house to persuade me to go back." "Don't worry lad, I booked you a room here last week, I booked for us all." Arthur, happy with his rejoinder, added with a beaming smile, "I hope you've brought your debit card."

The first dining night of the 'Grey Haired Knights' was fit for the most fastidious of gentlemen's or military clubs. Tristan, who had spent his life in bars, restaurants and hotels, could not fault it. The Crown Inn at Scagill had always been the hub of the town's social whirl, the venue for the most important occasions; Society Balls held in the fifties through to the sixties, Old Time and Modern dances in the seventies, even the Party Discos of more recent years. Scagill Rotary met at the Crown. Round Table and the Lions met for their more relaxed evening dinners at the Crown. For most Scagill Mothers, the Crown was the only possible setting for the reception following the wedding of her precious daughters.

While Arthur and Geraint were drinking an after dinner brandy apiece, Percival sipped at a cherry brandy that he did not really want. He had ordered it because he felt obliged to keep up with the others. While he savoured a very large, very old, very expensive port Tristan stood up to launch into one of his critiques. What followed was not, as was his habit at the Laurels, a rant dismissal of the staff, food or fabric of the place; it was a eulogy in praise of the Crown Inn.

"You can tell whether a hotel is in the top echelon, as soon as you are three paces in off the street. It embraces you; it welcomes you as an old friend, even if it is your first time over its threshold. It has to do with the smell of the place, the feel of the fabrics, the leather, the lighting, and the quiet hum of background noise that allows one to speak normally, not in the hushed terms used by visitors to cathedrals and museums. It is to do with the work of generations of owners, managers, receptionists, housekeepers, chambermaids, chefs, cooks, barmen, waiters, porters, potboys and cellar men compelled to whistle. It has to do with its history, the generations of guests who have made it their special place. All these, when cared for, aged and matured, make the perfect English hostelry.

My devilled kidneys were just sublime, just enough. I know of nowhere in London, France or Switzerland that does a better vichyssoise, or one that has a better pudding list. Arthur, you made a great choice. Bacchus has blessed the place where we have dined on food fit for gods, kings and princes. He has concealed it in the soft folds of Yorkshire's Pennine Hills, obscured from celebrities who visit restaurants, not to eat, but for fans to view them as icons. Its northern reach has hidden it from the ghastly London-centric food critics who scribble for Sunday supplements; ridiculous conceited sycophants whose published criticisms are not fit to wrap up a Whitby fish and chip supper. This special place will be my beacon, a candle in the window. It will call for me to return on the Saturday after next year's summer solstice, as we all have vowed to do. "Tristan raised his glass, "Arthur, or should I call you Merlin, because you have woven great magic. You have drawn three not fit for purpose old men into your circle. By your decree, you have set us free, free to have a new life, but bound to return one year hence. I salute you, whatever challenge life may set for me, I shall welcome it." He drained his glass, looked steadily at each in turn before he said, "I shall not see you tomorrow, I have things to do." He turned, to walk out of the restaurant. He did not look back.

Percival was next to go. No rhetoric, just a quiet, "Well goodnight you two, I'm off too. It has been a funny old sort of day. I am tired, however, come what may, I must write a letter of resignation to the Chairman of the Antiquarian Society before I retire. I don't know what they will do. They will think me a perfect fool. Goodnight Geraint, goodnight Sir."

Geraint spoke quietly, as was usual for him, in a steady measure. "I'm glad he has decided to join us, if that's the right word to use about four peculiar old men who have forsworn each other's company for a year. I hope he will be all right. As you know, he has led a quiet life. Not like me, I have travelled a lot; I have lived in many places amongst many different people. Come on Arthur, the staff want to go home, we are the only two left. Come my liege, lets to bed."

Comfortable in bed, with the lights out, Arthur savoured the privacy that both the hospital and the rehab unit had denied him. He exulted in the bed linen, crisp white cotton sheets made up with boxed corners, covered by pure wool blankets, so different to the mixed fibre sheets and covers he had had to put up with for the last six months.

He worried about what he had done to inspire three good men to forsake comfort, shelter and possible unfinished clinical treatment, to risk the unknown. It concerned him that, unwittingly, he was their leader. Tristan's wonderful eulogy in which he referred to him as Merlin, together with Geraint's only half-mocking 'My liege' taken together with Percival's simple, 'Goodnight Sir' disturbed him. As he dozed into a fitful sleep, for the first time since his wife Jenny had died he prayed aloud. "Please God, preserve us, lead us all safely to the destiny you have chosen."

Chapter 4

After long weeks in the dreadful Laurels rehabilitation unit, unused to the late hour of dining, draft ale and Brandy, Arthur Thomas slept fitfully after the inaugural dinner of the Grey Haired Knights.

His mind fought to differentiate what he thought most likely to be a dream from the possibility that he had again taken the chance to walk up to the moors at Halter Top to think about a possible cause he might follow as a suitable quest.

Whatever it was, sleepwalk or dream, the moonless night was dark. The white ground mist that swirled about him had confused his sense of direction.

Ahead the track separated into four different paths and he had no idea which to take. He felt no sense of unreality when a bearded yet ageless man came out of the mist to join him at the spot where the path separated.

Arthur was sure that it the same man, or a manifestation, that he had, or had not met on Halter Moor, when he had slipped out of the Laurels to regain his memory of incidents that - occurred when he was a policeman; incidents that he could embellish as stories to entertain his friends.

The night he had arrived back at the Laurels, cold and wet, unsure whether he had slept and dreamt as walked, but sure that he had not picked the four unexplained sprigs of white heather he now carried.

Arthur spoke first, "I am lost, there are four ways ahead and I don't know where I have come from and I don't know which path to take."

The old man smiled in a vague sort of thoughtful way before he chuntered, a bit like a startled jackdaw, "Always difficult that one Arthur, very. Often one learns to regret the path not taken. These days I can never remember where he has sent me, where I am going, or what I am supposed to do when I get there.

That is if 'These days' means anything at all since that time long ago, or is it yet to come, when I lost the idea of correlated space-time. No matter, whenever it was, I never fully grasped the idea. Even Einstein got it wrong; string theory got its self in knots, wormholes never went anywhere and Hawking organised chaos. Nevertheless, I will come with you for a while, which itself is a relative indefinite."

Arthur remembered how the ageless little bearded man, who still wore a wide stitch brimmed hat, had scolded him about living in the past. How he had told him that if he put his mind to it, he could do great things with the rest of his life. He could become part of a new order, a new age of chivalry, a present Camelot.

This prompted Arthur to tell the stranger how he and his friends had pledged, as Grey Haired Knights, to go alone to seek adventure, which was why it was so important that he choose the right path. The old man had nodded several times before he said, "I am glad that you remembered what I told you last time we met; to stop banging on about what you have done. Done is done when all is said and done and there is nowt to do about it. I told you to think about how you could make your mark in a new Camelot, not that you could know about King Arthur's Camelot. Nobody told the story quite right, certainly not that Welsh ninny Nennius, or the misplaced Mabanigion. Bishop Geoffrey bowlderised it. Creation copied it and Mallory was morbid. They were all far too miserable, except perhaps Tennyson and that un-happy man White. He at least told of the happy times Arthur and I had when he was a boy."

The strange little man talked in a peculiar slightly Welsh accent, punctuated by squeaks. He fidgeted and fiddled with scraps of paper, and little notebooks that he took from one pocket, read, and put back into another pocket in his coats of many pockets. "I know I have it here somewhere," he said, "I came specially to tell you about some bother or whatever it was or is, I can't remember. I won't have lost it, far too important. Perhaps I left it with her underwater, sorry Arthur," he said, "I can't recall for the moment what it is I have to tell you, but I have remembered where I was going. I have to see to a sick brachet. I will get back to you when I have found, or I have remembered, what I have forgotten.

As usual, I have muddled the two possibilities, to find or to remember and never even thought about a third option, to recover whatever it is. It will come back to me, or catch me up, it usually does."

Not watching the rocky path, Arthur tripped and fell.

The sudden shock of a falling sensation that usually ends a dream shocked Arthur hard, but did not wake him. He felt lifted to his feet by the stranger who clucked and laughed as he shouted into the wind that had suddenly blown up to scatter many of his bits paper into the darkness. "You must watch your step when you go questing. Deny it who can, it tests the blood of an English Man. Not much chance of that in these days of yours though, what with 'Elf and Safety' being what they are. Sad thing though, for one of you Grey Haired Knights, I do not remember who, I cannot be there for him at the end. He will be a true knight and rest with Arthur in Avalon."

The curious old man had almost blurred into the background before he shouted, even louder, "Arthur, stop, I have it! Yes, that's it. I have remembered, now so must you. Your quest begins with a source of much trouble. If you can penetrate an impenetrable thorn, draw base metal from a stone to fashion a sword and fight like a dragon, you will both free and bind a lady.

Dawn broke. Shafts of golden light broke through the clouds to touch the moor and the single familiar path that Arthur had often walked. The old man faded away into the folds of the grey curtains of Arthur Thomas's bedroom in the Crown Hotel, Coopers Yard, Scagill. It was the dawn of the year's longest day, the summer solstice.

Arthur Thomas, the seventy-year old retired police Superintendent, stared at the curtains, dry mouthed, gasping for breath. A dread induced cold sweat made the whole of his upper body gross. Tangled in his bed sheets, he sensed that he smelt like a hob ferret. Only once before had he experienced such fear. That was many years ago when he faced the spout-end of a service revolver, the butt end of which was held by a disturbed young soldier.

Whatever had disturbed his usual quiet unbroken slumber, Arthur never quite understood. He knew for certain, that it was no ordinary fleeting soon forgotten occurrence. It had connections. He could remember the smallest detail from when it began, to its curious end; a thing he thought not possible with a dream. Even after Arthur had made himself a cup of tea, every detail of whatever it had been, remained clear in his memory.

When he tried to make sense of what had upset him, Arthur realised that he had two events to consider because, during whatever had occurred during the night, the strange man had referred to their meeting on Halter Moor, two weeks earlier. Arthur still thought it possible that the man on Halter Moor might not have been a dream figure, despite Tristan's raised eyebrow that inferred he had been dreaming while sleep walking.

He had had to agree that the evidence of his muddy shoes, dew damp coat and four sprigs of white heather only proved that he had been out walking during the night. He recognized that the stranger's sad prediction that he might not be there, at the end, for one of the Grey Haired Knights, who would become a true knight and rest with King Arthur in Avalon, had been the cause of his panic attack. It had changed his optimistic mood to one of deep anxiety. It now concerned him that his idea of a new Camelot had been reckless. He thought that he had been unwise to persuade his friends, including the vulnerable Percival, to leave the Laurels rehabilitation clinic.

He thought himself a fool to ask men of their age to think of themselves as Grey Haired Knights, able to take on a quest. He felt responsible that they had taken a vow to return to Scagill one year hence, to tell true tales of their adventures.

He realised, for the first time, that the vow had turned a fanciful idea into a commitment that might drive them to take undue risks. He knew that in Arthurian legends many brave knights fell to treacherous foes.

Arthur feared that he might be the cause of any one of his friends standing into mortal danger. It bore down on him that it would be his fault if any of them, in pursuit of their chosen quest, receive a mental or physical injury, or God forbid, suffer a premature death. He did not worry for his own safety.

After a second cup of sweet tea, Arthur thought that memories of Arthurian stories he had read, films he had seen, or tricks of his own imagination, had created the images that troubled him. He persuaded himself that the cause of his panic attack was not whatever it was that had occurred during the night, but simply a reaction of the drugs prescribed to treat his memory loss, with the unusual amount of alcohol he had consumed during the inaugural dinner of the Grey Haired Knights. "After all," he said to the bathroom mirror, as he wet shaved, "We did eat a lot later than the usual time for the Laurels meagre suppers and I did enjoy a full four-course dinner that included a lot of cheese, and I downed three pints of ale, followed by a double brandy. However, whatever had caused the two incidents; they had a powerful sense of reality.

To put his new worries out of his mind Arthur took a long hot bath, followed by a cold shower. Comfortable that the bath, shower and a generous splash of 'Old Spice' aftershave had rid him of the sweat smell of fear, he dressed in his casual trousers, hush puppies, clean white shirt, demure tie and sports jacket.

Before he left his room, he jotted down in his sketchbook the unfathomable words the curious old man had shouted into the wind and told him to remember, because he knew how words could fail his memory. He wrote, 'Your quest begins with a source of much trouble. If you can penetrate an impenetrable thorn, draw base metal from a stone to fashion a sword and fight like a dragon, you will both free and bind a lady'.

In soft pencil Arthur also drew several sketches of the strangely dressed old man who seemed ageless. He hoped that one day he would use them, as an inspiration for a large oil painting.

After a quick mirror check, he made a steady progress to the restaurant. For the first time in many weeks he was alone at breakfast. To treat himself he ordered a 'Full English'. Arthur believed a Full English breakfast a misnomer, as he believed they only existed in Yorkshire, Lancashire and Cumberland. He only included Cumberland for its sausage and Lancashire in tribute to Bury, for its best of all black puddings.

A spry lady waitress dressed in a smart blue overall, who was almost of his age, greeted him warmly. "Hello Inspector, it's good to see you again. I am glad that you have not lost your appetite. I like to see a man set himself up for the day with a good breakfast. I always got my Alfred one before he went off to work."

"Well lass it was Superintendent before I retired, if you don't mind," Arthur said, "And it is not for just a day for which you have to set me up. I'm off for a year long adventure. I start just as soon as I have paid my bill. I don't know yet where I am going, perhaps where breakfast is continental; wafer thin cold meat, cheese-parings, croissant crumbs, and coffee; not much else. Just because I have a pension, it does not mean I cannot have a

'Gap Year'. I think I have earned it. These days' young people take them on credit before they start to earn a living."

The waitress laughed, "Eh Inspector, just you be careful, I don't know what your Jenny would have said, you going off gallivanting at your age."

Arthur, who remembered that Tristan had called him Merlin, took it as his cue, "You just watch it young lady; I refuse to grow old. When I reached sixty, I took an idea from T. H. White's book, the 'Once and Future King'. Like his Merlin, I decided to live my life backwards. Consequently, I have reached retrospective fifty-years of age." "Go on with you, you daft old beggar," she said, "Two of your friends left ages ago, they asked for 'Just coffee'. I took them lots of toast with pots of butter and marmalade and, as I knew they would, they did not leave a crust." Arthur replied, "Yes, they have much to do. We said our farewells last night. I do not think that any one of us wanted more drama this morning."

After his leisurely breakfast, Arthur changed up a gear, cleared his room and booked out of the Crown Hotel before ten o'clock. With his small case in hand, he walked up to Victoria Square, where he caught the number 29 Booth Road bus to take him to the end of Wellhead Lane. His solid little pebble dashed nineteen thirties bungalow stood half way along the tree-lined lane.

Mindful that the 'Jobsworth' managers of the Laurels, their paperwork assessment of patients incomplete, might come to the bungalow to look for him, Arthur did not stay for a minute longer than necessary at his home. He only went inside to pick up the car keys for his quite new, only one previous owner, 'Ford' four-door saloon.

Prior to the planned mass defection from the Laurels, he had spent a busy week to make what arrangements he could for the year ahead. As a first priority, he had arranged for his local Ford garage to Service his car. He was relieved when it started at the first turn of the ignition key.

Arthur drove slowly back into Scagill where he paid to park close to Scagill's town centre pedestrian precinct. He soon found what he wanted, a busy newsagent's shop. In the shop, he did not just browse, he searched but failed to find. Eventually, frustration led him to seek help from a girl shop assistant.

"Miss, have you got any magazines about motorhomes?" His frustration increased when the girl went straight to the shelf where he had been looking, to pick out three different publications, all of them with articles and adverts about caravans or motorhomes. The girl recommended MMM because it specialised in motorhomes, rather than caravans. She told him that her Dad said it was the best.

After he paid for the magazine, and a 'Daily Telegraph', Arthur felt unsettled. He knew that he was still within easy reach of the managers of the Laurels rehabilitation unit. He thought that they may have reported him missing to the police, even though they would be acutely embarrassed to admit losing four long term residents in their care.

Without further faff, he drove out of town, happy that any road out of Scagill would take him up onto the Pennine Moors. Parked up, safe in a viewpoint, he began to study the MMM magazine adverts for second-hand motorhomes. Within a few minutes, he realised that he had a dilemma. Those he could reasonably afford did not suit his purpose; those that did, he could not possibly afford.

One double page advertisement did catch his eye. All over it, 'Brownhills' claimed to be the biggest U.K. retailer of motorhomes, both new and previously owned. They offered hire purchase and part exchange on cars, or boats. They advertised that their main site was on the Great North Road. This claim irritated Arthur. He was fond of pointing out to anyone unfortunate enough to live south of the River Trent that the eastern carriageway of the M1 or A1 was a Great South Road.

With a purposeful look, in the rear view mirror, at himself, not the view behind, Arthur Thomas unconsciously performed a lifelong habit of which he was unaware. He swept the left side of his neat moustache with the forefingers of his right hand and the right side of his moustache with the forefinger of his left hand. Satisfied, he set off for Newark to find Brownhills motorhome showrooms.

Even though he drove fast, it was mid-afternoon before Arthur negotiated the last of many roundabouts into the Brownhills site, where a red and white pole barred his way.

A florid faced uniformed gatekeeper approached him with a great smile of welcome. He asked if he could help. "Well, I think I want to buy a motorised shed on wheels," Arthur replied. "Well you have come to the right place," the gatekeeper said, "We have hundreds of them, all shapes, all sizes, most new, some previously owned, we don't do second hand. Some are good, some not quite as good, but none that are old or not fit for purpose. First, you must park your car, before you wend your way over to the sales office over yonder, can you see? They will do you a good deal."

A salesman, no less cheery than the gateman, picked him out. He soon understood Arthur's predicament, not able to afford any new unit that might suit him. "Why don't you go to have a look around outside where you will be able to get a feel of value rather than cost? You will find a range of earlier used units that we guarantee for a year. You can buy an extended guarantee if you wish. Try to get a clear idea of what you need rather than what you think that you might want. Think about why you wish to own a motorhome." After half an hour Arthur had seen a unit he thought best for his purpose, but its price was well beyond what he dared to pay.

The salesman who had kept an experienced eye on Arthur was ready; "So this is the one is it?" "Would that it was," replied Arthur, "It's just right for my purpose, regrettably I can't afford it; there's the rub." Un-phased, his practiced answer ready, the salesman said, "Well, let us see whether we can erase the rub shall we. Come into the office. We could take that nice Ford of yours in part exchange. We do a very special rate on hire purchase for senior citizens."

It took less than half an hour for Arthur to hoc a good part of his state pension and trade in his car to become second owner of a five-year-old Hymermobile Mercedes automatic diesel powered two-berth motorhome. He dismissed all morbid thoughts about the hire purchase company funding a ten-year loan on a five-year old vehicle to a seventy-year old man. In fact, it put him in good heart; it was for them to worry about, not him.

It was just before six o'clock when he drove gingerly to Brownhills site exit. The gatekeeper smiled at him, "That's a good choice of vehicle you have made there sir, your very own take it anywhere sleepover. It will take care of you if you take care of it. In future every night you will be able to scratch, comfortable in your own cot. You are free to go when or where you wish." Arthur recognised that it was just good sales talk that Brownhills had schooled the gateman to say to all new buyers. All the same, the patter made him feel good.

Because it was the longest day, Arthur realised that he had time to drive back in daylight to his bungalow in Well Head Lane. As soon as he was on the road home, he began to decide what to transfer to his new home. Clothes, pots, pans, pillows and paraphernalia that would make his gypsy life comfortable.

In the Brownhills shop, he had bought himself a luxury sleeping bag and an ingenious toaster that worked over one of the cooker's gas rings. He knew his passport, valid for about three more years, was in his bureau at home.

With funds in the bank, passport in his pocket, debit card in his wallet, he agreed with the Brownhills' gateman . He would be able to go when and where he wished in Britain. He knew that he could also roam the continent on the same terms, if he dared to drive on the wrong side of the road.

Even though it was the longest day, it was almost dark when Arthur pulled up outside his bungalow. He immediately began to transfer all of what he thought might be necessary for his physical comfort. Finally, he loaded what he thought most important for his mental well-being, his sketchbooks and box of paints.

During the journey home he had decided to call his shed on wheels 'Tootsie', because although she was a land ship, he was sure that she must be feminine. He considered its continental built carapace to be his tortoise shell. The alliterative Tootsie the tortoise suited his mood.

It was completely dark when for the last time he finally locked the door of his house that was to stay fixed in Well Head Lane, while he travelled, as a true Romany travels, in his new foundation free motorhome. Three or four times he had been about to leave when some other necessity came to mind. Each time he had to climb down from Tootsie to unlock the front door of the bungalow, to find, or fail to find, or decide not to bother, muttering to himself, "I'll get one on the way." He had not realised when he said it, that he had no idea of where the way might be.

When he finally left Well Head Lane, he drove up to the moors, to a disused quarry. Tired by his long eventful day, Arthur resolved to leave it until morning to plan his gap year.

It was late when Arthur woke. When he looked at his watch, he was surprised to realise that he had slept for a solid nine hours. However, he was annoyed that he had no fresh milk or milk of any kind for that matter. Lack of a forward plan reduced him to instant black coffee from a sachet, a poor substitute for his usual first morning cup of Yorkshire tea. Frustrated by lack of both milk and sugar he took out his sketchbook to make a list of everyday necessities he would need on his journey.

When he opened it, he felt all effects of his minor stroke, loss of memory, and palliative drugs evaporate. It was as though a fog had cleared. For the first time since a policeman had found him wandering, he felt fully alive, complete with all his faculties.

The catalyst to his recovery was the note he had written to record what the little man of his nightmare happening had shouted into the wind. The incomprehensible message that started, 'Your quest begins with a source of much trouble'.

In an instant, the single word 'Source' made clear what his quest must be. He must strive to find and recover the still missing stolen masterpiece, 'La Source', Jean Auguste Dominique Ingres's masterpiece.

He had often day dreamed about it, as other people dream of winning the lottery, or used to dream of a win on the pools. Arthur knew that there was a reward of two-million pound offered for information leading to recovery of the painting.

He also knew where he must begin his search. Peter Bainbridge was the starting point, the key to forgotten files, the blue touch paper to launch his adventure.

Peter was an old friend, a colleague from when they had joined the county police force together. After several years, Peter had transferred to the London Metropolitan Police to work with Interpol. He had helped to bring to justice a London based gang who had stolen La Source from the Musée D'Orsay in Paris. During the robbery, the thieves had murdered a museum guard.

Peter had recently told Arthur that although the French courts had sentenced those of the gang they had caught to long terms in jail, only one remained incarcerated. He had added, bitterly, that European human rights law had allowed him to serve the latter part of his sentence in British custody and in an open prison at that.

Peter had also told him that the whole affair had been a complete farce. Although Interpol had alerted the French police that a British gang of art thieves planned to steal an important painting from a gallery in Paris, they had failed to prevent the robbery and murder. Both the French and British police were convinced that they knew who had murdered the guard, but they did not have the necessary witness, forensic or circumstantial evidence to bring the murder charge.

Arthur, who had a passion for painting and paintings, had read that many scholars, art historians and dealers, believed that Ingres's pubescent nude, if ever brought to auction with good provenance, would fetch more than would Leonardo's Mona Lisa.

Over the years, Arthur and Peter had exchanged Christmas cards and holiday postcards, with short messages included to keep in touch. As is often the case with old friends, they met most often at funerals. The last three occasions were at memorial services for senior police colleagues. Before that, it was at the cremation of Arthur's wife Jennie. Although they met infrequently, they both knew that their friendship was one upon which they could rely in time of need.

When Arthur checked Peter's address and telephone number in his address book he thought, "By heck Peter you've done yourself right well; Wicket Gate Cottage, The Green, Lurgashall, Near Haslemere, West-Sussex, must have cost you a bob or two." Arthur knew that Peter had retired with a substantive pensionable rank of Assistant Commissioner before he joined the Swiss insurance company that offered the two million pound reward as their 'Head of Property Recovery'. "Right Tootsie old girl," Arthur said to himself, but out-loud, "That settles it. We are off down south."

Always a romantic Arthur eschewed England's 'M' roads and duel carriageway A roads. He preferred to take the historic routes, even those he called rural ride dual carriageways, because they had grass that grew in the middle. "I'm in no hurry, I want to see a little of England on my way south," he said, again aloud.

He took from his brief case a blank sheet of paper on which he wrote down the principal towns on his route south; Huddersfield, Holmfirth, 'Last of the Summer Wine' country, over Holme Moss for a last view of Yorkshire, before the road would take him into Derbyshire's Peak District.

After Ashbourne, it would be dull Midlands before he could join the Fosse Way to roam along that old Roman road through the Cotswolds. He planned to drive across the folds of Wiltshire's wide acres to have a look at Stonehenge.

After further study of his map, he picked out a way east that bypassed Winchester, onto Haslemere, then finally to Lurgashall, where he hoped to beard Peter in his den. "That will do me, give or take a few excursions, diversions or other considerations," Arthur again said all this aloud, but only to himself.

He often talked aloud to himself, not because he felt lonely, it was his habit. He called it, 'thinking aloud'. From the very start of his journey, when he eased Tootsie out of the quarry, he had felt a sense of purpose to his life that had not been there since Jenny had died.

It was already middle day when he stopped in a small car park at the summit of Holme Moss that marks Yorkshire's boarder with Derbyshire. He stepped out to breathe the moorland air and to take a last look at his beloved county that lay stretched out below him.

In the clear air, he could see the industrial conurbation of Holmfirth, Huddersfield and Scagill, all that had been his bailiwick for the whole of his working life. Beyond, in the far distance, the blue smudge that marked the start of the Yorkshire Dales lured him to return. His commitment to his determined quest overcame the temptation; it stiffened his resolve.

Back in the comfort of his driving seat, he drove the few yards over the crest of Holme Moors into the High Peaks of Derbyshire where the scene was very different.

The huge forbidding dark mass of Kinder Scout threatened all who passed. It imposed on Arthur the truth - that the quest he had chosen had its dark dangerous side. Someone in the gang who stole La Source had murdered the prison guard, but all had his blood on their hands.

Blind justice would soon release, on parole, the man still in prison. His police experience told him they would kill him, without trouble to their conscience, if he threatened their chance of profit from the theft.

When he started on the steep drop into Derbyshire, Arthur knew that he had chosen a true quest, worthy of the idea of a new Camelot.

He began to wonder about the cryptic message with the unresolved words, base metal, fire and the contradiction that he would both free and bind a lady.

Chapter 5

The first real test of Arthur's competence at the wheel of his new command was the long steep descent from the summit of Holme Moss. It tested his nerve and Tootsie's capability. After a quick selection of low gear followed by a touch on the breaks, then four or more, he felt confident that the vehicle did all that he asked of her. He laughed aloud because he considered this an unfeminine trait. He thought briefly that he might change her name, to one of masculine gender, to the name of King Arthur's charger Passelande. However, because his new shed on wheels had provided him with comfort in the night, he dismissed the thought. He could not then know that major events in his life would bring about a change in less than a year.

As he neared the bottom of one of England's best hill-climbs for keen cyclists, Arthur saw a prominent sign, 'Escape Route'. Exhilarated by the steep decent coupled with his newfound freedom he shouted aloud, "That is my route. I will take the high road to escape from the immutable slow road that leads through boredom via senility onto death's low road". At the bottom of the hill, when he reached the junction with the main road, he let out a joyous 'Poop – Poop' in honour of Mr. Toad, his favourite character in one of his favourite books. Mr. Toad, fellow adventurer, fellow escapee.

Arthur felt that he was once again in control of his future. He enjoyed the huge difference as he drove with his eye level some eight feet above road level, instead of the less than the four feet in his Ford Mondeo. It opened up new vistas, not just the road ahead. In the country, he hedge farmed the beasts and the crops. In the suburbs, he judged the gardens and valued the properties. When he drove past the Toreside reservoirs, on his way to Glossop, he could see wind surfers skim over the peat brown water past sailing dinghies that appeared to be dead in the water. From his mobile high-seated vantage point, he spotted a van invisible to any passing car that sold burgers, hot dogs and bacon buttys.

Because he had no food on board, he stopped to buy a cup of tea and a hot dog. A dull uncommunicative youth served him with a foam plastic beaker part full of hot, not boiling, water, in which floated a tea bag. The hot dog was a bland plastic cased simulation of a Frankfurter trapped in an unbuttered bread roll that had the texture of a crêpe bandage. Back in the driving seat, he spoke severely to himself. "Arthur, there is a lesson learned. In future, you must brew your own tea, prepare your own breakfast and skip lunch. In the evening, you must find a pub where you can have company, a drink and a bar meal. If funds allow, you may treat yourself to an occasional restaurant dinner."

After he discarded the bread roll in the waste bin, Arthur studied his map. With plenty of daylight left, he reckoned he could be through the barren midlands into the Cotswolds before nightfall. When he noticed that Stratford-on-Avon was only just off his most direct route he decided to stay overnight by the river, after he had stocked the fridge and cupboards with staple foods; bread, cheese, milk and beer. Many times before Jenny died, he had promised her that one day he would take her to the theatre at Stratford to see one of Shakespeare's plays, but what with one thing and another it had never happened. Free to do as he pleased, he decided that if he could get a ticket, he would go to see whatever was playing.

After he learned that supermarket car parks do not provide for motorhomes, Arthur spent an hour in and out of high street shops to buy supplies, making it just after half past six when he pulled over to the side of the road in sight of the brick built theatre. His first reaction was that it looked like a superannuated cinema converted into a bingo hall. Disappointed, but not dismayed, he took the shallow steps to the main entrance that he had correctly assumed led to the ticket office.

When there, he was frustrated to learn from the large notices posted that the play on that night in the Shakespeare Memorial Theatre was by an author unknown to him, with a title he did not recognise, that featured actors of whom he had never heard. Other less conspicuous notices advertised that the RSC was to perform 'King Lear' in the 'Swan', with the performance to start at seven p.m. Arthur wondered whatever and wherever the Swan might be. As he only needed one seat, he was able to buy a returned ticket for the performance.

The cost of the ticket shocked him. He thought it far too steep for a second hand ticket for a second best show in a public house. The lady at the ticket counter did not improve his temper with her sniffy dismissive answer to his question, "Pray madam, where and what is the Swan?" "The Swan is the company's theatre immediately next door left; you will have to hurry."

Nearly four hours later, Arthur came out into the cool summer night air. His heart pounded his pulse raced. At first, he had been deeply disappointed at the stark décor and seating arrangement of the Swan Theatre. He had groaned, inwardly, when the play started with no fanfare or rising curtain. The players had simply walked onto a bare stage dressed in some curious almost modern clothes that were hardly worth the term costume, certainly not the garments of a medieval court.

Later, when he thought about the performance, he realised that within minutes, the spoken word of Shakespeare's drama had held him enthralled and he had not been aware of the theatre and audience around him. Although he had not understood all of the play, he had understood enough. For the first time Arthur knew why Shakespeare was so important.

He wondered why he had not written a play about the tragedy of King Arthur. He thought that Shakespeare would have known far more of the story of King Arthur, Guinevere, Lancelot and Mordred than that of the mysterious King Lear, both of which have the same drama of deceit.

The next day Arthur drove past Cirencester and later swung around Swindon's ring road with its many roundabouts before he crossed the Salisbury Plain to look at Stonehenge. He thought the blue and the Sarsen stones too small, too shabby to warrant the fuss made about them. After he left the stones, he decided that he would have to forego his rural rides if he was to make progress in the South of England.

Arthur chose Winchester for his next lay over, because his map showed it to be as far south as Lurgashall where Peter had made his home. He hoped to be there by nightfall so on the following day he could take the easy road through Petersfield on to Midhurst to arrive in Lurgashall in time to surprise Peter in or from the local pub.

He felt sure his friend would not have settled in a village that did not have a decent hostelry. He was not a bit bothered that Peter might not be at home, or that he might be on holiday, or in the City on business. Arthur knew that he had 362 days left to wander abroad before he was committed to return to Scagill for the reunion with his friends, Tristan, Percival and Geraint.

The more Arthur thought about his plan to recover 'La Source', Ingres's masterpiece, the nubile nude, the more it suited his romantic nature. He convinced himself that the principal cause of his quest must be to bring a heinous murderer to justice, not merely to find information that would lead to the recovery of the painting and the rich reward.

He accepted the risk of pitting himself against a gang of thieves who had already committed murder. He believed it a cause worthy for a Knight of any age or time. He did however realise that he would be at risk if ever the gang who stole the painting should learn of his identity and his intention to recover the stolen painting. The memory of the strange old man and of his still unexplained nightmare dream, who had shouted into the wind that he could not be there, at the end, for one who would be a true knight and rest with Arthur in Avalon, added to his concern.

An hour's drive short of Winchester Arthur pulled into a good clear lay-by where he made himself a cup of tea and a sandwich. The sandwich was a doorstop of bread, butter, spam, lettuce and tomato, dressed overall with Heinz Sandwich Spread. When he sat down at his small table to eat, he said aloud, "Eh Arthur Thomas you are common. Fancy, thick bread, spam and sandwich spread, without a knife, fork or plate. It just won't do; it is not the behaviour of a parfait gentle knight." While he ate, he referred to the Caravan Club handbook. In it, he found details of a club site located just outside the city that accommodated touring vans.

Arthur thanked modern technology, when he used his mobile phone to make a reservation for a one-night stay, with a hook up to electric power. At eighteen pounds a night, he thought he had better not stay for more than one night in three on club sites.

Arthur took a taxi into Winchester to look around the Cathedral. After the cathedral visit, he enjoyed a pint of beer, or was it two, to cool a vindaloo curry in a cosy pub, before he returned to the caravan park by the same taxi. Before he slept, he lay in his sleeping bag and thought of the great change he had made in his way of life.

He decided that he was content with his decision to travel in his mobile home. He delighted in the liberty it gave him. However, he realised that liberty came at the cost of loneliness. He missed the friendship of Tristan, Percival and Geraint, his companions during the long months they had endured incarceration together.

On the third morning of his journey, after a light breakfast of cereals, fruit and toast, Arthur left the site quite early, but not before he ticked off all domestic duties from his checklist. On his way to Peter's home, he stopped to buy his morning paper in Petersfield, and for a cup of coffee in a quaint little bakery come teashop in Midhurst.

He approached Lurgashall village about half an hour before mid-day. Road signs he had never seen before, 'Danger: Road width suitable for vehicle under six feet wide only', twice stopped him from entering the village. "Blimey Peter," Arthur said aloud, "I thought you were a retired copper, not a fugitive from justice, or a witness in need of a safe house."

Eventually he found a notice 'Single track road with passing places'. Arthur reckoned that the village must have a pub; furthermore, the pub must have a weekly drop from a brewery dray, if so, this must be a safe way in to the village, if not to Brigadoon.

When Arthur drove out from the dark tree screened lane onto one of England's most beautiful village greens, he saw the expected pub. It was set well back against the trees on the far side of a great open space. He pulled off the narrow road to park on the edge of the green that sloped from north to south in undulating folds. It was big enough to accommodate the swards of both Lords and the Oval cricket grounds, with enough space between for Twickenham's rugby pitch.

Around the green were mature detached houses, with none like any other. Arthur got out of the driving seat to stretch, put on a good pair of shoes, and his linen jacket, before he stepped down from his mobile home the onto the green.

When he got closer to the pub he could see the church, almost hidden in trees. Alongside the church, which had its own proper wicket gate, he saw 'Wicket Gate Cottage', Peter's home.

Arthur had expected to find a roofed gate but it was a small gate cleverly made of cricket gear. From a bright red cricket ball in the middle, straw-coloured stumps radiated like spokes of a wheel with bails drilled through and threaded on a thick wire forming the rim of the wheel. Whoever made it had squared off the gate with white painted wooden slats that could once have been part of a side screen.

Beyond the gate Arthur could see that a Breeden gravel path lead though a well-kept garden, with a water feature, to a thatched house far too big for the name cottage.

Arthur noted that Peter had indeed done very well, far better than most retired peelers. He did not go straight to the house; he went to the pub so that he could invite Peter to join him there. He though it tactful to give Mrs. Bainbridge, Anne, time to 'plump the cushions', because he was certain that if they were at home, not off gallivanting, he would be invited into the house.

He bought a half of beer that he took outside to one of the many tables spread out on the green. He had not forgotten to take with him the piece of paper on which he had written Peter's telephone number. Using his mobile phone, he rang to find out if the Bainbridge's were at home.

To his delight, Anne answered his call. Arthur spoke in as flat a tone as he could manage, "Could I speak to Mr. Peter Bainbridge please?" He was thrilled when without hesitation she called, "Peter it's for you," followed by, "Here he is." No cautious response of "Who is it?" or "Can I help you?" Arthur's police brain told him, to his great satisfaction, that all was well in the Bainbridge household.

"Hello, Peter Bainbridge here," Peter said, "Well now, is that so," Arthur tried to mimic PC 49, "I am sorry to disturb you sir, but this is a police matter, Superintendent Cockleberry here. I am investigating the theft of a quantity of stumps, bails and a ball, stolen from Yorkshire County Cricket Club." "Arthur, is that you, you daft old plod?" Peter sang out, "Where are you?"

"I am outside the pub, on the green, looking at the swag. I wish to interrogate you that is if Anne will let you off the household chores." Arthur heard Peter say, "Anne, Arthur is here; I'll go to get him," before the phone clicked in his ear.

In less than a minute, after a quick bear hug, a long firm hand-shake closed the gap of the years since they had worked together. Both men tried to question each other at the same time. Eventually Arthur managed to ask, "Can I get you a drink?" Peter replied, "Just a half please, bitter, as a rule I don't drink at lunch-time." "Nor me either," replied Arthur, as he went into the pub to get the beer.

When Peter noticed that his old friend's half was hardly touched, he thought of the many times, when off duty, they had each shifted a gallon or more when out in the Dales on their motorbikes.

The two sat and talked together, comfortable as old shoes, until Peter asked, after a careful look around, "How did you get here? I don't see any cars that I don't know all about." "Tootsie brought me; she is over there in the shade of the trees on the other side of the green." "Well for goodness sake," Peter said excitedly, "You sly old dog, what do you mean by leaving a girl on her own. I know; you are still worried that I could pull the birds better than you?" "Neh Lad," Arthur said, "You couldn't pull my four wheeled floozy, not now, not any day. She is that horseless caravan over there, my carapace, my wandering wonder wagon, my Mercedes motorhome."

Peter who was obviously astonished said, "Well I never, who would have thought it; I had you down as a stick in the mud since you retired. Well-done Arthur, now let us go over to my little pile of bricks and straw to see if Anne can rustle up a cup of tea with a biscuit or three. How long can you stay? You will have din-ner with us tonight, won't you? You had better bring your floozy nearer to the house. The village posh will have fits if they think that the gypsies have come to take up residence."

All this talk tumbled from Peter who was not just pleased to be with his old colleague again, he was thrilled.

When he brought Arthur into the cottage Peter said, "Anne, look who I have found in his cups on the green." Anne said serenely, "Calm down Peter. Hello Arthur, it is good to see you." She took both of Arthur's hands in hers while she gave him a long careful look. It pleased him that she was not the air kissing type. Smiling, Anne said, "Peter often talks about the good times you two had together. Come through to the garden, I have made tea, Yorkshire Tea. It's all he will let me buy, even though we have been here in the south for more years than I can remember."

They spent the afternoon in the garden. Peter showed off all that he had built or grown since Anne and he bought the property ten years previously, to be ready for his retirement from the Met. Arthur was anxious to hear about the insurance company job that Peter had taken on. Peter was more than happy to tell him. "It was a piece of luck really. It happened not long before I planned to retire. I had already done more than my thirty-year stint. I was working with a chap called O'Rourke, on a suspected fraud case involving arson. He was a man I had a lot of time for, very Oxbridge, obviously tipped for advancement. He was younger than I was, easy to work with.

Well one day he asked me to stand in for him at a meeting with Swiss Mobius, a major re-insurance company. They were suspicious about the cause of a fire that had burnt out several factories before the fire brigade could bring it under control. As the prime underwriters of the factory where the fire started, other insurance companies had mounted claims against them that amounted to many millions of pounds. Anyway, that is by the by. During a break in the meeting with Swiss Mobius, one of their staff introduced me to their Chief Executive Officer. I believe he thought that I was O'Rourke.

I heard no more about it until a month or two later when I received a letter that invited me to their Zurich office, all expenses paid, to discuss what they called 'An opportunity'. What they wanted was an in house linkman to deal with police forces worldwide where there was a possibility that a claim against a policy underwritten by them might be fraudulent. They thought it wise to have a man on their staff who knew how European, American and Asian forces worked. They had done their homework. They knew that I had been on the Mets Interpol team for a few years and that I had language skills. Of course, I took retirement as soon as possible. After a month's holiday, I joined Swiss Mobius on condition that I could live here in England."

Arthur smiled before he trotted out one of his favourite aphorisms. "Neh lad, it wasn't just luck. I used to tell all young recruits to the force that the harder they worked the luckier they would get.

Now then, my little Swiss chard, can I take you and your beloved edelweiss out to dinner tonight. I presume that in this affluent part of the south of our beloved country you must be surrounded by a veritable rosette of suitable restaurants." "You'll do no such thing," Anne broke in, "You two can go over to the pub about seven, but you must be back here at eight sharp for dinner." Peter shrugged his shoulders, "Don't waste your breath Arthur, 'She' has spoken." Arthur acquiesced, "I shall repair to Tootsie where I shall freshen up. Peter I will see you in the pub at seven. Cookie, on the strike of eight we shall return, clean, cold sober and hungry."

The pub was both cool and comfortable. Arthur took the opportunity, to tell Peter the reason for his visit. He briefly told him about his minor stroke that caused a temporary loss of memory, his time in hospital and in more detail about the dread Laurels rehabilitation clinic. He was embarrassed when he told Peter how he, and three other residents in the clinic, had decided to take on the mantle of Grey Haired Knights of a new Camelot and escape from the Laurels, before the ennui of their incarceration caused them to lose the will to live.

He told Peter of their vow that each man would go his own way, to seek a quest to follow and return to Scagill at noon on the Saturday after the next summer solstice to tell true tales of their adventures.

He was too embarrassed to mention that the inspiration for the idea to go questing came from a strange backward skipping, ageless, snow-white bearded moustache-chewing little man who he had or had not met on Halter Moor.

Pleased that Peter had not laughed at his story, Arthur continued, "Peter I need your help to get me started. I have decided that my quest is to recover the Ingres Painting, 'La Source', for which your company offers a huge reward for information leading to its recovery." He did not mention that his equal intention was to bring the murderer to justice.

Arthur had spoken with such obvious determination that Peter, although anxious for his friend, did not object to his idea. "Well Arthur old friend," he said, "Of course I will do all that I can to help. I know my company will be supportive. The reward is less than three percent of what we have had to pay out on that one theft alone.

If you can recover the naked nubile water carrier, and I do not mean that you should give her new clothes, I am sure we can get some other missing masterpieces back where they belong. We are convinced that the same gang have nicked most of the famous paintings that have gone missing since 1985 apart from 'The Scream'.

However, I must add a serious word of caution. You must not take any risks. We believe the bad bastards who did the theft are bloody dangerous. Regrettably, we did not get them all banged up. Anne will kill me if you get hurt. Be careful tonight; do not be too specific about your plans. I don't want Anne to worry about what you will be doing. I will be doing enough of that for both of us. We will go to the office in London tomorrow, on an early train from Haslemere. I will arrange for your education in art appreciation, restoration, and conservation. You will also have to learn the techniques used by those who deal in fakery and forgery. The gang who stole the painting is an evil nest of vipers if ever there was one. It is London based, even though most thefts have been in France, Holland, Germany and Italy. I will show you what I believe to be their nest that is also their alibi."

With little notice, Anne produced a wonderful dinner. She served a lightly curried soup, followed by Coq au Vin with rice, with poached pear in sweet cider sauce as a dessert. A bottle of good red wine with the meal, followed by a glass of port made it a meal complete.

Arthur was able to recognize that Peter and Anne Bainbridge had made for themselves a very comfortable way of life. They had invested in superb furniture, some antique, some top class reproduction Georgian, real silver cutlery, solid silver sauce bowls, a fine china dinner service complete with tureens. The glassware was even finer. Together it showed their good taste afforded by their joint income.

Arthur was aware that it was all the result of years of hard work, by them both. Neither had come from families with money. Peter's police pay, put together with the pay from Anne's career as a teacher all carefully managed had provided the comfort they deserved.

Arthur had been Peter's best man at a simple church ceremony after which the happy couple had paid for the reception. It had been a simple affair, held in the upstairs room over a local café, with paper plates for the finger buffet, trifle in wax cartons and cups of tea in thick white pottery. They had begun their married life in a rented flat over a shop in the centre of Scagill.

After Peter's caution, Arthur was happy to let the conversation drift along in happy recount of their early adventures, without mention of his current or future plans. Peter told Anne that he had to go to the office in the morning. He added, too casually, that Arthur had decided to tag along to shop in the metropolis.

A little before midnight, Arthur heaved himself out of the deep armchair to declare, "Thank you Anne that was good. The witching hour is near, so if you will excuse me, I will amble to my peripatetic annex where I shall turn in for a good night's sleep. What time am I on parade tomorrow Peter?" "Better make it seven on the sixth pip." Peter replied, "I'll pick you up from your door step." Anne, for about the fourth time, said, "Arthur, I have made up the bed in the quest room; you really are most welcome to stay." Arthur replied. "Anne my dear, old men like me are too fixed in our ways. I rest easy in my own cot."

Comfortable in his sleeping bag on the large firm bed, Arthur was pleased he had taken another step on his road to adventure. Following police practice, he had secured an inside contact.

In Wicket Gate Cottage, as she worked with Peter to clear the table, load the dishwasher, and put the furniture back in place, Anne probed, "What are you two old rouges up to?" "Nothing dear," Peter lied with practiced ease.

Chapter 6

On the morning they were to go to London, Peter Bainbridge did not have to knock on the door of Arthur's motorhome. Arthur called to him from his open door, "Are you the man from the Pru, if you are mi Ma says she's not in." Anne Bainbridge had already driven a new or nearly new 'Lexus' out of their double garage ready to drive them to the station. "Wonderful dinner you put on last night Anne" Arthur said, "I remember I said in my 'Best Man' speech that you were too good for him." She seemed to be pleased with Arthur's compliment,

On the way to the station, Arthur ran his hand along the burr walnut trim of the door and the cream leather of the back seat. "Lexus, very discrete, more Bentley than BSA, the motorbike and sidecar you two used when you were courting." It was Peter's turn to be pleased, "Yes, it is one of the company perks; you may have noticed that it is registered in Switzerland. It keeps 'traffic' off my bumper. If they do stop me, I smile and speak French or German. Invariably they decide that I am too much trouble and send me on my way rejoicing."

When Ann dropped them off at the railway station, she waved a cheery farewell before she drove away at speed. At the station kiosk, Peter bought the Financial Times. Arthur, true to his habit, bought the 'Daily Telegraph'. Astonished at the cost, Arthur used his debit card to buy a return day ticket to the city; Peter calmly used his season ticket.

On the train, comfortably seated in a first-class carriage, Arthur used a pencil and a ballpoint pen to attempt to complete the crosswords. He did not read the news. For Arthur, crosswords came first. During the journey he noticed that Peter carefully read the F.T. news and business columns, and that he marked details that interested him with a gold fountain pen.

Outside Waterloo Station, they were lucky to get a taxi without much delay. After Peter had asked the cabby to take them to an address in the City, Arthur took the opportunity to suggest an idea. "Peter, at your suggestion, we told Anne that I wanted to shop in the metropolis today. As it happens, I do, and with good reason. If you can spare me for an hour before we leave the City, this high rise filter that is clogged with grime and crime I want to buy an artist's travel easel, some prepared board, good brushes, oils, pigments, paints and a palette knife. I've done quite a few pictures using oil paint since I retired. Last night, I thought about the job in hand. I reasoned that while I search for the siren La Source I could make my hobby my invisibility cloak. It will give me good reason to spend un-natural periods of time in peculiar places."

Peter, who was a bit puzzled, asked, "How will that happen?" Arthur explained, in thoughtful tone, "Say you chose to stand or sit alone, for more than ten minutes, in a public place, in any city street, or open meadow, some curious or nosey individual will ask you if you are alright, or a jobsworth official will tell you to move on. A respectably dressed old gentleman like me, painting a canvas set on an easel, explains everything. No busybody or jobsworth will disturb me. They will accept me as an artist, or dismiss me as an eccentric. No one will bother me, other than those who may try to take a surreptitious look to judge my work.

Even the bad lads who steal paintings will not believe that someone well over police retirement age will search for their stash of stolen goods. As I see it, the only risk is that I may be reported to the police as a dirty old man, or even a paedophile, if anyone notices that I take too close an interest in paintings of naked young ladies."

The luxury of the Insurance Company office reception area reinforced Arthur's already high opinion of his colleagues career move. Marble floors, glass and stainless steel everywhere, conveyed an atmosphere of City efficiency, rather than bank building opulence. The only strong colour Arthur noticed was the lipstick worn by the young lady receptionist who greeted Peter pleasantly. "Good morning Mr. Bainbridge, will you please ask Mr. Thomas to sign the visitors book."

This made Arthur realise that security must be tight in the City and that Peter must have been busy before they left Lurgashall. The receptionist already had a printed nametag ready for him to pin to his coat. With the formalities completed, an express lift took them to the seventeenth floor. The two men soon settled in comfortable chairs at a side table in Peter's large office, not at his desk.

A young man came to ask if they would like coffee. Peter's reply to the young man was brisk, "No thank you lad, however a pot of tea would do the trick." To Arthur he said, "The firm may be Swiss, but we are native English chaps here in London. Coffee is head-office stuff." Arthur, who was in reflective mood, talked half to himself, with the balance for Peter's ear. "Your firm would not have deemed fit for a broom cupboard, the office I shared with two other superintendents in Scagill police station."

When the young man brought in a silver tray set with a silver tea set and fine Worcester porcelain Arthur shook his head in disbelief. He told Peter that to get his last cup of tea in police service he had had to fetch it himself, in a plastic cup, from an automatic vending machine that charged 50p per cup and did not give change.

Peter ignored Arthur's muttered comparisons. "I had a word with head office in Zurich before we left home. I have been authorised to give you as much information as possible. The company will not pay you; they will however stand some costs to help you with your efforts to find the stolen painting.

We hope that the thieves will have left DNA traces all over it. If they have, it might help us to get the murder conviction we want. Whatever happens, their theft of the painting involves blood money. It may have reduced the price that they could sell it for, or it may have caused them to destroy it, to prevent it being used in evidence, if we, or the police, ever find it.

On balance, we think that it still exists. The gang is both arrogant and greedy. It has made too big an investment in its acquisition to destroy it. Part of their investment was murder. For them it means that another murder is immaterial. Swiss Mobius will help you, but cannot protect you.

Today I will arrange for you to spend a few days at the National Gallery with the conservators. Apparently, the gallery abjures the term restorers. They will show you the most up to date techniques used in their conservation work. Inevitably, criminal forgers have also learned to use the same techniques when they knock out their forgeries and fakes. Forgeries are copies; fakes are new paintings created to pass off as a recently discovered unknown work of a famous artist, for which the clever crooks create an appropriate provenance.

You should pick up some tips on how to recognize an original and spot a wrong un. I have also arranged for you to spend some time with a private security company we use. They will bring you up to date with current surveillance, espionage and security techniques. Friends of mine at Scotland Yard have agreed for you to have a long hard look at photographs of the people we collared for the theft, plus a few more we know to be part of the racket. Most important of all, I want you to go to an open prison in Derbyshire to get a good look at the king rat in the pack, one Terrance Servient-Higgins. He is due for parole quite soon. I know the Governor of the open prison who has to keep him within what puny boundaries are available to him. I will call in a favour he owes me to let you in to see Higgins, on the pretext that you are a new volunteer prison visitor under instruction. I do not just want you to see this man; I want you to hear him, smell him, and touch him, even if it is only a handshake. I want you to be immediately aware if he ever comes near to you, however far into the future that may be. You must have the sense of his evil presence, whether he is in disguise, or in the dark, or whether you are drunk, sober, asleep or unconscious. I want you to know immediately should he come near at anytime, anywhere, indoors or out. Only then will I be able to relax, confident that you will be prepared."

The force of Peter's plea startled Arthur. He said, "Good God, you sound like Ian Fleming's M combined with Q." Not put off by Arthur's levity; Peter was brusque, "Well heed my words mister nascent 'Double 0 Arthur Thomas. Make no mistake; he is a cold evil vicious killer. I am sure that Higgins shot the guard, without pity, at point blank range, in a struggle for the painting. The guard died soon after, although not before he told the Paris Police that he had fought with a skinny youth who wore a balaclava mask with a ponytail stuck out of the back. Horrible Higgins has a ridiculous greasy rat-tail that sprouts from the back of his head. If he rumbles you, before we have him locked away, committed to a full life sentence for murder, he will kill you himself, or he will have you killed. To have you killed would be his second choice for he is a corrosive slick of bile mixed with spite. Although I can give you many things, I cannot give you police protection or even a shoulder holstered potato gun."

The company have however, given you this much better tool, it is a simple mobile phone fully funded for use all over the world. Put it in your pocket. Keep it with you, fully charged at all times. I have already plumbed in my telephone numbers: home, mobile and office. Do not use it for any other purpose.

The two men spent most of the day to organise Arthur's crash training course. Finally, late in the afternoon, Peter let him go, by taxi, to buy his oil paints, brushes, pallet and travellers easel. He insisted that the young man, who had earlier in the day brought in tea, act as his escort to the shop that his secretary had sourced, as the best for artists in London. Once the mission was complete, to Arthur's satisfaction, Peter had ordered the young man to bring him safely back to the office.

Peter, ever the efficient manager, had rung Anne to arrange for the three of them to have dinner at a restaurant between Haslemere and Lurgashall. Always thoughtful, he had even booked a taxi to wait for them at the station, so that Anne could drive straight to the restaurant.

Arthur began to realise why Peter had done so well in the Met. His admiration for his efficiency and attention to detail made him acutely aware that he must take his dire warning about Servient-Higgins seriously. However, he had noted that Peter had not tried to turn him from his chosen quest.

That evening, Arthur enjoyed the company of his friends. He rated the restaurant dinner better than good, however not a patch on the Crown in Scagill or Anne's home cooking. He thought the beer only as good as it could be, south of the Trent.

Back outside Wicket Gate Cottage, although pressed, he declined the invitation to come in for a nightcap.

After he took leave of his hosts, he happily unlocked the door to his private quarters to press the button that lowered the steps; it never failed to amuse him. Not used to late nights, Arthur was tired, so tired that he forgot to set his alarm clock before he fell asleep.

A gentle tap on the door woke him. He was acutely embarrassed to see from his wristwatch that it was almost ten o'clock. After he put on his dressing gown, he opened the door to find Anne who held a tray set with scrambled eggs, bacon, toast and a pot of tea.

"Good morning Arthur, she said, "It is time you were on duty young man. Peter has left you sealed orders. Have your breakfast in peace before you come over to the cottage. Today you can help me in the garden."

Although Anne had left the cottage door wide open, Arthur knocked before he went into the house to return the breakfast tray. He could see that Anne was already in the garden clipping the lawn edges. "I don't know what you must think of me," he said, "Ten o'clock still bed-locked. I do apologise," "Don't be daft Arthur," Anne said, "You boys need a sleep out every now and again." Arthur remembered that his Jenny used to say the same when he had a lie in, after a spell on night duty. "

Tell me Anne, what I can do in the garden that does not need green fingers," he volunteered. Her pert reply was, "Nothing, just settle down over there to read your sealed orders. Being a bobby's wife, I will not pester you to find out what you two tough guys are up to. Whatever it is, you must remember that you are no longer in the first flush of youth." Arthur grinned because, at last, he had remembered the name of the film with Burt Lancaster and Kirk Douglas. The film that he thought had inspired his original idea to leave the Laurels rehabilitation clinic. He did not know, nor would he ever know for sure that other forces had been in play. Anne had just said it, 'Tough Guys', yes that was it, Tough Guys.

The caution that Peter had given him yesterday made him realise that he was no tough guy. Although not feeble, Arthur had to acknowledge that he was no longer strong or agile and that age did occasionally weary him. What concerned him most was that unlike the tough guys in the film, he had no partner.

Obedient to Anne's instruction, Arthur went over to the comfortable garden chair with a side table. On the table, he found a large brown envelope on which Peter had written in large block and very small letters, using a fountain pen.

Part time seconded non pensionable 003½ Arthur Thomas
FOR YOUR EYES ONLY
GLASSES NOT PROVIDED

In the envelope, he found a précis about the murder and theft of the stolen Ingres masterpiece, as well as the criminal record and CVs of all those sent to prison for their part in the theft. There were also letters of introduction to the Head of Conservation at the National Gallery, the Technical Director of the security company Peter had told him about, and to the Governor of one of HM Prisons in Derbyshire.

Also in the envelope, Peter had put a detailed programme of activities he had arranged for him. In a separate envelope he found an open first class return rail ticket from St Pancras to Derby stuck with tape to a bundle of ten pound notes marked 'Five Hundred' on the blue wrapper.

In the parcel, he also found a pack of business cards that intrigued him: 'Dr Edward Davenport PhD. The Open University (Attached) Forward Programme Planning Dept.' It gave no other details. In a separate small envelope he found a debit card in the name of Dr Edward Davenport PhD and a note stating that he was to hand his own debit card in, so that the new card could be linked to his account. There was also a note to empty his wallet and clothes of anything that might identify him as anyone other than Dr. Edward Davenport.

Arthur was impressed to say, "Gracious heavens Anne, did Peter get any sleep last night?" Anne admitted, "Well he did stay up late and he was up early. Do not forget, at this time of year, Zurich is an hour ahead of London. His staff over there typed all the letters before they emailed them here. I printed them out. Peter did the hard job; he put them into the envelopes. A man on a motorbike delivered the other packet just before I disturbed your slumbers."

Arthur stood up to stretch before he said, "Well Anne, I have my orders. I must go before English Heritage hound me out of this area of natural beauty that includes the resident beauty who kindly brought me breakfast.

Your husband has arranged that on Monday I start on two weeks in the wicked city, busy with things to do. In consequence of which, I must take my leave of you. I need to find a caravan site near to the suppurating city, in order to be ready to join the daily commute of millions from suburbia to central London.

Before I go up to town, Tootsie shall take me to the seaside. I have not had a paddle for years. I am sure that a breath of sea air will do me the world of good before I have to join in the choke in the 'Smoke.'"

Anne appeared grave as Arthur made his way to the door. As she had when he arrived, she took both of his hands in hers. "Arthur, I guess that whatever it is you are doing with Peter, it has to do with Servient-Higgins.

Peter has never forgiven himself for failing to make the murder charge stick. It still worries him, which worries me, and now I shall have to worry about you, best of all 'Best-Men'. Take-care Arthur; I can understand that you do not want to settle for a quiet life, not after all those years in the force, but in your search for a new challenge make sure you do not get dead in the doing of it."

Arthur was soon on the road, headed for the coast. But as soon as he had the opportunity, he pulled over into a lay-by where he sat for an hour deep in thought.

He realised that Anne had awakened in him memories he had suppressed since his wife Jenny had died. Although he was in no way jealous of Peter, he recognized that he did miss married life.

Anne's feminine touch in all things, the warmth with which she had greeted him and her tender yet formal leave taking, with both of her hands holding his and no false empty air kisses, were things almost too hard for Arthur to bear. "Best make yourself a cup of tea Arthur Thomas," he said aloud, "Can't have you maudlin when you have to go questing, or as Tristan would have it, 'Questin.'"

When Arthur drew up onto a car park, facing the sea, at Bracklesham, it was already mid-afternoon. Because the adjacent public lavatories were still open he was able to service all the necessary cabin side facilities of what he thought of as his beach hut.

With both batteries fully charged by the run down from Lurgashall, he was fully independent.

Arthur was happy with the prospect of Friday night, and all day Saturday to explore a part of England new to him, while he lived rent and rates free. He planned that if he left the coast early on Sunday morning he would be able to set up on a caravan site, near to London, ready to meet the appointment that Peter had made for him at the National Gallery on the Monday that followed.

He spent a pleasant Friday evening on a visit by taxi to Chichester. All day Saturday, he spent on Selsey Bill engrossed with his newly acquired paint box. For his subject he took the posts and boards of a black wooden groin that contrasted with the grey beach pebbles leaving out any suggestion of sea and sky. It was a statement that he was a painter not a watercolourist.

Early on the Monday morning on his way to the National Gallery, even though it was high summer, Arthur felt raw cold while he stood at the bus stop, a few hundred yards from the Caravan Club site at Crystal Palace.

The club's guidebook indicated that it was their closest to Central London. He had joined the regular seven o'clock in the morning queue of sleepy eyed silent commuters, all of whom seemed to be on autopilot. Arthur was fully awake; the prospect of time spent at the National Gallery excited him.

He had called the Bainbridges on the Sunday evening to thank them both for their hospitality and to confirm that he was in place, ready to commute. Likewise, Peter had confirmed that there was only one change to the arranged programme. He wanted to meet him for lunch on Wednesday in two days' time, to show him, during the afternoon, where he and the police thought the gang of murderous thieves had their den, and alibi.

After Arthur had presented his letter of introduction and a director of the National Gallery introduced him to the staff of its conservation department. He was impressed by the knowledge, skill and technique displayed by the team of conservators. All of them chatted happily with him while they worked, except for one woman who seemed to have a problem with everyone, including herself.

The conservators all referred to him as Dr. Davenport, or Edward. Their Director had told them that he was a 'Forward Planning Manager' attached to the Open University film unit engaged to carry out research for a projected television series. He had added that his research would include other galleries in the UK and the Continent.

Peter's notes had warned him about this necessary alias because it was important that his connection to Swiss Mobius remain unknown to anyone associated with the arts.

Arthur thought Peter had been clever to choose the Open University for his alibi. Because the O.U. organisation was almost undefined, it would make it virtually impossible for anyone to check his status. The O. U. was very different to Oxford, Cambridge, or even the new Red Bricks, where a quick check on the internet would establish the truth or dishonesty of his claimed credentials.

On his third day at the National Gallery, somewhat diffidently, Arthur took with him his paint box.

The techniques his teachers at night school classes had taught him, his new tutors brushed aside. First, they showed him how to set up his easel, at the right height and angle whether he needed to sit or stand. They recommended he stood to paint. They told him how to hold his brushes, also his pallet knife.

They taught him how to mix paints, and ways to prepare both canvas and board the professional way.

They took pleasure when they taught him to look at paintings in a critical not an emotional way; to look for clues in the brushwork in paintings by the same hand in order to be able to spot repairs, or work of a different hand in background detail. They taught him how an old master could be veiled or hidden by another painting without any permanent damage to the original.

The conservators made him practice techniques they had demonstrated to detail folds in velvet, clear glass, reflections and shadow. They gave him tips on the correct brushes to use for skin tones and texture. He felt his time so well spent he decided that, once he had recovered 'La Source', he would return to the National Gallery to work as an unpaid porter, or cleaner, so that he might have opportunities to watch the conservators at work.

As arranged, Arthur met Peter in a small Italian restaurant in Knightsbridge, where they had a light, though Arthur thought it a very expensive lunch. Peter had to endure the enthusiastic bursts from Arthur about his discovery of art. His new obsession obliterated all previous passions. Painting on canvas, or board with a pallet of oil paints was the only thing that a chap should do.

Peter let him ramble on until the waiter had served them both with coffee. Peter explained he had ordered coffee because although Italians may be great cooks, they knew nothing of tea. When they had finished the coffee Peter said, "Come on, we are about to test your invisibility skills at a posh shop that calls itself, 'Faux Art Works'.

"Now Arthur," Peter commanded, as though he was about to instruct a small boy, "You are to promise me to curb your enthusiasm. You must let me take all the attention of the creeps who run the shop. You will be a bored bag carrier with no interest in the art works; do you understand? I don't want anyone who works there to notice you this afternoon, or ever to recognise you in the future. You have just this one shot to take in as much as you can. We are sure that Faux Art Works are in the Premier League of fine art fakes, forgery and theft.

Do not be fooled by the bum starver jackets and pin stripped trousers. The obsequious bastards are, to a man, pure evil. Any tart who works there is complicit in their iniquity. Yes, I want to get the paintings back, that is my job, but most of all I want the thieves locked away for the rest of their miserable lives.

I want them tried, proven guilty of murder and conspiracy to murder. The guard they killed at the Musée D'Orsay had just retired from the French Gendarme. He was part of our team, a good man with a wife and three children. It should have been straightforward because we were on to them before the heist. For us it all went horribly wrong. We lost a good man; they got away with the painting. Brutal callous greed made a wife a widow and orphaned three children.

Because we could not prove who or how or from where the murderer fired, the shots, we failed to get a murder conviction. We still hope that some future information or evidence might let us bring a murder charge without the problem of double jeopardy. The trial was in France. To my regret, they no longer use the guillotine. The French Court sentenced Servient-Higgins, who we think was the prime suspect, to a long term in prison. The European agreement allowed them to offload him onto our prison system. The law will soon release him on parole, perhaps even in weeks, if he cons the parole board to believe that he has shown remorse. Any remorse he shows will be left at the prison gate"

Viewed from the pavement, the double fronted shop in Knightsbridge astonished Arthur. The shop that sold pictures and sculptures, the prime subjects of the visual arts, had no windows. The designers had had the shop front faced with panels of cream brown veined marble. The middle third of the marble panels sloped inwards to a smoked glass double door emblazoned with a gold leaf faux coat of arms.

A doorman, who attended the entrance, wore a green frock coat trimmed with gold, white gloves, and a black silk top hat. Arthur's detective eyes spotted a clue that the business might not be top drawer. The cheap shoddy black trousers and worn down dirty shoes that made up the rest of his uniform would not have passed muster outside any half-decent store or hotel. The only signs to indicate the nature of the business were two small discrete engraved stainless steel plates, one on each side of the glass doors: 'Faux Art Works - London - New York - Paris - Rome.'

When Peter moved towards the door, the doorman asked if he had made an appointment. Peter answered dismissively, "Sir Ralf Connisburgh to see Charles Higgins." The doorman glanced at a clipboard in his left hand, "Oh yes sir, I have it here," before he opened the door with his right hand. He called out to some unseen person inside the gallery, "Sir Ralf Connisburgh with his man."

Inside, Arthur had the first surprise of the afternoon. Fixed to a panel immediately inside the door that screened the interior, the gallery had on display Leonardo's un-mistakable Mona Lisa, complete with her enigmatic smile. To demonstrate the skill of their copyists, on the same canvas, the gallery had had a replica of Edward Munch's 'The scream' painted to look over the Giaconda's shoulder. The astonished, "Good Lord," from Arthur brought a quick glace from Peter that cautioned him to silence.

A black bum starver jacketed, pin striped trouser wearing, pale faced weasel of a young man, who had bad teeth and worse breath greeted Peter with an unctuous welcome. "Good Morning Sir Rafe, I believe this is the first occasion that we have had the honour to show you the exhibits in our humble gallery of faux art work masterpieces, although many critics think that they are masterpieces in their own right."

He continued, in a voice that made Arthur think of Uriah Heep, "Would you care to take sherry. We have a fine old Manzanilla, a special favourite of their Lordships." Peter with genuine patrician style brushed the man aside. "No, I will just take some time here to browse. I wish to determine if there are any canvases or pieces that might suit my latest project." "Certainly Sir Rafe, I shall be at my desk, should you have any questions." Peter said, "I have just one; if I buy a particular copy, can you assure me that you will not create other similar copies?"

Higgins junior replied, "Of course Sir Rafe however, I am sure that you will understand, it will add a premium to the purchase price, particularly if we have another such work in stock that would have to be destroyed." "Quite," was Peter's only response. The young man left Peter to browse.

The gallery walls were stark matt white with the larger paintings well hung and cleverly lit. The gallery was much larger than the frontage had led Arthur to expect.

The shop fitters had arranged screens to break up the space to allow for the exhibition of different schools of painters, the Pre-Raphaelites, Dutch Masters, Impressionists, with a whole section for Picasso and another for Warhol and yet another to contrast Bacon with Freud.

By the side of each painting, at eye level, a white card, with copper plate script, gave details of the work. The original artist, the date of the original painting, the size and material of the original, the scale of the copy and how many copies had been released. There was no mention of the name of the copyist or of the price.

There was only one other customer in the gallery, a loud individual who kept the Higgins fellow busy with endless banal questions. Arthur thought him a brash nouveau rich fellow marked out by his open neck raw silk shirt, medallion, cords, sandals and gold Rolex.

Arthur shunned the watercolours, the abstract and the modern. He spent almost twenty minutes in a detail study of a superb full sized copy of Ingres's 'Odalisque with a Slave'. The painting had a photograph of the original by its side, taken from a folio issued by Harvard University. The card by its side stated that the original was on public display at the university's Fog Art Museum.

To copy the original correctly, 'Faux Art Works' had had it painted on board without a frame. The faux painting overwhelmed Arthur. The beauty of the skin tones brought out by the technique of the copyist both amazed and depressed him. The more that he studied it, the more he felt that the standard achieved by the copyist who worked for Faux Art Works, or who was commissioned by them, made it impossible for an amateur like himself to identify original, fake or forgery.

After almost an hour, Peter signalled to leave. When they were in a taxi, on the way back to Peter's office, it became obvious that Peter was very pleased with himself. Arthur challenged, "My not yet dead police nous tells me that you have been up to some mischief." "I have that," Peter replied, "I am dead chuffed; didn't the boy do well?" "Who?" Arthur asked, completely at a loss. "Why the loud mouth braggart in the shop. That was Sergeant Cooper of the fraud squad." For the second time that day, Arthur's surprised comment was, "Good Lord." Peter who was excited, rattled on, "He kept the little chap so occupied that I got a moment or two to myself in the small office behind his desk. I gave the blond bimbo who was in the office a fifty pound note and asked her to nip across the road to buy me a box of 'Rennies' as my lunch had upset my delicate indigestion.

I struck gold; I took the sales record books for the year that the Servient-Higgins gang stole 'She who you seek' and another that covered the dates on which two other stolen paintings in which Swiss Mobius have an interest. They are all on one shelf, in date order, beautifully bound and dated. They must use the books that do not show the price paid as a sales aid, or they have an interest in where the buyer will display his or her chosen faux work of art. I suppose they do not want any of their customers to pass off, as genuine, any of their 'Faux' works. All we have to do is to get the books back onto the shelf, after we have copied any record that is relevant to our search. I will leave that to the sergeant or one of his men.

You too did well Arthur, you may be six foot four and seven-teen stone, but I don't think that anyone noticed you at all. It was always the same when we used to chase the girls on our nights off. By the by, you might like to take this back with you to your land yacht, as a bit of homework for tonight; it is their current catalogue, but don't stay up too late; tomorrow you have a busy day.

Do you know that the cheeky sods charge twenty-five quid for a copy? I bought it with the change from the fifty I gave to the girl. It left me a bit skint, as she said the Rennies cost a tenner. "Good Lord," Arthur commented, for the third time that day.

Chapter 7

The last two days that Arthur spent with the conservators at the National Gallery were not the pure joy for which he had hoped. The senior man was a bit pedantic when Arthur, without thinking, referred to his work as restoration. He took Arthur's naïve use of the term particularly hard.

He declaimed, "We are conservators not restorers. Restoration is a last resort, damn near to forgery. Curators must record, in detail, any work that goes beyond the norms of conservation, which in general terms means cleaning and protection only. You will no doubt see the difference when you continue your research in Paris, particularly at the d'Orsay, where that incompetent charlatan d'Chasterlain loses rather than conserves paintings. Although Arthur felt the boss had ticked him off, he was still enthralled while he watched the conservators at work. He still enjoyed dabbling with the set pieces they gave him. A small event had however, made him a little wary.

It was only by chance that Arthur saw one of the women conservators drop a copy of the expensive 'Faux Art Works' catalogue. It interested him that she far too hastily picked it up, to stuff it hurriedly into her workbox.

The habits infused in Arthur by thirty plus years police work came powerfully back to mind. 'Check everything twice over, facts, alibi and motive, test the evidence, examine events; trust no one until they have been proven true beyond doubt'. It intrigued him that she had been so quick to conceal an innocent catalogue.

He thought the woman to be in her middle to late forties. He categorised her as an un-tamed shrew that would never have her portrait done as an oil painting. She was an overt feminist who looked almost like a man, emphasised by Doc Martin' boots, thin frame, slack jeans, collared shirt, woollen tie and thin mousey hair drawn back to a short pony tail held with a postman's red rubber elastic band.

Later in the day, Arthur also found in her workbox a thick wad of superb colour photographs. He did not find them by chance; he went to look. They were all the same size; each one appeared to be an enlarged section of a painting that he did not recognise. As far as he could remember, he had not seen it in the conservators' workshop, or in the National Gallery. The photographs were marked with fine red lines that gave dimensions between critical points, in millimetres. His discovery disturbed Arthur. It made him wonder if any of the team of skilled restorers who worked for the National Gallery could be moonlighting for Faux Art Works.

He thought of an even worse conjecture. Could a member of the team also be a member of Servient-Higgins's murderous gang of thieves? The incident made him realise why Peter had arranged for him to use an alias to keep secret his identity and real purpose, even from such an august body as the National Gallery.

On Friday afternoon, prompt at twenty-minutes past four o'clock, the workshop closed for the weekend. When Arthur bid goodbye, with many an expression of his appreciation, most of the conservators wished him well.

The woman who had alerted his suspicions with the content of her workbox did not smile, nor did she offer to shake his hand. Conversely, she gave him a long thoughtful look. Arthur thought that it was such a look that an artist would use to commit to memory features of a life model. It was a cold look. It sent a chill through him.

With no appointment, or demand on his time until the following Monday morning, Arthur realised that he was free to do as he pleased. He ignored Dr. Johnson's aphorism; he realised that he was tired of London, a life he could ill afford. Neither did he see London as Wordsworth saw it.

After only a week of commuting by bus, he considered Noel Coward's London Pride was well past its sell by date. He believed 'London Blight' rather than 'London Pride' a better term to describe what Cobbet's 'Great Wen', in modern times, suppurated over, rather than handed down.

As soon as Arthur got back to the Crystal Palace Caravan Park, he reserved a pitch for the next week, Sunday to Friday. The weather being full summer, he first thought that he might go to the coast. He put aside the idea because he did not want to spend the weekend driving. The coast to Arthur was the rugged North Yorkshire coast, or the coast of Northumberland from the Tyne to the border with Scotland. He thought the concrete promenades of the south coast, with their formal flowerbeds that fronted hotels converted to flats, were the habitat of the self-satisfied that made them dull company.

He considered the long dreary marshes along the banks of the Thames estuary fit only for wading birds. That settled, he decided that as he was already south of the river he would push southeast, away from London, into rural Kent. He planned to find a village with a traditional village green, where he could paint. Wherever it might be, he would set up his easel to practice the tricks, or were they techniques, he had learned from the conservators at the National Gallery.

He also wanted to test the idea he had mentioned to Peter that his artist's easel would be his invisibility cloak, behind which he could hone his observation skills.

A little after six o'clock Arthur was on the road, clear of the site. He knew he still had almost four hours daylight to find a place to park up overnight.

It took him far longer than he had hoped, in both time and distance, to clear the slough of London's suburbs. Because of the delays, he took the precaution to buy provisions at a late night shop that had an off license. Most important to him, he purchased six bottles of bottled conditioned real ale.

He made a fuss about the beer. He insisted that the young shopkeeper did not shake them and that she keep them upright. To transfer his precious bottles to Tootsie, he paid a little extra for a cardboard carrier designed to carry six wine bottles. He carefully stowed the bottles in a bottom cupboard, stuffing the carrier with newspaper to stop the lees at the bottom of the bottle from being disturbed. When Arthur went back to the shop, to pick up his bag of assorted groceries, he casually slung it over his shoulder, as would a sailor home on leave.

It was mid-summer dusk before he found a village suitable for his needs. It fell a bit short of his ideal. There was no pub, however it spread out around a green big enough to have a cricket pitch where the boundaries would make a four difficult and a six only possible for a mighty blacksmith. Satisfied with his recognisance, and sensitive not to alarm village residents that he might be the advance party of a group of travellers, he turned back from the village to park in a lay-by outside its curtilage.

He spent a pleasant late evening listening to the radio, while he made a macaroni cheese. He ate his simple supper slowly. Later, he drank one of the bottle-conditioned ales that his careful packing had kept in good condition.

The next morning, by ten o'clock, Arthur had set up his easel. By eleven, he had completed several sketches of views from the village green. The sketch with which he was best pleased was of a horse chestnut tree that shrouded an old thatched house, part hidden behind a thick mixed hedge of green holly that fought for space with copper beech. He chose to paint his subject on a twelve inch by eight inch prepared board.

It was well after two o'clock before he realised that he had observed nothing, nothing at all. He felt guilty. While he painted, he had planned to hone his surveillance skills. He called himself a useless old fool.

He thought that for all the good he was at observation, without him noticing, the village maidens could have erected a maypole, and danced around it, naked. Concentration on the painting had made him oblivious to his surroundings. When he reached forward, to try a touch of sienna on the gable end of the house in his picture, he was again lost to the world.

A gentle cough, followed by a soft feminine voice just behind him said, "We thought that you might like a cup of tea, you must be ready for one. You have not stopped since early this morning." Arthur, shocked back to reality, jumped to his feet. The sudden movement knocked over his collapsible chair. "Good heavens; what time is it?" he said abruptly, because he had been startled. He quickly corrected himself to say politely, "Oh, sorry ma'am, thank you, thank you, yes, yes indeed, you are very kind."

His thoughts collected, he used his proper name to introduce himself. The lady continued, "Come on over to the garden to meet my husband. He was becoming quite worried about you." "Thank you, a cup of tea would be grand." Arthur said. Although his manner was easy, Arthur was not a happy man. He realised that he was an unwise monkey. He had heard nothing, seen nothing, nor had he spoken to anyone, whereas a couple he had not noticed had observed him for several hours.

An hour later, after he thanked the hospitable couple, he told them he had to return to the city to attend to dull business. Only when he drove out of the village did Ex Superintendent, ex Detective Inspector, now private investigator, Arthur Thomas notice the sign, 'Stelling Minnis - A neighbourhood watch village'.

On the Sunday evening, after a day spent painting on the bank of Bewl Water near Ticehurst, Arthur was again parked at the Crystal Palace Caravan Club site.

At ten o'clock Peter rang. In answer to his question, "Have you had a good weekend?" Arthur replied "Curate's egg," before he asked, "Is all still in accord with our list of instructions?" "Yes," Peter replied with a voice of authority, "As listed, Monday and Tuesday with the Techno-boffins, Wednesday with me in the office. I have arranged for your further education about La Source. Thursday you go to the Yard to meet an old pal of mine to study photographs. Friday you go to Derbyshire to meet the prime suspect. Saturday, not listed, Anne insists that you come down to the cottage. She has arranged one of her special dinner parties. She will not let me do a barbecue. You had better invent some plausible tale to tell her how you have spent your days." "All right 'Gov'; Wednesday it is then." Arthur put the phone back in his pocket.

The Techno-boffins, as Peter called them, were good enough citizens. They were however, not at all Arthur's cup of tea. They enthused about gadgets, usually the newest and smallest. Some, Arthur found quite frightening, particularly the eves dropping microphones that could hear through walls of stone, and the digital cameras that could see in the dark.

The prototype remote DNA testing devices alarmed him most. Unknown to a visitor they could register an individual's DNA when he, or she, entered a building. The device automatically transmitted collected data to a central database. Within minutes, the system could identify any person who had had his, or her, DNA previously recorded.

The gadgets were all very small big-boys toys, of little interest to Arthur.

He made excuses to leave early after lunch on each of the two days that Peter had arranged for his technical brief. Using the afternoons, as he thought to more advantage, Arthur improved his knowledge of painting. He visited the Tate Gallery, not the Tate Modern on Monday, and the National Portrait Gallery on Tuesday.

On the Wednesday, in a small conference room next to Peter's office, Arthur met the three experts who were there to advise him of how he could identify a painting of La Source, as genuine, or as a forgery or a copy.

A thin nervous man introduced himself as Jacques Dupont, the Deputy Head of Security of the Musée d'Orsay in Paris. It was from there that that the gang had stolen 'La Source' and during the theft callously murdered a museum guard. He then introduced an expert on Ingres that he had brought with him from France, whose name Arthur immediately forgot. The third man introduced himself.

He was an elegant elderly man who explained that his old friend Peter had asked him to help with clues to identification and translation. The elderly man's business card identified him as a partner of 'Bonham's' (Ret'd). Soon after the theft, the two scholars had worked together to compile for Swiss Mobius a most scholarly document worthy of a Doctorate at either Oxford or Cambridge.

To Arthur's relief, they recognised that he was an ex policeman, not a trained artist. To help him they had compiled a concise readable summary of their almost impenetrable greater work. They aimed to give Arthur clues that would enable him to authenticate the original Ingres masterpiece, and techniques to identify forgeries, fakes, or copies. The guide to help him identify the original went into detail about previous known conservation. It gave particular detail of critical measurements.

The definition of detail relied on the background, not the figure of the water carrier, but in the leaves on the vine, the little daisy like flowers, points that the tired copyist might overlook. All three experts told him to look for the enamel-like colour of the skin tones, yet unmatched by any artist.

They each told him it would be worth his while to visit, the Louvre to study the composition and commit to memory other nude subjects painted by Ingres, particularly the 'Valpincon Bather' and 'The Turkish Bath'. They gave him a copy of what they believed to be the most-perfect colour photograph ever produced of 'La Source'. The Musée d'Orsay curators had commissioned photographs of all their important works before the Germans occupied Paris. They had feared that Albert Speer would have taken the best to the chateau at Berchtesgaden for his Führer's private pleasure.

Although he listened carefully, Arthur thought it unlikely that any study by him of Ingres's technique would help. Conversely, he was confident that if he used the photograph correctly, a simple metric ruler would provide answers.

The curators who commissioned the photograph had marked and recorded in millimetres the distance between several flowers on the original painting. It reminded Arthur of the photographs he had found in the workbox of the pony-tailed women conservator at the National Gallery.

His engagement with the experts went on after lunch, into the afternoon. As a result, it was not until about four o'clock that Arthur went to meet Peter for further instruction.

"Well, we got the sales record books safely back on the shelves of the Faux Art shop," beamed Peter. "An official spot check visit from a VAT inspector about a claim made by one of their clients saw to that. Their record books helped me with an idea that I have been working on. It is usually a small event, a bit of paperwork, an overheard conversation or something missing that provides an important insight into how the criminal mind works. Once we understand their mind-set, it helps us to understand their method. It becomes easier to bring them to justice. The books show that Faux Art Works are expert with smoke and mirrors; now you see it, now you don't. I am now almost sure that they have a sting that has confused the forces of law and order. I will explain, so listen carefully. I shall be asking question later"

Peter leaned back in his chair, steepled his fingers and began, "When Servient-Higgins chooses a particular high value painting to steal, and he first commissions one of his retained experts to create an as near perfect copy of the original as possible.

He specifies that the copyist include one or two deliberate errors in the background detail that would go un-noticed by any art expert, except for an Ingres specialist. Only then do he and his gang of thugs steal the original.

With the hullabaloo and publicity about the theft, Faux Art Works put the near perfect copy on sale in their gallery. The publicity enables the gallery to offer it at an extortionately high price.

Now comes the clever bit, the sting. To hide the original that they have stolen, they deliver the original painting, not the copy, to the unaware purchaser of the copy.

With the original safely stored, Servient-Higgins can wait until after the hoo-ha about the theft dies down, and all insurance claims are settled, and the police case shelved. As the law has had him in prison, for seven years, all that has already occurred.

When released on parole then has two routes to the pot of gold. One would be to recover the original and to sell it to an unscrupulous collector.

This would take a long time and be dangerous because Higgins would have to be sure that the unscrupulous collector would not have a fit of conscience and inform the police or beat down the price and claim the reward for himself.

The second less remunerative, though safer way to a substantial income, would be for Higgins to claim the reward from the insurance company." Peter explained, "The usual method is that the thieves come up with a credible story that an agent has contacted them offering to arrange to recover the stolen painting from an anonymous third party, if the reward is paid, in full. I know some museum curators, even government arts ministers, who have reacted more hysterically to receiving a fragment of a masterpiece through the post, than they would have done if they had received a gory ear cut off one of their own children."

"Do you really seriously believe that Higgins could do that," Arthur got in at last. "Oh yes," Peter replied. "On two occasions, Swiss Mobius has paid out princely ransoms to what they believe to have been agents of Servient-Higgins. As yet, we have not been able to prove the connection. You see Arthur, there have been many famous paintings stolen in the last ten years, other than the one in which you have such a special interest. For example Edvard Munch's 'The Scream', stolen twice, though why anyone would want to hang it on his or her wall is beyond rational thought. We don't think they are stolen to order, the popular conjecture of the tabloid press, we believe they are stolen for stock, investment stock."

Peter went on, "I repeat, having stolen their chosen work of art, the thieves sell it, as a copy, to a rich collector or to a large company to hang in their boardroom. Higgins would know that the high value put on it by Faux Art Works would mean it would stay with the buyer, as a prized possession, even though they bought it as a copy. The purchaser, could exhibit the original when and where he wished, in a private house, on a millionaire's motor yacht, or on the wall of a swish hotel, all places where the gang could easily steal it. If Higgins and his gang steal the painting again, they might try to throw sand in our eyes by switching the genuine painting, sold as a copy, with the copy. The owner, who had bought the painting, believing it to be a copy, would never know that he had been in possession of the original. Recovering the original from private or corporate possession would be far easier for them than to steal it from a museum or a stately home. Security on a copy would not be secure.

The gallery has built up such a solid business dealing in declared copies that the cheeky sods put on a show of absolute confidentiality for the buyers. They undertake never to disclose their names or particulars of the price paid for their purchase. In return, as a condition of sale, I believe that they go through a charade with each buyer that requires them to sign an undertaking never to 'Pass off' the copy as an original. They also ask for an agreement that if at any time in the future the client should decide to sell what they think to be a copy, they will give Faux Art Works the first opportunity to buy it back. Because the copies are high-value, the Faux Art works price includes delivery and the service of expert hanging, thus the customer would never know if the company had delivered and hung the original and not the copy. To provide an easy opportunity to recover an original, sold as a copy, Faux Art Works offer a cleaning or conservation services. They also offer a package to reframe and stretch any painting that they have previously sold.

When the honest buyer leaves the gallery his purchase of a copy completed, the shop manager writes down in their sales record books, the ones that I borrowed, all the details of the sale, including the customer's name and address, and where it will be on show. In fact, all we need to know. There is however a problem; I found no record of a sale of a copy of La Source. Nevertheless, the books may contain a clue in what is missing. Three pages have been torn out," "What have they to do with the price of Sugar?" Arthur broke in. "Well perhaps not a lot really," Peter admitted, "However each missing page falls between recorded dates not long after the theft of a genuine old master in which Swiss Mobius have an interest; a Velasquez, an Utrillo, and Ingres's La Source. I am concerned that because we have twice paid out ransom money, Higgins believes that we are a soft touch. He may have inside knowledge of which paintings Swiss Mobius have insured. Nothing connects the owners who insure the paintings, so it is unlikely that they are the source of any leaked information. It puts security at Mobius in a bad light. Putting two and one together, I am pretty sure that Servient-Higgins organised all three heists, and sold the originals, as copies, for safe storage at someone else's expense. I think that they keep the copy in the gallery, but put on it a little red dot to mark it as sold. Once that little runt Terrance Servient-Higgins leaves prison, he will be off like a starving squirrel to recover his hidden winter hoard of originals."

Arthur sighed, his shoulders slumped, "I get it" he said, "All that I have to do is to find the picture that could be on display anywhere in the world, or in some private study of a wealthy collector, and get to it before squirrel Nutkin."

The reply he got did not raise his shoulders or his spirits. "Yes, we do want you to find the painting. Once you have done that you will have done your job. You must clear the field. Swiss Mobius will arrange with the owner to take possession of the original. I plan to use a reverse sting. With help of the boffins and with the agreement of the museums and the police, we shall switch the stolen original for a copy that we believe to be the best, most accurate, copy of La Source ever made. If the gang's copyist has concealed or shrouded some part of the original, we will have to wait until our copyist replicates his or her work, before we make the switch. That taken care of, we will wait for Higgins's, once he is out on parole and reunited with his gang, to steal our copy that he believes to be the original. We shall arrange for the boffins to record the theft using their most up to date cameras and microphones. Even though we shall have the evidence for a successful prosecution, we shall not move to have the thieves arrested.

We shall wait for Servient-Higgins to send one of his 'representatives' to claim that he represents an anonymous source willing to return the paintings in return for reward money somewhat in excess of that offered. After some negotiation, we will pay out the reward. I will suggest, privately, that the anonymous party might wish to do other deals. We will have to wait patiently until they bring in all three stolen paintings, the Velasquez, the Utrillo and La Source. When we have recovered all three paintings, we shall have the evidence we need to put Servient-Higgins and associates in prison for long enough to take them all well past their retirement age. If, as we hope, La Source yields sufficient forensic evidence, we shall be able to bring the murder charge that we all want."

Still despondent, Arthur asked, "What happens if I don't find it?"

"In that case, we are still stymied my dear Arthur," Peter replied, "But be of good heart for we are just about certain that the Faux folk are the villains, and that Horrible Higgins is 'Mr Big', as the coppers say on the television. If what I believe to be their 'Modus operandi' for safe storage of their ill-gotten gains is correct, all five foot of the pubescent lass is hanging around somewhere, waiting for you to pick her up. The crooks running Faux Art Works are successful because their shop is in the right place, they advertise and promote their wares; they make themselves known. If you visit the right places, if you ask the right questions, you will make yourself known. Word will get about that you are interested. People may tell you they have seen a copy that was 'So good you would think it is the original'. The Servient-Higgins gang may even think that you are working for someone who might want to buy it. They might even think that you are a modern day bounty hunter,"

Peter stood up to stretch before he said, "Enough of this overlong brief; you had better toddle off. You have not yet been to the Yard to see the photographs. They expect you at half past ten tomorrow morning. Ask for Detective Chief Inspector Gordon Gordon-Smith, his family is so posh they named him twice. He is a bit grand, but he is good at his job."

"Just one thing before I go," Arthur said, "Who is the artist who as supplied your near perfect copy of La Source?"

Fully engaged Peter asked, "Why?" "Well," Arthur replied, "I think one of the restorer conservators at the National Gallery, whatever they are, may be moonlighting for the 'Faux Folk' as you called them."

Peter grinned, "You mean the skinny gender obscure bird with prominent teeth, skimpy hair, with dirty fingernails; about forty five going on a bit?" "Yes that's her," Arthur said, once again at a loss, "How did you know that?" Peter smiled, "We've been onto her for long enough. Well done Arthur, you have not lost your touch. She only looks ratty, as well as miserable, because she has an itch. She has been without a man for almost seven years. She calls herself Edwina Masterman. It is her sick joke. She is, in tooth and nail, Mrs. Elizabeth Servient-Higgins. Servient was her maiden name. She is such a feminist tartar that she made him take her name in exchange for his. As my mum used to say, 'they don't spoil a couple.'"

Arthur's visit to Scotland Yard gave him pause to reflect about his career in the force.

To reach the Detective Chief Inspectors office, a clerk escorted him along dull corridors before he had to climb staircase after staircase, because the lift was out of order.

He began to wonder why he had stayed to do his thirty years plus four and not joined a company in the private sector, as had Peter.

The CDI's office was no better than his had been, probably worse. On top of one of several filing cabinets, a collection of empty foam plastic cups, obviously dispensed by the automatic machine he had noticed in the corridor outside the office, spoke of economies. "This is a tradition taken too far," he thought, "Nothing has changed, there is no progress. It even smells the same as my old station used to, moreover that was only a tad better than the Laurels."

Gordon Gordon-Smith was helpful. In a modified 'Kim's Game' he used a set of ten photographs of eight men and two women thought to be responsible for the theft of La Source, and complicit with the murder of the French museum guard.

Most were standard police photographs; full face, left and right profiles, with a few informal shots that showed Higgins full length, in different attitudes.

Arthur had to remember their features ready to call out their names when the CDI turned them face up, for a second or two only at an ever-faster pace. When Arthur had satisfied his tutor, at that stage of the exercise, he made him repeat it with each photograph partially obscured.

Arthur was tired and hungry when he finally got away from Scotland Yard. As he could not face the bus ride, he hailed a taxi.

He was lucky that the cabby agreed to take him as far south of the river as Crystal Palace. Arthur asked the driver to drop him off at the door of an Indian restaurant that he had noticed was only a few hundred yards from the entrance to the caravan park.

Two poppadums', one naan bread, a Chicken Madras, cooled by a pint of Cobra beer restored Arthur to his usual good humour. Before he left the Indian Restaurant, he asked the waiter for the number of a local mini-cab company. Using his own phone, he booked a mini-cab to pick him up at six-thirty a.m. to take him to Euston Station to catch the train to Derby.

The people at Scotland Yard had given him a full set of the photographs, an action he felt sure broke a hundred rules. He had promised to destroy them once he could go through the pack, each time able to recognise each person and remember their name without failure, confusion or hesitation.

Conscious that he had to be on the train to Derby, due to leave Euston at seven forty three, he was in bed by just after ten, still turning over the photographs.

Each time he turned up a photograph of the woman who Peter had told him called herself Ms. Masterman, who was in fact Mrs. Servient-Higgins, he felt sure that she was not the sort of girl he would ever have taken home to his mother.

Each time the photograph he turned up was an image of Terrance Servient-Higgins, her husband, he could not understand why Peter had called him pure evil. Arthur thought that Higgins could never be type cast as the bad guy. He was of medium height; the police database had him at one meter-seventy, slightly built, with a smooth, tanned, clean-shaven face.

The artist in Arthur judged his finely boned facial features almost patrician, the sort of face portrayed as the hero on the covers of 'Chick Lit' paperback novels. He did not see any feature that marked the man out as a villain, or even mildly horrible. The photographs did not show the aura of evil that Peter had led him to expect. However, like Peter, he did not like the man's hair. It was thin, jet-black, smoothed back with some type of jell into a ridiculous rat-tail, held by a clasp set with jewels.

Arthur remembered that a postman's red rubber band held back Higgins's wife hair. The jewelled clasp that her husband wore disturbed him.

After his early start, the mini-cab had delivered Arthur to Euston Station well before the train to Derby was due to leave. At a bookstall, he bought a Daily Telegraph. At one of the many coffee counters, he purchased a cup of tea and a satisfactory looking large sausage roll. The young man behind the counter heated the sausage roll in a microwave oven. It did not improve the unconvincing filling although it did ruin the pastry.

Peter called on the Swiss Mobius mobile phone while Arthur waited to board the train. Peter said, without pause or introduction, "I have arranged for you to be picked up at Derby Station. With the prison not being one in your bailiwick, I could not trust you to find your way to meet the evil one. You will be using your own name. You may remember it as Arthur Thomas. Do make sure that you get off at Derby, not at Leicester, Nottingham or Sheffield. Remember, Anne expects you Saturday, if you manage to talk your way out of the open prison."

Peter closed the one-way call before Arthur had chance to reply. Prior to getting back to the crossword, Arthur again thought about Peter. He admired his attention to detail, and his influence that did not seem diminished since he had left the force.

With too many distractions to observe from the window, Arthur had not finished either crossword when the train stopped in the once great railway town of Derby.

In modern railway speak the train was 'On Time', as it was only nine minutes late. The woman driver, who the prison service had arranged to pick him up, spoke hardly a word during the twenty-minute journey.

When they arrived at the open prison, the driver handed him over to a prison officer who took him straight to the Governor's office. Arthur was not required to produce any identification, submit to a body search, or sign a visitor's book. "Clearly, I am a non-person today," he thought. He wondered again about Peter's influence.

The Governor's greeting was cheerful, "Welcome Superintendent." "Ex Superintendent I am afraid," grinned Arthur, who was still not sure if his visit was official, or not. "No matter, if an Army Major can keep his rank, I am sure a gazetted Superintendent can keep his title," the Governor said. "I understand that you have come to visit one of our model prisoners; Terrance Servient-Higgins no less.

You look astonished Superintendent however, my remark is technically correct. Since he joined us, he has been careful not to put a foot wrong. He has done excellent work in the library. He has conducted many fine art classes for other members of our flock. I do not like to use the term 'Inmates'. With all the regulations that constrain me, I find it difficult to keep them 'In' and 'Mates' of mine they are not." The Governor's smile disappeared, "Superintendent, make no mistake, he is an evil cold hearted psychopathic killer. I would not go alone with that man into the exercise yard, let alone a jungle. I do not know how he radiates hate, but he does, even though his manner and language are always controlled. None of the other prisoners will associate with him. When he is up for his regular parole assessment, the psychi-

105

atrists are scared witless. They are the ones disturbed after the interview. Mr. Thomas, your escort whom we wait for is Mr. Tony Long. He is an architect, a magistrate, and our most experienced prison visitor. He will take you round. He is also a golf partner of mine. I have been able to tell him that your visit is important however, I had to admit that it is not genuinely kosher. He understands. He won't ask you any questions. I understand that it would be unwise for Higgins to pay you too much attention in case he remembers you on some future occasion. For this reason, I have arranged for the oldest trick in my book. It will mean that you will pass un-noticed amongst us."

Arthur was intrigued, "How is that to be done?" The Governor smiled again, "It's over there, the wheel chair with the rug. Tony will push you around during his visit. I have this ratting cap for you to wear to cover your distinguishing silver hair. You will have this on your lap, under the rug. When Anthony talks to Higgins, you will record him. It will enable you listen, and listen again, until you will recognise the signature of Higgins's voice intonation, even if you cannot see him". The Governor passed to Arthur a most up to date very small sound recorder; it was the best that the Techno-Boffins had shown him in London.

After a brief knock on the door, a man that Arthur correctly took to be the golfing architect breezed in.

"Hello! Here's a lark, my name is Anthony Long, Tony for short. I take it that you must be Mr. Thomas. Talking of the long and the short of it, I hope that your first name is John." He beamed "Hello George," at the Governor, before he turned to speak again to Arthur, "How about I bring in an old niblick of mine to break both your legs. Method acting is the thing these days. No? Come on then, if you cover yourself up in this splendid chariot, we can go out to play with some of my best friends. If I could get the 'Gov' here to fix a nice little nine-hole course here in the park that surrounds us, I would give up architecture to do prison visits full time. Come along Mr. Thomas; we have work to do."

The little man Long astonished Arthur. The unpaid volunteer visitor was a joy to meet. He knew many of the prisoners by name, and he had a joke for everyone. He clearly had genuine concern for their personal worries, with even more for their concerns about their families.

He was not often able to reassure them however; he seldom failed to amuse them. Arthur thought that if all prison visitors were as effective, as was Mr Long, there would be a marked decline in recidivists.

In the library, Arthur immediately recognised Servient-Higgins. He wore the black slacks with a white open necked shirt of a 'trusty'. He gave Mr Long a practiced sarcastic greeting, "How kind of you to visit old chap. I believe you are long overdue on the return of the paedophile porn book you took out, a penny a week is the fine you know. Who is the cripple in the cart, not a geriatric 'Ironside' I trust. Not that I trust anyone in this colony of crooks." For Arthur's benefit he added, "Of course, I refer to the guards not the incarcerated."

In his wheelchair, Arthur felt far from safe from recognition. He did not like the long appraising look that Servient-Higgins gave him. It reminded him of the look his wife Greta Servient-Higgins gave him, as he said his farewells to the conservators of the National Gallery.

He knew, from that single look, that the photographs he had studied did not lie; they hid the truth. This man did have an aura of evil about him, more powerful than the heavy perfume that hung on him like a shroud. Mr. Long ignored the question, but he kept Higgins talking about nothing at all. He only made an occasional innocuous reference to 'His colleague'. He told Higgins that he would be a visitor in Manchester Prison. Mr. Long, who seemed to Arthur to have a quip for everything, laughed at his own joke, "I suppose that 'Her Majesty's Prison Service' had to change the name Strangeways to Manchester because the P.C. police deem no behaviour, however deviant, to be in any way strange".

After the badinage, Mr. Short asked a direct question, "How long before your parole Mr. Librarian? I understand that if all goes well you will be out before Christmas, is that right?" Higgins's reply was sour "You are correct Mr. Long, but there is no right about it. "A corrupt frog judge banged me up for almost seven years after collusion with a corps of crooked coppers who fitted me up for a crime that I did not commit. They were in cahoots with a bent examining magistrate. As you already know Mr. Long, I had nothing to do with it. I was on holiday in Paris, studying the romantics. I shall not tell that to the parole board. I shall sob with more remorseful tears than Alfred Jingle shed on Pickwick's shoulder in the Fleet Prison. One lie deserves another does it not Mr. Long. Please tell the pupil in the pushchair that I have a good business to go back to, a loyal wife, my son and many friends. I am better placed for a pension than anyone else in this cage without bars, including my mate the Governor."

Arthur nearly choked, but hoped his bucolic colour would go un-noticed. "Well, we must get on," Mr. Short exclaimed, I want to see that man who is building a scale model of the guillotine out of matchsticks and looking for razor blades. Cheerio Mr. Librarian, see you next Friday, if you have not decided to join the monkey run." "Not me Mr. Long, I am almost out of here. They will not get me back behind bars, no way, however much the screws goad me. Push off pupil; I trust that we shall not meet again".

Arthur had another chance to observe Higgins, while the prisoners ate their lunch. He noted that no one sat near to or spoke to him, nor did he speak to anyone, not even to the men who dished up his lunch.

After they had watched the feeding of the three hundred, Mr. Long took Arthur back to the Governor's office where he embarrassed and worried him by recounting the experience.

"You know George," he said, "When Higgins accused the judge of corruption, Mr. Thomas here went bright purple, thyrotoxicosis I believe the quacks call it. I don't think that Higgins fell for our ruse. He certainly took a long hard look at our friend. I had better take him out in the wheel chair as far as my car. Pound to a pinch of snout Higgins will be watching."

The record made of Higgins's conversation with Mr. Long was excellent. Arthur assured the Governor that the mini-disc was all he needed because his friend Peter seemed to be able to provide all that he required.

It was almost seven o'clock by the time Arthur arrived back at Euston and almost two hours before he was back on the caravan site. He took care of all his domestic requirements and Tootsie's service necessities to be ready to leave after breakfast in the morning.

Near to the Indian restaurant, where he had eaten the night before, he had noticed a 'Late Shop' with a cash dispense machine.

After he drew sufficient cash, he bought ingredients to treat himself to a grand 'Fry-Up'. He told himself he deserved it because he had only had a soggy sausage roll for breakfast, no lunch, and the Eccles cake he ate on Derby Station, while he waited for his train, had been short on currants and starved of butter. He was satisfied with his supper, except for the plastic cased fat free so-called black pudding. "They don't make them proper in London," he muttered.

Jenny's early death had left him a widower for nigh on twenty years. During that long time, of necessity, he had become a self-sufficient creature of habit. Routine came naturally to him. After he had washed the dishes and neatly packed everything away in the right cupboards, he set the alarm for seven thirty.

Sitting on the edge of his bed, as he peeled off his socks, he knew that his two-week long brief was over. "You are on your own now Arthur old lad," he said aloud. "This is a right caper you have gotten yourself into. You are an old fool, aged three score year and ten, about to set off on a quest to find a painting that could be anywhere.

If you are not careful, you will have the added frisson of a gang of murdering thieves on these heels of yours. I don't know how I can be careful if, as Peter suggests, I put it about that I am interested in Jeanne Dominique Ingres's stolen painting, La Source."

Despite these thoughts, Arthur Thomas slept well undisturbed by any manifestation, hallucination, nightmare or dream. He only woke when his early set alarm clock rang.

Chapter 8

Arthur was an early riser on the morning after his two-week crash course to convert him from retired policeman, to a freelance undercover agent with a one off task to recover a stolen Ingres masterpiece.

This day he had to drive less than a hundred miles from the caravan site at Crystal Palace to the Bainbridge's dinner party at Wicket Gate Cottage.

On days when he moved to a new site, he planned his route with meticulous attention to detail, after taking account of the weather and traffic warnings on the radio. On a plain white post-card, he wrote out, in large capital letters, the names of the towns he needed to go through, or past if possible, with the letter and number of their connecting roads. He excluded motorways. He avoided, where practical, any A roads with only one or two numbers.

In the caravan site shop, when he bought his morning Telegraph, on impulse, Arthur also bought a device used by typists to hold paper documents upright in line of sight.

Using 'Blu Tak', he stuck his new gadget in front of the steering wheel. Before he set off, he lodged his prepared route card firmly into the curved slot in his four centimetre high grey plastic dome.

It amused him to think of the simple low cost, low-tech device, as his 'Head-Up' navigation system. He imagined himself as a 'Top Gun' pilot. Arthur had been lucky; he had never lost a childish enthusiasm for simple things.

After a pleasant uneventful drive, broken only by a short stop along the way to buy flowers for Anne, Arthur pulled over into a field gate a mile short of Wicket Gate Cottage.

He set up his camp chair in the sun, ready to read the newspaper, after he had discarded its many unwanted supplements.

He only read the news and opinions in newspaper after he had completed the quick crossword and the proper crossword, usually complete, but sometimes abandoned short of a word or three.

He planned to arrive first for the dinner party, although not too early. He knew that if Peter saw his peripatetic bungalow parked outside on the green, he would insist that he come into the house where he would be in the way of Anne's busy preparations.

Any formal dinner party was a greater challenge for Arthur than his recent prison visit. He was out of practice.

A widower in Scagill does not get many invitations to private dinner parties. Experience had taught Arthur that a policeman's irregular shift pattern made it impossible for him to accept more than two out of three invitations that did come his way. He had long since understood that two or more RSVP regrets meant that further invitations would be unlikely.

A dinner party with friends of friends who Arthur, did not know, intimidated him. Like many men, widowed for a long time, and working mainly with men, he had become socially shy. He was painfully uncomfortable in female company.

Feminine gender speak was to Arthur a foreign language. He did not understand feminine subtleties, nuances, inflection or gestures.

Dressed in a clean shirt, his only suit, a discrete tie and highly polished shoes Arthur drove the last mile to Wicket gate Cottage to arrive prompt at seven o'clock. His final action to make himself ready was his habitual crosswise sweep of his index fingers to smooth his moustache. With the bunch of cut flowers that he had bought for the occasion in hand, he crunched in quick march up the gravel path to the cottage. Arthur was amused that Anne greeted him with the usual female response to a gift of flowers; "Oh Arthur, you shouldn't have". He knew she would have been a little miffed if he had not brought some small token gift. For such occasions, he thought fresh cut flowers were always preferred to a bottle of wine, or a box of chocolates.

As the first guest to arrive, Arthur was pleased. It would mean that Peter would introduce the other guests to him, not him to them. He found such an arrangement more comfortable than if he had been a late arrival into a room full of strangers. He was also pleased to notice that Anne had set the dining table set for eight.

He thought eight the best number possible. Six was too intimate, twelve split into two completely separate conversations. Ten was neither one thing nor the other. Eight was right; the head of table could manage eight.

Peter welcomed him warmly. Arthur was astonished that even though Anne had set the table for a formal dinner, Peter was casually dressed. He wore light grey cotton slacks, an open necked rust coloured raw silk shirt and white canvas shoes. It made Arthur acutely conscious that he was out of touch with the modern mores of the people who dwell in rural Sussex, East or West.

When Peter noticed Arthur's reaction he said, "Come on Arthur, let me have your jacket and tie lest you put us all too sartorial shame." Arthur kept his tie, but when he reluctantly relinquished his coat, he felt self-conscious about his corpulent middle.

Peter took his arm and said, "Come on through to the garden. I have some beer, but first I must have a discrete word in your ear, a word of caution. Anne has brought you here as a sacrificial lamb. She has invited one of her vagabond widow friends to correct the gender imbalance caused by your single status. Three things you must know; she is as rich as needs be, she spends money like a drunken sailor, she is man mad. You must be on your guard. I do not want a middle aged woman, however well turned out, to turn my highly trained bounty hunter from his task to rescue a painted lady."

"No chance of that," Arthur said, shaking his head, "She may be sexually active, but if I ever I was, I have forgotten what it meant. My id has lost its I.D. My ego has lost its go." Peter grinned, "I wonder; just you wait until you see her?"

Anne, the skilful hostess, made sure that the evening went well. Despite Peter's warning, Arthur was able to relax. Peter told stories about the miss-spent years he and Arthur had spent as young constables when they had shared digs in a station house.

Arthur capped them all. The two couples that the Bainbridge's had invited were good company. One couple was Peter's golf partner and his wife who did yoga and ikebana; the other was a teacher friend of Anne's and her husband, a senior commuting civil servant. The honey blond 'gender balance' challenged Arthur's modest demeanour.

Slim as a twig, she was in her middle fifties. Her skin was as gold as a September sunset. She wore gold, gold jewellery, lots of it, a gold pencil slim skirt, gold-strappy shoes with very high stiletto heels. She wore no stockings. Of these, she had no need. Her still pretty legs were sun tanned gold. She had even polished her fingernails as well as her toenails with gold lacquer. The blouse she had chosen was a cleverly folded gold organza confection with a décolleté that invited admiration and wonder because there was no visible means of support. Throughout the evening, her part in the conversation had been sexually provocative.

It was obvious to all the guests that, to prepare for the occasion, Anne had worked all that day in addition to most of the previous day. Given the chance, Arthur would have marked her efforts, 'Ten out of ten', plus a tick for neatness. Anne had cooked

114

and presented, without pretentious fuss or elaboration, carefully chosen superb ingredients.

It was a little after midnight, as the party broke up, that clear for all to hear, the lady in gold called out, "Arthur, can I give you a lift? I drove over in my Bentley Continental, it's the new convertible." Arthur blushed. His hosts added to his embarrassment. Waving his hands across his chest, Peter mouthed a silent, urgent, "No – no." With a twinkle in her eyes, Anne pointedly looked at her friends plunging neckline, before she urged, "Go on Arthur, a breath of fresh air would do you good, it will blow way the cobwebs. I am sure that Jane will want the top down."

"No, er, no," stammered Arthur, "Thank you, most kind, but my shed is just outside. Tomorrow I must be up be-times. I have the English Channel to cross. It is already late for me; I had hoped to be tucked up in my bed before midnight." "So had I, so had I" the golden beauty sighed.

Thirty plus years on shift duty had conditioned Arthur to wake when needed. The weeks spent in hospital, and the months he had spent in the rehab clinic, had refreshed the habit of early starts to the day.

The day after Anne's dinner party, he woke to the dawn chorus. He woke with a clear sense of purpose. He knew that he must put clear water between himself and the man mad marauder.

Her advances had been harmless enough, but they had reminded him of when Percival had told him that a predator's hand on his knee had persuaded him to throw in his lot with the Grey Haired Knights. Arthur determined to be on the road before anyone in the village was awake.

In a short letter of thanks to the Bainbridges, Arthur thanked them for the fine dinner complemented by good company. For fear that any comment might be misunderstood; he deliberately did not mention the lady in gold.

In a post-script, he promised Peter that he would keep in touch, particularly if he had news. In order not to wake the household, he walked quietly along the grass by the side of the gravel path. He trapped his letter in the spring flap of the letterbox to prevent it from landing noisily on the wooden floor of the hall.

By ten in the morning, Arthur was well on the way to the channel ports, or the channel tunnel; he had not yet decided whether to go under or over the water, however he was inclined to the latter.

He planned to stop over for the night near to Folkestone. To satisfy the clear sense of purpose that he had, when he woke, he was determined to cross over to the continent, if not that day, within days.

He weighed the possibility of seasickness nausea, with the certainty of tunnel-induced claustrophobia. He smiled to himself when he added to the sum of his reasons that a breath of fresh sea air would do him good. On reflection, he did not know whether, when he declined Anne's suggestion that a breath of fresh air would do him good, he had missed a golden opportunity or escaped a tender trap. He decided to opt for the sea voyage.

Before he could go anywhere, Arthur realised that he would need time to make plans.

The experts Peter had arranged to brief him had followed the advice of the conservators at the National Gallery. They too had recommended that he extend his knowledge of Ingres's technique by a visit to the Louvre and the Musée D'Orsay.

Arthur knew that both galleries were in Paris. He also knew that Paris was in France. For further study of Ingres's work and artefacts, the document prepared for him by Peter's experts suggested that he visit the Ingres museum at Montauban. Montauban was also in France. Consequently, despite a lifelong reluctance, Arthur decided he must go to France.

The prospect that he would have to drive in France, particularly in Paris, concerned him. He imagined it would be worse than the hostile environment he had experienced on the outskirts of London. It had seemed to him that most London drivers had anger management problems. On the French side of the Channel, he wondered how he would manage to drive on the wrong side of the road.

With French road signs written in French, he felt sure he would be confused. He worried about his ability to compete with French drivers. He had heard were all hand on horn aggressive.

While he still drove comfortably on the left hand side of a quiet English Sunday morning road towards Hastings, Arthur wondered how he would cope with the practical difficulties of finding his way in a foreign land.

Although he had never been a gadget-minded man, he decided he would buy one of those tacky spherical plastic highly coloured compasses, to add to his 'Head up' navigation system.

He felt sure that after Calais, if he followed a compass in a general southerly direction, on minor roads, he would eventually reach Paris.

From Paris, if he continued on a southerly bearing, he would find the Ingres museum at Montauban. "After all," he said aloud to keep himself company, "I have all year to faff about in France, or Italy, or Holland or even further afield, before I have to honour my sworn pledge to take my part in the reunion of the Grey Haired Knights, back in England, back in Scagill, back at the Crown Inn."

As he drove, Arthur regretted that, since he had left Yorkshire, he had not thought much about the other Grey Haired Knights. He worried about Percival, the least suited to adventure. It still concerned him that his idea of a new Camelot might get the mild antiquarian into a situation with which he would not be able to cope.

He was sure the other two could look after themselves. Geraint the well-travelled practical engineer would take no chances. He thought that if Tristan flaunted his Stewart Granger looks, he would probably do best of all, if he did not succumb to liver failure, go broke with bad bets, or get himself shot by a jealous husband.

To emulate Peter, the consummate planner, Arthur realised that he would need to buy many things new to him; French maps, guidebooks printed in English, Euros and Tootsie would need headlight beam deflectors, adaptors to cope with continental electric systems and gas bottles. "If I had a mind like Peters," Arthur thought, "I would have sorted all this out when I bought Tootsie at Brownhills." What most concerned him was that he did not have a clue where the stolen Ingres painting he sought might be displayed, stored, hidden, or even if it was still extant.

Arthur considered the possibility that, in the inevitable panic that would have followed the murder of the guard, the gang might have burnt the painting to destroy evidence. He decided however, that because the crime was committed not long after DNA evidence had proved useful in the prosecution of criminals, the gang would not have understood that the painting, or its frame, might yet identify the murderer.

Arthur thought that the prospect of lucre would have persuaded Servient-Higgins not to destroy the painting. He remained convinced by Peter's idea that the object of his quest waited for Servient-Higgins to retrieve it from the innocent person who had bought it as a copy from his Faux Art Works London gallery.

The first two caravan parks that Arthur rang, to book a pitch for the night, were already full. A third that took his reservation told him that he could only stay two nights, as it was high season. When Arthur arrived at the site, he was disappointed.

Dozens of motor homes, some large, some small, were already parked amongst hundreds of caravans interleaved with cars that stretched in serried ranks across acres of English Countryside.

It reminded him of a badly laid out council estate. Arthur's concept of a caravan holiday was to get away from people and places. This site had created an urban conurbation around a small shop. It provided however, just what Arthur needed, a location near to a bus route that linked it to the ports of Dover and Folkestone.

Two days on the site was all he needed to book a ticket for Tootsie and himself to cross the Channel and to collect the necessary items for her 'Frenchification'.

The most difficult item to find proved to be the tacky 'compass in a sphere'. He finally purchased one from a Souvenir shop in Folkestone.

The woman at the ferry office queried Arthur's request for a one-way ticket, Dover to Calais. "Yes, single it is Miss," Arthur laughed, "You see I am just about to start my gap year."

The women could not raise an eyebrow; she had plucked both clean away.

She had pencilled in, on the 'Botox' frozen space created, distressed arches that reached almost to her hairline. Nevertheless, she did manage an expression that said much, none of it sympathetic.

Arthur had chosen to sail on a ferry that left Dover, mid-morning, after his second night on the caravan park. He spent most of his last day in England with travel agents to collect English guides to the French countryside.

Anxious to have enough English books to keep him occupied during the late evenings when it would be too dark to paint he, found time to browse and buy in bookshops.

As a gesture to the supposed 'Entente cordial' he went so far as to buy a 'Penguin' pocket French / English – English / French dictionary, although it went against the grain to do so. The most expensive item he bought was a high-powered battery operated radio.

The shop assistant assured him that he would be able to listen to the 'BBC World Service', wherever he went in Europe. His facetious comment, "We mustn't miss 'The Archers' must we sir." annoyed Arthur.

After much thought, Arthur reluctantly decided he would not take any beer with him. He resolved that wherever he stayed he would take the popular drink of the local man. He did stock up with four bottles of 'HP Sauce'. He thought them more essential than any beer or wine.

He stowed three of the precious bottles in the external luggage locker. To keep one handy, he put it in the dry goods cupboard. An elderly man in one of the travel agents had told him that the sauce, although made in France, was still difficult to obtain over there. As he stowed away the sauce with a tin of dry English mustard powder, he thought that to absorb some French culture might be one thing; to abandon his Yorkshire roots was quite another.

He worried about how long his two boxes of 'Yorkshire Tea' would last. Each one contained only five hundred treasured bags. He calculated that it was not sufficient for two pots of tea a day, with one bag for him and one for the pot. He realised that he would run out, if he had to spend the full year on the wrong side of the Channel.

It rained heavily during the July morning that Arthur crossed to France. When he approached the ferry terminal concourse, with the windscreen steamed up and the wing mirrors of little or no use, he began to wish that he had chosen the tunnel route to take him to France.

The direction signs, posted in more than one language, confused him. He held up traffic when he had to get the ticket from his wallet to remind him, which ferry company he had booked to take him across the water in pursuit of his quest.

The men who directed traffic wore luminous yellow jackets with reflective silver strips. They disconcerted him by their apparent anger. He thought that they shouted at him alone, amongst all the others.

When he finally understood what they wanted, he was able to park in a queue of assorted trucks, and vans. His pulse raced, although he was reasonably confident that he was in the correct place to catch the ferry for which he had bought a ticket.

From where the marshals had put him, he could see, coming into dock, what he presumed to be the ferry that would take him to France.

The vessel did not look like a proper ship. He thought looked like a monstrous blockhouse, or a pre-war Glasgow tenement building. After a long wait, punctuated by the clatter of the berthing process, a fleet of cabs, without trailers, darted into the dark open maw of the vessel. Almost immediately, just as the whale regurgitated Noah, the ferry spewed them out.

As if by magic, each one hauled an articulated trailer.

After a short lull, cars, trucks, Lorries, busses, motorbikes, a few motor homes, and many caravans spewed from the ferry's different levels. They came in continuous streams. They were so many that he began to wonder if he had made a mistake.

He thought that the marshals had put him to wait at the mouth of a newly opened second Channel Tunnel controlled by traffic lights. He watched the traffic streams slow to a dribble before they finally petered out. There was a brief hiatus before the men in luminous jackets, with reflective strips, began again their 'Nutcracker' ballet movements to feed the ferry with ribbons of vehicles. Arthur thought, "Surely, we cannot all get on this one vessel.".

A few minutes later, he drove off English concrete onto the cold wet steel of one of the sea-monster's many decks. All over the walls, in many languages, notices forbade smoking and prohibited passengers to stay in their vehicles once the vessel was under way.

Arthur thought the supposed luxury facilities were almost as dricht as the tween decks.

After an exploratory wander, he found the ship's shop where he bought a copy of the Daily Telegraph.

The crosswords only taxed him until the vessel was part way to Calais. Enthused by the novelty of his first crossing, he went on deck to take a first look at France. The 'Tannoy' squawked its recorded message, 'Passengers with vehicles must return to them without delay, ready to disembark.' Arthur observed that nautical expressions still ruled, 'Disembark' not 'Drive off'. It pleased him that to comply with the officer's command he had to wind his way down companionways, not staircases.

When he tossed the newspaper into a waste bin, it began to dawn on retired Superintendent Arthur Thomas that in France he would face many changes to his 'life-style', as the Sunday Supplements expressed it.

Everyday day since he retired from the force, he had taxed his mind with the crosswords of the Daily Telegraph, or its Sunday sister paper. Only after he had solved, or nearly solved, all the clues, did he read the newspaper.

He assiduously read the front page to the letters page, and all of for the obituary page. He seldom bothered with the sport, reviews or Art pages.

In France, Arthur knew that he would have to get along without his daily news update. The Alzheimer prophylactic of the puzzles would no longer steal his time. He would have an extra hour or more each day to do useful things, to paint, read and perhaps to make some progress with his search for the Ingres stolen masterpiece.

Back in the driving seat, Arthur took a deep breath before he started the engine.

When he engaged gear to follow the line of what had been vehicles, but was now traffic, French traffic, he said aloud, "Oh lordie, be prepared for the big cross over to drive on the right hand side of French roads while you still sit in Tootsies right hand drive seat; do be careful."

He noticed his pulse rate was definitely a little faster than usual. What he did not notice was his habitual nervous habit of the cross over index fingers that smoothed his moustache.

A moment later, with a jolt, he landed in France.

Chapter 9

When he landed on French soil, Arthur Thomas needed time to adjust to the French custom of driving on the wrong side of the road. Without a care for direction, he decided to follow, for an hour, any small car that towed a large caravan, wherever it might lead him.

He reasoned that it would be unlikely that anyone could drive such a rig as fast as the other vehicles of all types that swarmed around him.

The drivers who overtook him signalled their displeasure at his dilatory progress in what Arthur took to be true Gallic fashion. There was no hint of an 'Entente Cordial'. Their two-fingered gestures were definitely not Churchillian. He took their single finger gestures as a declaration that the cannon at Castillon had not ended the 'Hundred Year War'.

To his relief, before he left the dock area, a small Renault car coupled to a large caravan overtook him. In a 'Walter Mitty' moment, Arthur assumed a top gun pilot role. He 'Locked on' to the Renault rig. Tailgating helped, except that the occasional stolen glance at his head up navigation system compass showed him that he had chosen to follow a caravan going north, not south towards Paris. Nevertheless, he determined to follow his target for an hour.

It was not to be. Arthur learned that 'Sod's Law' rules world-wide. When he left the port of Calais, he had tripped his odometer, which measured distance run in kilometres, not good English miles.

After thirty-five of the short measure, the indictor on the caravan in front warned him that its driver was about to turn off the road into a well signed entrance to a caravan park. Inside the perimeter gate, signs in both French and English indicated where new arrivals should park.

Arthur saw that the driver of the Renault was a woman, almost of his own age. He followed her into the reception office in the hope that, as she had come from England, she might be English or speak English, and might help him. In a cool friendly enough voice, in English, with a French accent, the women asked, "Have you followed me you funny English man?" A little embarrassed Arthur replied, "Well er no, not really, although I suppose yes I have. You see, I have never crossed the Channel before. I followed your caravan to get used to the deviant French custom of driving on the wrong side of the road."

The woman laughed, as she took up Arthur's challenge, "There you are, I knew it, you are a funny Englishman. In all of Europe only the English drive, a gauche, on the left side of the road. You will have to change." "Madam," Arthur replied happily, "You must know that Europe is altogether too small to dictate on such important matters.

It is land locked to the Indian sub-continent, where live millions more rich and middle class people than all of the population of all classes of geographical Europe. Soon, they will have as many cars per family, as have mainland European families. They are on our side, as are the Japanese, Australians, Indonesians, and most countries on the African Continent, also the Channel Islands and the Scilly Isles. They outnumber Europeans. They drive on the left side, the correct side, our side. There are no car ferries from the Americas. If change is needed, Europe will have to change." Arthur was relieved to be on equal terms.

The dour concierge spoke to him rapidly in French that was 'All Greek' to Arthur. The woman laughed, "He has just asked you if I am your wife. Do you want me to book your wagon in for tonight?" "Oh! Yes please," Arthur replied, "I shall be most grateful. You see as an English man, I only speak English. I have to shout to be understood."

"It will cost you twenty Euros, for which you will have electricity. He will give you a key to use the shower block." The women talked rapidly, in French, to the man at the desk, before she wished Arthur a bright, "Bon soir Monsieur; welcome to France."

The twenty Euros that Arthur paid was all he needed to become a resident of France, if not a citizen. With Tootsie safely parked, connected by a new adaptor to French electricity, Arthur walked back to the site shop where he bought two small bottles of French beer, a tub of pâté, a petit baguette, and a pre-pack of Salad Niçoise for his super.

The next morning Arthur rose, very early, to a bright sunny day. He had enjoyed his 'dîner', but he was hungry. He breakfasted on all of the English food left in the fridge, eggs, bacon, black pudding, and pork sausage.

It tempted him to catch the next ferry to go back home to England. "No lad," he said aloud, "You are on a quest. For a while yet you will have to put up with their funny ways, funny food, awful beer, and with their fixed habit to drive too fast on the wrong side of the road."

If anyone had asked him whether he said this to himself, or aloud, he would have had had no idea.

Because he did not have the Daily Telegraph, as his usual breakfast companion, Arthur had tuned into the 'World Service' on his new radio. He had listened to the news with more than usual interest because he was, for the first time in his life, 'A listener overseas'.

It was already later than nine o'clock by the time Arthur had done all his routine chores and studied the map to plan his route to Paris. Careful study made him decide to take two days for the journey. He divided the distance shown on his maps in kilometres, by eight then multiplied by five.

The sums done he deduced that if he drove all the way on the A 16, Paris was about 175 miles almost due south of the campsite. If he chose to follow his compass's directions, along minor roads, it would take more than 200 miles.

He decided that to drive 200 miles was too much for a retired English speaking copper, a novice driver of a right hand drive motorhome in a left hand drive country where the signs are in French.

Cost considered, Arthur resolved that he would not use a campsite until he was in the Paris area. He made up his mind to find a village with a restaurant where, after he had sampled some of their famous French regional cuisine, the Patron, given a satisfactory tip, would allow him to stay overnight, on his car park, free of charge.

Arthur's recent experience of an English lay-by burger van persuaded him to stop to have lunch, on-board Tootsie, somewhere before Amiens.

Using the last two slices of bread bought in England, he made a decent pâté sandwich, which he enjoyed with a pot of his precious Yorkshire tea.

By early afternoon, Arthur started to enjoy himself. He began to master the skill of cack handed driving. He even drove for a short distance on the A16, a road where the big boys play. The juggernauts that tailgated him soon confirmed his resolution to keep to rural routes.

When Arthur passed a signpost, 'Paris 80 kilometres', he decided that it was time to look for somewhere to spend the night.

After he parked up, in a tidy little lay-by, to study his large-scale map, he decided that Vernon on the Seine would be ideal.

The French regional tourist book that he had bought in Folkestone recommended Vernon as, 'A picturesque excellent stopover on the way to the capital'. The guidebook also mentioned that on the opposite bank of the river Seine visitors could find, in the village of Giverny, the famous home and garden of Monet, founder of the impressionist movement.

It was late afternoon when Arthur drove into Vernon. He realised that he had spent almost seven hours on the road, without running into anything other than the bad temper of several drivers who had indicated that he was a senile menace.

Near to the town centre, he noticed what he took to have been, until earlier in the day, a stall market.

A few cars, vans and small flatbed lorries still littered the area. The casual parking convinced him he would be safe to park there overnight. Arthur was surprised at the size of Vernon, a town of which he had never heard. The massive church that faced the even taller city hall closed the shorter two sides of the elongated ancient town square'. The longer sides of the square had at least two banks, a small supermarket, and what he thought might be a French estate agent, spaced amongst many shops and offices.

On roads that lead off from the square, Arthur could see other shops, two small hotels, and several restaurants, some of which had tables set out on their wide frontage pavement. All had cool dark interiors to invite the weary to rest out of the sun.

"All life is here," mused Arthur. When he looked at the graveyard full of larger than life memorials, he added, "Also the dead." He decided that Vernon, including Giverny with the Monet Garden, would be a perfect place to acclimatise to French customs.

Vernon would be his toehold in France where he could paint and practice observation, before he set out on the next stage of his quest. He promised himself that he would return to Vernon after he had made known his interest in Ingres's La Source at the Louvre and the Musée d'Orsay in Paris.

The ambiance of a small café restaurant, that was obviously popular with tourists, tempted Arthur not to cook his own supper. He thought the food expensive, although the wine he chose was both reasonable in quality and price. That the menu was transatlantic surprised him but did not concern him overmuch.

He recalled that he had had many poor meals in English restaurants catering for tourists. What did bother him was that sitting alone in an English restaurant he had rarely felt lonely. In England, he was able to earwig other people's conversations, often finding himself drawn into their chatter. Occasionally, a party dining at another table had asked him to join them. During this night, his second night in France, he connected with nobody; he felt lonely, he felt a long way from home.

Finding that he was unable to use his mobile phone to make a reservation to stay for a week on a caravan site near to the centre of Paris gave Arthur his first real problem with language. His guidebooks listed several sites that claimed to be the nearest to the city centre, close to the metro.

Despite several attempts, including a raised voice, he had not been able to make himself understood. He realised that even if he could make clear what he wanted, he would never be able to answer the rapid-fire questions asked in return to his simple question. "Without doubt," he thought, "No one in England speaks English as fast as the French speak French." He cautioned himself, "Use your brain Arthur Thomas. In Paris, there is the Eiffel Tower, a structure almost twice as high as the Blackpool Tower. Surely even I will be able to find it. At the tower, there will be a Bureau Tourisme. The staff there will speak English. Go there and let them book a site for you."

The next day, when he set off from Vernon on his way to Paris, Arthur's luck changed for the better. A hundred metres or so along one of the old streets that lead out of the town he noticed a 'Tricolour' hanging above the door of a very old curiously constructed half-timbered house that bore a sign 'Bureau Tourisme'.

After he found a safe spot to park, he hurried back to this most welcome sign. Sure enough, it was what he wanted except that the leaflets on display were all in French, as were the displays on the wall. The only human presence was a thin middle-aged woman who did not seem to be fashion conscious.

She had secured her combed back thin mousy coloured hair with an office bulldog clip. She sat; her posture rigid, at a desk, engaged with a computer screen full of French text. She did not move. She did not make eye contact. She did not appear to notice him.

Arthur coughed. He coughed again, twice. The femme still did not stir. "Pardon moi madam, Je, er, I" Arthur began.

Although the woman checked him with a stream of French, spoken in a non-too friendly tone, he struggled on, "Je suis Anglais. Parlez vous Anglais? He tried in English, "Can you help me please?" "None," was the abrupt reply. The woman, who did not look at Arthur, picked up a phone into which she gabbled a stream of uninterrupted words faster than a tape recorder on rewind.

She replaced the receiver before the party to whom she had spoken had the opportunity to reply. Arthur, at a loss, was about to leave when a short on stature, tubby, broad shouldered, florid faced man burst from a door at the back of the room. The few remaining thin strands of dark hair flew about his head in disarray.

With a great grin across his face, he took Arthur's hand to shake it warmly. "Hello, I saw you in the market place yesterday did I not? You must be the Englishman the miserable cow over there would not attend to."

The woman's head jerked round to glare at the two men. "You see, she does speak English," he laughed, "It's not that she lacks the fluency in your language, or confidence. The Bureau has not given her the rise in pay that we earn by being able to speak more than one language. I suppose she is what you English people call, 'Working to rule'. In France, we call it 'Pipi dans le vent', or as you might say it, 'To piss into the wind'. By the way, my name is Alaine Cartet. You are?" "Arthur, Arthur Thomas," Arthur replied greatly relieved.

"Well Mr. Thomas," enthused the tourist officer, "What may I do, or can I do, or perhaps even better, help you to do, to make your stay in la Belle France an experience that you will remember with affection, even joy? In other words, "What's up?"

An hour later, after Arthur had told this engaging man about his abject failure to make an advance reservation to park his motor home on a campsite near Paris, he had it all sorted. Arthur felt that the hour spent with Alain Cartet had taught him more about France, the French, and Paris, than all his years at school had taught him, or his later reading of Balzac and Guy de Maupassant.

Monsieur Cartet kitted him out with a large cardboard folder full of information about the Louvre, and other French galleries all printed in English, unlike the leaflets on the bureau shelves. With customary Gallic habit, the Tourism Officer again shook Arthur's hand, while he added an invitation to join him for a drink at the Brasserie Julienne. He suggested sometime about seven o'clock when he would have reverted from his weekday artifice of a stuffy formally suited officer of the Bureau Tourism to a happy French peasant.

Arthur decided the man was a character who would be a good friend to have in France. It reaffirmed his intention to return to Vernon. It also encouraged Arthur to stay another night in Vernon.

It was with renewed confidence that he drove the short way back to the deserted market place where he settled to read his newly acquired leaflets. He also took time, before the shops closed, to see what he could find for a decent non-continental breakfast. Le bouchère, le boulangerie, le épicerie all interested him, although they were too exotic for his taste. He did not recognize some of the produce they had on display. When he ventured into the small supermarket he had noticed when he first arrived, he was able to get most of what he wanted.

He found eggs, bacon and loaves of sliced bread in a wax wrapper, similar to those sold by Tesco or Sainsbury in Scagill. He thought the sliced bread better for toast than French baguettes that dried too quickly. Arthur could not find any pork sausages so he went back to the épicerie, where he bought a sort of black pudding, 'Bourdon Noir' they called it. All in all, he was well satisfied with his sortié.

In the Brasserie Julienne, when the remarkable envoy for French tourism asked Arthur what he would like to drink, he asked for a beer. It was not good. When Arthur asked the patron for wine for Alaine and for the friends who had joined him, no mention was made of payment.

Arthur did not want any more beer so he asked Alaine what wine he should drink. The little Frenchman smiled. He shrugged his shoulders, as only a Frenchman can. He raised his open hands, palms upwards, shoulder high. "Just ask the Patron for wine, red or white, it's all we ever do. We leave it to him. If you ask for a particular wine, whatever you ask for, the wicked old scoundrel will pass off anything that he wants to get rid of from his stock. He will swear it is the wine that you asked for, but with a different name.

He hates pretentious wine snobs; just ask for wine. He will never give you a bad one. If he did, he would lose all his local customers. He does not do tourists. That is one of the many reasons why I come here; I do not like to mix pleasure with work."

It was about eight o'clock when Arthur noticed that, although nobody had ordered food, a well-rounded girl, who wore a long black apron, put eight large white cloth napkins around a large wooden table. On each napkin, she placed a knife, fork and soup-spoon. Few came from the same set.

The girl set plates by each napkin. All the plates were undecorated white. They also did not make a set. Many had different rims but all had deep bowls. By the side of each plate, the girl placed a chunk of course brown bread as big as a London brick. Without ceremony, the Patron set on the table two large rustic brown ceramic bowls full of stew, rich with meat, haricot beans, and sausage.

The girl followed with tureens of new potatoes and green French beans that gleamed with melted butter.

Alaine called Arthur to join them when he and his friends sat at the table to eat. Each man used a pair of crocodile clips, to secure one of the large napkins to the collar of his open necked shirt.

When Arthur looked carefully, he could see a small enamel badge on each clip with the motif VCC. Alaine told him it meant 'Vernon Cassoulet Club'. He explained that they met once a week at the brasserie, except of course in August, when Cassoulet was out of season.

The casserole was as good as great casseroles get. Arthur noticed that in each rustic bowl the cook had added a pig's trotter and two goose legs to enrich the dish. They explained the rich gelatinous feel of the casserole on his teeth.

When each man paid into a deep plate, an equal number of Euros for their share of the meal, without regard to how many or what drinks each had consumed, they allowed him to contribute his share without a fuss. Arthur took it as a compliment that they treated him as a friend, not as a foreign guest.

With less than sixty miles to drive to Paris, with a detailed route written by Alaine Cartet on a card already wedged in the 'Head Up' navigation system, Arthur took time over his part full English, part Continental breakfast.

He also set up his easel to rough out several sketches of parts of the town square. With his delayed start, it was early evening before he set out on the last leg of his journey to a caravan site on the outskirts of Paris. In his wallet, he carried a card that confirmed his reservation for seven nights on the site, the maximum it allowed.

A better card, also in his wallet, was the business card given to him by the extraordinary French tourist officer who called his assistant a 'miserable cow' without bringing down on his head calls for his dismissal on the grounds of harassment.

On the back of the card, Alaine Cartet had written his mobile telephone number.

Arthur knew that he had made a friend. It honoured one of the vows of the Grey Haired Knights that help, if needed, must come from new friends made along the way.

The last part of the journey into the city of Paris was difficult. The need to change lanes across multi carriageway avenues and negotiate wrong way round roundabouts confused Arthur.

Twice he pulled over into a side street to check again the route through the city outskirts that Alaine Cartet had set down for him. It was much later than he had planned before he finally arrived at the caravan site.

Using his pre-booked reservation, he managed to make himself understood at reception. He also managed to find his way to his allocated hard standing. Daylight had faded to midsummer dusk when he lowered the steps, ready to hook up to the electrical supply.

He stopped in the doorway. His heart missed a beat. He could clearly see the flood lit top of the Eiffel Tower.

Chapter 10

During Arthur Thomas's fourth morning in France, while clearing his breakfast things he said aloud, but to himself, "Now what?" As though in reply to his question the mobile phone supplied by Swiss Mobius rang.

Within the first three sharp tones Arthur answered the call, "Peter is that you?" "Peter replied, but his tone was unusually flat, "Yes it is me. Where are you Arthur, are you still good? "

Alarmed by Peter's voice, because it lacked its usual bantering tone, Arthur replied, "I'm fine Peter, honest. I am already on the outskirts of Paris. In fact, from where I have parked, I can see the top of the Eiffel Tower. What's up?

Peter continued to sound serious, "Well old lad you must listen to me, and pay attention. Despite thinking ourselves to be a couple of clever cops, it seems that we have been rumbled. Late last night the Governor of the open prison, where you went to see Servient-Higgins, rang me. He told me that the rat-tailed Higgins has formally complained to the Inspector of Prisons that the Governor, conspiring and conniving with outside interests, has allowed them to spy on him, his business and his family. Thinking about it, someone in the prison may have remembered your very noticeable silver grey hair, your moustache, your policeman's feet and Yorkshire dialect. It could have been a long-term prisoner, who you had put away years ago, who put it about that you were a nark, an ex-policeman. However, I think it more likely that after your visit to the National Gallery, the distaff side of the Servient-Higgins marriage talked to her husband. Pound to a penny he has a mobile phone. Perhaps we were wrong to try to pass you off as an intellectual. Your beat flattened feet and wind chilled complexion give you away; you still look like P.C. Plod.

Whatever, we are sundered, you are too exposed, and it's a right balls up. You can't go bounty hunting when you are the quarry. The people who stole the painting are a dangerous murderous crew. Anne says that you must come straight back to England. If it is excitement that you crave she says you could not do better than settle for the vagabond widow."

Arthur slumped into the driving seat. After taking a long time to react he replied, "Nah, can't do that. Don't need to. From day to day, I don't know where I will be. They can't possibly know where I am; I often don't know where I am myself.

I feel a bit like a chap I met in a dream I had recently. It is all part of living in a peripatetic wander home. I shall just have to be a little careful which name I use, and when. On campsites I shall be Arthur Thomas, P.C. Plod retired. In the galleries, I shall continue to be Dr Edward Davenport of the Open University. It could be a good thing if they think that I am a threat and come looking for me."

Peter, who sounded more anxious than before, cut in to say, "Arthur, I am serious, how can that be?"

"Well, as I was about to say," Arthur continued, "It will be like the old children's party game of 'Hunt the Thimble'. If I am cold, they will leave me alone, but if I get warm, they will start to get all over excited like little children do at parties.

Perhaps they will try to discourage my interest by a bribe, or more likely threats, but they will not risk killing me. It would link them to the murder of the museum guard. We will know then that I am on the right track. If I get hot, by getting close to finding the genuine Ingres painting, they will have to act quickly to get there before me.

Any activity of theirs in my vicinity will confirm my findings. If I follow their movements, they will lead me to the painting. I will be able to tell you where it is. I will then bow out, leaving you to take over."

Peter was now truly cross, "It's not worth it Arthur, you will be like a forward observation officer calling down an artillery barrage on his own position. My company only gives rewards of money, not awards of medals. Madam, the neé Servient, will know that you told her boss of your plan to visit the Louvre.

Yes, you may be right, at first, they will probably try to scare you off, but if that fails, if husband Higgins thinks you can get to the La Source before him, or reveal evidence that he murdered the guard, he will try to kill you himself, or have you killed. Honestly Arthur, he is a cold killer with connections to villains of his ilk all across Europe."

It took a long time before Arthur could convince his old friend that he was determined to continue with his search for the stolen painting.

He had to promise to call regularly to report what he was doing, that he would not take risks and would take every care to stay out of trouble. However, when Arthur finally pressed the disconnect button, he sat for a long time wondering whether he should take Peter's advice to pack it in, or find another quest to follow.

However, he could not get out of his head the dream he had of the strange old man who had shouted to him "Good thing to go questing, can't be denied, it tests the blood of an English Man."

After the disturbing call from Peter, Arthur truly felt that he was a stranger in a foreign land. Knowing that he would find the day to come a bit difficult, he planned to use it for reconnaissance only.

The caravan park Alaine Cartet had booked on his behalf was well organized. In the reception office, to his delight, Arthur found that the girl behind the counter spoke faultless English.

She had the same charming French accent that had delighted him when, as a young man, like many others, he had had a crush on Brigitte Bardot. That was when he went to see Vadim's film 'And God Created Woman'.

The receptionist gave him a folded full colour leaflet about the 'Louvre'. It contained instructions, in English, of how he could get there using public transport, bus, metro, or riverboat along the Seine.

Although tempted to the river trip, Arthur decided to take the metro because the caravan park ran a shuttle bus service to the metro station, from eight in the morning until eight in the evening.

After some difficulty with change for the ticket machines, and a couple of missed turnings before finding the correct platform for the train going in the right direction, Arthur arrived at the entrance to the Louvre just before eleven in the morning.

Even though he had worked at the National Gallery and visited the Tate and Portrait Galleries in London, he was impressed with the sheer size of the Louvre.

The people who formed the small slowly moving queue wending into the museum through an out of place glass pyramid intrigued him. Arthur thought the entrance no better than a potting shed with delusions of grandeur, a conceited gratuitous insult to history wrought by an arrogant modern architect.

The people moving gently forward into this garden centre glasshouse were a polyglot population of different age, gender, colour, race, affluence and interest, in contrast to the predominantly white middle class patrons of the London galleries.

Alaine Cartet, manager of the Bureau Tourisme in Vernon, had suggested that he should ask at the pay kiosk for a special rate for a weeklong pass, but warned him not to ask for a reduced rate for pensioners.

With feigned superiority he had declaimed, "We logical French citizens subsidize our young people, as an investment in the future, any reduction for the ancients would only be a consolation prize." The six-day pass he bought saved Arthur a deal of Euro.

Once inside the great palace Arthur bought the essential glossy guidebook. He decided to put aside his lifelong prejudice against the French, and to allow himself a free rein to wander and wonder at their collected glories.

He almost walked past the Mona Lisa, the Museum's star billing, because a small crowd standing in silent homage to Leonardo's enigma had it almost obscured.

He felt a sense of disappointment that, despite the crash course in the National Gallery, he did not immediately see any difference between the genuine 'Giaconda' and the copy he had seen on display in the entrance to Faux Art Works, the thieves kitchen located on one of London's most fashionable streets.

Despite his early decision to wander freely, he spent the better part of the day studying both 'The Valpincon Bather' and 'The Turkish Bath', the two best examples of Ingres's art in the Louvre's collection.

A sandwich, bought from a kiosk, at exorbitant cost, but no different to any he could have bought in an English petrol station, eaten while taking a breath of fresh air in the Garden des Tuileries at the far end of the palace, made a poor lunch.

That there was no tea, just bad coffee dispensed in a paper cup from an automatic vending machine, did not improve Arthur Thomas's temper, or digestion, but it did dissipate any 'Francophile' tendency that the museum had engendered in him during the morning.

Hunger forced Arthur to leave the Museum before it closed. He was intent on eating early so that he could catch a metro train that would connect with the last shuttle bus to the caravan site. After traipsing for several hundred yards, none of the bars or bistros he passed attracted him, but eventually he found that which he sought, a restaurant that was not part of a chain.

It was sheltered in a narrow side street, marked only by a simple sign over the door, 'Bien-Découplé'. The lights in the widow made it look warm, also welcoming.

Through the window he could see that it was old fashioned. It had wooden floors and some good paintings on the wood panelled walls.

The tables were covered with deep red cloths hemmed with tassels, part covered by clean starched white runners. Shining silver cutlery and gleaming glassware illuminated by bright table lantern lights completed the setting. "Well, Englishman abroad," Arthur said to himself, "You either face up to embarrassment, or starve."

After straightening his back and pulling back his shoulders, followed by the inevitable unconscious left and right index finger smoothing his moustache he braved the threshold barrier by pushing open the door and stepping into Bien-Découplé.

The two waiters, both leaning on a service bar, concerned to maintain the status of their calling, did not spring into action. Neither of them reacted to his diffident question, "Are you serving dinner?" Neither waiter moved to show him to a table or to offer him a menu.

Annoyed by their behaviour, he was about to leave when, as if from nowhere, an explosion of energy in the form of a grey haired tidy little woman in her late fifties appeared. Full of feminine Gallic charm she almost sang her welcome, "Monsieur, my poor man, obviously you are hungry, and also tired. You are in need of food, a glass of wine, or perhaps a beer. These ignorant men ignore you because you are English. Crétin - they are too young to remember the war, the occupation, the liberation.

My father died fighting with the maquis. I could understand their attitude if you were German, but not this, they will hear more from me."

The little bundle of energy rattled on, "I am Madam Déclâre, Yvette. This is my restaurant since two years ago when my husband, the Patron also Chef de Cuisine, did me the great disservice of making me a widow."

As she guided him to a table she asked, "Wine or beer monsieur, we have French wine from many regions, some so called 'Supérieure', too expensive, some we call 'Pays', often not worth it, some 'Table' always acceptable at the price.

We do not have any wines that are not French, but we have some British bottled Bass or Irish Guinness." "Oh the beer please," Arthur responded with delight, forgetting his resolution to drink only the wine or beer of the region.

There followed a stream of French directed at the two now rather cowed waiters who, to Arthur's amusement, shrugged as only Frenchmen can.

One brought an opened bottle of Bass with an appropriate glass, the other handed him the menu on a large card. Arthur said, "Madam, despite my obvious age, I am a novice, an innocent abroad. I need some help here.

Please choose for me a substantial meal, but with two courses only, first and then main. I wish to learn about how the French eat, and to know how and what to order, but please don't tell me what I have eaten until I have cleared both plates."

Madam Déclâre made a great fuss of Arthur, even though her restaurant slowly filled with what were obviously frequent customers, each of whom received a genuine welcome.

As soon as she had cleared both of Arthur's clean plates, Madam Déclâre described, in detail, the ingredients her chef had used, where they came from, and how he had prepared both courses.

After he had paid his not expensive bill, Arthur explained that he was studying at the Louvre for the rest of the week. He asked her whether he could come again for further instruction on matters gastronomique. "Of course monsieur, I shall be glad to be your tutor, but first you must tell me your name." "Well," Arthur replied, "It's Arthur Thomas for my sins." "Nonsense," was his host's sharp response, "Arthur was a pure knight, a noble King and without doubt, Thomas is a good name." She followed her admonition with a parting friendly, "À bientôt!"

On his way back to his mobile home, Arthur realised that he was tired, and a little overwhelmed by the day, but the journey was uneventful. He did not have to wait long before the shuttle bus came to pick him up from the metro station.

He did not mind that the driver waited another ten minutes, for other passengers to arrive, before he drove back to where waited his well fitted out and equipped van that he was genuinely beginning to think of as home.

Before turning in, relived to find the milk was still fresh, he made a pot of his precious Yorkshire tea, while listening to the BBC Overseas Service.

When he lay comfortable in his bed, he felt secure; he had no fear of Servient-Higgins, or his gang of thieves.

He also felt a little less of a stranger in a foreign land; he had made two French friends, Alaine Cartet and Madam Déclâre.

Thinking about the poor coffee, and expensive sandwiches he had bought at the Louvre, he decided to buy a thermos flask to carry boiling water to make tea. He also planned to buy ingredients to make sandwiches for his lunch, as he had done for years after Jenny died, while he was still in the force.

He also decided to buy a box to contain his lunch to stop any leaks damaging his brief case. Satisfied with the day, he set the alarm for seven. He was asleep in as many minutes.

Arthur spent the next few days in the routine of a commuter.

Up early to shower shave, dress and then polish his shoes, before making a simple breakfast, using convenience foods he bought each evening from the little shop on the caravan site.

After breakfast, he made sandwiches and filled his thermos with boiling water. The thermos had arrived courtesy of Madame Déclâre.

When he asked her where he might buy one, she bustled into the kitchen to come out with a flask, claiming that she would be glad to get rid of it because, kept on a shelf in the kitchen, it needed cleaning every day.

Under her expert guidance, Arthur began to learn how to understand a menu, and how to spot a chef's guile, or even trickery, in the 'Daily Specials'.

He began to enjoy ordering a meal without falling into the traps laid by waiters who inveigle customers to choose the most profitable items on the menu, or wine list, or the dish that the chef had told them to get rid of before it reached the end of its sell by moment.

Arthur's study of some of the world's greatest works of art, including sculptures as well as paintings, did not discourage his desire to paint, to paint using oils. His few short lessons in technique with the conservators in the British National Gallery had given him an appreciation of the skill with which great artists used brushes, pigment, and pallet knives.

He longed to set up his little easel, to try to copy some small detail of a Titian, or a Velasquez, or better still a fraction of the Ingres masterpiece, 'The Valpincon Bather'. He wanted to attempt to reproduce the skin tones that the guidebook said were, 'Unequalled by any artist since his time'.

Each day had so enthralled him it was not until the Friday afternoon that he realised his allowed seven days at the caravan park was running out. It meant that he would have to leave before middle day on the coming Sunday.

While he was enjoying his dinner at the 'Bien-Découplé', he told Madam Déclâre of his sorry plight. He had to do this in short bursts as she darted around the tables, like a little bantam hen looking after her brood of guests, while all the time chasing the ever-indolent waiters.

For the first time Arthur did not leave the restaurant early to catch the metro connecting with the last shuttle bus to the caravan site.

He lingered, hoping to ask Madam Déclâre for her advice. He needed to know where he might move to in order to continue his studies.

He wanted to spend another few days at the Louvre, followed by at least two days at the musée d'Orsay, on the opposite bank of the Seine. "Pouffe!" she exclaimed, "Not a problem, my lovely husband was not only Chef Patron for this restaurant; he also had a team of chefs. They made high-class charcuterie and patisserie for sale to other restaurants around central Paris.

He should have had a 'Michelin Star' of his own, made up from fragments of the Michelin Stars of the restaurants he supplied. I do not know whether too much work killed my poor Jacques, perhaps he was just too big. A magazine review described him best; 'Built like a bear with a voice like a bullhorn'. He was a lovely big fellow in frame and personality. That is why we named this restaurant 'Bien-Découplé'. It was his sense of humour, it means, 'good - well built - well set up' – Bien-Découplé was how do you say, his nickname.

He had a great high-sided van that he used to deliver the produce he made each day. We parked the van overnight in the kitchen yard. It has a high wall, so who is to know what it may conceal.

There cannot be too much difference between a truck and your funny little home on wheels, can there? We do not open on Sundays. Accord! I will come to find you at the gypsy camp where you have kept your vardo. You can then follow me back here. From the metro, you have seen nothing of Paris. If you behave anything like my Jacques, you will be too proud to ask for directions, and you will get hopelessly lost if you try to find my restaurant by yourself. Mon Dieu, you cannot yet speak French; it is decided, I will lead, you will follow, just as it was when I danced with Jacques.

There is electricity in the garage to connect to what will be Découplé's new outhouse. It will make you comfortable."

All this came out in an uninterrupted stream, without pause for breath. Arthur just stared at her, wide eyed, before he said, "That would be wonderful, but you must let me pay the same rent that I would have to on a caravan site." "We'll see," Madam said, "Maybe lunch next Sunday. That would seem about fair with the prices most places charge these days."

Arthur was elated at the thought of another week in Paris. It meant that, without the drag of commuting, he would be able to study at the museums during the day and continue his instruction in gastronomy during the evenings at Restaurant Bien-Découplé.

Arthur was also grateful that, other than when he was in either museum, the high walls of Bien-Découplé would hide him from any accomplice of Servient-Higgins who might logically search for him in the caravan sites of France.

It was late when Arthur came out of the metro station, too late to catch the shuttle bus that had made its last run of the day. Missing the bus set Arthur a challenge.

To walk all the way to the caravan park was physically impossible. To make things worse, try as he might, he could not remember the name of the campsite; funny French words did not seem to register in his memory, as did proper English words.

He damned himself for a fool for having a senior moment, but cheered himself, as he always did, by thinking it better than a teenage dysfunctional day.

He therefore did what any sensible English Man would do in a crisis abroad, in lieu of a pub, he went into the nearest café-bar where he sat at an empty table and ordered a beer.

He systematically emptied all his pockets, then his wallet, onto the table, searching for something that would identify the caravan site where his comfortable bed waited for him. He found nothing to help him communicate, absolutely nothing, not even his little French English–English France dictionary.

Then, to his relief, in his pack up lunch box he found a half-eaten packet of biscuits on which a small stick on price label gave him the name of the caravan site that he had been unable to recall.

Ten minutes later, after many thanks to the Patron who had called and given instruction to a taxi driver, Arthur was on his way home.

Tipped out at the gate of the caravan site he felt as though he had just come off the big dipper at Blackpool. It was true, he thought, French taxi drivers are modern day Valkyrie who have swapped broomsticks for super turbo charged Citroens.

He was so tired by his long day and alarmed by the bolting taxi that his chosen nightcap was not a cup of Yorkshire tea, but a good measure of Scotch whisky, the first out of the bottle he had brought from his bungalow in Scagill.

The following morning, Saturday, Arthur took courage to carry with him, as well as his brief case containing the thermos flask and his lunchbox, his little travelling easel, pallet, brushes, and paints, all of which fitted in a rather smart attaché type case.

At the entrance to the Louvre, in that horrid glasshouse insult to history, two security guards asked him to open his cases.

They checked the contents of both very carefully, but after a few questions, which he did not understand, or to which he made no reply, they let him pass.

Arthur again made his way to the Ingres masterpiece The Valpincon Bather. After he asked permission from a museum attendant, she allowed him to set up his easel with a sight line to the painting. It gave Arthur the opportunity he wanted; a chance to study and copy the technique Ingres used to represent skin.

The Louvre's guidebook quoted a critic's analysis, 'As smooth as the skin of an onion.' Arthur reckoned the painting to be about half life-size, but unlike the anorexic size zero models cruelly used by modern day couturiers, it showed the unadorned back of a healthy woman.

His plan was to spend the day trying to replicate, by many attempts, just one small part of the painting. He wanted to find out whether he could ever reproduce the enamel like colouring of the skin tones that were Ingres's unique signature. Arthur felt compelled to do this if he were ever to authenticate the stolen original of 'La Source', the object of his quest.

Arthur realised that by concentrating on Ingres's paintings he was broadcasting his whereabouts to other people with the same interest. He was content to think that he might already be 'It' for Servient-Higgins's gang of thieves playing 'Hunt the Thimble', following his moves, but he worried that they also played another more adult party game, 'Murder'.

Arthur had not long been back from his half hour lunch break in the Tuileries Garden when he became aware that a tall man, with a thin drawn face, was closely observing him.

Arthur had been up and down, peering then painting, trying unsuccessfully to copy the Ingres technique. In answer to Arthur's shy smile, the man said in a cold voice, but with a wan expression, "Doctor Andrew Davenport I presume." "Er no," Arthur replied, immediately kicking himself, he stuttered "Oh er sorry, yes, yes indeed, sorry, I was miles away.

People at the office rarely call me Doctor they usually call me 'Sofa'. It's their little joke picked up from the American TV they watch. Do forgive me."

The tall patrician extended a hand in greeting, "It is a pleasure to meet you Doctor. My name is Charles d'Chastelain; I am the Director of Security at the Musée d'Orsay. I believe one of my staff, Jacques Dupont, met you in London. He thought that I might find you here. Perhaps you will allow me extend the Musée's courtesies to you.

Our Monsieur Renan, with his team of conservation technicians over the river, will be able to help you with your research. That is if you will desert your shameless model here to spend some time with us next week. I am afraid we have lost our equally shameless nubile nude, 'The water carrying nymph, which is a source of great trouble to us. We hope it will be a source of much trouble to others in the future. Even so, we may have a little surprise for you. I will leave a note about you at the enquiry desk in the reception hall.

When you arrive, just tell them who you are, and one of our English speaking staff will come to collect you. Bring your little easel, paints and brushes with you, but for now Doctor, I will leave you to your studies."

Arthur could not offer anything but a simple "Thank you Monsieur, I shall be most grateful. It will be a wonderful chance for me to further my research for the programme. I shall be there on Monday, first in the queue waiting for the Musée to open." Ah no monsieur, I regret that the museum is closed every Monday, we have to give our staff some time to themselves." "Well then, Tuesday it will be" replied the ex-Superintendent of Police.

At the same time, he felt a chill of fear that d'Chastelain had been tipped off by someone, that Doctor Davenport of the Open University was in the Louvre.

Arthur did not take to d'Chastelain, he almost felt threatened by the man. He sensed there was something cold in his manner, something not quite genuine. He remembered the warning Peter gave him, 'Not to take anything, or anyone, at face value'. He decided he would ring Peter at his home, around six thirty British Summer Time, to ask him whether he had told d'Chastelain that he might be found in the Louvre, or whether he thought the 'Hunt the Thimble' party game might have started.

As instructed, Arthur kept the phone fully charged. He had also bought, for not much money from a petrol station, a kit to make the phone hands free, so that when on the move, it became part of his 'Head up navigation system'.

'Chastelain, invitation to visit the 'technicians' at the d'Orsay worried Arthur. His concern was that d'Chastelain was responsible for security when the odious creature Terrance Servient-Higgins had callously killed a security guard.

Even gunshot and murder had not prevented him from getting one of the world's most valuable paintings out of the gallery, past d'Chastelain's security.

The heinous crime had succeeded, despite Interpol having Servient-Higgins's gang under surveillance. It troubled his policeman's nous that even though Interpol had alerted d'Chastelain to the possibility of an imminent attempt at robbery, he had failed to prevent it. Possibly more alarming, he had still kept his top security job.

Arthur feared that d'Chasterlain's had invited him to the Musée d'Orsay to find out how warm he was, or whether he was still cold.

Chapter 11

d'Chastelain's invitation for Dr Edward Davenport to visit the Musée d'Orsay had broken the rhythm of Arthur Thomas's week. He had enjoyed the days spent in academic study of Ingres's technique in the Louvre, followed by evenings engaged in practical study of French gastronomy at Restaurant Bien-Découplé, under the expert guidance of Madam Déclâre.

The interruption had made Arthur uneasy, and unable to settle again to his studies.

Frustrated, after packing up his easel, pallet, paints and brushes he left the Louvre well before it closed, and long before he thought it the best time to ring Peter Bainbridge. He walked slowly back towards the restaurant Bien-Découplé, but stopped at a shop to buy flowers for Madam Déclâre. To kill time, because the restaurant would not be open until six, he sat at a pavement table of a bistro.

The unexpected visit by d'Chastelain made it clear to him that his quest was not a superficial light-hearted adventure; it had a deadly undertow. He knew that modern forensic science might find matching DNA traces on the painting, if he were to find it, and that such traces could lead to a successful prosecution of Servient-Higgins for the murder of the museum guard. It occurred to him that such a success might be Pyrrhic, putting his life in danger, perhaps mortal danger.

While he sat thinking about this, he could almost hear again Anne Bainbridge's plea, "Look after yourself Arthur, I can understand you not wanting to give up on life, but make sure you do not get dead in the doing of it."

Arthur realised he would have to find something to occupy him for a couple of hours until he could make his early evening call to Peter Bainbridge about d'Chastelain and before returning to the restaurant Bien-Découplé. Almost automatically, he unlocked his case of paints, and then set up his easel ready to paint.

To practice a technique the restorers at the National Gallery had taught him about painting glass, he chose for his subject a dark green frosted glass bottle, and several empty wine glasses, that idle staff had left on a nearby table.

He was soon lost in that special world of the artist; the wholly consuming world of effort, snared by self-criticism, leading to frustration; the angst common amongst painters, sculptors, composers and authors. Nobody bothered him. Apparently, he bothered nobody.

It was almost eight o'clock when a waiter, with a less than discrete cough, brought Arthur back to the streets of Paris from the garret of his imagination. The waiter followed a second cough with his practiced sarcastic prompt. "Perhaps monsieur may like to consider ordering a coffee, or would you prefer to pay rent?" "Oh sorry, pardon," spluttered Arthur. "No, no coffee, I am hours late, I must go. Thank you for bringing me back to reality; I have things to do."

As soon as he had packed away his portable painting kit, Arthur left the bistro without hearing the waiters dismissive, "Vaurien Anglais". He soon found a vacant bench on the bank of the Seine from where he phoned Peter Bainbridge, who he liked to think of as 'M', his spymaster.

He was not surprised to find that Peter had recorded each number twice in the Swiss Mobius phone's memory. The second number having the country code for the United Kingdom already entered. The phone only rang three times before Anne answered, "Bainbridge Lurgashall." "Anne, its Arthur, I am in Paris, sitting by the Seine. Could I please speak to Peter? Is he at home?" "Yes and yes he is," Anne replied, "But you can't speak to him just yet. First you must speak to me, you rude un-communicative Yorkshireman. You must tell me, truthfully, what you have been doing. Peter tells me that you should come back to us here, safer to risk the advances of the merry widow, rather than risking your life to recover a rude nude.

They may both be painted ladies, but the only risk with the Lurgashall lady would be that she might kill you with kindness." Arthur was not a raconteur on the phone. He thought phones were to pass or receive messages, no more. However, before Peter came on the line, Anne had dug out of him, in about five minutes, much of what he had done since leaving Lurgashall. Peter then interrupted, "I have been listening on the bedroom extension to your hopeless flirting with my wife; there is no need to repeat your unlikely tales.

Will you be going to the musée d'Orsay on Monday?" "No" replied Arthur. "But I shall be there, Tuesday until Friday, they shut shop on Mondays.

The d'Chastelain chap you told me about, the d'Orsay's negligent security chief accosted me in the Louvre. I did not take to him; he seemed to be a cold fish. Did you tell him that I was there?" "No I did not." Peter answered. "His mates in the Louvre must have told him that they had an old English deviant weirdo ogling pictures of naked young ladies. He would have been onto you straight away. Your dirty mackintosh must have given you away. I told you, anyone who wanted to find you could easily do so. The art world, like all worlds, is very small."

Peter continued the call in a serious vein, "Now pay attention, I have had a meeting with my friends at Interpol. We are not sure about the integrity of the people working in the musée d'Orsay, not even the careless d'Chastelain. If you are still intent upon finding the painting, do no more than observe. Be discrete, do not push or pry. Ask about the theft, but do not show too much interest. Remember, you are an academic planning a TV series for the OU. You have an interest in Ingres, but it is across his complete canon, not just the missing jade with the jug. Call me every day or two. Let me know about everything that you do, and about everybody that you meet. I do mean everything and everybody. I want to know about what you have seen, particularly things that you may not have seen, but those that you sensed. I know many unimportant things that might connect with things that you might consider unimportant, but when taken together might be important. Do not take any chances; remember to keep your phone with you at all times, always fully charged, in case I have need to talk to you."

When Arthur finally reached, what he hoped would be the sanctuary of the Bien-Découplé, because it was Saturday night, customers occupied every table. Madam Déclâre was too busy to greet him with her usual warmth. She did however accept his flowers and waive him to a high cane stool set against the small dispense bar.

In a moment, by some form of magic, he had before him a glass of Bass. "Drink that and starve you rude un-communicative Englishman. You are late. I had to let your table go to proper people. You will have to eat leftovers with me after the last customer has gone."

Arthur drank slowly, appreciatively, thoughtfully. He was thoughtful because within less than thirty minutes he had been called rude and un-communicative by two ladies; two of only a very few with whom he found it easy to talk. Too long a bachelor too set in my own little word he concluded. He cheered up while watching the mannerisms of Madam Déclâre's clientele.

He thought their behaviour very different from the English in a similar class of restaurant. Here was noise, gusto and laughter. Food was 'polished off', fingers used, plates scraped clean with bread. Compared with the English attitude to wine the Bien-Découplé customers were irreverent, without regard to ice buckets or napery.

Here, the diners poured out wine, straight from the bottle, without waiting for a wine waiter, or a clean glass. Many added water to their wine from the carafe on their table, provided for that purpose.

It was almost eleven o'clock when Madam put Arthur's glass, on a tray with his third bottle of beer, to set both down at a corner table. Auguste, the Head Chef, of an age with Madam, came to sit with him.

A few moments later Madam Déclâre joined them and put on the table his flowers, now beautifully arranged in cut glass vase. The second chef, a thin rake of a man in his thirties with sloping shoulders and deep-set dark eyes, brought from the kitchen and set before them a deep bowl, full of mussels, almost swimming in a creamy garlic sauce. Alongside this steaming bowl, he set a plate piled high with sliced fresh bread hewn from a grand baguette.

Because the waiters and the second chef had gone home, Chef Auguste brought in the main course in a well-worn red enamelled cast iron tureen with a close fitting lid. With the lid removed it revealed a casserole of lamb hocks that he had cooked slowly in the oven, together with button onions, root vegetables, celery, haricot beans, leeks, peas and mushrooms.

Arthur assumed that he had used everything that needed using up, because the restaurant would not open again until Monday evening. All of this fresh natural goodness was in a rich deep brown sauce, thick as double cream, and with a glaze the equal of a majolica vase. Chef put round the table three deep soup bowls, plates, knives forks, and spoons. When the three had eaten their fill, with hardly a word spoken, Arthur leaned back in his chair to declare, "Chef: that was good."

Looking straight at her Head Chef, Madam Déclâre smiled. She then said, "Yes, this poor old man has not learned anything new, not in forty years, not a thing; not since he came in off the streets, to work for my husband Jacque, as an apprentice. It has been the salvation of Bien-Découplé. All around us in Paris, and beyond, are young pretenders in their brightly lit showroom restaurants of chrome and glass.

Their tables are too small to have side plates or elbowroom. To fit more customers at each table the chairs have no arms. They cook only, as you say in England, 'Flash in the Pan'. They would not recognise a stockpot, or a stove; not even if their mothers boiled their brat heads in a brat pan or burnt their bums in boulangerie. Excuse my vulgarity but I fear that it will be the end of France."

Madam then said, again with a smile, "It's no good you looking at your watch Englishman, it is too late for you to go back to your little home on wheels. It is 'le weekend'. At this time of night, the metro is not safe for you. If you were lucky enough to find the one taxi driver in Paris who would take you so far north, it would cost more than to stay for the night, in a suit at the Hotel Ritz, on the Place Vendee. You will stay with Auguste. We have it arranged. Just round the corner, he shares a big flat with his brother. It has many rooms that he lets out to his staff and to other chefs for huge rents. He is richer than I am, although he has much less to do. Come back here tomorrow morning, not too early, about ten o'clock, after I have been to Mass. I shall then take you in my little Renault to your encampment. You can follow me through Paris to arrive back here by mid-afternoon. It will be fun."

Somewhere around the middle of Sunday morning, Arthur knocked on the door of Restaurant Bien-Découplé, but he received no answer. After a couple more attempts at knocking that produced no acknowledgement, he wandered along the street until he found a way round to the back of the restaurant.

It was easy enough for him to recognise the back entrance because of the unusually high wooden double doors set in an equally high stone wall. When Arthur gently pushed at one door, it swung open to let him walk through. What he saw inside the gate impressed him to a point beyond amazement. He thought that it could not possibly be the back yard of a restaurant in the middle of a city. He had pictured a concrete yard with bins and detritus; similar to the yards he had seen when he was a constable patrolling town centre beats in Scagill.

This yard was different. It was a courtyard fit for a Florentine Palace. Its creator had built it on several levels, to feature stone walls, cobbled paths, balustrades, a wrought iron pergola and a fountain flowing into a cascade dropping into a small lily pond in which coloured carp took lazy turns round a central stone pagoda. Cleverly placed tall evergreen cypresses, Mediterranean shrubs, and herbs, planted in terra cotta pots, or wooden tubs on castor wheels, created vibrant contrasting colours. In one corner, a vine trained to overhead wires provided shade.

The garden courtyard was clearly a creation of skill, love and devotion. A Palladian façade masked a large garage. On the highest level, Madam Déclâre presided over her realm in a high backed wicker chair. She was dressed for summer in a brightly coloured dress and a large, very large, white wide brimmed sun hat. "Bonjour mon brave" she sang out, "You found your way through our Parisian back streets. I knew that you could and would. I did not worry. On Sunday mornings only, the streets are safe from the druggies, muggers, buggers, pimps and prostitutes who corrupt the sole of Paris." Arthur replied, "Madam, this is a surprise, it is an oasis fit for Cleopatra."

Madam was obviously pleased, and said, "Yes it is. My lovely Jacque had it built to celebrate our twenty-fifth wedding anni-

155

versary. It gives me much pleasure; unspoilt by drudgery. All my plants, apart from the vine, are evergreens in pots, and with the whole area paved, it is easy to keep tidy.

Unlike English men, who spend all summer Sunday mornings edging and cutting lawns, and all autumn weekends burning bonfires, I am free for the day, but first we shall have a glass of wine." Arthur could not remember having spent such a pleasant day in the company of a woman since his wife Jenny died. He was surprised at how relaxed he was and how easily conversation flowed between this busy little French bundle of energy and himself, a reserved elderly Englishman.

On their way to the caravan park, as he expected, Madam Déclâre drove with élan through the streets of Paris. She acted as a voluble tour guide by taking many diversions to improve Arthur's understanding and appreciation of Paris.

Because Madam had given him the 'Grand Tour', it was already mid-afternoon when they finally reached the caravan park. Arthur was pleased that she approved of Tootsie. He was even more pleased when she told him that it had been an ambition of her husbands, when he retired, to convert his delivery van into a mobile home in which they could tour Europe.

Following Madam Déclâre's red Renault, Arthur drove, without mishap, on the journey through Paris. She demonstrated her skill as a lead driver, never going too fast, never losing him, but even so, Arthur found the traffic daunting. By the time he had reached Bien-Découplé, parked in front of the garage, and then hooked up to electricity, it was already early evening. Arthur wondered how he could repay his host's many kindnesses. Long a widower, he was nervous of being too familiar.

He was totally at a loss of where he might suggest taking her, or even if he should presume to ask to take up more of her precious spare time. He realised, as soon as she came bustling out into the courtyard, that he need not have worried. "Come along," she trilled, "Will a charming Englishman not escort a girl to parade on the boulevards of the most romantic city in the world?"

She had changed into a very smart suit. Her hat was now very elegant, though pill box small. In a word, Arthur thought her 'Chic'. Together they had a lovely time doing what Parisians have done for years on summer evenings.

First, they chose to promenade, to look down on and criticise those people who were sitting, eating and drinking, at tables set on the pavement outside cafés. Then, noticing that Arthur was flagging, Madam suggested that they sit at a café pavement table, under a warming light, to drink wine, while criticising the promenading Parisians.

Because the musée d'Orsay closed on Mondays, Arthur decided on a different sort of a day, a day he would spend painting rather than studying the work of other artists. Anxious to get on with his plan, he skimped a bit on breakfast. However, as always, he made sure that he was showered, shaved and smartly dressed, and with everything left tidy before stepping out into the courtyard garden.

He had no difficulty in choosing a subject. It was all around him. The garden was bright with mid-summer morning sun. The sunlight stimulated his ideas by contrasting the warmth of the stone walls with the shadows cast by the tall deep green cypresses and Mediterranean shrubs. On the highest level a huge umbrella, its panel's wasp like, alternating black with yellow, shaded Madam Déclâre's unoccupied high backed wicker chair. After a careful look around the garden, he chose both his subject and a clean prepared board.

The board was a small thing, about as big as a family sized corn flakes packet. By nine o'clock, comfortable in his folding chair, he had boldly struck his first charcoal lines to set the outline of what he hoped would be a fair representation of a corner of this very private courtyard garden; a garden hidden in the heart of Paris.

Using a separate already used board, he quickly daubed paint trying to record the bright yellows and dark greens of the morning light because he knew that, as the sun progressed, the colours would change. He wanted his picture to be a summer morning picture, a detail of the courtyard garden, as he had first seen it.

When Madam Déclâre plonked a wide brimmed floppy white hat firmly on his head, Arthur realised that his whole life was changing.

He felt that he had a purpose beyond his quest to find the stolen Ingres painting, claim the reward and bring to justice the murderer of the guard.

His love of painting was developing into a passion. He had not heard his charming hostess come into the garden.

The deep frustration with his oils, paints, and brushes, that would not do what he wanted them to do, had muted his senses. "Now my little Cezanne" Madam burst out with her usual whirling energy, "You must take a break. It is almost lunchtime.

You have not moved for more than three hours. You must wear this hat against the sun; it was one of Jacque's. He does not need it now that he is cooking for the angels. In heaven, he will have an air-conditioned kitchen.

Your lovely silver hair is too thin to provide any protection. Too much sun will give you a headache. Come inside for Déjeuner, with a glass of your English beer. I hope you had a good breakfast. If you are going to paint well you must eat well, with lots of fish to encourage your little brain cells. Oh Pardon, what am I saying? It is the fault of your back to front language. I'm sorry; I know that you have a big brain, only the cells are little."

The weather in Paris held bright and sunny all week. Each day, before going across the Seine over the Pont Royal to the musée d'Orsay, Arthur spent a good hour working on his painting of the garden, but twice he restarted on a clean board.

Dissatisfaction with his progress led to him using his pallet knife to scrape back fist sized areas of misbehaving brushwork to the bare board. Each time he scraped away a patch, he was thankful that he could not afford to paint on canvas. To use stretched canvas meant that each brush stroke had to be right 'First go'.

Arthur did not like to see any oil painting on which paint that had been overworked, or pushed about by an uncertain hand until it was tired.

Arthur spent his days at the musée d'Orsay between picture gazing and watching the technique of the conservators. Their patience with their work, also with his questions, was truly remarkable.

He could not believe his good fortune. La Source was still missing, but the surprise d'Chastelain had hinted at was in the restorer's workshop, set up without a frame, to rest on a solid wooden structure.

It was the Ingres masterpiece, 'Odalisque with a Slave'. It dominated the main room of the workshops. It was one of the artist's most sensuous paintings, his depiction of a Turkish concubine. Arthur remembered from his brief study that the painting normally hung in the curiously named Fogg Art Museum at Harvard University, in the USA. Monsieur Renan, the slight, elderly, now frail Head of Restoration recognised Arthur's astonishment.

He told him, in perfect Maurice Chevalier English, that the University had sent the painting to him, "To give the old scrubber a wash and brush up." Arthur was excited, because Renan told him that Ingres had used the same style and technique when he painted the Odalisque as he had when he painted La Source their missing painting.

Playing the part of the serious minded researcher from the Open University, Arthur spent as much time as he dare talking to Monsieur Renan, while the conservator worked, with an assistant, to reveal the Ingres painting as it was when first exhibited.

He finally plucked up courage to ask Renan to demonstrate how he would restore a damaged part of the painting had it been an area of skin. Monsieur Renan, flattered by the English academics attention to his work, gave Arthur a 'Master Class' in how such work should be done.

Renan copied from the original several small details onto a small board. His copies were not only exact in their detail, but they also reproduced the delicate skin tones that were Ingres signature.

On the last day of his visit to the musée d'Orsay Arthur finally overcame his shyness. He asked Monsieur Renan, apologetically, but in general terms, for some help with his little painting of part of Madam Déclâre's garden.

He asked how he could paint the cypresses and herbs to reveal depth and texture so that they did not look like cardboard cut-outs, without depth or substance. Inevitably, his newfound passion to be an artist took a hard knock.

Without a word, Monsieur Renan took the little board, and pinned to one side of the frame supporting the Ingres masterpiece. With a sinking heart, Arthur thought the expression 'Sublime to the ridiculous' apposite. Within seconds, Renan mixed oil and paints on his pallet. Setting up a similar sized new board above Arthur's painting, with seemingly effortless strokes of brown, followed by light and dark greens, then flecks of yellow, he turned an initial flat outline similar to Arthur's flat outlines, into a living shrub.

He went on to do more, fiercely demanding that his pupil, "Look, watch, copy, remember, then practice, practice, practice. Practice until you understand. Use good brushes, oils, pigments, paints, all of the quality I use. Wear the brushes out with practice, and then buy more. Paint a hundred different cypresses on one board. Burn that; then paint a hundred more. You will soon get the idea. Then do the same with the details of your stonework."

He made a few brush strokes to create an exact copy of a small detail of the wall that Arthur had painted. He then added strokes from another brush, almost too quickly for Arthur to follow, that gave a warm texture to the wall, revealing the warmth of morning sun.

Renan hurried on, enthused, excited, "You have already got the shade about right, leave it. You have chosen a good subject. Was it just imagination or have you recently been in Italy?"

Sensing Arthur's mood, he said with a smile, "Cheer up, you are never too old to learn. Your picture has good composition and perspective. You have talent, only technique is lacking. Technique you can learn from a good teacher or you can get it with much practice. Beg, buy, borrow, or if necessary steal, books with photographs, explanation and critiques of paintings by the great masters. Monet was good with cypresses, so was Van Gough in his early years. Visit as many galleries as you can; copy, copy, copy. By doing this you will master technique; eventually you will develop your own signature. I have technique. I am a master technician, one of the very best. The art world recognises me for what I am, but not as an artist. You see, I have no imagination. Every Sunday when I go to Mass, I thank God for my lack of imagination. People often ask why I admit to such a failing. My answer is always the same. I have no shame, because during all of my long life, I have earned a steady honest income. I have had a quiet untroubled domestic life. Had God imbued me with talent, creative thought, and imagination, I would have joined the shoals, not schools, of artists who driven by their calling often starve and are usually dead before they get recognition, and they are few. Sadly, greedy fraudulent critics, agents and gallery owners, dupe collectors into believing that a painter's work has hidden meaning. They corrupt the artist into painting canvases that he knows have no worth by offering to pay them as much as forty percent of the obscene prices they trick buyers into paying for their work. Other artists, in order to pay the rent, resort to crude pornography or primitive daubs, distorted imagery, or worst of all, craft pictures shaped by using protractors, compasses and stencil sets. From all of this seedy manipulation my lack of imagination has saved me." Renan then shook Arthur's hand and said, "Please forgive my diatribe, it is the one passion that I have about art, the wish to do away with cant and corruption. Doctor Davenport, stay true to yourself, be true to your talent."

Arthur took leave of Monsieur Renan and d'Chastelain with mixed feelings. He realised that Renan was a natural mentor from whom he had learned much, but of the Director of Security his doubts had increased, though he could not fathom the reason.

Monsieur Renan had told him where, nearby to the museum, there was the best shop in Paris to buy artists' materials. He had scribbled a note listing items that Arthur should buy; brushes in particular. Arthur bought the items suggested, adding to the list a stock of prepared boards of different shapes and sizes.

Lighter in pocket, but heavy with luggage, he took a taxi to what was now his artist's studio, as well as his mobile home.

Arthur set his mind to leave Paris on Sunday evening, after taking his hostess to lunch at a restaurant where the reckoning would be at least equal to a week's tariff for a motor home on a campsite.

Dinner was not an option; most of the Michelin Starred restaurants closed on Sunday evenings. In fact, Arthur found out that most restaurants closed all day Sunday and Monday. With Chef August's help, Arthur reserved a table for two at 'Grandual' on the Avenue de St Andere.

August assured him that he knew the chef who had held two of the coveted Michelin stars for several years. Arthur was a bit concerned when, after making the reservation, August said, "I hope your bank account is flush with many Euros. Don't order caviar or truffle, and watch out for his wine waiters. Don't let them talk you into a Premier Cru; if you do you will walk out needing a win on the lottery."

All day Saturday Arthur used his new brushes, on a new board, to try again to paint the same part of the garden he had shown to Monsieur Renan. On a separate board, he copied, many times, the shrub Renan had painted.

He also tried to copy the patch of wall that Renan had brought to life. He wore Jacque's old floppy wide brimmed hat and walked around the garden for five minutes every hour or so, but only because he set his little alarm clock to prompt him. By eight in the evening, Arthur had his picture.

Madam suggested that they eat together, 'scraps from the rich men's table', as they had on the previous Saturday. August objected. He insisted that to stave off dementia he would grill the sardines he had bought from the early morning market with his own money.

He said a light first course was necessary to leave room for a grand Cassoulet du Languedoc that he had had on the go for two days.

Arthur smiled, remembering Madam fondly telling him what a blessing it was that August had not learned a thing about cooking for forty years.

While Madam and Chef sat quietly, after a most convivial meal, Arthur stood up from the table to announce, in formal terms, "Madam, tomorrow evening I shall decamp; taking my leave of you, but grateful for all that you have done for me, a miss-fit; an English man in France. I have a quest that I must follow. Like Odysseus on his odyssey, I must break free from the siren pleasures of your wonderful restaurant and garden before they capture me forever. However, I shall not go before I pay the fee that you suggested when you so generously let me park my studio in your lovely Italianate courtyard. Tomorrow you and I will lunch at the two Michelin stared Restaurant 'Grandual.'"

In the Taxi to Grandual, Arthur and Madam Déclâre chattered happily, relaxed in each other's company. Arthur had never seen anything so opulent in a restaurant, the overwhelming furnishings, chandeliers, gilded mirrors, above all the magnificent golden cockerel defining the Frenchness of it all.

The lunch was good, in a minimalist style, but needed a good breakfast to support it. The service was faultless in technique but obsequious, even ingrate, in manner.

The wine he chose was good but hugely expensive, even though it was one of the cheapest on the card. What killed the occasion for Arthur was the ambience. Not one person laughed; waiter or customer.

There was no music. Every chair that squeaked, every knife that scratched a plate, or glass that clinked made every head turn. There was no gustatory indulgence possible. It was as though they were not dining, but taking part in a solemn ritual.

In the Taxi, on the way back to the Restaurant Bien-Découplé, Arthur was quiet, Madam Déclâre was quiet, neither spoke. The experience had squashed flat their mutual delight in anticipation of a special celebration. It had been wrong. Arthur thought the Grandual customers, though French, behaved like the pearls and twin-set patrons of a stuffy English country house hotel.

Finally, he broke the silence to say, "I am so very sorry Madam Déclâre; that was not what I wanted for you. You deserve a better mark of my appreciation of what you have done for me."

For a moment, there was no reply, then for the first time Arthur heard her use a low quiet sad voice. "Arthur Thomas, please don't say another word, or I shall do one of two things, both of which will embarrass you. I shall either cry, or sing 'La Marseillaise', at the top of my voice. I told you, these people with their silly food fashions, they will be the end of France."

Early during the evening after the disappointing lunch, Arthur had backed Tootsie out through the large wooden gates into the street behind the Restaurant Bien-Découplé.

Madam came to say goodbye, or as she insisted, 'Au revoir'. Arthur was shy. He took out his still not yet dry painting of the garden. "Please Madam, Yvette; I would like you to have this. It is not good, but my heart is in it. I am told that if I practice for ten years, and then some, I might one day get it about half right."

"Oh you lovely ridiculous grey haired man," Madam replied, "Until I met you, I did not know that there were romantic Englishmen. If you had not given me your lovely painting, I would have wept when you had gone. I now have something to remind me of a very happy time. I shall have it in my sitting-room, just as it is, with no frame."

She put the painting carefully down onto a low wall. After taking both of Arthur's hands in hers, she said, "Mr Englishman, Mr Arthur Thomas, I don't know what this quest of yours is about, but remember life is for living, take care of yourself so that you will be able to come back to Bien-Découplé." Picking up the painting, without looking back, she was gone in her customary whirlwind.

Arthur only drove just beyond the street before pulling over into a safe place to park. For a long time, he sat quietly thinking. He could not get out of his mind that when madam had taken both of his hands in hers, counselling caution, it was just the same as when he had left Anne Bainbridge, Peter's wife, two days before he left England.

From his wallet, he took the bill, 'le Addition' the reckoning, from the restaurant Grandual. He looked at it then gave a wry smile. Its total, with 'le Service' was much more than what it had cost him to stay for a week at the caravan site on the outskirts of the city.

He lit one of the cooker's gas rings to ignite one corner of the bill. He took the burning paper onto the street where the wind took hold of it. He watched, as the pretentious gold-bordered scrap drifted away, out over the river, hoping that it would take away with it all memories of the poor meal that had marred what had been two very happy weeks of good company and many truly satisfying dinners.

Arthur climbed stiffly back into Tootsie, eased himself behind the steering wheel, checked his head up navigation system, then whistled a few bars from 'La Marseillaise' before pulling out into the traffic. He was determined to meet again with Alaine Cartet, in Vernon.

Chapter 12

It was already dark when Arthur reached Vernon. He parked on the empty market place, in a quiet corner where he had parked before. He quickly turned his mobile artist's studio into a bed-sit. Tired to the point of exhaustion, he chose to go straight to bed without a calming cup of tea or even a tot of whisky.

The following morning, after a long sleep undisturbed by dreams, Arthur had just finished his first cup of life restoring tea when his Swiss Mobius mobile phone rang.

"Yes Peter, what's up?" he asked. Peter Bainbridge's reply was unusually direct, "Arthur you must seriously consider your position. Servient-Higgins knows too much about you. He even knows that you read the Daily Telegraph. I told you that if he connected you to me, that before killing you, he would probably try to frighten you off. Well old lad, he has already started his terror campaign. This morning I received a 'deep throat' call suggesting that I read the 'Personal Notices' in the Telegraph, your usual morning read. My colleague brought me a copy, which I read while drinking my morning cup of 'Twinings English Breakfast'. The phone call drawing my attention to the notices was deliberate; it was their way of telling me that they know of our connection. They hope, and I hope, that it will convince you to give up bounty hunting. I will read it to you. '*For Dr Edward*

Davenport of the Open University, currently touring European art galleries. Your programme has a fatal error.

Arthur did not immediately respond. He took a deep breath before he told Peter that he would call him back, after he had had time to give the matter due consideration.

Taking account of the threat, Arthur went part way to following Peter's advice. It fell in with his idea of staying in the area until the end of September, and preferably at Giverny, the village across the Seine from Vernon.

He knew that Claude Monet, a founder of the impressionist movement, had made his home in Giverny for more than forty years and it was where he had created his 'Garden of a hundred thousand flowers'.

Arthur rang Peter back later that morning to tell him he that he would not give up his quest to seek the Ingres painting, but for the time being, he was prepared to put his search 'On hold'. He explained to Peter that he felt confident that if he showed a genuine interest in Monet, who had no connection with Ingres, he would be cold in the deathly game of hunt the thimble, and would be of no interest to Servient-Higgins, or any hired assassin,

Alaine Cartet, the bustling genius from the bureau tourisme, was ever helpful. He arranged for Arthur to park in the grounds of a gîte on the outskirts of Giverny, near to the bridge over the Seine. Ever practical, he also persuaded the lady who owned the gîte to do Arthur's laundry.

Living in the village, rather than in the bigger town of Vernon, suited Arthur. He was not a city man. Being close to Monet's garden encouraged him to fill his long delayed gap year by learning how to paint. He was truly happy.

Each day, the only meal that he prepared was his breakfast of cereal, tea and toast. He was able to walk to nearby restaurants for a light lunch, and for dinner, he drove into the countryside to seek out unpretentious restaurants where the chefs did not

167

bother with fashion, but changed their limited menus when the seasons changed.

Once a week, Arthur joined Alaine at the Cassoulet Club in Vernon, where both the ambiance and food were not just better than average, they were better than good. At the club and while shopping in Vernon, he began to pick up some ability with French conversation.

Frequently Alaine picked up Arthur in 'Dolly', his old "Citroen 2CV, to take him to places that he knew would foster his interest in painting. Like Arthur, Alaine had time to himself. He was also a long time widower.

His children were living their own lives in big cities, far from Vernon. "More fool them," Alaine often said, "One day they will come to their economic and cultural senses, and return to Vernon. Here there is everything a man needs without incurring the hassle or expense of city life. All people who live and work in big cities are impoverished. A metropolis denies its residents a good life. There the dark fogged air of the narrow slab sided canyon streets allow the sun to cast its light but weakly, and briefly, into their day. It gives them little time to stand aside, to think, to look afresh, or to understand. In the country the sun, shines brightly into broad fields and cottage gardens. It measures the day by its wide arc, from horizon to horizon, allowing plenty of time for all to ponder, to find their way, to thrive, to prosper."

One morning, a couple of weeks after arriving in Giverny, Arthur took out pencil and paper. Instead of sketching, he spent the morning working out his average monthly expenditure. Rent to Madam Savary, owner of the gîte, for parking, electricity and laundry was reasonable. Food for breakfast did not amount to much. The cost of his lunchtime snack was minimal. His biggest local expenditure was for dinner and wine in restaurants and they were cheaper than in UK.

After he had totted up all the details, and added the cost of diesel for his trips around Giverny, his snap audit showed his expenditure to be just a little over half of the police pension that the authority paid each month into his bank account.

His state pension took care of the hire purchase charges on his dual-purpose mobile home, lately come artist's studio. The result came as a relief. Even after payment by direct debit of the dreaded, income tax, council tax, insurances and the weekly cleaner for his almost forgotten bungalow in Scagill his income, minus expenditure, left him with a clear margin to spend as he wished.

Arthur was as happy as Wilkins Micawber was with a spare sixpence. He had enough to spend on paints, brushes, oil, cleaning spirit, and boards, lots of boards.

With the quality he wanted, such things did not come cheap, particularly as he preferred to buy prepared boards. He did not see himself ever choosing to paint on canvas. He thought it too much trouble to cope with stretchers and the preparation needed by such a change. However, he did make one big change. In addition to the usual white boards, he also bought some boards prepared with colour, choosing ochre, red, blue and even black. He also bought, new to him, a sketchbook, made up of a range of coloured cards, and to use with it, a box of oil based crayons.

Although he had taken time out, Arthur had not given up on his quest to find the Ingres painting stolen by Servient-Higgins.

To further his cause he spent time with Alaine Cartet, in his office at the bureau tourisme, working out a detailed route with both overnight and longer stay parking strategies for his journey south.

Arthur wanted to go south, to Montauban, the town where Ingres was born, so that he could study at the town's museum of Ingres artefacts. Arthur reasoned that it would be a test of any network used by dodgy dealers if, using his Doctor Davenport alter ego, he could spend a week of unbroken days studying at the Ingres museum.

If he did not attract any unusual or inexplicable attention, it would be a sure indication that on their radar, he would be a non-combatant far from the stolen painting. If he did attract unusual or inexplicable attention, it would mean that he was at least getting warm, andpossibly even close to finding La Source, but it would also mean that he was standing into danger.

Arthur found from Alaine's notes that Montauban was on the river Tarn, a tributary of the Garonne, the last boring alluvial plain before the Pyrenees. It meant that to reach the Ingres museum, he would have to go a long way south, at least eight-hundred miles, passed Orleans then Limoges, but Arthur was content with that.

He was in no hurry; he knew that he had used up only a fraction of the time before he had promised to return to Scagill to tell the other Grey Haired Knights the tale of his quest.

Alaine Cartet wrote letters of introduction, and made suggestions about where there were views to paint, and museums and galleries to visit. Just as important, he marked the towns, places, and roads to avoid.

Alaine arranged private parking for Arthur's mobile home at farms and gîtes, on the same terms arranged for his stay at Giverny. He explained that in France most caravan sites closed at or even before the end of September.

By the early days of September, Arthur had used many prepared boards on which he had painted more than two hundred Cypress trees, large and small. He had then painted as many stone walls, and even more cobbled paths.

Because he was in Monet's village, trying to master the impressionist technique, he had also painted more than a hundred floating water lilies.

On rainy days, he sheltered in Tootsie, his artist's studio, copying details from a series of good reproduction large souvenir postcards of Monet originals.

Arthur was happy doing it. He was following the advice of Renan, his mentor, 'Copy the masters, practice, practice, practice. Wear out your brushes with practice and then buy more brushes and practice some more'.

One evening, before Arthur and Alaine set out together to find a recommended restaurant, new to both of them, Alaine, who had been looking through a pile of Arthur's painted boards, challenged his friend. "Arthur, what sort of an artist are you? You have not painted one complete picture in all the time you have been here." "True, you observant cultured critic," Arthur sang out happily, "You must understand, at my age, I am running out of road. If I am ever going to paint a half-decent picture, I have to get the years I missed at art school crammed into the next few months.

I haven't even thought of attempting skin yet. One day, I want to paint nudes, nubile nudes, and voluptuous nudes, nudes in the romantic style of Rubens, Valasquez, Hunt, or even better, Ingres the master. I do not understand the modernist fashion; the cruel studies by Lucian Freud or the grotesques of Francis Bacon." "Is there a difference between nubile and voluptuous?" Alaine laughed, "I've forgotten."

Near to the end of September, Arthur's idyll was disturbed. It occurred while he sat in his comfortable folding chair, painting an unused wooden gate in the stone wall of the Monet garden.

He had painted the gate many times, usually in the morning when the light was best, but all his attempts had failed to satisfy him. He had over-painted, scraped or scrapped many boards. Like all painters who worked alfresco, Arthur had become used to the occasional person stopping to look over his shoulder to judge whether he was just another amateur, or perhaps a real talent.

Usually they did not speak, but after a few minutes, they would quietly leave him to work on, alone. However, on this particular morning, a man did speak. To Arthur's surprise, he addressed him by both his proper name and alias. "Mr Arthur Thomas, sometimes Dr. Andrew Davenport, I believe."

Arthur's chair had sunk into the grass, which made it necessary for him to stand before turning to see who had spoken. "Sorry to disturb you Mr Thomas," the man said, diffidently, I hope that you will remember me, Jacques Dupont. Your colleague Mr. Bainbridge introduced us in the Swiss Mobius London office." Arthur, not knowing quite how to react, stumbled a bit with his reply. "Well, well I never, well, yes I do remember, yes, yes indeed, you were most helpful. I am sorry that I missed you when I visited the musée d'Orsay. I spent most of my time there with Renan and his conservators. Are you here to visit Monet's garden?"

Before he replied, Jacques Dupont looked steadily into Arthur's eyes, without embarrassment, but clearly nervous.

"No, I am only here as a messenger. As you already know, d'Chastelain is my boss. He is Head of Security where I work as his deputy. His recent behaviour worries me. I am sure it would worry you if you were there to see it. Since your visit, he has become a nervous wreck. He behaves illogically, erratically, secretively, and he has become paranoid. He trusts no one. Much of the change in him seems to be a result of your visit. He has told me that Servient-Higgins is due for parole very soon. He did not find it difficult to locate you, but for some reason, of which I have no knowledge, he chose not to come himself. He implores you to stop your search for the painting. He says that if you don't, you will compromise the current investigation by the museum's security, the police, the gendarmerie and Interpol. He has told me to tell you to go home, to leave it to the professionals. He wants you to understand that the criminals who stole the painting know all about you. He said that they could find you, as easily as he did. He believes, if you continue to seek the reward, those who stole the painting will kill you, or arrange to have you killed."

Arthur, thinking the whole outburst peculiar asked, "Why do you think d'Chastelain is paranoid? Why are you afraid?"

Dupont was losing control, when he blurted out, "Because he is telling lies. The insurance has paid out on the claim. My god, I am deputy head of security and I know that there is no current investigation by my department at the museum or by the police.

Unless there is any new evidence, we can do nothing; the case remains on file, but is inactive. d'Chastelain's behaviour can only mean that he was involved. Perhaps the thieves bribed him to look the other way. You must understand that they, whoever they are, have him scared out of his reason. He believes that if you get to the painting before they do, or even if you only compromise their plans, they will kill him. When I report to him about my meeting with you, I will tell him that I have passed on his message, but if I do anything to make him suspect that I believe him to be part of the robbery, I will fear for my own life. I intend to find an unconnected excuse to resign; I want out."

Arthur, who felt sorry for the excitable Frenchman, said, "No need for that old chap. I shall up anchor today. You can tell your boss a porky, une craque. Tell him that you never found me. Tell him that I had already left Giverny. Tell d'Chastelain that the local gîte owner, where I had been staying, told you that I had become bored with both Ingres and Monet and that I had told her I intended to go to Picardi, to study Mattisse at his hometown museum. That cannot possibly be more removed in subject or distance from Ingres."

Arthur was happy to fulfil his promise to Jacque Dupont. He decided to leave Giverny immediately, and to head south to Montauban, but not before calling at the Bureau Tourism to say goodbye to Alaine Cartet.

The two friends parted with a Gallic handshake. Arthur was touched when Alaine then took both of his hands in his to say solemnly, "Take every care my elderly English gentleman. Come back to Giverny when you have done whatever it is you have to do. I shall miss your good companionship. Who knows, one day you may have a completed picture to show me."

Arthur enjoyed the journey south, a journey smoothed by the hard work that Alaine Cartet had put into the itinerary he had prepared for him. He had bound it in a very official looking folder, supposedly for issue to VIP visitors only.

Arthur set the style of his journey south to Montauban, the birthplace of Ingres, as soon as he left Giverny. Determined to keep clear of the main roads, he relied less on Alaine's bound itinerary than he did on his 'head up' little compass to guide him along the minor roads shown in his large scale English language map of France.

He drove along minor roads through small towns and villages, but always generally in a sort of southbound direction. Occasionally he detoured to visit towns and villages with nice sounding names, and he always stopped at the places where Alaine's itinerary suggested that there was an interesting museum or art gallery.

When visiting the galleries, he made a point of telling the officials of his interest in Ingres generally, and La Source in particular. His questions made him feel a little nervous. He felt like the runner laying scent for drag hounds, unable to see or hear hounds, but sure that they would soon close on him.

It took Arthur almost ten weeks before he reached Cahors, his last planned stop before Montauban. He had spent most of the time devoted to improving his painting technique by experimenting with different brushes, and his pallet knife, to apply pigment-tinted oil paint to prepared boards.

Nervous of attempting a big picture, he was content to copy and practice details only. He had delighted in what he thought of as his compressed student years. He thought them a preparation for his life as an artist, not caring that at his age it might be short.

The thought of life expectancy did not bother him, but it made him think of Tristan, Geraint and Percival, his three friends who had taken up the challenge to quest as Grey Haired Knights.

During his stay in Cahors, an event interrupted the pattern of his new life. It came as a chilling reminder of the danger he had chosen to face. It started in the town's municipal gallery, where he had already spent two days trying to copy a detail from a painting of evening sunlight falling on corn stooks casting their shadows on a field of stubble.

During the morning of the third day, while he was quietly continuing his studies, two men wearing dark raincoats approached him. They asked, first in French, and then in Franglaise, whether he was Doctor Edward Davenport of the English Open University.

Arthur, with thirty plus four years' experience in the police force immediately thought that they might be detectives.

It was something in the way they were dressed, and their confident approach. One man was clearly in charge, and the other in support. "Yes I am he," Arthur replied, but somehow he felt nervous responding to his alias. "Any identification?" the older man asked, without any manners or humour. "I have," Arthur replied, adding with a grin, "Have you?"

Both men produced cheap imitation leather cases that held what anyone unfamiliar with French police identification cards would accept, though like all such cards, even their mother's would have had difficulty recognising the full-face photographs. "Your passport please," the younger of the two detectives asked, adding, "I am sure that you did not leave it in your little caravan." "Ah, I see that you already know who I am," Arthur replied with a sigh. He slowly took out his passport from an inside pocket in his jacket, and handed it to the senior of the two men. "Who is this Arthur Thomas?" the man asked. "Also me," Arthur grinned again, trying to establish an equal, or even a friendly relationship. "You will see from my occupation that Arthur Thomas is a Superintendent of Police, now long since retired." "That may be monsieur," the detective's tone remained formal; "You will come with us to our office where we can clear up the apparent difficulty with your identity." Arthur replied with a tinge of apprehension in his voice, "I will come with you, but it will take me just a moment to pack up my painting kit."

Arthur was far from happy because it had crossed his mind that the plain-clothes policemen might be plain-clothed crooks intent on kidnap, or worse. He was therefore relieved when, after a short drive, the two men took him into a building where men and women in police uniform were doing what policemen and policewomen do.

In desperation, after failing to explain to the detectives that he was in France seeking to recover the stolen Ingres painting for Swiss Mobius, the insurance company, Arthur told the po-faced Frenchman that he wished to use his mobile phone to call a colleague in England. With a Gallic shrug, the senior man granted his request.

Peter answered the call almost immediately. Arthur almost shouted, "Peter, it's me, Arthur. The French police have just taken me into custody for telling fibs about my being Doctor Edward Davenport. Please have a word with them to confirm who I am, and what I am doing in France."

Peter laughed, "Who, er, who is this speaking please? Is it Arthur, or is it Edward Davenport, never heard of either of them, or the doctor?" Arthur voice went up in pitch and volume, "Peter, this is no time to muck about, this is serious." Peter did stop teasing.

"Where are you?" he asked. After Arthur told him that he was in Cahors, just north of Montauban. Peter took over. "Right, now listen; because I am not known to them it will not be much use if I tell them that you are kosher. Ask them to speak to me. Tell them that I am your solicitor, no try advocate. I will ask them how I might contact their chief. Once I know that, I will not bother to speak to him, but I will immediately talk to my connections in the Paris Sûreté. I am sure that they will be able to get you out of nick in time for Christmas. Now let me speak to whoever is the most senior officer." Arthur passed over the phone to the older of the two detectives. He was relieved but not surprised to hear Peter speaking what he thought must be fluent French.

Less than three hours and several cups of coffee later, a man wearing plain clothes came into the office extending a hand in greeting. Arthur was relieved to find that the man was obviously 'On side' when he said, "Superintendent, I am Charles Fontaneau of the Sûreté. I am so sorry that you have had to wait so long. I have come from our regional office after receiving a call from Paris. Our people have been watching you since you were in Limoges. We have asked all museum and art gallery staff to report any unusual interest in Ingres. In particular, we have asked them to inform us about anyone asking questions about the missing painting. You see, when we botched our attempt to catch the thieving bastards in the act, we lost a very good man, a husband, a father of children, a retired policeman, one of us. We shall never close the case until we have a conviction for his murder. By the way, your colleague Peter Bainbridge asked my boss to pass on a message. He has asked me to tell you that someone known to you as Servient-Higgins, known to us as Charles de-Vere Tolemache, is out of prison. His probation conditions do not allow him to leave England, not even the London area, but your colleague doubts that he will take much heed. Now, you must be tired and hungry, I have my car outside; let me drive you back to your housevan. My wife and I are going to get one when I retire in two years' time. We are determined to sample all the varied cuisines of our European capitals. We also want to compare and contrast the peasant food of the mountain regions with that of the river plains, before the bloody bureaucrats in Brussels reduce all foods, by their ridiculous regulations and directives, to a common pre-digested pap. My wife is sure there is a bestselling book in it."

On the short journey, Monsieur Charles Fontaneau of the Sûreté insisted on stopping at a café so that they could share for a bowl of Mussels, with chips and mayonnaise, and then again at an auberge, where he wanted Arthur's opinion about the new wine of the district.

When he finally dropped Arthur off, Fontaneau got out of the car to shake hands and to wish Arthur well, but in very serious terms he warned, "Be careful my retired crime fighter, things have changed. There are no gentlemen thieves any more. The villain associates of your Servient-Higgins, our de Vere Tolemache, are evil He has no friends, but those about him fear him and their loyalty to his money means that they would not hesitate to kill you if he simply raised an eyebrow. For that man you are a troublesome priest and his acolytes could misunderstand such an inflexion."

With a wry smile, Arthur thanked Fontaneau for releasing him from police protection to be quarry of a known psychopath, or worse, unknown assassins. Before turning in for the night, Arthur made himself his usual pot of tea, but instead of milk, he added a dram of whisky from the bottle he had brought from his home in Scagill.

It was at the end of the first week in December when Arthur drove into Montauban. His first task was to find a garage to fill up the empty fuel tank with diesel, and to exchange an empty gas cylinder for a full one.

He asked the man who was taking payment for the fuel where he might find a caravan park near to the city, one that would be open at this time of year.

The man, who spoke good English, introduced himself, with a handshake, as Paul Lenormand, owner of the garage. He showed a genuine mechanics interest in Tootsie, and he amused Arthur with his variation on what he had heard so often, "When I retire, such a Mercedes mobile fishing lodge is just what I want; free to go fishing whenever and wherever I please."

He then told Arthur that there was no such thing as an open caravan park in Montauban, or even one within 30 kilometres of the city. "No problem though," he said, "You can park your van for free, behind my garage. I'll hook you up to a power point. In fair exchange, you can be my irregular night watchman. Recently, some youthful vandals have caused some trouble. I have done my back in, by sleeping in my office chair, trying to catch them."

However, the garage owner insisted, "If the 'voyou' make a nuisance, they will wake you. You must ring the police, but you must not try to deal with them, you must not get involved. Let me have your phone, I shall put the police number into its memory for you.

If you do have to ring them you will find that they are very helpful. I shall let them know you are a friend doing me a favour."

It turned out to be a particularly useful arrangement for Arthur. He reckoned that Montauban, although a city with a cathedral, was about half the size of his hometown, Scagill.

The streets in the city centre seemed as old as the Shambles in York, but in Montauban, the medieval craftsmen had built the houses using beautiful dark pink brick.

This gave the city a warm glow, even in the late afternoon sun of mid-winter. Across the road from the garage, a small general store sold bread, milk, and cereals, all that he needed for his breakfast.

He was able to walk to the museum in less than ten-minutes. It was an exercise regime he thought would do him some good, but it made quite an inroad into his savings. The cold winter weather forced him to buy a hat, a warm overcoat, a scarf and leather gloves. For this excess, he called himself a forgetful old fool. It rankled with his Yorkshire thrift that he had left behind in Scagill a beautiful 'Cromby' overcoat, several hats and many pairs of police issue officer's leather gloves.

Arthur made it a discipline to go to the museum every day that it was open. He realised, on the first day, that it was really only of interest to those who wished to study the minutiae of Ingres's work.

It was in an ancient palace, once home of the Bishop of Montauban. Arthur had studied at the museum for two days before his regular attendance and obvious serious study brought him to the attention of the Curator who, in near perfect English, asked if he could be of assistance. Conscious of his lead role in his idea of

Hunt the Thimble, Arthur felt a twinge of nerves when he introduced himself as Doctor Edward Davenport of the British Open University.

When he explained that he was researching Ingres for a programme planned for BBC Television, it worked a magic more powerful than Abanazar's 'Open Sesame'. Arthur told the Curator of his research at the National Gallery in London, the Louvre, and the musée d'Orsay in Paris, dropping as many names as possible.

When he mentioned that Monsieur Renan was his mentor, the Curator received him into the inner circle. Renan had been one of his tutors.

The museum staff accepted Arthur, as the learned doctor. They gave him full and free access to the museum, which allowed him to set up his easel whenever and wherever he wanted during museum opening times.

The three attendants and the security guard invited him to join them in what was in effect their common room, where he could eat his pack up lunch, drink coffee and, when he remembered to bring his precious tea bags, make a proper cup of tea.

The curator also allowed him to study a portfolio of the master's work provided he wore surgical gloves.

This heavy volume rested on a cathedral sized lectern illuminated by a discrete picture light in the museum library. It was a priceless folio of original details and sketches by the master including plates of Ingres's paintings, reproductions, and photographs sent by collectors, museums and galleries from all over the world. It was a folio for the people of Montauban, the city of his birth, representing the full canon of his work.

The Museum did not allow the public visiting the library to touch the book. A carved oak rail, the equal of many a cathedral alter rail, prevented any unauthorised person from coming close.

For a normal public view, each day, one of the museum attendants turned over one page, as though it were a book of remembrance. Arthur concentrated his study on the portfolio. The details held him engrossed, oblivious to his surroundings, while he marvelled at the technique of the nineteenth century French champion of traditional values.

Late in his fifth day at the museum, a day that had started routinely enough, a spell, of which he had no knowledge, turned Arthur's already exciting quest into one of drama and high romance.

He had set up his easel, to give him a good sight line to the lectern. Arthur waited until after the attendant had turned the daily page and left the library, before he turned the pages back until it was open at a fine reproduction of 'La Source', the stolen masterpiece, the object of his quest.

On one of his larger prepared boards, he had outlined, in charcoal, ten-times over, the same detail. That of her right arm with the fingers of the hand just touching the clay water pot held, almost upside down, on her left shoulder, letting water stream out.

He was determined to find out how, with such subtle, almost unnoticeable shading, Ingres had achieved such depth to show how the arm connected naturally with the shoulder, even though it was in such a strained attitude.

He was standing at the lectern, peering closely at the picture, locked deep in thought, tired after hours of unproductive work, frustrated to the point of anger at his failure to get anywhere near to the Ingres signature of perfect skin tones when it happened.

"She is lovely isn't she?" the simple phrase, spoken in English, with a lilting Italian intonation penetrated Arthur's concentration barrier like a laser cutting through fog.

During the last hour, as he searched the painting for clues to Ingres's technique, he had not even been conscious that two anxious nuns, nervous that their charges might notice the naked nymphet, had hurried a class of about twenty giggling girls passed him.

He also had no idea that a lady had been quietly standing behind him, but to one side of his chair, for more than quarter of an hour, absorbed in him, rather than the reproduction of La Source.

It was as though Arthur had touched a live high voltage electric wire. In his confused state, turning to see who had spoken, he knocked over his folding chair. Rather than her taking his breath away, he gave an involuntary double intake of breath. He knew, in that instant, she was the most attractive women he had ever seen, imagined, or thought possible.

Her poised natural elegance unnerved him, the more so, by the teasing laughter in her eyes. She reduced him to a bumbling blushing fool. "Er, oh pardon, oh dear, I'm so sorry, I was in another word, a cruel world I am afraid. I just cannot fathom how he did it, oh dear." Then looking again, he paused, for a moment, before he softly said, "No, it is not the girl in the painting, it is you who are lovely."

He then broke into a babble, "Oh bother, what am I saying, I do beg your pardon that was very ill mannered." Confused he twittered on, not recognising that she had spoken to him in English. "I am afraid I am English, so I don't speak French. Oh damn, I am making a fool of myself, please forgive me." He felt his cheeks blush with an intensity that made them burn.

The lady then spoke in a voice that enchanted him, "No, sir, it is I who must ask you to forgive me. I broke your concentration. It was unforgivable, but please forgive, I am Italian; we are impulsive. Please, may I introduce myself? I am Galiena Vercente."

Arthur prattled on, "Oh bother, and I don't speak Italian either. As I said, I am English; we are not very good at these things." Eventually, a little more composed, careful not to break his cover with the museum staff, Arthur introduced himself as Doctor Edward Davenport.

He was deeply embarrassed because this elegant creature had watched him poring over the pubescent nude. "Please do not think that I am peculiar, I am researching Ingres for the English Open University.

La Source, this immodest young woman here, is reputedly one of the greatest of his works. Sadly, the original is missing. Some years ago it was stolen from the musée d'Orsay in Paris." Galiena Vercente said, "I am sure that you are right to choose her for your research, she is very special. I know the painting quite well. Now, I must leave you to your study." She smiled, and then went quickly away, leaving only a zephyr of perfume.

He did not recognize the fragrance, but he was sure he would remember it, for the rest of his life.

After righting his chair, Arthur slumped down onto it, desolate. He wanted to follow her, run after her, chase after her.

He wanted to take her into his protective custody, this Galiena, something or other, whatever name she said, he had forgotten. He desperately wanted to find out who she was, to talk to her, just to be with her.

He needed to obliterate the total hash he had made of their meeting. From that moment he could not get her out of his mind, he could not concentrate on anything, least of all 'La Source'.

Even though she had admitted that she knew the painting quite well, it did not occur to Arthur that her interest in him might connect her to the evil of Servient-Higgins or that she might be part of the Hunt the Thimble game.

Chapter 13

By speaking to him in the Ingres museum at Montauban, the fragrant Galiena Vercente had disturbed more than Arthur's deep concentration.

She had disturbed the whole of his disciplined ordered life by bringing back, in one instant, emotions that he had put away when his wife Jenny had died. A time now so many years ago that such feelings were unknown to him, all long forgotten.

Arthur did not go the museum on the day after his meeting with the lady who had enchanted him, but who's second name he could not remember.

He went about the city in the streets and broadways, hoping to find her. He looked into cafés, hotels, churches and shops, but without success. He justified his out of character behaviour by assuming that he must have offended her when he had blurted out, 'No, it is not her, it is you who are lovely'.

As a Grey Haired Knight-Errant, he was desperate to make a formal obeisant apology.

The following morning, after spending a miserable lonely night, Arthur determined to work himself out of his dark mood. He was encouraged by his memory that Winston Churchill, the man he most admired, painted to rid himself of his black dog.

He returned to the museum where he set up his easel, close to the lectern holding the portfolio. He reconciled himself to the fact that he was just an old man, infatuated by a vision induced by his single-minded concentration on Ingres's idea of classical beauty.

However, dream, vision or reality, he decided that Jean-Dominique Ingres's claim that his painting, La Source, was the 'Image of Perfection' was time expired.

He thought her no match for Galiena's beauty. By mid-afternoon, he had become completely engrossed with his paints, oils, spirits, and brushes, but frustrated by the results of his efforts. He was sitting in front of his easel working on a detail of a shadow of the clay water pot, his tenth attempt to get the correct soft change of texture, when his heartbeat raced and his skin shivered.

Galiena Vercente had said nothing to penetrate the concentration barrier that kept Arthur enclosed, isolated from all but the painting, but her perfume spoke for her.

At first, he wondered if it was a dream or hallucination, but when he turned his head, Galiena was there, smiling. Her teasing lilting voice broke the silence, "Were you playing truant yesterday, you were not here."

For a second time her appearance shattered his composure.

This time, careful not to knock over his chair when he rose, he involuntarily kicked a leg of his easel. The freshly painted board fell to the floor. "Damn, jam side down as usual," was Arthur's automatic response.

It was his salvation. It allowed him a moment to recover a little of his usual urbane equanimity, a characteristic that had served him well when on police duty.

"Oh er, hello you, no, I was not here yesterday. I tried to find you in Montauban. I wanted to apologise for my behaviour. I was rude; you must think me a bumbling old fool." Galiena, shaking her head, gently replied, "No, I told you then, it was very wrong of me to shock you out of your world of work. I know about not waking sleepwalkers. Your intense concentration must be the same. I did not think. You were not rude, how could you think so. No woman could take offence at a handsome English gentleman telling her that she is lovely. Today, I have been very good. I have been here for more than half an hour, as quiet as a mouse."

Arthur said, "It was your perfume that gave you away. Please assure me that you are real, not a figment of my over excited imagination. I had begun to think that my mind had been playing tricks again. You see, it was a strange dream encounter, or perhaps a vision, or manifestation, that set me on the road that has brought me to Montauban."

Galiena put her head on one side and she looked pensive before she said, "Perhaps my coming into the museum was more than serendipity. I had not thought of coming to the museum until a strange old fellow, who was standing outside in the square, pointed his thin stick, first at me and then at the museum door.

He looked old, but ageless, if that is possible. I do not know what he said, because he was not only muttering into his beard, he was chewing the ends of his moustache. It was most odd, he might have been speaking in Latin, or very old French, but I sensed that he wanted me to visit the museum. Arthur said nothing in reply, but a shiver ran through him.

Arthur forced himself to put aside the restraint he had practiced for years when talking to women of any age. He felt as nervous as he had been when, aged sixteen, he finally plucked up courage to ask the girl next door to a Christmas party.

He stumbled to say, "C, cou, could you, er we, I mean, perhaps go somewhere for afternoon tea, no, not a good idea that, they don't do afternoon tea in France. Better idea; possibly we could share an early evening glass of wine somewhere, but oh dear, I mean, only if you would like to? It would not take me a minute to pack up my painting kit."

To Arthur's joy, the stunning creature replied, her eyes full of fun, "Yes I am real, yes I would like to share a glass of wine with you, but perhaps to share a bottle would be an even better idea. I have my little car outside; we could drive to the river at Villeneuve where I know there is a nice quiet little restaurant."

The early evening drink turned into a long unhurried dinner at the restaurant, followed by a late leisurely walk by the river, even though it was bitterly cold.

Throughout the evening, they never stopped talking. They interrupted each other with countless questions, but found that they had nothing, absolutely nothing, in common, except for two things.

The first was that each had been on their own for a long time, she a widow he a widower. The second was that neither wanted the evening to end. Finally, just before midnight, Galiena Vercente said, very formally, "Dr Edward Davenport, if I do not take you home soon, my family will consider me compromised. I am on my annual pilgrimage to spend Christmas with my aunt, my dear late mother's youngest sister. She has a lovely flat in Montauban where she will be waiting for me to return. Aunts never believe that their nieces can be all grown up or that they should stay out after midnight".

On the drive back to Montauban, Arthur used his ability to tell a good story. He explained his gypsy status and elaborated by telling a few white lies about his research for the Open University's intended film about Ingres, but he had difficulty when trying to explain how an open university operated.

He told her about "Tootsie" who had shared his adventures, sheltering him for half a year, while he followed her head up navigating display, always taking roads south, but allowing for many minor detours, before reaching Montauban.

He was a little surprised when his lovely companion complained, "I think I am a little bit jealous of this "Floozie" of yours." Arthur smiled inside himself, wondering why it was that the ladies he had met called his mobile home "Floozie" when he always introduced her, quite clearly, as "Tootsie."

187

When Galiena pulled her little Fiat onto the garage forecourt, it was after midnight. Arthur struggled to get out of the low seat, but like a dancer, she moved effortlessly, gracefully, to her feet. Standing close, she thanked him for the evening they had spent together. Then, in a little girl voice she asked, "Do you have to go to the museum tomorrow? It will close early; tomorrow is Christmas Eve."

Without waiting for an answer, Galiena continued, "I would like to take you to a gallery owned by a cousin of mine. We Italian families have many cousins. He has some wonderful original paintings, an eclectic collection of old masters, impressionists and modern art, displayed together with some limited edition prints. You must bring some of your studies. I know that he would be interested to see them. He has launched several previously unknown artists onto successful careers. Perhaps he will offer you some commercial advice. From what little I have seen of your work I can tell that you have talent."

Again, not waiting for an answer she gave him the most dazzling radiant smile he had ever seen, before she said, "Well that's all settled then isn't it; ten o'clock tomorrow morning, here at the garage. Get your chores done early, don't be late, and wear a suit if you have one."

His fragrant elegant companion of the evening left Arthur so emotionally overcome that he could not speak, his mouth was too dry, the connective synapses of his brain cells were in such confusion that he was unable to find the right words to say. He yearned to touch her, but dare not.

When she drove away, he just bowed his head to her. While watching her car's lights disappear into the night he said aloud, "Goodnight my lady, here is a change I did not expect. I was content to quest as a Pellinore, now surely I am required to be a Lancelot."

Before eight o'clock on the morning of Christmas Eve Day, nervous as a teenager on his first date, Arthur was showered, breakfasted, washed-up, tidied-up, and ready for inspection. Satisfied that all was in good order, he hurried to the shops, arriving before most were open. However, he found a flower shop, preparing for the big day, where he bought a cleverly made posy of Christmas roses.

Next on his shopping list were several essential items, a new shirt, also a discrete blue tie to go with his suit that had hung at the back of the wardrobe, untouched, since the days spent with Peter in London.

Shopping done, Arthur was safely back before ten o'clock, ready for his date; shoes polished, suit brushed, wearing his new overcoat against the cold, but without his new hat. When he had looked in the full-length mirror, for a final self-inspection, he thought that the hat made him look like a Crown Court Bailiff.

Prompted by Galiena's suggestion, Arthur had selected and packed into his little carrying case what he thought to be the best dozen boards of his detail studies.

With a quick left and right forefinger to smooth his moustache he was ready. When he stepped out into the cold air, he was in time to see the little Fiat pull off the road onto the garage forecourt.

His materialised vision was out of the car in an instant. Galena Vercente gave him no time to say hello, bon jour, or to give her the posy of Christmas roses, before she took command.

She gave him no greeting, except her dazzling captivating smile followed with instructions, "If you are going to fit in to my little car, you had better put your coat and jacket in the boot; we have quite a long way to go. Hurry, it's cold out here, but you will be warm in the car." Arthur just had time to hide the little posy of Christmas roses in a corner of the Fiat's boot. Galiena was obviously excited when she pulled out into the traffic, "We are going to Andorra la Vella, just across the border into Spain. It is about 160 kilometres; you have your passport, Si?" "Yes, I always keep it in my jacket inside breast pocket, together with my volume of

Rupert Brook's poetry; one never knows when one might need either or both."

Arthur added, half aloud, half to himself, "Last night I was compromised by a beautiful woman. This morning the same stunningly attractive lady seems determined to abduct me across the border into a foreign land. I have never been so pleased."

Arthur had two good reasons to be pleased. Sitting close to Galiena was one. Her pleated skirt that barely covered knees, her elegant tanned legs and trim ankles, set off in the sheerest nylon stockings, brought back good memories of long forgotten attractions.

On her small high arched feet, she wore soft leather driving shoes. However, Arthur noticed in the door pocket, a stylish pair of very cut away, very high heeled shoes.

The other reason to be pleased was that the lady drove with the flamboyance of an Italian racing driver. Arthur could see that she enjoyed overtaking any male French car driver who dared to share the road with her.

However, with lorry and van drivers, other lady-drivers, even tractors drivers, she had no quarrel. Arthur did not enjoy sitting so close to the ground. He missed not being able to look over the hedges and walls into fields and gardens or to see into people's homes.

The guards at the French / Spanish border waived them through without any fuss or delay. Galiena parked the Fiat in Andorra la Vella, some way along the avenue past the gallery where she wanted Arthur to show his studies to her cousin.

Because they had taken some time to put on their coats, and for Galiena to change her shoes to walk to the gallery, it was just after middle day.

True to the Spanish custom of siesta, even though it was winter in the foothills of the Pyrenees, the gallery had already closed for lunch. Galiena was not put out, "Never mind, I know where Pablo will be, come on, we will drive there, it is not far."

Before getting back into the car, Arthur took off his overcoat and jacket. To avoid creasing his jacket in the boot of the little Fiat, he shook it out, and from the inside pocket his passport flew out.

To his horror, it fell at Galiena's feet. Before he could retrieve it, she had picked it up with cat like grace. With her natural feminine curiosity, she looked for his photograph. Immediately Arthur was desperate; he was unable to speak. He saw the laughter in her eyes fade. It was as though a dark ice cold waking kraken had clouded a clear sparkling sea.

Galiena looked closely at the passport, slowly turning the pages, before she asked in a voice that he hardly recognised, "Who is this Arthur Thomas who has stolen your face? Who are you, a Doctor from a university, or as it says in this horrid little book, a Superintendent of Police? Oh dear, oh dear, I was so happy, but now I have every reason to be frightened." Distraught at the sudden turn of events Arthur said, "Galiena, please, don't be alarmed, there is no need. I want you always to be happy when we are together, as we have been. If I have hurt you, I shall be desolate. It is right that you should know that I was born, Christened and remain Arthur Thomas. I never was, nor ever shall be, Doctor Andrew Davenport. Please, can we go somewhere where I can explain why, for some time yet, I must use the alias Doctor Davenport?

In a small café, warmed by a huge log fire, Arthur ordered coffee for them both, though he craved for tea, hot sweet tea, the universal panacea for trauma.

They sat opposite each other, at a small round table. Again, although desperately wanting to take her hands in his, he dare not. He dare not look into her eyes for fear of seeing cold rejection. However, he was determined to convince her of the realty of his identity.

In calm measured tones, he related something of his early life and police career. He described the Laurels, the dreadful rehabilitation unit that had held him for far too long after his brain had put itself back in good order, following the disturbance of a haemorrhage.

He told her about Percival, Geraint, and Tristan, with whom he had become good friends while incarcerated, and how he had had the idea that they should all tell stories to keep up their spirits, like the travellers in Canterbury Tales.

Arthur then grasped the nettle. He said, without looking up, "Galiena I told you that a strange dream encounter, or perhaps a vision, or manifestation, set me on the road that has brought me to Montauban.

Well there was rather more to it than I suggested. Whatever it was, vision, manifestation or dream, or just another malfunction in my head brought about by the drugs and treatment of my condition, it led me to the idea that that we should vow to take on the mantle of Grey Haired Knights, ready to seek adventures fit for a new Camelot.

Somehow, spurred by the idea, I persuaded the others to break out of the Laurels with me, prepared to put aside old age and our infirmities, and each to go alone to follow a personal quest. I chose, as my quest, to recover the stolen Ingres painting, la Source.

All that was good, but we also vowed to return, at noon on the Saturday after the next summer solstice, to tell true tales of our adventures. I now deeply regret the idea of a reunion. It changed my fanciful idea into a commitment.

You see, the last words that the strange ageless eccentric shouted to me in my dream were, something like, 'Sad thing, I might not be there for one of you at the end'. Galiena, each time that I remember the dream, which is often, I worry that I may have stood my friends into danger."

With his eyes, still cast down, Arthur continued, "To help me, my old police colleague and friend Peter arranged for the underwriting insurance company involved to support my search. They came up with the idea of my pseudonym, Doctor

Edward Davenport, an expert in neo-classical and pre-Raphaelite artists, carrying out research for a BBC television programme for the Open University. It was simply a ruse to get me known to both the good and shady side of the art world. To give me easy access to art galleries, museums and to those who curate them and those who restore and conserve great works of art. Unfortunately, we were not clever enough. The thieves have rumbled the ruse, but it might still work to our advantage. I am banking on them getting into a flap if I get near to finding the painting. They will make haste to move it, and in making haste, they might make a mistake that might lead us to the true Source."

Arthur took time with his account of how he had made friends with Alaine Cartet in Vernon and Madam Déclâre owner of the Restaurant Bien-Découplé in Paris.

He was enthusiastic about the days that he spent at the Louvre and the Musée D'Orsay, but was candid about his moments of fear during his near arrest in Cahors, just days before he arrived in Montauban.

To complete his plea for Galiena's understanding, Arthur said, "I am compelled to continue my search for la Source. You see no one else is looking for it. It is a closed case until there is new evidence. But, if we can recover the painting, there is a possibility that with the advances in DNA profiling, the police might be able to prove, beyond reasonable doubt, that Servient-Higgins murdered the museum guard."

Arthur told his story solemnly, earnestly, with the clarity of truth, as he would have done if giving evidence before a senior judge in a murder trial.

He was desperate that she would believe. Although he had not yet recognised that he was in love with Galiena, he knew that he must regain her trust to secure his future happiness.

He did not realise that he had talked, without stopping, for almost an hour, but when he finally lifted his eyes to look into hers, he could see that Galiena had understood, that she did believe him, and was no longer afraid.

She returned his look with such compassion that he could not hold her gaze. He dropped his eyes again.

Galiena said quietly, "I do not think that I like anymore this Dr Davenport, I used to know. He seems to be too clever by half. He lives too near to danger with too many 'mights' to have a real chance of finding the painting. I have decided that I shall leave him here in Spain. I will take this Arthur Thomas, Chief of Police, back across the border to France. Then I will be happy again."

Encouraged, Arthur looked up to see that she was smiling. If possible, her smile was even more compelling than before. It was a confident warm embracing smile of acceptance. Buoyed up by her smile, though still absolutely drained, Arthur laughed, "I think we should order more coffee, this is stone cold; we have not touched it." Galiena replied, "May I suggest that we have a little Strega to go with the new hot coffee, please?"

Arthur's heart lifted, her little girl pleading voice was just the same as the night before when she asked him not to go to the museum. They lingered over the hot coffee. Galiena raised her glass of Strega, the stringent yellow liqueur.

Arthur raised his glass to touch hers. She looked over the raised glasses into his eyes, this time her deep brown unflinching eyes held his gaze.

In the 'Gallery Castanos', Galiena was gay. Before she was able to introduce Arthur to her cousin, the gallery assistants greeted her as though she was royalty.

Eventually, she was able to say, "Pablo, please let me introduce Doctor Edward Davenport from England. He is making a television programme for one of their universities, a funny one without a campus or anywhere for the students to live. Working for such an institution has made him a little confused. I think he may be a better artist than he thinks he is. Please appraise the few little painted boards that I made him bring to show you".

Arthur, acting the erudite Doctor, took out his twelve selected boards to arrange them on the floor, in a semi-circle.

Galiena picked up his latest work to show it to her cousin, adding, "I am responsible for these little specks of dirt and this smudge down here. I am afraid I made him jump; it landed jam side down."

After several minutes of picking up then putting down, Pablo returned his attention to the first board with its several detail studies. To Arthur's delight he said, "This is quite good; I believe they are details from a copy or photograph of the missing Ingres. You are beginning to master technique, if you show talent in composition; we may be able to arrange a small exhibition. I am sure Galiena will keep you in touch. Now because it is Christmas Eve, I am going to close early. As my present to you dear children, I shall throw you out onto the cold street to encourage you to go home before the snows come to hold you here until the spring. Spring comes late in Andorra."

On the drive back to Montauban, Galiena questioned Arthur. "Because your friend Peter and the insurance company gave you a pseudonym to use when you travelled in search of a lost painting, they tell me that what you are doing is dangerous. I do not like that, but perhaps I can help. I told you that I already knew the painting; well, I do know where I could show you a copy that is almost life size. I saw it many times when I visited my cousin Prince Paulo Borghese in his beautiful palace in Rome. That was before he decided to change it from a palace into a casino. You see the building was falling into ruin. Poor cousin Paulo had to do something to preserve his family fortune. He now has all sorts of pictures and statues in his casino, many of them bought when he was in London. He served our country as an air attaché. Most of them are of ladies who must have played the tables in the casino and, as you English say, 'Lost their shirt'; they have no clothes to wear."

Arthur exaggerated astonishment, "You mean you have a cousin who is a Prince, yet here you are with me, a pauper gypsy?" "Oh, don't be silly," Galiena laughed, "Italy, although supposedly a republic for generations, has many princes, most of them Borghese or of Savoy. For every prince there must be at least ten lesser titles. I have a title, though I seldom use it. My aunt uses hers when in America; it impresses them no end because they have never had any of their own."

Arthur tried to sound calm, "Well, I would like to see your princely cousin's painting. It sounds very interesting. It ties in with some of the clues we have already. When was your cousin in London?"

"Oh, let me see, he was there in the late nineties I think. I am sure he opened the casino for the millennium. If you want me to take you to see it, you will have to race me to Rome, you in your tortoise, me in this hairy little motor. To make it fair, I will give you a start, the whole of Christmas day, promise, 'eyes shut, count one Mississippi to ten Mississippi'. I won't leave Montauban until after leftover lunch on the twenty-sixth."

Arthur affected a shrug, "How will I find you, I don't know Rome and I am no good in city traffic." Although driving at speed, Galiena Vercente fiddled with one hand in her handbag to pull out a card, "This is my address in Rome. If you do not find me, I shall come looking for you. I suppose it is not quite 1,600 kilometres on the Autostrada.

I usually stop over in Alassio, with yet another cousin, so I will be home on the 27th." "Well now," replied Arthur. "Two-hundred miles a day is about my limit, so don't expect me in the Eternal City until the New Year.

It was cold and dark when Galiena pulled onto the garage forecourt. Without giving Arthur chance to talk, Galiena demanded his phone. "I will enter my home number and my mobile number so that you can call me if you need help".

That done she was out of the car in a trice with the boot open, offering him his jacket and overcoat. It was then that Arthur remembered the posy of Christmas Roses. "Galiena please let me thank you for leaving Doctor Davenport in Spain and forgiving poor old P C Plod. I promise, no secrets from now on, but do not go just yet; I have a little Christmas present for you. I bought it early this morning, at the flower shop"

He reached into the corner of the boot to pick up the posy. The keen mountain frost had nipped every petal. All that he had in his hand were the bare stalks, still bound by a ribbon. Disappointed, Arthur said dully, "Oh, damn and blast it, I should have known. This little miniature broomstick was once a posy of Christmas Roses. I did want you to have it, it was lovely."

He was about to throw the thing away, but Galiena quickly took it from his hand. She smiled at him with that particular expression of hers that was to Arthur, for now unknowable, but it pierced his heart. Then in a quiet thoughtful voice she said, "Arthur Thomas, my brave Chief of Police, remember, it is always the thought that counts. I shall press these stalks between the pages of my bible. When they are dry, I shall have them arranged and framed under glass. I will keep them always, so that I shall never forget this best of all presents". Without pause for breath, with her voice back to its usual lilting tease, she said, "Good - now I wish you a happy Christmas, until we meet in Rome in three days' time, ready to celebrate the start of a new year, a new time in our lives. Go in now to your great tortoise shell, it is almost Christmas day, you will catch a chill without a hat".

She was in the little Fiat, her chosen hare for the race to Rome and was away before Arthur could reply.

197

Chapter 14

Arthur felt very much alone after Galiena Vercente had dismissed him to his 'tortoise'. His only two comforts, a cup of his precious Yorkshire tea, and the BBC Overseas Service failed to cheer him.

He understood that the BBC must have recorded their English language Midnight Service from the Holy Land, because of the time difference between London and Bethlehem, the birthplace of Jesus. However, he enjoyed the music, but he hardly listened to the words; he was too deep in thought.

For the first time in many years, Arthur was not content to be alone on this special night. It was more than quarter of a century since his wife Jenny died. Every Christmas Day, since that awful time, he had not minded being on police duty. Content within himself he had never felt the need for company.

Because he was a widower, with no children, he always volunteered to work on Christmas Day. He had occasionally worked a double shift to allow colleagues, with young children, to be at home with their families.

This Christmas night was the first time that he could remember being lonely. He wanted to be with Galiena Vercente, a woman he had known for only a few days. He realised that in those few days she had him spellbound, but he was aware that the spells that bound him to her came from a different world to his.

He imagined her world to be the glamorous international socialite scene of Italian aristocracy, a dignified cultured way of life, not the 'Dolce Vita', the highly charged, corrupt, oversexed version portrayed in Fellini's post war film.

He knew that his life, as a plodding Yorkshire copper, was no match for her status.

When the midnight service came to its end, with the priest chanting the ancient blessing, 'The Mass is ended, go in peace', his spirits dipped further. The word Mass made him realise that religious dogma would be a further barrier between them. Galiena would almost certainly be Catholic, Roman Catholic.

She was Italian; she had mentioned her bible. His own christening, confirmation and marriage by the Church of England made him undeniably a thrice-certified Protestant, however lax his attendance had been at church services, other than funerals.

He thought the differences in culture and creed that their separate lives had imbued in them, meant that there was no chance for their brief friendship to have a future.

He slumped on the side of his bed, his elbows on his knees, and his face covered by his hands. He did not just feel lonely, he felt excluded.

As he thought about recent events, Arthur remembered the shiver that ran through him when Galiena had described how a curious old man had somehow persuaded her visit the museum. She had called it serendipity. Her description of the man as old, but ageless, brought back vividly into Arthur's memory the squeaky voiced backward skipping man that he had met or imagined on Halter Moor, half a year ago.

He clearly recalled the man's admonition, given before he disappeared into the mist. He had said that he must stop banging on about the past, but think about what he was going to do with the life still left to him.

That there was still time to do great things, to make a mark, to be part of a new order, a new age of chivalry, a present Camelot.

The memory changed Arthur's mood, it changed his attitude and gave him hope. He switched off the radio, paused to think, then he jumped of his bed to say aloud, "Damn it, I am not only a Grey Haired Knight, I am Yorkshire born, Yorkshire bred, winner of the world first prize. For me there is every chance. Right then my lady, I said it would take me into the New-Year to reach Rome, but you have decreed three days; so be it. The race to Rome is on."

Determined to take advantage of the thirty-six hour start Galiena had promised, Arthur prepared a simple breakfast ready for an early start.

He wrote a letter of thanks to his host, the garage owner, Paul Lenormand. He studied his map of France for a direct motorway route to the Italian boarder. By the time, he had finished his preparations it was already two a.m. but he set his alarm clock for six a.m., giving him just four hours to sleep before taking to the road.

While he slept, his body clock worked with precision. He woke in time to shut off the alarm a minute before it would have rung. After a quick cup of tea, followed by a bowl of cereal, he shaved then dressed hurriedly. After checking that he had secured everything in the accommodation side of what was now to be his racing tortoise, he unhooked then stored the umbilical cord to the electricity supply.

At six-thirty precisely, he tripped the odometer to zero, started the engine, engaged gear, and drove off the garage forecourt on his way to Rome. Five minutes later, he pulled back onto the forecourt, jumped out of the cab, leaving the engine running, to post his letter of thanks to his host.

That duty done, setting aside all thoughts of an onset of Alzheimer's disease, he drove off again, determined to make it to the Italian boarder in one day, Christmas Day.

It was cold and dark with the outside temperature indicated on the control panel showing minus four degrees Centigrade, but the roads were ice-free. They were also very quiet. In his clever little cardholder, part of his head up navigation system Arthur had stuck a simple white card on which he had printed his chosen route to Ventimiglia where he would cross over the border into Italy.

Altogether, the distance charts at the front of his map indicated a huge span of about 640 kilometres. Arthur felt a little better when he converted this to four hundred of his more familiar miles, but still a challenge when he thought of it in terms that he could understand; driving from Scagill to London and back in the day; a journey he usually made by British Rail cheap day return.

Using the almost deserted duel carriageways, he estimated that he could achieve an average of almost fifty miles per hour, while on the road, making the travelling time about eight hours.

After every two-hour stage of driving, he planned to rest for at least half an hour. He calculated that with two breaks separating three two hours spells on the road, that he would be somewhere in the region beyond Aix-en-Provence, by early afternoon where he planned to take a long break, to eat, then to sleep for two hours, prior to driving the last leg into Italy. For this last leg, similar to the first, he knew that he would be driving in the dark, but he still hoped to be over the border in time to find a good restaurant that was open on Christmas day, where he could eat, and park overnight.

It did not rain, it did not snow, consequently his pre-determined journey plan worked well.

At each stop, he made a pot of tea that he drank while listening to the World Service. When he awoke, after his planned two-hour nap at Aix, he turned on the radio. A simple act delayed his start on the last leg of the day's journey.

He chose not to drive while listening to the Queen's Christmas message to the Commonwealth. Not forgetting his vow to be a true knight of a present Camelot, Arthur felt compelled to stand to attention during the National Anthem.

There were no checks at the border. Arthur drove into Bordighera just after seven in the evening where he decided, enough was enough. He pulled onto the little promenade that was typical of many promenades of small seaside towns on the English south coast.

The front was as deserted as a plague village, with not even a man walking a dog in view. Although he walked the full length of several streets set back from the sea front, he did not find a restaurant, or a shop, that was open.

In desperation, he went into the Hotel Bristol thinking that someone in a hotel with that name might speak English. The Italian restaurant manager came to meet him in the foyer. He was typical of his trade, rude to his male customers, and a flirt with the ladies.

Speaking to Arthur, who was unmistakably English, the manager spoke in exaggerated Italian English. "I am so sorry senor, ere on Christmas Day ze hotel only serve our resident guests, you understand, Si."

Arthur, who understood perfectly, took out his wallet. It immediately brought about the required change in the manager's attitude. "Ah, but so sorry, of course, I believe you are in room one hundred and one, is it not. Si, it must be so. I will have your table ready, pronto, mille grazie." Arthur tipped, very much in the spirit of Christmas.

The waiter did not give him a menu, or a wine list; the food, all six courses, just came one after the other. The bottle of Montepulciano d'Abruzzo complimented it perfectly but Arthur, who wanted a clear head first thing in the morning, drank half the bottle only.

With the promenade still deserted, and being full of good food, good wine and good humour, he did not bother to look for a formal parking lot for the night, but determined to win the race to Rome, he set his alarm for six a.m.

Tired, but content with his day, Arthur Thomas was asleep well before midnight.

In the morning darkness of the following day, Arthur realised that he would be flying blind. He did not have a map of Italy, in English or Italian. He was already off the pages of his English map of France.

He thought it worse that the folder prepared by Alain Cartet was of no further use. However, the road signs had told him that beyond Bordighera lay Sanremo.

He remembered from school maps of Europe that somewhere further along the coast was the port of Genoa, located deep in the groin of Italy's leg. He also knew that Rome was on Italy's west coast, somewhere around the kneecap.

The lack of a map did not worry or delay him; a clear memory from his school history books assured him that all roads lead to Rome.

Arthur reckoned that his Christmas Day driving had completed about half his journey to Rome, but because it was no longer Christmas Day, and it was raining, he thought that he would not be able to achieve an average speed of fifty mile an hour.

He therefore decided for this second day he would drive three, two and a half hour stages, and take longer rest periods, hoping that on the third day he would need to drive just one stage before he could enter the 'Eternal City'. Arthur was anxious to maintain the fable by being the tortoise that beat the hare, hoping to arrive at the appointed rendezvous, before Galiena Vercente got there in her little Fiat sports car.

Leaving Bordighera before seven on Boxing Day morning, Arthur took the road to Sanremo, where he found the road sign-posted to Genova that he confidently took to mean Genoa.

On the outskirts of the great city port, huge signs lead him to the A12, the Blue Freeway Autostrada, to Roma.

His felt justified in his confidence that all roads would lead him to his rendezvous, but he worried, that using the Autostrada, in his right hand drive motor home made in Germany for sensible English roads, he would be on the wrong side of the toll-booths in Italy.

He also worried whether he would have sufficient Euros, in the correct denomination, to pay the correct toll. He coped; his day went well.

When the light began to fade, he left the super highway to drive the few miles to Orbetello, where he laid up for the night overlooking the sea. A walk in the rain failed to find any shops or restaurants open. He therefore dined, very frugally, on tinned corned beef on toast, grilled in the oven. After a long day of driving in the rain, he turned in early. He was so tired that he forgot to set his alarm clock.

When Arthur woke, it was already daylight. Intent on reaching Rome before mid-day, he decided to miss breakfast. By late morning, due to lorries and heavy traffic being back on the road, and causing him to make slow progress, he was becoming anxious. But, when he approached the dull outskirts of the city, still on the motorway, his heart skipped a beat, his spirits soared and a huge grin spread wide across his face.

Through the spray and rain, he had seen a small white Fiat car, with flashing headlights, parked on a slip road leading out of a service station. The little car came onto the road behind him, but was quick to overtake, with the driver's hand waving from the side window.

His great wide grin broke into an excited shout of joy when he saw, written in red on a white card in the rear window of Galiena's little car, the simple instruction, 'Follow Me'.

Arthur had to drive hard to keep up on the last stretch of the Autostrada, but when Galiena led him into suburban Rome, she took care not to lose him.

Arthur thought that he must have driven round all the Seven Hills of Rome before the little car slowly moved over to the kerb in a quiet broad tree lined avenue. Galiena slid out of her little car to waive Arthur past, indicating that he should turn into an entrance leading to a wide double wrought iron closed gate.

As he slowly moved past the Fiat, he could see that behind the gate a long drive led to a large formal detached house with an equally formal beautifully manicured garden. As though by magic, the gates swung slowly open to allow him to drive Tootsie through to park on the drive. Engine off, handbrake on, gear safely in park, he stepped down to meet the woman who had captivated him.

Galiena was first with her greeting, "There you are, the tortoise has beaten the hare; the finishing line was the gate."

Once again, Arthur went to pieces. All that he wanted to do was to embrace her, but uncertain of her feelings he was terrified of rejection. The best that he could manage was a feeble 'Hello you,' not even a handshake. He was not an air kissing man.

His first plebeian question to the aristocratic beauty was, "Am I alright to park here?" Galiena smiled, "Well, I dare say the neighbours will make a row about gypsies camping in the avenue, but I don't think the owner will mind. Later, we will hide your movable address round to the back of the house, by the old stables. First, you must come into the house to rest; you must be tired. Rome in two and a half days, I knew you could do it. I cheated yesterday; I left early in the morning, not after lunch, but I did have my fingers crossed behind my back when I promised you a thirty-six hour start. I stayed over with my cousin in Genova. You did not see me overtake you on the Autostrada; it was about half an hour before I took you in tow. I came past on the outside lane, sheltered by a line of trucks in the middle lane. I was quite proud of my cunning. It gave me time to mark the card for the back window, but it cost me a whole lipstick to draw the letters big enough for you to read."

All this Galiena said, at speed, in her lovely teasing way. Arthur realised that he did not mind that her chatter made it difficult for him to make sense of everything that she said. When she led him towards the door to the house it also opened, miraculously, this time not by electricity, but by a housemaid dressed in black, with a traditional housemaids white starched cap and apron.

A stream of Italian from Galiena to the housemaid was incomprehensible to Arthur, but one word in the maid's equally rapid reply he did understand. It dashed the hope; rekindled by his stubborn Yorkshire pride, that their friendship could continue, perhaps develop.

The word he did understand was 'Contessa'.

With a parting dazzling smile, Galiena was gone, leaving only the perfume of memory.

The housemaid showed him into a small room overlooking the side garden. Within minutes, she brought in a very English silver tray, set with a Georgian silver teapot, hot water jug, matching sugar tongs and teaspoons.

A second maid followed with a tray on which was set delicate china cups, saucers and milk jug. Arthur was surprised that in the very short time that it had taken the maids to set the trays, brew the tea then bring them into the room, Galiena had re-joined him, already changed into a beautiful Yellow suit with matching shoes and handbag.

Galiena said, "I'm sorry, the tea will be 'Darjeeling', I remember in the café in Andorra you told me you had a favourite tea, Yorkshire Tea I believe. Do you know I never knew you had tea gardens on those bleak northern moors of yours?"

"I don't remember telling you that," Arthur replied, "And we -" here he stopped himself, just in time, realising that she was teasing him.

What she said next made Arthur conscious of how quickly she could change from her natural gaiety, to a quiet introspective mood matched by a subtle change in her voice. "You may not remember telling me," Galiena said, "But I remember every word of your soliloquy in Andorra. I was downcast when I saw your passport; I was frightened. You did not look at me once during your explanation of your need to be the too clever Doctor Davenport while you search for the missing painting. We let the coffee go cold. After you ordered a fresh pot of hot coffee and I asked for Strega, Arthur Thomas, my brave policeman, looked into my eyes when we drank the liqueur of the witches of Benevento. All things were set to rights; I was happy again."

Galiena's lilting enthusiastic voice was back. "Are you hungry? I am. I skipped breakfast this morning. I could get cook to prepare lunch, but I am sure you would rather see something of Rome. I like to go to a little restaurant that is not far from here; they spoil me. They serve pasta and salads for lunch. It is so near, we can walk. Today will be a pasta and salad day. We will go as soon as you have finished your second cup of the poor week tea Maria prepared for you, but not before you go back to your Floozie with her winning ways to get your coat and hat. Although it is not far to the restaurant, it is cold. You must look after yourself. If you will let Mario have a spare key to your racing machine, I well ask him to take it round to the stable yard; that is if you don't mind."

Arthur was relieved that despite the morning rush he had left everything ship shape. When Arthur was back in his mobile home, he was beginning to appreciate that it made an excellent annex to other people's houses. He again tried on the hat he had bought in Montauban, but vanity forced him hide it in a top cupboard.

A middle-aged man with a military bearing, who Arthur took to be Mario, was standing with Galiena waiting for him on the drive.

After handing his spare keys to Mario, Arthur managed to get in the three short words, "Right I'm ready," before Galiena was once again in charge. "You must wear a hat in cold weather; cold winds can cause the blood in the head to form platelets. They can block the flow to parts of the brain. Perhaps that is why you had to spend time in that horrid place, rearranging your little brain cells. We must go shopping tomorrow, we will choose you a hat that befits the dignity of a chief of police, perhaps one like the man wears on the Moretti beer bottle labels."

Arthur's shock at the housemaid's use of Galiena's title, 'Contessa', doubled when they arrived at the restaurant. He noticed that the owner greeted her warmly, but with deference. He called out for all in the restaurant to hear; "A table for Contessa Emilia Romagna." Conscious that Arthur seemed worried by her title, Galiena whispered, "Don't let the title frighten you, I am by birth entitled to the courtesy rank of Contessa, but honestly, since the Republic, it does not mean anything."

Then in a mock aside, she said "But as you can see, it is useful in restaurants; also for theatre bookings."

Lunch was a delight. They ate a simple farfalle con salsa pomadoro, followed by Insalata alla Roma, the house special salad made up of sliced tomatoes over spinach dressed with freshly torn basil, rich with an olive oil dressing cut with tarragon vinegar.

They shared a bottle of wine chosen by the Countessa because she said, "It comes from the Province Emilia Romagna, where my family have interests, although it is in Italy's North East, a long way from Rome where most of us live.

While they ate, Galiena made plans, "Now, about my cousin's naughty picture. The casino will be open tonight, but not until ten o'clock. I could give him a ring to arrange a visit this afternoon, if you feel it would be better to meet him first. He is very nice, really, but his parents brought him up to think that he is rather grand."

Galiena, who gave Arthur no chance to comment, went on, "No, that will not do at all. If, by any chance, La Source is the Ingres original, it might be better if Paulo did not know about it until you have been able to make plans, with your friends, for its recovery. If it is just a copy, as it almost certainly is, then there is no need to involve Paulo. We will have to keep looking."

Arthur was thrilled that Galiena had said, "We will have to keep looking." He thought that perhaps they might be able to continue to be friends if she played Watson to his Holmes. Galiena interrupted his daydream, "We will go tonight. Now, we will walk home, where I will take my usual siesta. Today you too must take a siesta, after our early start; it is going to be a long day."

As they approached Galiena's grand house, she offered Arthur one of the guest suites, but he mumbled his excuses, and repeated, several times, that he would prefer to be in his Romany 'vardo', a term Alain Cartet had taught him.

Again, he noticed Galiena's head tilting to one side, as she gave him an enigmatic smile that tore his heart, but she nodded, accepting his decision, and did not press him further. Arthur was embarrassed, but did manage to ask, "Is there anywhere that I can hook up to an electrical supply? Galiena's smile immediately changed to radiant, knowing that she was again in charge. "I believe that Mario will have done that already. I hope you do not mind, but I have also asked Maria, my personal maid, to turn down your bed. Happily, Maria is Mario's wife, she will have arranged for one of the housekeepers to take care of any obvious laundry she could find. Please forgive me, but you looked so tired this morning. I was naughty, I should not have said three days to Rome, a week would have been better. Be rested, ready to come at seven, from your house to my house. We will have dinner here at about eight before we go to see the lovely lady."

When Galiena left him, Arthur was surprised to hear her humming a simple tune that he knew he had heard before, but he could not put a name to it.

Arthur found Tootsie parked behind the house where there were old stables, new garages, and an old stone built cottage that looked as though it had been empty since cars replaced horses. He lay on his bed, wide-awake, staring at the ceiling. He was thinking carefully about what Galiena had said about going to see the painting.

She had addressed the issue better than he would have done himself, in a fraction of the time that it would have taken him to reach the same, the correct, decision.

He rejoiced in her radiant smile, her perfume, her obvious vivacity, but that other smile, that other voice, made him acutely nervous, afraid even to take her hand.

Five minutes before the appointed time of seven o'clock, Arthur heard a firm knock on his door. Outside, he found Mario holding a large umbrella that he seemed to be using to shelter a small dog from heavy rain, rather than protecting his own head and shoulders.

He introduced Arthur to the dog as 'Attimo'. It took some time, because the little fellow fussed all round Arthur, taking in and memorising all the recognition signals that dogs use to discriminate between friend and foe.

Mario explained that the dog was his companion, a mongrel, but a supreme champion guard dog. He had called him Attimo in recognition of his capacity to see off, in 'quick time', any living stranger, ranging from a rat, to a cat, to an unknown dog of any size, even to intruders with criminal intent.

However, the appearance of the little dog was more of a genial intellectual, rather than a bruiser. The only rough thing about him was his brindle white and grey coat. His deep brown eyes, framed by bushy eyebrows over a droopy moustache, inherited from his families Schnauzer line, gave him star quality, but a gene pool deep enough to drown a Great Dane ravelled the many other lines there were to his mongrel pedigree.

Mario explained that now he had formally introduced Attimo, he would accept Arthur Thomas without further fuss.

Leaving the little dog on guard, in his wooden kennel by the door, Mario escorted Arthur through the rear entrance to the house, and on through the vast kitchen area and then through the green baize door to the reception rooms.

"The Contessa is waiting for you in the Blue Room sir, dinner will be at eight in the small dining room," all spoken in perfect BBC English. Arthur, somewhat surprised, asked, "Mario, your accent is more the perceived pronunciation than my vulgar Yorkshire tones. Where did you learn English?" Mario's reply was formal, "I was with the Contessa's late husband during the time they were at our Embassy in London. He was military attaché. I was his aid. He was very young when he died. It seemed correct that Maria and I should stay with her. It is an arrangement that we all respect."

The warm elegant Blue Room was big enough to have a high double door in the centre of the wall opposite the great window that overlooked the front garden.

When Mario opened one side of the door Arthur could see that the Contessa Galiena Vercente was sitting, regally, on a high backed silk upholstered chair. On this occasion her beauty did not make Arthur draw a double breath, she took his breath away.

He thought her more beautiful than any flower in the several different arrangements of fresh flowers that gave life to the room.

To his delight, a Christmas tree with a train of lights sparkling on exquisite glass baubles shone in one corner. Arthur said, quite genuinely, "Oh how lovely, a Christmas Tree, I thought it was only we Teutonic tribes that had them."

Galiena said, "When we were in London, we always had a real one, much bigger than this poor little artificial thing, but I am glad that you like it. Now, in exchange for your Christmas gift to me, I have a present for you. You must get it from under the tree, there, you see, the little red box."

Arthur stiffly bent on one knee to retrieve the box. Overawed by the occasion he was hardly aware that Galiena helped him to get back to his feet. He sat awkwardly, on the very edge of the twin to the chair on which Galiena resumed her place, properly at ease.

When he un-wrapped the box, it revealed a pair of cuff links, each made with two enamel rectangles linked by a gold chain. The enamel on one side of each link was fashioned as the green, white and red tricolour flag of Italy, on the other the Union Jack.

"I hope that you don't mind, but I have not had time to shop. They are second hand, but undoubtedly the better for it, because they belonged to my father. He was with the diplomatic corps in London, after the war."

The gift reduced Arthur to bumbling again. As he heard himself, it made things worse. He thought he sounded like a good actor reading, from 'The Wind in the Willows', giving voice to the unhappy mole. "But oh dear, oh bother, it makes my ruined gift to you such a poor thing, inadequate, insufficient to match your kindness, oh drat."

"Shh, no more" Galiena's quiet voice commanded, "Come here." Galiena led him to a small occasional table to the left of the great doors.

Her heavy black leather bound gold embossed bible, fit for the Vatican, lay upside down on the table. After turning it right way up, she opened it to show Arthur that the pressed bundle of twigs, once a posy of Christmas roses, rested on the first page of the 'Book of Ruth'. "I told you I would find my big family bible to press them ready for framing. Now sit down again so that I can fit your new cufflinks."

Arthur was relieved yet mortified at the same time. He was relieved that his new shirt did have holes for cuff links, although he had only used the buttons, but mortified that the cuff was not a double cuff.

Galiena unbuttoned both cuffs, frowned, then from an occasional table drawer she took out a small pair of scissors to cut off the shirtsleeve buttons. After threading the new cufflinks, she was obviously pleased.

"There, you are now linked with chains of gold to Italy. I am sure my dear Father would approve." Arthur was very steady in his reply, trying to remember exactly what she said about the ruined posy. Finally, he found the words, "Remember, Galiena, it is always the thought that counts. I shall keep them always, so that I shall never forget this special day of Christmas, this best of all presents."

To his delight, he knew from her eyes that always said so much, that she understood his echo of her acceptance of the frost-ruined posy that had been Christmas roses.

Maria, Galiena's personal maid, served dinner. It was a series of light delicious courses, with strange to Arthur's custom, the cheese served before the dessert.

As soon as they had drunk coffee with 'Strega', the curious yellow liqueur, Galiena was on her feet, as lissom as a leopard.

Maria came into the room with a coat for her mistress. Arthur did not know much about fur, but from his experience of a theft of furs that he had dealt with years ago, he thought the coat might be sable, the most expensive of all furs. The coat was fashioned like a full-length cape to touch the floor.

Galiena called out, "Come along, Mario has the car waiting. I am sure my cousin's den of iniquity will be seething with gamblers making him rich.

Please, I do not want to stay to play the tables, I think that gambling is greed. We will just look at his pseudo art collection, and take one of his free champagne cocktails, before making a dignified exit."

"That will suit me fine," Arthur nodded, "But I might need a little time to look at the painting. If I think it could possibly be the real thing, I want to be sure enough to call Peter who will arrange for experts to examine it."

The entrance to the casino was very grand. A top hatted, frock coated, doorman, wearing white gloves, opened the door of Galiena's coach built Fiat.

This was not to Mario's liking. He was out of the driving seat faster than an American President's security guard, ready to hand out Galiena, under the shelter of his ever-handy umbrella. Galiena asked, "Mario, please wait if you will be so kind, we will only be a little while, Mr Thomas and I do not gamble."

Inside what had once been a minor palace, the Prince's architect had had the large marble-floored reception hall, extended to provide, on one side a cloakroom for gentlemen, on the other, a cloakroom for ladies.

However, Mario had left the car to follow his mistress into the foyer to suggest that he should look after her coat. At Galiena's suggestion, he was also about to take Arthur's coat, when a thin badly dressed middle aged women with prominent teeth, and thin hair scraped back to a bun, came close.

She greeted Arthur in a nasal grating voice, "Good evening Doctor Davenport, how very interesting to see you here. Perhaps you have come to study the paintings. I am sure you will find the stakes even higher than merely playing the tables."

Galiena was immediately very concerned. She saw Arthur's usual ruddy complexion drain so quickly that she thought he might be seriously ill.

He replied, completely to Galiena and Mario's surprise, "No, er, no madam, how strange, we had hoped to meet friends here, but we have just been told they are not able to join us, so we are leaving." As he said 'leaving', he looked imploringly at Galiena who understood that, for some reason, Arthur was in trouble. Taking an instant dislike to the creature that had clearly unsettled her brave policeman, she added more than a pennyworth.

"Yes, I think we have better ways of spending our time than with grotesques who gamble and letches who leer at lewd pictures. Mario, we will go directly on to party at the Embassy. I am sure that my cousin the Prince will forgive us for not contributing to his personal fortune." Yes Contessa, of course." Mario replied.

Arthur noticed that Mario had interposed himself between the woman and Galiena.

As soon as they were back in the car Arthur burst out "I don't need to see the picture, it is the real thing for certain. Your Prince Cousin has what I have been looking for, the original Ingres masterpiece, 'La Source', sold to him as a copy. It is worth millions of pounds. I must speak to Peter. Oh, can we skip the Embassy party, please?" Galiena seemed to be electrically charged, "Don't worry, there is no party, I just made that up for that dreadful harpy wearing trousers. I am surprised that the Prince's staff allowed her into the casino. The woman looked like an out of time, out of sorts, morning cleaner. What has happened, how is it that you are certain, without even having had sight of it, that you know the painting is the original, and not a copy?"

Arthur paused for quite some time before he turned awkwardly in his seat so that he could look directly at Galiena. "You are right; she is a dreadful woman, truly dreadful. She is, Mrs. Greta Servient-Higgins. Servient was her maiden name. She is not only the wife, but also the accomplice of Terrance-Servient Higgins, whom we believe killed a good man to steal the painting. What makes me more certain was that I caught sight of a man hovering in the background. His photograph was in the pack of cards that the Special Branch in New Scotland Yard made me commit to memory.

He is one of the gang who stole the painting from the musée d'Orsay. His name is, er, I know, Peter Bond, known as 'bull-neck' by his associates; he does not have any friends."

Chapter 15

The shock of meeting Greta Servient-Higgins changed everything. Arthur Thomas was sure, beyond doubt, that the stolen Ingres painting was somewhere in the casino.

The discovery forced the relationship between Arthur and Galiena to a level more highly charged than when they drank Strega in the café in Andorra and she had held Arthur Thomas's eyes with hers.

He had never dared to flirt with her, or to touch her, but her instant demonstrative dislike of the Servient-Higgins women, made him hope that there might yet be a chance for a bond between them, despite their different backgrounds, he almost a gypsy, Galiena Vercente, Countess Emilia Romagna, almost a princess.

In the Contessa's car, driven by Mario an expert security driver, Arthur felt safe, for the time being, but he realised that the nursery game of hunt the thimble was over.

Greta Servient-Higgins, in the company of Bull-Neck Bond, had seen him in the casino where the gang had undoubtedly hidden the painting.

This unfortunate chance meeting meant that he was in trouble, serious and immediate trouble. Peter Bainbridge had warned him that because Servient Higgins had fouled the theft of La

Source with heinous murder, he would not hesitate to kill him, if he thought that he might frustrate his plans.

Arthur was pleased that the hours spent doing his homework with the set of Scotland Yard photographs had enabled him recognise Bull Neck Bond, but he worried that he did not have a complete set of cards for all the Servient-Higgins's gang, or for any of the wild cards of Italian Mafia assassins that Higgins might hire.

Arthur had more concern for Galiena's safety than he had for himself. Galiena had been there when Greta Servient-Higgins had confronted him. He felt sure that this unhappy accident put the Contessa in danger.

Arthur felt certain that Terrance Servient-Higgins would assume that he and the Contessa were working together because of her close relationship to the Prince, who owned the casino, and who had bought the painting from him thinking it to be a copy.

It was almost midnight before Mario had them back inside the gates of the Contessa's beautiful home. Arthur felt that he would be secure, parked out of sight, behind the house that had the aura of a small European embassy.

The house stood in the middle of a tree-lined avenue of equally grand houses. He was sure the owners of each house would have their own security, particularly as, during their walk to her favourite restaurant, he had noticed discrete brass plates confirming that many houses were no longer family homes, but head offices of corporate businesses, financial or charitable institutions.

Mario, umbrella to hand, escorted Galiena and Arthur from the car to the front door. Once again, as if alerted by some extra sensory perception, her personal maid Maria opened the door before her mistress had even reached the steps.

For a moment or two, the Contessa spoke rapidly to Mario in Italian. He nodded gravely in what appeared to be consent. He then walked back to the car, leaving Arthur alone with the Contessa. Galiena tried to persuade Arthur to move into one of the guest suits, to be safe, but he even refused her invitation to join her for coffee and Strega.

He said, reluctantly but determinedly, "No, you have done enough for me already. I have much to do tonight. I will contact Peter Bainbridge who is the old friend I told you about, the one who looks after security things for the insurance company.

Now that we have found the painting, he will take charge of recovering it. With luck, because the UK is an hour behind Italy, he will not yet have gone to bed. I shall be busy until the early hours. Just one more thing before I go; may I please ask Peter to meet me here, when he gets to Rome? I do not think that I should be seen out and about, not until we can sort something out."

Galiena gave her reply in serious tones "Of course your friend must come to meet you here, where else?" Then, for the first time that he could remember since they were together in the café in Andorra, she used his name. "Arthur, please rely on Mario, let him be your Italian brother. He is discrete and is very loyal to me. He will be helpful to you in all things. You must take care; you are not to tangle with these awful people. You must leave it to the professionals. You have done what you charged yourself to do. You have found the stolen picture. The quest that you told me about in Andora is now over. I am sorry if I offend; I know that you are a proud brave man, but you must now leave it to the young ones. They must make plans to take back the painting. They must arrest the thieves. It is their time to take the risks."

For once, her lovely face was not smiling, her eyes did not spar-kle, but they looked deep into Arthur's eyes, pleading for him to take her advice. Then she was gone, except for her perfume that clung to his coat. Together, in the large coach built Fiat, they had been close, though not touching.

Mario had waited to drive him round to the courtyard at the back of the house, where he had hooked up 'Tootsie' to a water-proof electrical supply on a garage wall.

Long ago, the stone buildings had been mews for carriages and stables for the horses, giving a clue that the house was quite old, certainly well established. "How does your misses always know when to open the door for the Contessa?" Arthur asked, feeling slightly uncomfortable, because he realised that it was the first time he had referred to Galiena by her title.

The question raised a contended smile, "That is our little secret; I have a radio button in all the cars, one I also keep in my pocket. It rings a pager that Maria wears around her neck. It is in the form of a crucifix. I give one long buzz for one minute, or five short for five minutes. The security boys at our foreign office, those who look after our embassies, keep them serviced for me. You must understand that the Contessa is much admired, very well connected, and still a likely kidnap target, although kidnap in Rome is not as bad as it was in the seventies."

Arthur's expletive "Oh hell" was savage, but he calmed down to tell Mario of his concern. "Greta Servient-Higgins and Bull Neck Bond saw the Contessa, with me, in the casino where the painting is on show. I think that it has put her into greater more present danger. It has certainly put the wind up me. I must be getting past it."

Mario's smile broadened, "I did notice you got a tad nervous when that ghastly woman accosted you, but you are not past it, not at all. Now that we are to work together, I can tell you. I did ask my old colleagues at the diplomatic to run the usual checks on you. That was yesterday, when the Contessa brought you to her home, unannounced. You have a good record. You also have powerful friends. The Frenchies are still embarrassed about feeling your collar in Cahors." "Good God," was all that Arthur could splutter before Mario continued, "Don't worry, I have not mentioned any of this to the Contessa, nor shall I, there is no need." Arthur replied wryly "I suppose you would have told her if I had been black balled at your club." Mario admitted, "Well, put it this way, if there had been a breath of scandal, you would

219

not be sleeping here in your gypsy caravan. For now, good night, I know you have calls to make. Tomorrow I shall have cameras and security beams around the courtyard. If anyone should want to have a look at you, or your nice little home, I shall know all about it. By the way, rather than letting him find his own way when he arrives, I think that it will be better if I pick up your friend from the airport. The Contessa will agree. When you learn his flight number and ETA, let me know. Tell him that I shall be waiting at arrivals, waiving a card mounted on a stick marked 'Mister Alfred Marks: IDT Guest'.

Left alone, Arthur fell back on his old habit of thinking aloud.

"First things first Arthur old lad, brew a good pot of hot sweet tea to calm your nerves, they have not had such a shaking for many years." He finished his second cup before settling himself comfortably in his dressing gown, prior to ringing Peter.

The phone rang several times before Peter answered, "Arthur, sorry for keeping you waiting. I am in the car. I had to pull over because my hand free set is not compatible with this phone. I keep this phone exclusively for your calls."

Arthur burst in, "Yes it's me, sorry to ring so late but we have found her for sure. I did not stay to view the naked lady; I did not need to. That is the good news; the bad news is that Greta Servient-Higgins was there with Bull-Neck Bond. He saw me; and worse still she talked to me."

Peter's expletive brought a smile to Arthur's face. "Bulls-eyes and Bust a Frog, that is not what we wanted at all. Look old lad, we will be home in five minutes, hang up now but stay awake. I will call you in ten," but before he cut off the call, Anne was speaking, "Oh Arthur, you clever old thing, but do be careful," then the phone went dead.

After Arthur cleared his tea things, he sorted out pen and paper to take notes. He found the address Galiena had given him for their rendezvous in Rome, ready to pass it on to Peter.

He waited for the return call, knowing that it would take longer than ten minutes, but this did not worry him.

He guessed, correctly, that Peter would be speaking to Swiss Mobius, his Head Office in Switzerland, to New Scotland Yard, and possibly to the Home Office, to check on the whereabouts of husband Higgins.

While he waited, he dozed, thinking of Galiena. He thought it curious that he, a broken down old copper, had been befriended by an eccentric French Tourism officer, sheltered by a lady restaurateur in her courtyard garden in the centre of Paris, and protected by an Italian Contessa in a stable yard in the middle of Rome.

His half-awake thoughts took him back to his roots in Scagill. "Eee Lad, you must have had something going for you. With the reward coming for finding the painting, you will no longer be just a poor retired copper."

However, he concluded, grumpily, "Still too poor to throw your cap at Galiena, the Contessa Emilia Romagna." As he drifted near to sleep, he thought of his friends, the other Grey Haired Knights.

He wondered if they had found adventure, put aside old age to live life to the full, as he had done, in part at least. His thoughts ran on, Tristan; no need to worry about him, an acerbic streetwise loner. He would survive. He would find someone to do his washing.

He had no worries about Geraint, the engineer, youngest, most competent of them all; he would cope, he had already survived an epic pirate adventure.

However, he did worry about Perceval, the retired teacher antiquarian with his risk of recurrent gangrene, difficulty in walking, and natural diffidence.

He hoped that he had not caused him to risk too much, just to be able to tell a tale at the re-union.

It was just after three a.m., the Devil's hour, when the phone rang.

Peter said, "Arthur, well done. You will be rich, no doubt about that, but for all our sakes make sure that you do not become 'Dead rich'. Sorry to be so late, I had to waken quite a few Home Office chaps, who in their turn had to waken probation officers. The bad news, though not unexpected, is that Higgins is not at home. He did not report to his probation officer last week. He frightened the silly moo so much that she thought she would not report his absence until he had missed his second appointment, which is due tomorrow. Scotland Yard have alerted all ferries and airports, but fat chance there, what with all these low cost flights to the continent that can be booked on the Internet. The tunnel trains are as bad, they leak illegal immigrants, both ways. Anyway, he probably has half a dozen passports, all with different names; he is a forger after all. Remember what I told you, I want you to be aware if he comes anywhere near you, whether you are asleep, drunk or sober. You must understand, he will try to kill Doctor Edward Davenport now that Greta has told him you have found one of their major investments, la Source, now once again a source of much trouble. Let us hope he never connects the erudite doctor to the bounty hunter Arthur Thomas. Find some different clothes, wear a wig, put on dark glasses, shave off your moustache, grow a beard, speak French, have yourself cut off at the knees, anything to disguise the unmistakeable policeman. Remember your disguise failed when you visited him in the open prison. When Higgins reunites with Servient, which will be in the next day or two, if he has not already done so, you will be in great danger. Do not let them find you. You can be sure that already he and his associates will be looking for you. Now, tell me, where are you?"

Arthur, who was now wide-awake, replied, "I am in Rome; the painting is somewhere in a rather posh Roman casino. The casino belongs to a cousin of someone I have met."

Peter cut in "I shall come straight to Rome to direct company operations, and to liaise with both the Police and Carabinieri. I shall call you tomorrow morning, sorry this morning, to tell you my flight number and arrival time. Now tell me, where you are parked up, are you still in your motor home?" "Don't worry about that Peter," Arthur replied. "I have a friend who will pick you up at the arrival terminal. He will be waiving a card on a stick, as they do. It will say, 'Mister Alfred Marks IDT Guest'. He will bring you to me.'"

Peter was impressed, "Gracious Canterbury, that is a blind used by the diplomatic corps. What have you been up to?" "Never you mind Mon Capitaine, just get yourself to Rome, tomorrow," was Arthur's now cheery final instruction. "And so to bed, little sleepy head, and about time too" was his quietly spoken lullaby to himself.

He decided not to set his alarm clock.

Arthur woke to the compelling ring of his telephone.

He scrambled across to where he had left it on the table, by his notes, and assuming that it would be Peter calling, he said, "Hello Peter, what time is your ETA." He was hit with an adrenalin rush as Galiena's delicious exciting Italian English voice said "What a way to greet a lady who has been anxiously waiting for signs of life from the gypsy camped under her castle wall."

The call flummoxed Arthur, "Oh, damn, oh gosh, marvellous, yes, of course it's you. I'm so sorry, I was expecting a call from Peter; he is flying in sometime today." Galiena said, "Calm down Arthur. Cook is making a breakfast for you. Please come straight away, before I go mad trying to work out how we are going to get the painting away from the Prince who will want to keep it."

Arthur, now collected, was able to reply happily, "That sounds wonderful, but ask cook to hold on the eggs. I am hungry, but I must shower, change and shave. Give me fifteen minutes, please; I did not get to bed until well after three." "No, I'll give you ten." Galiena replied, then she hummed a few notes of a melody that was familiar, but there was not enough for him to remember where he had heard it.

Cook had indeed prepared a breakfast, half a pink grapefruit, scrambled egg with chopped smoked salmon, dry cured bacon, toast made with supermarket sliced bread, butter, Coopers English Marmalade and tea. His hostess, wrapped in a silk kimono style housecoat, her hair immaculate, her flawless skin barely touched with makeup, did not eat.

She sat wide-eyed, watching him attentively, like a cat watching a bird perched low in a tree. She said not a word until he had finished eating.

Then she spoke eagerly, "I'm glad you have a good appetite. A man should set himself up for the day with a good breakfast. My late husband never lost the habit he made in London; he always ate a cooked breakfast before he went to the embassy."

Arthur grinned, because he remembered the breakfast conversation he had on the first day of his quest. "What are you grinning at, you night owl?" Galiena infected by his grin feigned a comic scowl, "Oh nothing, only that is exactly what a waitress I knew said to me, when I ate my last Yorkshire breakfast, before I set off on my quest to find a beautiful lady."

"You mean the painting? Galiena asked coquettishly. "I don't quite know, yet," Arthur replied. Then, embarrassed, he blushed and stared hard into his empty cup, as though he was trying to read his fortune.

Desperate to get back to their usual level of conversation, because his brief venture into a possible flirtation had brought back all his fears of rejection, he retreated to Galiena's earlier question. "You mentioned earlier, about us recovering the painting, well I must wait until my chief in this caper arrives. We must do nothing. Peter will have to liaise with the authorities, but I am sure he will have a plan, so there is nothing we can do about the painting until he arrives later today. You will like him. We joined the police force together, far too many years ago.

Galiena frowned, and then leaning forward, she spoke in a voice that demanded attention. "Look at me Arthur, you won't find your future in the tea leaves. Cook has gone all modern; she only uses tea bags. I think that you may have missed an important detail. I am afraid that I was deliberately rude to that horrid woman at the casino. I am sure that she will have asked the attendants to tell her who was the lady with the sable fur coat. I have to tell you, that even though I have never been there since the Prince turned his home into a casino, at least one of the attendants will have recognised me, and told her. I am sorry Arthur, we both played games with our names when we first met. I am Angelina Galiena Elizabetha Ruth Sophia, Vercente – the Contessa Emilia Romagna. I am afraid that my six names followed by a title will have compromised our security. You see, occasionally, because of my title, there are pictures of me in the papers, also the silly gossip magazines. The woman will already know where I live, when I am in Rome. We must move. I will arrange to borrow one of my cousin's country retreats; like the Pope, we will go to Castel Gandolfo. It is not far. I have so many cousins, each with many retreats, that for those killers to find you, it would be like, as I think you English people say, 'looking for a pin in a pigsty', isn't it?"

Although he had taken in the grim circumstances Arthur laughed, "Well near enough, you are right, I had not thought of that. Peter did suggest that they may try to do me some harm, but I cannot risk putting you at risk. I must go alone." Do not worry, replied Galiena, laughing, I have compromised you enough already. I told you in Montauban on Christmas Eve, if you remember, my family would believe I had compromised you. You do not know Rome, so you cannot go alone, but you can take your 'Floozy' with you.

Despite the seriousness of their situation, Galiena had him laughing with her reference to Floozie. "Tootsie," if you don't mind," he replied. Galiena said, "Well, fiddle de dee, now that we know that we are both in trouble, I shall go and change, ready to walk with you to the restaurant for pasta and salad. Perhaps we will have a glass each of Gavi from the Piemonte, where my family also has interests.

The woman may know where I live, but she will not have had time to make any plans, not yet."

Peter rang before Galiena had returned ready for their walk to the restaurant. "I am still in the office in London," he told Arthur hurriedly, "I am booked on Flight BA 927, due to arrive in Rome 18.45. I shall be staying at the company flat. There is a lot to do, and with precious little time to do it. We must have a meeting, tonight for sure."

"Alright Peter," Arthur relied, "I shall be waiting, and I look forward to having you with me, but where that will be I have not yet been told. Mario, my friend's driver, will know." "What? Do I detect that someone is running your life? It must be a woman, whatever next." Arthur just laughed before switching off his phone.

Lunch was a delight; Salsicce e Conghiglie, great shells of pasta in cream with lots of cubed garlic sausage, followed, this time, not by a salad, but Cappuccino Frullato, a coffee mouse sprinkled over all with grated strong bitter chocolate, served in superb stemmed glasses, shaped like a tilted double diameter champagne saucer.

When they came out from the restaurant into the sun, fussed over by the patron, Galiena said, a little surprised, "Oh, Mario is here."

At the kerb side, Mario had parked a Fiat limousine, even bigger than the one they had used the night before, with the back door open. It was sinister black, with black bumpers, black wheel trim and black windows.

Mario came quickly to collect the Contessa and had her and Arthur seated in its cavernous back compartment in quick time. In barely three minutes, he drove them back to Galiena's home, during which time the Contessa talked rapidly to Mario in Italian.

Once they were through the gate into the drive, Galiena spoke quickly to Arthur. "Stay in the car please, already you have had visitors. You are not to worry, Mario's brave little dog Attimo lived up to his name by raising the alarm.

He saw them off before they could get into your beloved 'Floozy', though they have broken a catch on one of the side windows. I shall go and make the necessary arrangements with my cousin to move house, but I shall not tell him about the painting until you tell me that it is safe for him to know. Mario will take you to Castel Gandolfo. He will then bring your friend Peter to you. With Mario driving, it is less than an hour from here. In the meantime, keep out of sight.

Mario will let me have your keys. I will arrange for one of the drivers from Fiat, to drive your little home north, well away from Rome, then around in circles, before delivering it, late tonight, to where we are going to stay."

Mario escorted her to the opening front door while she was singing nonsense, "Do di diddle um di." as though she could not remember the words to that same tune that seemed to be stuck in her mind.

When Mario returned it was clear there had been a change. "It is more than three hours until your friend arrives at Leonardo de Vinci. Because I have to do much work, the Contessa has just suggested a slight change of plan. She has asked me to take you to the Gallery Borghese. She knows that you will be interested in some of their paintings. The Contessa also likes to support the family business. Madam is sure you will not be bored or wander off. Stay in the gallery where you will be safe. The Mafia don't do galleries. You seem to have made an impression on the Contessa, my employer and benefactor. That is good; she has been too long on her own. She does not make friends easily. You must leave the gallery exactly at a quarter to six; it closes at six. Stay well in the shadow of the colonnade until I come to collect you. That will give us plenty of time to get to the airport to pick up your friend."

The paintings in the Borghese Gallery did engage Arthur's full attention.

He was oblivious to the passing of time, until he heard the public address system announcing, in English, after several other announcements that were all Greek to him, "The gallery will close in twenty minutes." Checking with his watch, he was relieved that he could still get to the exit in time to meet Mario.

He had only been waiting for two or three minutes when he saw the sinister black car draw up at the kerb side. He ran down the steps to find Mario already holding the back door open, but Arthur asked if he could join him in the front. "Yes, but get in quick, you will have to let Attimo sit on your knee. Next time, wait inside until I come to get you, do you English policeman have no training in security." "Sorry Gov" replied Arthur with mock contrition. "No I mean it," Mario said firmly, "Those Mafioso who came looking for you today are brutes, without fear or conscience. They would not hesitate to shoot you in the street, in daylight."

At the airport, while Mario went to collect Peter, Arthur moved to the back seat, leaving Attimo on guard in the front. Arthur thought that the huge beast of a Fiat might be armoured, but the thought did not take away all his worries.

Arthur was still thinking about Galiena when Mario opened the door to allow Peter to flop into the seat beside him.

While they shook hands Arthur was first to speak. "I'm glad to see you Peter, things are a bit pear shaped here at the moment, but first let me introduce you to Mario, my Italian brother, who has just collected a maybe Alfred Marks." "No need old chap" replied Peter beaming from ear to ear, "I met Mario several times, long years ago, when he was at the Italian Embassy in London. I was with Royal Protection at the Yard. He taught me a great deal, although we were then both young. He also taught me to drink

Strega. Of the two of us, I fear that I must be the worse for wear, I recognised Mario immediately, but it took me a little while to convince him that this old wreck really was Bainbridge of the Yard."

Then he spoke directly to Arthur in a censorious voice "Of course, I also remember the Contessa. Pray tell me, how did a low life copper, lately come gypsy, meet such an enchanting aristocrat?"

Arthur, delighted to have Peters with him said, "Shut up you, that is none of your business. You are here to recover the painting, give me the money, and to stop me from being late." "Late for what?" peter asked, puzzled. "Late for nothing; you must stop me from becoming the late Arthur Thomas. Mario tells me the Mafia are involved."

Chapter 16

Leaving the airport, with Attimo in the front with him and Arthur and Peter in the back of the car, Mario drove fast, but with great skill. Ignoring all speed limits, it took less than an hour before he turned off the main roads onto quiet country lanes and then into a walled estate.

At the gate, a uniformed security man waived them through without pause or question. Arthur guessed that the drive to the house was well over half a mile long. Mario stopped the car in front of a large floodlit rambling informal looking house that had twin Italianate towers and many terra cotta tiled roofs.

Although it was cold and wet, Galiena came out to greet them, shadowed by Maria her companion maid. Mario was quickly out of the car, holding his umbrella over the Contessa, and hurrying them all inside. It pleased Arthur to see that Mario was an experienced protection officer, dedicated to looking after Galiena.

It seemed that, whenever it rained, Mario always had an umbrella at hand. It gave him hope that Mario would have a gun in hand and Attimo on hand, should a Mafia gang ever attempt to kidnap the Contessa.

In the large reception hall, Arthur formally introduced Peter. "Contessa, may I introduce my friend Peter Bainbridge, an ex-Metropolitan Police Commissioner who now works with

Swiss Mobius, the insurance company with an interest in the stolen painting."

Peter was quick to respond, "Good evening Contessa, I believe, in fact I know, that we have met before. Although it was some time ago, I see that the rough winds of winter have not shaken your beauty, nor has it been dimmed by the too hot sun of summer's short lease." Galiena looked hard at Peter before, to Arthur's delight, she put him down by mocking his poor effort at flirting.

"Yes, perhaps I do remember. You were then in your third age; sighing like a furnace with woeful chat up lines, upsetting the female members of our embassy staff. Even now, in your sixth age, you pipe and whistle incorrectly the words of Shakespeare's eighteenth sonnet, the one that every educated Italian girl knows by heart."

"Ouch," cringed Peter, making everyone laugh. Although amused with Galiena's putdown of his friend, Arthur thought her obviously superior education was a further barrier of thorns between them.

Un-perturbed, Peter immediately became serious, "Contessa, Arthur, please excuse Mario and me for a few minutes while he helps me to get organised. I want to talk to the people in our Rome office.

They will arrange for a car and driver to come here, wherever here may be. I must also speak to our office in Basle and then, of most importance, to my boss back home in Lurgashall." Galiena said impishly "You can tell your people that if it were summer we would be next door neighbours to his Holiness the Pope. We are in one of Prince Borghese's family homes, near to the village of Castel Gandolfo."

When Mario and Peter returned, Galiena took them to the library where there was a beautiful rectangular baroque table, large enough for them to sit in comfort. Mario did not sit; he stood immediately behind his mistress. Peter asked the Contessa

231

if there was a chance that Prince Borghese could join them. "You see," Peter included them all, "The fact that La Source hangs in the Prince's casino is problem both to us and to Servient-Higgins, who even now is busy attempting to recover it. He now knows that he has to steal it. All his other options, such as offering to clean, re-varnish, or re-stretch it, have been frustrated. Because his wife Greta and bull neck Bond saw Arthur in the casino, he must have realised that we know it to be the original. If we simply reveal to the world that Arthur has found the stolen painting, Higgins will give up trying to get it back, and we lose the chance of using our well-planned sting.

The Prince will have had installed a high level of security alarms with cameras covering all public and private areas throughout the casino building and grounds. All casinos are places of distrust and deceit.

When Horrible Higgins takes back the painting, he will have had to find ways around the problem. He will probably find it more difficult than the job he bungled at the musée d'Orsay. For us, there is the need to act quickly. We must arrange to swap the original with the perfect copy my company has commissioned. We must do so, before they make their move. We must make the switch without the casino security staff knowing. Frankly, without the Prince's help, I do not see how we can pull off the sting."

Galiena frowned, before asking, "What is this picture swap, some sort of adult 'Pokemon".

In contrast, Arthur smiled before he said, "Well it is Peter's idea really, and you will see that he is not so daft after all. It is, as he says, 'A sting'. Before Higgins can do anything, Peter will arrange to swap Ingres's original painting with a very accurate copy.

If it works, all will be good. Whatever method Higgins chooses to take back the painting, the Prince's security guards, the carabinieri, and the police, must not stop him.

Nothing must stop him believing it to be the original Ingres masterpiece that he sold to your cousin, as a copy.

The museum will get back their original Ingres masterpiece. Swiss Mobius will get back the insurance money. The forensic chaps will have the opportunity to examine the painting to see if they can find any DNA to link Servient-Higgins to the murder."

Peter took up the story, "Countessa, we hope that the sting will bring more results. I am reasonably confident that, in time, after Higgins has taken back what he thinks is the original, he will arrange for a third party to approach Swiss Mobius claiming that for the rewards offered, they can secure the return of La Source, and two other stolen old masters.

After some negotiation, Swiss Mobius will accept the deal. When all three stolen paintings have been recovered, the police will have sufficient evidence to arrest all those involved and claw back the reward money."

Galiena smiled, "Goodness the games you boys play, not so much cops and robbers more Machiavellian double dealing. I will go and phone the Prince. The poor man has no idea that he has been exposing a masterpiece worth millions of Euro to his silly gamblers and their cigar and cigarette smoke.

I am sure that had he known its value, he would have hung it somewhere for his exclusive pleasure, but I doubt that the Princess, who is my half cousin, would have allowed it."

Later, when Galiena re-joined Arthur and Peter she had changed into a full-length evening gown made of flame coloured silk with long sleeves drawn into a tight cuff at her wrists.

Around her shoulders, she wore a wide stole of the same fine silk. Maria had swept her hair up into a complicated multiple bun, into which she had wound a string of pearls. Galiena spun around to say with mock hauteur, "When I dine with Paulo, he likes me to dress for the occasion.

He genuinely believes that he is rather grand, but you have no need to worry, he is too self-centred to notice any gentlemen guests. He would not notice you if you wore white tie, black tie, boiler suits, or the full dress uniform of the Swiss Guard."

Peter was fascinated to observe, from her glances and body language, that the Contessa had not changed her dress and had Maria fashion her pearls like a coronet, to indulge her Prince Cousin. Peter was certain that she had done it for Arthur, the pauper gypsy.

The Prince arrived about forty minutes later. After rather formal introductions, for which they all stood, the Prince automatically sat at the head of the library table. Galiena sat opposite him. Peter and Arthur took station either side. Mario remained standing behind his mistress. The Prince began, "Now gentlemen; the Countessa, my cousin, tells me you have news of some importance concerning my casino. I hope that you have not discovered a way to break the bank."

With his usual command of good manners, Peter responded. "Prince Borghese, I hope that you will let me outline the story so far, including the part played by your cousin the Contessa Emilia Romagna, and my colleague Arthur Thomas. I then wish to discuss with you our hope that you will assist us in our continuing operation.

After receiving a slow nod of assent, Peter began at the beginning. He told the Prince about the theft from the musée d'Orsay of La Source, the Ingres masterpiece, during which the thieves had murdered a security guard.

He accounted for the police failure to find sufficient evidence to bring a charge of murder. He detailed his theory about the swindle used by the gang of art thieves, of how, when they had stolen an original valuable work of art, to avoid the police catching them in possession, they sell it on as a very expensive unique copy.

Because of the high cost, even though they sold it as a copy, the gang would always know where the paintings would be on display. They would also be confident that those who had purchased the unique expensive copy would keep it secure. Their idea was that when the stolen painting was no longer 'hot' they could easily arrange to steal it again.

At the same time, they would steal some obvious but minor things such as computers, jewellery, even televisions. A crucial part of their scam was that during this second theft, having removed the original painting from its frame, they would replace it with a copy, accurate in every detail, including aging.

By this simple but effective ruse, the police would treat the theft as a low priority case and the victim would not notice that the thieves had changed the painting. Peter then calmly told the Prince the painting he had bought from the Faux Art Works shop in London, as a copy, was in fact the original that had been stolen from the Musée d'Orsay, and that to get the painting, one of the thieves had shot and killed a museum guard.

The Prince, being rather grand, cast a serene smile around the table "It just goes to show," he opined, "I have a genuine connoisseur's appreciation of the beauty of the subject, together with an understanding of the technique of the artist. I suppose that is what tempted me to pay so much, even though I thought the gallery owner an odious vulgar person. Of course I knew nothing of the robbery and murder."

Peter carefully explained, twice, that the painting in the Prince's possession legally belonged to Swiss Mobius, because they had paid out the insurance to the museum.

However, he was quick to reassure the Prince that his firm had no intention of proceeding against him for receiving stolen goods.

He went on to explain that they would seek to recompense him for any trouble that recovery of the painting may cause. Peter asked the Prince if he could arrange for Swiss Mobius to exchange the original painting with a perfect reproduction, as soon as possible, and with absolute secrecy.

He explained that some time ago, Swiss Mobius had had such a copy painted by a Norwegian, a sort of present day Tom Keating, a master forger, and that the copy was already on its way to Rome, in the care of the artist.

Peter explained that the artist would have to study the original, now hanging in the casino, so that he could replicate the disguises that the Faux Art Works gallery would almost certainly have made before selling it to the Prince. He also told the Prince that the plan was to switch the copy into the existing frame so that any marks that the thieves might have deliberately made on the frame would still be there to reassure them that they had taken back the original Ingres painting.

The Prince's brow creased into many lines. He looked a worried man, "Are you sure the robbers will dare to try to steal it again? It is most unfortunate; I do not want them to kill any of my guards. I have spent a great deal to protect my investment with the most up to date security devices. There are recording security cameras all over the palace. They cost me a fortune to buy and even more to maintain."

Peter was also serious, "Oh yes, they will get the painting back, one way or another, as we want them to do. Of that, I have no doubt, but hopefully, only after we have affected our switch. How they will take it back concerns me because they have a double problem. They are aware that Mr Thomas, whom they know as Doctor Andrew Davenport, suspects that they are the gang that committed murder to steal the painting. Because they saw him and he saw them in your casino, they must also realise that he will tell Swiss Mobius that they are in Rome planning to take back the original painting. The thieves must therefore act quickly. As you have rightly pointed out, their second problem is your security. They must make their exchange, swap, switch or whatever they call it, without you, or your staff at the casino, knowing anything about it. I think that these two things work to our advantage.

Once we have the original safe in our possession, and our fair copy in its pace, all that we have to do is to be vigilant. We must note any variation in normal casino routine. Any change, or a novel approach for access, will mean they are about to make their switch. I do not think that we need worry about them trying a smash and grab exercise."

The Prince responded, "Thank you Mr er, Bainbridge, er, Peter, for your masterful summary of a complex problem. I shall be glad to help in any way that I can. We must put these people out of temptations way, for good." He then turned to speak to Galiena, "Now, if you will excuse us, dear cousin, I would like to discuss confidential arrangements with Mr Bainbridge in order that we can ensure that we deal properly with the issues. I understand that dinner will be served in the small red dining room, please attend to our guest."

Galiena was pleased with the end of formalities, but she could not resist a tease. "Paulo, we will have to start dinner without you if you take too long to convince the recently retired Metropolitan Police Commissioner that you really did not know that the painting they sold you was the original, and not a copy. He will be thinking it strange, because you have just told us that you have a genuine connoisseur's appreciation of the beauty of the subject, together with an understanding of the technique of the artist."

When the Prince reached the dining room door, Mario asked the Contessa to excuse him. Getting the nod, before leaving the room, he gave Arthur an encouraging wink. Arthur presumed the wink meant that Mario would be off duty, able to spend time with his wife Maria.

In the small red dining room, Galiena asked Arthur to sit at what was obviously the head of the table. She took the opposite end. Arthur struggled, "Should I not leave this seat for the Prince?"

Galiena's answer was decisive, "No Arthur, please indulge me, I have a little plan. The Prince is currently screwing a great deal of money out of Swiss Mobius. As soon as he has secured a deal, to his advantage, he will come through the door wreathed in unctuous smiles. He will be talking, pompously, about acting for the public good. He will look at me, to check that I have dressed for the occasion, even though it is only a family supper, without the Princess. Only then will he notice that you are sitting at the head of the table. He will be shocked, but too embarrassed to say anything. He will immediately make an excuse that he cannot stay for dinner. Once he has left, we three can have a fun time."

It was as though Galiena had read, or more accurately written, the script. The Prince came through the door, ahead of Peter, still addressing rather than talking to him. "Well we must all do our part, 'Pro bono publico', as we Romans have said for more than two thousand years. He then half froze, stammering, "G, g, goodness, the time, I really must get back to Rome, I had no idea; there is much to do. Please excuse me cousin.

Galiena sang out, " ciao Paulo," after the retreating Prince. Arthur blushed, deep red, matching the curtains. Peter just looked baffled by their uncharacteristic behaviour. It was the first time that Arthur heard Galiena giggle. "Come and join our table, friend of Arthur, old acquaintance of mine.

First you must have some wine, and then I shall insist that you tell us just how much my cousin's public altruism cost your firm; only then we can eat."

Galiena made sure that dinner was a fun meal. She sparkled, teased, and charmed both men. Peter became sure that her feelings for his old friend were, at the least a warm genuine friendship, but probably more. It worried him that Arthur did not respond to her many invitations to flirt, although it was clear that he adored her.

Peter's long friendship with Arthur made him careful not to interfere. He counselled himself to take care, believing that there was more at stake in this affair, than in the affair of the stolen painting.

Without knocking, Mario came into the room to announce, cheerfully, "All is in order Mr Bainbridge, your car and a driver are waiting for you outside. I have given him a sealed note for you, just useful addresses, telephone numbers, and the usual et-cetera. Your case is already in the boot."

Then Mario smiled at Arthur, "For you my Italian brother, your relocated home is now waiting, tethered in the stable yard. I do mean stable yard, the sort that still has horses. There you will be safe. The stable lads live over the horses, never sleeping. They guard them with their lives. I have asked them to extend the same courtesies to you, their new, though no less thoroughbred heavy hunter."

Peter, anxious to leave the field clear for his friend, was quickly away. He ducked out through the door, followed by Mario, leaving Arthur alone with Galiena.

However, it was only for a moment or two. Arthur just looked at her, blushed again and bumbled, "Thank you, yes, splendid, excellent, thank you, it was quite an occasion, oh dear, I had better catch them up. Goodnight, er, Contessa, I mean to say, Galiena." When Galiena was sure that he would not hear, she smiled wistfully and sighed, "Silly old bear."

Arthur slept soundly, but he woke when the stable lads brought the horses out onto the cobbles ready for their ride out, but it was still dark.

While he lay awake, the gentle noises of the horses mingling with the preparations of the stable lads did not disturb him. He took the opportunity to take stock of his situation.

He knew that protected in the estate grounds he was safe. He decided he would stay in Rome until after the Servient-Higgins pair made their move to take, by whatever means, the Norwegian's copy, not knowing that it was not the original Ingres painting, for which they had committed murder.

He hoped the sting would eventually lead to the re-arrest of the odious Terrance Servient-Higgins', this time leading to a safe conviction on a charge of murder. He decided that he would leave Rome, as soon as the threat to his life was not critical. He determined to spend the rest of his life painting, to help him forget his hopeless, ridiculous, no chance to go anywhere infatuation with the Contessa Emilia Romagna. "That's it," he told himself, "Work yourself out of your misery; pursue your only credible passion, painting, painting in oils, maybe in time painting on canvas, perhaps one day exhibiting."

He promised himself that in the morning he would start to paint again. He felt sure that somewhere in the grounds of the estate, he would find cypresses and rough stone walls, a place similar to the courtyard garden at the restaurant Bien-Découplé in Paris. Yes, that was it, his only hope of a cure. He tried to convince himself that by committing his daily routine to painting that one day in the future he might find contentment.

It was late on, during the following morning, when Galiena finally found him. He was still in the estate grounds, but a long way from the house.

He was sitting on his folding wood and canvas chair, wearing his new overcoat, a scarf, and the hat he did not like to wear, because he thought it made him look old. He was staring blankly at an old stone wall. Set on the easel before him, a new white board was almost as blank as Arthur's stare.

The air was so cold that he had hardly been able to squeeze paint from the tubes onto his pallet. The paints had become as tough as 'Plasticine'; they would not flow or mix. His hands were stiff and blue with the cold. He was miserable. His plan was not working, he was thinking of Galiena.

Galiena was truly cross, "What do you think you are doing, it won't be the Mafia who kill you; it will be the old assassin, pneumonia. Come inside at once. You must leave your chair, the easel and paints; leave everything.

I will have one of the gardeners bring them to you. If you must paint, you can work in the library where it is warm and the light is good. You can copy the impressionist Cézanne; he was good with gardens. The Prince has two in the music room. I will have them brought to you, they are only small."

Arthur was too cold to put up any defence. He did not notice that Galiena had his arm firmly linked in hers as she supported him to the house where Maria was waiting. When he saw the anxious look on Maria's face, he began to understand why the Contessa was scolding him.

Within minutes, he was sitting in a high winged chair, close up to the huge log fire that warmed him through and through. Maria quietly brought in a tray of coffee. She apologised "So sorry Mr Thomas, the Prince does not have tea anywhere in the house; he is a Roman." Galiena did not quietly enter the room, she swept in like a Diva in grand opera, holding aloft a balloon glass of what Arthur thought would be brandy, but it was Strega, the stringent rich yellow liqueur.

"Mario says you are to drink this, he says brandy is for old men, and it would send you to sleep. Strega will give you inspiration, also the strength that you need. It is a secret potion from the witches of Benevento. I am trusting them to work their magic for us both. The Prince has some made every year to give out as Christmas gifts, but of course, the usual brew is not good enough for him, he has a special batch made called 'Superior' that is made to be seventy not forty something, or other, whatever that means."

Without pause Galiena continued, "Arthur Thomas, now that I can see that you have defrosted, lost the blue tinge and regained your rosy hue, it is safe for me to leave you. I am sorry, but Mario, Maria and I must leave Castel Gandolfo.

Your friend Peter requires us to go back to my home in Rome. He says that for us to be safe everything must appear to be normal. Apparently, this morning, there have been more visitors. They wore dark blue suits, shades and old-fashioned felt hats. They asked cook where they might find their friend Doctor Andrew Davenport. Peter does not think that they were Jehovah's Witnesses. We know that they were a bad lot because Mario's little dog Attimo bit one of them on the ankle. I will only be gone for two days, at the most, because we have persuaded the gossip columns of the newspapers, including 'Collezioni', a top fashion magazine that is published tomorrow, to announce that I am leaving tomorrow to join a photo big game safari in Kenya's Rift Valley. The rubbish these magazines do publish. I suppose I shall have to give them an exclusive at some future event in my life. I wonder what, when, or even if ever that may be." The radiant smile was back, her laughing eyes teasing. Then she made an exit matching her diva entry, singing that fragment of a familiar tune.

Later, as Galiena had promised, a gardener padded in, in his socks, having left his boots at the door.

He brought Arthur's easel, brushes, paints and his pallet, lumpy with frozen paint. Even the oil in its bottle hardly moved when he shook it. "Well half an hour should do it," Arthur said aloud to himself. "Si?" replied the gardener, as a question, not an agreement. Arthur smiled, and put his thumbs up, a universal gesture indicating in any language that all was well. He was no longer miserable.

When the gardener left, a rather elegant woman came into the room, followed by two men, each of whom carried a painting by Cézanne. Arthur reckoned that the paintings must be originals because they handled them with considerable care. One was a still life with apples, the other, a river scene. Arthur tried several detail studies of the parts of the river scene trying to copy the brushwork that Cézanne had used with such certainty.

Arthur soon became absorbed, losing track of time, but he was aware that someone watched over him because, quite frequently, the door opened and closed without revealing who was there.

Several elegant trays of coffee followed, one after the other, until at last a maid brought in a tray set with a silver teapot around which she had set all things necessary to restore a weary Englishman abroad. "Cook has been into the village, I do hope it is satisfactory," the maid said, in good English. After starting to pour out the tea, Arthur lifted the lid of the teapot. "Oh yes, this will do very well, for now, but would you very kindly, also tactfully, ask cook to use two tea bags in the pot, after first warming the pot with boiling water.

If she can do that, she will make a true English cup of tea. If she tries it herself, which all good cooks must do, she will probably never drink coffee again."

The girl laughed, Arthur, laughed with her, and then he turned back to his painting, but as the day moved on into evening, the light made it impossible to paint.

Later, dining alone in the red room, waited on by a housekeeper, he was lonely. He ate a light supper before going out to the stable yard where he went early to bed. He fell asleep, listening to the radio. The day of concentrated study had tired him.

Chapter 17

The following morning Arthur was still asleep when Peter knocked loud on the door, calling out, "Come on PC Forty Nine, get on parade, the games afoot, the dogs of war have been slipped." The horses and the quiet murmurings of the stable lads had not woken Arthur, nor had the radio that was still playing.

He quickly pulled on his dressing gown, and then let down the electric steps, before opening the door to welcome his friend. "Come in Peter, we do a right good pot of tea here. Sit down over there; you can tell me all about it, while I get dressed." He said all this, while lighting a gas ring, putting on the kettle, and adding another cup and saucer to the tray he had prepared before going to bed.

"Well Gov, what's afoot, Arthur asked, drinking his tea while shaving?" Peter, who was obviously excited, said, "You will remember that I said we must be vigilant, ready to spot the unusual. Well, I was right; would you believe it? An obscure local fashion house has approached the Prince with a proposal.

They want to have access to the Casino, on the first day of the New Year, from eight in the morning to six in the evening. They told him they want to use it as an elegant setting for a photo shoot using some of Italy's top models, ready for their spring collection.

During the day, the casino sleeps; only a minimum of security guards watch the monitor screens. They are offering good money to the public-spirited Prince for his permission. He is, of course, only too happy to be of service.

We are sure that Servient-Higgins is behind the fashion house proposal. It will give them the opportunity to switch their fair copy for what they believe to be the Ingres original."

Arthur asked, "What happens after they have what they believe is the original painting back in their possession.

Peter was less confident with his answer, "Well, we have to hope that no-one in the Servient-Higgins gang will spot that the painting they have nicked is a copy, not the original. I think that is the easy bit.

We have had the Norwegian's copy looked over by experts and even they admit that they would need to do some further examination with X-rays to be sure; even the canvas is the right type and age. The tricky bit is that everyone on our side must play their part correctly. We have to persuade the museum, also the Prince, to keep shtum about the recovery.

The police must do their forensic tests without any leak that they are reopening the case of the missing painting, or of the murder. I am sure the museum will co-operate, they will be too busy to do otherwise.

They will have to raise funds to repay the money Swiss Mobius paid out before they can get the painting back into their collection.

As I told your friend the Contessa, we must wait for an approach from someone offering to bring us the painting in exchange for the reward money. We must play on their greed by weaving into the sting the other stolen paintings, the Velasquez and the Utrillo. By the way, our Norwegian Keating has arrived. He assures me he can have all the necessary adjustments made to his copy, aged, ready for us to fit it to the existing frame, tomorrow afternoon, which is New Year's Eve.

At our suggestion, that includes our picking up the cost, the Prince is arranging for a small New Year thank you party for all the casino staff, including the security guards.

The Prince will hold it in the room where there are slot machines, well away from where the picture is hanging. He is going to take the opportunity to give a short pep talk, the excuse for making attendance compulsory. This will allow our experts to make the switch without fear of interruption.

A blown circuit breaker will take care of the cameras for the time we require, we think about eleven minutes. For what I have already learned about the Prince, he will talk for at least twice the time that we need. After that, all we have to do is to watch. The Prince has co-operated with us by telling his security force that the security camera company are to do maintenance work on the cameras.

That has given my people the chance to do a few modifications to the wiring. It is most important that we do not give Servient-Higgins and his crafty crooks any clue that we are with you and ahead of the game. This supposed photo shoot is such a neat idea it has to be that of the up-market forger. I'm sorry old lad; you will have to stay here and keep your head down. I only came out to keep you informed of what we are doing, but now I feel compelled to suggest that you grasp the greater opportunity that you seem wilfully to reject".

Throughout the whole of the following day, New Year's Eve, Arthur was not a happy man. He had agreed with Peter's idea that he must stay confined to Prince Paolo Borghese's retreat at Castel Gandolfo, for the good reason that Servient-Higgins, given the opportunity, would kill him, or take the easier option, to have him killed.

With time on his hands, Arthur had other thoughts about Peter's idea that Galiena should return to her home, and when there, to act normally. Arthur was not sure that Peter was right. He had only agreed, believing that Servient-Higgins, as all criminals of his kind are selfish, would assume that Doctor Davenport would not have told the Contessa of his suspicion that the stolen Ingres painting might be in the casino.

He thought that the gang involved in the theft would not share a packet of crisps, let alone the reward on offer from the insurance company.

With no Doctor Davenport in his motor home parked behind the Contessa's house, Arthur hoped that Servient-Higgins would assume that he had fled Rome to avoid any further contact with his wife, or Bond, before reporting his unconfirmed find to the insurance company.

However, Arthur was deeply worried that Servient-Higgins's evil criminal mind might think differently.

Because his wife had seen the fraudulent Doctor Davenport with the Contessa in the Prince's casino, he would think that the Contessa must know of the possibility that the painting was not a copy, but the Ingres original.

For Higgins it would be the only possible explanation of how the crooked Doctor Davenport could have ingratiated himself with a person so much his superior in social status. Arthur thought that it would have reassured the Servient-Higgins partnership that when challenged by his wife, the Contessa and he had hurriedly left the casino. Their abrupt departure would have given them the idea that Doctor Davenport was not yet certain of his facts.

Arthur reasoned that Higgins, who did not have charitable thoughts, would assume that the Contessa would drop all association with Doctor Davenport, tell the Prince, and demand a share in the reward. Arthur's thoughts troubled him; if his reasoning was correct, the Contessa was in even greater danger than he was.

It was of little consolation to Arthur when he realised that the sting could still work. Servient-Higgins would think that he had time to take back the original and leave his copy in the frame, even if Doctor Davenport told Swiss Mobius of his unconfirmed suspicions.

He knew that any insurance company would need several days, if not weeks, to verify his claim. The same would apply if the Contessa told the Prince that he was in possession of the original, and not a copy. The Prince would need to consult art experts and lawyers before making any announcement. It did cheer Arthur a little that Higgins would be gloating after he had carried out his planned switch.

The experts would confirm that the painting in the Prince's possession was the fair copy that Faux Art Works had sold him, thus frustrating Doctor Davenport. However, Higgins would not know that Peter and Swiss Mobius had tricked him into switching his copy for their Norwegian's copy, not the original.

Whichever way Arthur thought about it, he was deeply concerned that Peter might have misread the situation. He knew from experience that criminals like Servient-Higgins were not masterminds; they were greedy amoral creatures who thought and reacted in erratic ways unfathomable to normal honest men. Alone at Castel Gandolfo, Arthur was worried; he was not sure that Galiena was safe.

It irritated Arthur that Peter would be at the casino, witnessing the recovery of the original Ingres painting, the object of his quest. He felt side-lined; he was so out of sorts that he could not settle to paint. All he could think about were his plans to leave Rome prior to the Contessa Emilia-Romagna tiring of him, their holiday friendship having run its course.

Although Arthur thought their backgrounds no better or worse than each other, just different, she a vivacious Italian Contessa, he a worn out PC plod, retired, he was convinced that the difference put them too far apart to have any continuing bond.

Theirs was not a case of 'Vive la difference'. He thought that she might put him down more severely than she had slapped down Peter, a past master of flirting, if he presumed to develop their friendship. Arthur felt the difference between them insurmountable.

Because it was New Year, a time for new beginnings, he turned his conviction into resolutions. He resolved to leave the Eternal City, as soon as the Servient-Higgins gang had fallen for the sting.

He resolved to return to Giverny, where he could stay for a while to continue his studies, and to visit his friend Alaine Cartet across the river at Vernon. He resolved to visit Madam Déclâre at restaurant Bien-Découplé, where he would try, using his improved technique, to fashion a better painting of her courtyard.

Arthur knew that he had been happy in both Giverny and Paris. "Now that would be a match, a match of equals," he thought, "Alaine Cartet with Madam Déclâre - Madam Déclâre with Alaine Cartet."

Early on New Year's Eve, Peter came to visit Arthur to tell him that during the Prince's New Year party for his casino staff, experts from the musée d'Orsay had taken the original Ingres painting off the wall and out of its frame.

They had also taken it off its stretchers that they had then used to fit the Norwegian's copy into the frame, reusing the original fasteners in the same places. Peter confirmed that he had dispatched the original, under armed escort, to Paris and that the French police had agreed that before it would be lodged, undisclosed, in the vaults of the Bank of France, DNA tests would be carried out to help with their ongoing investigation into the murder of the museum guard.

Peter's news, though good, did little to assuage Arthur irritation that he had not been part of the action. He was also disconsolate because he had not heard from Galiena.

When Peter left, it was too late to paint. With nothing else to do, he spent the rest of the evening listening to the World Service on his radio. Just before mid-night he felt so fed up that, instead of toasting the New Year with a whisky and water, he made himself a comforting cup of hot drinking chocolate that he drank while sitting up in bed. When a silly thought came to him, he laughed for the first time since Galiena had left Castel Gandolfo to go back to Rome.

He had wondered what his police colleagues would have said if they could have seen Superintendent Arthur Thomas, sitting up in bed drinking cocoa to welcome in the New Year.

The following day, New Year's Day, Arthur felt more settled. He set up his easel, in the Prince's library, determined to work into a better mood by copying details from the Cézanne river scene.

Although he did manage to do some work, the day passed very slowly. He received no call from Peter to keep him informed about the Servient-Higgins operation, and as the day wore on, he became more discouraged because he also had had no word from Galiena.

That she had not spoken to him during the whole of this most important day, not even to wish him a happy New Year. The absence of communication of any kind confirmed his belief that there was no hope for an enduring relationship.

Arthur had dined alone in the small red dining room, before retiring early to Tootsie, parked in the stable yard. He was listening to a concert of choral music when Peter arrived. Only the outward opening door, and his full hands, prevented Peter from bursting in.

In one hand, he held a magnum of rare vintage 'Taittinger' crystal champagne, and in the other hand, two fine cut glass flutes. As soon as Arthur let him in, Peter, full of enthusiasm burst out, "Champagne, a late New Year present for you, from the Contessa. You are commanded to go back to castle Romagna to arrive about middle day tomorrow, but not before. Arthur old chum, it worked like a dream. I watched and heard the whole thing from a van parked in a street two blocks away from the casino. Somehow, the police techno-boffins, working with the Prince's security chaps, had hooked us up to the casino's security cameras. All the cameras were working for us in the van, but in the casino, all the screens were blank. The Prince had let the staff know that the fashion photographer had insisted that the manager switch off all cameras, 'Copyright darling', all that malarkey. They had no idea; it was thrilling, better than watching that film 'Topkapi' or 'Rififi' come to that."

Arthur eventually managed to break into the Peter's excited torrent of news, "How did they get the painting?" Arthur's question did not put Peter off, but he did pause to say, "Hang on a minute, let me get the bottle open, we have a victory to celebrate."

Arthur honoured tradition by touching his glass of champagne with Peter's, but he made no toast, his heart was too heavy, his face grim.

Peter's face had a grin wider than a commedia dell'arte mask. He continued, "The switch was pure scripted camp. The limp wristed director chap took a queer dislike to the painting, 'Take that fat cow down, I can't work with that vulgar pubescent tart staring at me. I want a shot of Nina where she is, against the fountain.' By the way, the Prince's interior decorator had had a nice little water feature built to look as though the water was flowing from the picture. It was in the plot, the excuse to take the painting down. That caused a hiatus, you see, six keyhole sockets secure the frame to the wall, but they have a clever sort of IKEA furniture device that requires a unique irregular five-sided 'Allen' sort of key to unlock them. The so-called security guard, actually an Italian detective, did not know anything about it. I knew where it was, because the day before, we had used it to take the painting down to make our swap. The whole thing was developing into a pantomime. I could see both the man Higgins and the woman neé Servient hovering in the background."

Arthur was surprised, "You saw them both?" "Oh yes," Peter replied, "I don't know which of them is worse, but neither looks good on camera. Ah well, as my granny used to say, 'They don't spoil a couple'. The Prince was in the van watching with us. Consequently, he had to scurry round prepared to act as though he was just calling in to see if they were satisfied with the arrangements. Bless him; he did well. He pottered round, all smiles and Princely courtesy. When they explained the problem, which of course he already knew about, he looked suitably vague, before he said he thought he might be able to find the key. He wandered off to take the key from a wall peg in the maintenance workshop where I told him he would find it. He came pottering back saying, 'Is this the thing you need? I have no idea myself. I am not good with mechanical things'. As soon as they had the key, they had the painting off the wall in no time.

The director had this poor size zero girl, posing by the water feature. The Servient-Higgins couple clearly intended her to distract all eyes. She was damn near as nude as is the girl in the painting. Lying against a wall, we could see a black canvas case, the type artists and photographers use. It had a zip around three sides. In seconds, they had taken out our Norwegian's copy of the painting from the frame and put it into this black case, but not before taking out their fair copy.

They had their copy fixed back in the frame ready to go back on the wall, I swear, all in less than five minutes. Of course, none of the models or crew saw anything of the switch; they were all too engrossed with the shoot and the nude. By God, they knew what they were doing, but they did not have to re-use the stretchers. There were a few distracting histrionics from the model, who complained of the cold. The technicians told me, as gospel truth, that she wanted to go to the loo because the noise of the flowing water made her want to pee. Honestly, we were in hysterics, the photo shoot was a pantomime, but the robbery pure cold professionalism."

Arthur had hardly drunk from his glass of champagne, but Peter was well into his second glass before he continued the story. "They kept up the charade of the photo shoot, on through the lunch hour, not finishing until after three in the afternoon. The black case was one of the last things they took away. The rat-tailed king rat Servient-Higgins carried it. They may be a murderous gang, but their attention to detail is admirable. We had a camera covering the street in front of the casino that enabled us to watch them put the case containing our copy into a Volvo estate, driven by that chap Bond. Oh how I wish that we had been able to hear their self-congratulatory gloating when they drove away."

"Is all that true?" queried Arthur. "As I live and breathe," Peter chortled, "We can both breathe a bit easier now the heist has gone to their plan and the sting to our satisfaction.

We are into the waiting game now. Oh! I nearly forgot; Mario sent you this map. With it, even you should be able to find your way back to the Contessa's house tomorrow.

I am sorry that she has not called you, be assured that was down to me. I persuaded her, with difficulty, not to call you. I feared that the Mafia might have a trace on her phone line, or even on the mobile phone that I gave you. I could not take the risk.

Now I am going to have more of that champagne, if you will stir yourself. I have my driver with me, so I reckon I can do half the bottle even though she sent you a magnum. Let's just listen to the music and get a bit sloshed. We deserve no less for our efforts."

The following morning Arthur rose at about seven ready to make careful preparation for the day. Before putting on his suit, he pressed the trousers using the iron he had brought from home.

He put on the shirt with cuffs secured by the cuff links Galiena had given him. When he insisted, that he wanted to clean his shoes himself, a maid, brought shoe cleaning polish and brushes with which he buffed his shoes up to parade standard.

On his way from Castel Gandolfo to the Contessa's house, he stopped at a supermarket to stock up with supplies sufficient for several days.

Arthur was intent on keeping to his New Year resolution to give up hope of a future with the women that he knew he loved, hoping that the intensity of his feeling might fade with time. He planned that, as soon as he met the Contessa, he would thank her for her help in recovering the painting, and then, without giving her any suggestion of his reasons, he would tell her that he was leaving Rome, to return to Giverny.

Unknown to Arthur, events were already happening that would dictate, for both him, and Galiena, a different destiny.

Chapter 18

Just before noon, Arthur drove into the tree-lined avenue where the Contessa's home lay well protected in the middle of other grand mansions. Arthur found it easy to park fifty meters short of the Contessa's gate as all the houses had long drives, and parking spaces, off the avenue. He did not wish to drive into the grounds of the Contessa's home, because he wanted least fuss when leaving.

He walked steadily up to the Contessa's gates, but found them closed against him. Before he pushed the button on the device that had voice contact with the house, Arthur thought he saw a bulky shadow of a man, wearing a hat, move across the Blue Room window. It made his flesh creep. Galiena, Mario or Maria could not have cast such a shape. Had it been anyone looking out for his arrival there would have been instant activity. The gate would have opened; Galiena would have come out to meet him.

He did not know why, but he felt sure that something was wrong, very wrong. It brought back his doubts about Peter's idea that Galiena would be safe if she returned home to act normally. He walked back to Tootsie, as quickly as his old bones could manage.

Deeply worried, he sat in the driving seat thinking hard, trying to work out his best option. He thought it a minor worry that he would make a fool of himself, if all things turned out to be normal in the house, and Arthur's instinct told him that something about the way the shadow moved was threatening.

His long service as a policeman sparked in him memories of how he had found in such minor oddities in movement, voice inflection, facial expression, even inappropriate dress, the first clue that after investigation had solved crimes and convicted villains.

The shadow of the hat convinced Arthur that the Contessa's life was in great danger. No invited guest ever wore a hat in Galiena's house.

One of the servants would have taken hat, coat, or umbrella from any guest before showing them to any reception room. He was now sure that the base mind of Servient Higgins had decided that the Contessa Emilia Romagna's only reason to associate with Doctor Davenport was that he had told her about the Ingres painting.

He decided, fool or not, to investigate before making any attempt to contact Galiena on foot, in Tootsie, or by phone.

To make sure that no one in the Contessa's house or grounds could see Tootsie, he reversed twenty meters then drove off the avenue, though the open gates of the property next-door to the Contessa's home.

A brass plate on the gate pillar indicated that the house was the headquarters of an insurance company. He drove, unchallenged, along the drive until he could park by the side of the house, out of site from the Contessa's house. His whole body tingled, stimulated by fear he could not explain, but he felt compelled to press on.

He stepped out to walk to the back of the house, where he met his first real, not imagined, problem.

A five-metre high-whitewashed wall topped with razor wire faced him. The fabled Arthurian impenetrable barrier of thorns that Arthur had often thought of being between him and Galiena was now a present reality.

It appeared to Arthur that the insurance company head office was empty. He assumed that the staff must still be on holiday and all security measures automatic, and he was relieved that he could not see any external surveillance cameras.

It did not take him long to go back to Tootsie, and then drive to the rear of the house where he parked up close alongside the wall that was the boundary separating the insurance company grounds from the Contessa's extensive property. Despite his difficulty with mobility, caused by his age, compounded with the residual effects of his minor stroke, by using the access ladder fitted to all Hymer motor homes, he managed to climb onto the roof, of what he imagined to be his siege tower.

Even from the roof, he still could not get over the wall. "Now what should a Grey Haired Knight do?" Arthur whispered to himself, using the sobriquet his friend Geraint had suggested when he and his friends decided to seek adventure. "This is a bit too much of a jump for your old pins. This is more of a job for a Lancelot or a Bedivere, not poor old broken down grey haired Arthur Thomas."

He climbed back down the ladder to get his sleeping bag. After a quick search through some out buildings, he found an empty wooden crate that had held a dozen bottles of wine.

Back on top of his siege tower, by standing on the crate, he was able to look over the wall. His view brought both frustration and what he hoped would bring him luck.

The frustration was that he could clearly see a double extending ladder that would easily reach the top of the wall, hooked horizontally to the wall of the garage block facing him. The thing that he saw that he thought might bring him luck was a deep heap of garden compost on the Contessa's side of the wall.

He climbed back down from Tootsie's roof to move her so that she was immediately opposite the heap of compost. Back on the roof again, trembling and seriously out of breath, he stood on the wooden crate to spread his sleeping bag across the razor wire.

By compressing the razor wire, followed by a supreme effort, he managed to heave his right leg over to straddle the wall. Taking a huge risk of losing his balance and toppling over backwards, or headfirst into the compost, Arthur swung his left leg over the wall until he was sitting, facing into the Contessa's grounds, more than three metres above the heap of compost.

His hands and wrists were bleeding where he had touched the razor wire in his clumsy manoeuvre. From his sitting position, the razor wire prevented him from turning to hang from the wall before letting go. Left with no alternative, he pushed himself off the sleeping bag, hoping that the compost would provide a soft landing.

He landed shaken, but unhurt, well up to his thighs in leaf mould and grass compost. It took him a little while to catch his breath before he recovered sufficiently to stamp the soft decomposed vegetation from his shoes and brush it off his trousers with his bleeding hands. "Damn and blast, I have just polished my shoes and pressed my trousers," he said to himself, "I'm going to look all sorts of a fool if everything in the house is normal. Here I am, covered in blood mud and white wash, in my best, my only suit and bleeding as though I have cut my wrists to make an end of it. Well, no turning back, at least there is no moat to cross."

The nearer he got to the servants entrance, the less certain he became that something was amiss until a stomach churning sight confirmed the worst of his fears.

Outside the door, by his kennel, Mario's wonderful little guard dog Attimo lay dead.

There was no doubt that Attimo was dead. Someone had cut the little fellows throat. He lay, callously discarded, in a pool of congealing blood. Arthur's trembling had increased to shaking.

He was sick with fear and worry, but stupidly relived that he had not made a fool of himself. He knew that he was standing into danger. However, because he was desperately concerned about Galiena's safety, he carefully worked his way along, close to the house wall, working his way towards the kitchen door through which Mario had taken him into the house.

He made sure to duck under each window that he passed until nearing the door he could hear voices.

He cursed under his breath that he did not know the language, but he did recognize fear. Arthur knew that fear speaks in tongues to all with experience who listen.

The fear was in Maria's voice. There was another voice, a thin cruel male voice. It was not much more than a sneer with the occasional sharp word or two. Arthur took them to be some rude Italian expression for 'shut up'.

It was clear, without looking through the window, that whoever was speaking had Maria restrained and little dog's mutilated body showed that the man had a knife, at least.

It was evident to Arthur that the man was not alone and that the intruders were assassins, not simply robbers or kidnappers.

He knew that modern assassins carry guns. He was also sure that somewhere in the building, others had the Contessa restrained. It did not make sense that it was a kidnap. Kidnappers would have taken the Contessa away, in a fast car, as soon as they had seized her.

There would be no point in leaving a guard on the servants for more than a few minutes, for even if they got themselves clear from their restraints, they would be too late to raise an effective alarm.

It was obvious to Arthur that whoever and how many the assassins were, he was their quarry and the Contessa their sacrificial lure.

Whether he took the bait, or not, he felt sure they would kill her and then come after him. He felt the evil genius of Terrance Servient-Higgins behind this dreadful situation. He reasoned that Higgins must have made a contract with the Mafia to kill Doctor Davenport, his other self, to stop him being a witness against 'Faux Art Works' and preventing their plans to take back their investment.

"Bugger reasonable force," Arthur thought, "I will first have to seriously incapacitate the man holding Maria and then decide what to do next." Over-riding all his thoughts was what he might do to anyone who harmed the Contessa.

Because he carried no weapon to overcome an armed man, and because his love for Galiena allowed no turning back, fear weakened him. Fear gripped his heart, it churned his stomach, and it raised his pulse until it banged inside his head. He was so high on adrenalin and endorphins that his brain played tricks; he began to hallucinate.

The strange man with an ageless bearded face he had met on Halter Moor and who he had dreamt of after the inaugural dinner of the Grey Haired Knights, still dressed from head to foot in green, still wearing the wide stitch brimmed hat, appeared directly in front of him. Obviously excited, the fellow was hopping, from one foot to the other, skipping backwards, leading him towards and pointing at the old stone house next to the stables, while still chewing on the ends of his moustache.

Arthur had never forgotten his strange meeting on Halter Moor or the words the old man had shouted to him in his dream; word that he had never been able to make sense of, but in his head, he recited them again, as he had done many times before. *'If you can penetrate the impenetrable thorn, draw base metal from a stone to fashion a sword, then fight like a dragon' you will free one lady and bind another'.* Arthur shook his head; the vision was gone, but it had taken away with it all his fear and weakness.

He straightened his back, and said to himself with quiet composed detached determination, "Arthur old boy, you are over the razor wire, the modern day impenetrable forest of thorn. Lead is base metal. Old buildings have lead pipes. A lead pipe used to be the favoured cosh of many a vicious thug before they tooled up with guns. That's my best chance." He made it to the old stone cottage beyond the garage and stable-block without evidence of anyone noticing.

As though in answer to his prayers, because he was praying hard, he found a lead pipe, thicker than his thumb, sticking out of the stone wall by at least half a metre. No longer connected to a pump, or to a tap, it stretched out over a stone trough. The adrenalin surging through his body did not fail him. Like Samson in the temple, he felt the raw strength of his youth restored. Even so, it took him a huge effort to pull the pipe free from the wall, but he knew he had drawn a sword from stone.

Arthur whispered to himself, "Right lad, you now have a weapon, not quite Excalibur, but good enough for its purpose."

He took a few minutes to get his heavy noisy breathing under control before he worked his way back to the door where he could hear the man guarding Maria whistling through his teeth.

He could not believe his luck, the man was whistling the Italian tune that Arthur, and everyone in Britain with a television set knew as, 'Just one Cornetto'. Thinking that a pebble slew Goliath, he picked up three pebbles from the ground before pressing himself against the wall on the hinge side of the door.

He then began to whistle, very quietly, taking up the tune. Many times Arthur echoed the same few bars before he heard a chair scrape and someone come towards the door. The man had stopped whistling. He grunted, three times, what Arthur assumed was Italian for, "Who's there?" Arthur continued to whistle.

The door opened slowly. First a gun barrel appeared, then a white hand, followed by a shiny black coat sleeve. To Arthur it was like the head of a snail emerging from its shell. Using his left hand Arthur threw a pebble across the door opening. His right arm was aching. For more than a minute, he had held it aloft, ready to strike. The noise of the pebble brought a sleek greased head of black hair into view. Finally, Arthur could see his target, the thin neck that held the hated head. For a second, all the time that Arthur needed, the head was looking towards where the pebble had fallen.

The man had made two fatal mistakes. First, because he was nervous, he had come out slowly, stooping. Secondly, he had fallen for the old trick to make him look the wrong way. Arthur made no mistake. He did not hesitate, or falter. He did not fail. His blow was savage. It was final. The man pitched forward, already dead. The only sound he made was the crunch of his lifeless body on the gravel.

Arthur did not need the police surgeon to tell him that he had killed the man. He had broken his neck, as cleanly as if a hangman had done it with a rope, an eight-foot drop and Pierpont's special insert in the noose.

Arthur had no regrets. He said quietly, "That one is for you Attimo." After picking up the gun, he unconsciously swept his index fingers across his moustache before he went quietly into small room from which there were doors to the kitchens and a green baize door connecting with the corridor leading to the reception rooms.

He put his index finger, vertically across his lips, to make sure that Maria did not cry out. The intruders had tied her hands together and her ankles to a kitchen chair. She was justifiably terrified. In a very low voice she whispered, "Mario, he is through there in the kitchen, but be careful." Arthur went quietly, cautiously, through to the kitchen. Mario's captors made Arthur acutely aware that he was dealing with criminals who dealt in fear.

They had blindfolded him by using a black woollen balaclava mask, put on backwards, and taped it to his neck. They had also gagged him with a woman's nylon stocking. They had made him stand on a kitchen chair, his hands behind his back, and ankles bound with gaffer tape. Around his neck, Arthur could see a noose, made from a thin climber's rope. They had tied the rope over a roof beam, leaving just six inches of slack. Arthur had never seen such cruelty; any loss of balance would have caused Mario to fall off the chair.

The short drop would not have broken the rope, or his neck to cause instant death. The noose would have cut deep and strangled him, slowly, to a painful choking death.

Arthur spoke quietly. "Mario, it's me, Arthur, I will get you down but first I must free your hands so that you can hold onto me.

It did not take Arthur long to find a sharp kitchen knife, one of many in the cook's wooden block, but it took much longer than he hoped, to cut Mario free. He was frightened that he might knock him off the chair while he climbed, with difficulty, onto another chair in order to reach up to cut the rope.

Once free, Mario just nodded to Arthur. Using the same knife Mario took less than half that time to free his wife Maria. Arthur asked, in a whisper, "Have either of you got a mobile phone?" Mario shrugged, "Sorry, they took them both, they also ripped out the wires to both the land lines." Arthur who was gaining confidence spoke softly to Mario, "Get mine; it is on the dashboard of Tootsie. She's parked against the party wall, at the back the house next door, that way." Arthur indicated the direction, adding, "Mario, we can't risk you running round the front of the house. I saw that you have a ladder on the garage wall. Use it to get over the wall onto Tootsie. Put the ladder where I have left my sleeping bag but take care of the razor wire, it's bloody sharp. When you have the phone, don't ring the police, but ring Peter. He plumbed his number in under Bainbridge. Tell him what is happening. He has influence. He will know what to do."

With Mario away, Maria was almost hysterical, but with great difficulty she was finally able to tell Arthur that two men, both with guns, had taken the Contessa to the Blue Room.

Maria was crying when she told Arthur that the men said that she would be untied, when Doctor Davenport arrived in his wagon, and that she must take him straight from the front door to the Blue Room.

They had told her that Carlo would be watching her, gun in hand. If she did anything else, or said a word out of place, they had promised to kill the Contessa, then Mario, then her. Through tears, despite the terror that was shaking her, Maria was able to tell Arthur that the men had said that they only wanted to take Doctor Davenport away for discussions.

Maria asked, "Mr Thomas, I don't understand, who please is this Doctor Davenport?" Maria was still shaking, when she said. "They are Mafioso; they will kill us all; it is what they do. Mario was out when they burst in. When he came back, he walked right into them. He did not have a chance to do anything because one of them had the barrel of his gun in my mouth. They are bastards; they made me take of my stocking to gag poor Mario. That Carlo was laughing when he killed little Attimo here in the hallway, in front of us both, it was horrible." Arthur tried to reassure her, "These men are useless, no good to society, they have no manners; we must teach them to behave. Don't worry Maria, we will pull through, Mario will be back soon. Where are cook, the housekeepers and the rest of the staff?"

"Cook has taken her assistant shopping, Martha and Sophia are on day off, and I don't know where the gardener is." Mario said this quietly, as he came silently into the room. "I spoke with Peter, the cavalry will be here very soon, but I have told them they must not approach until we signal that it is safe."

Arthur, though breathing heavily, looked ten years younger than he did ten minutes ago. His mood had changed to excitement. "Good, make sure Maria keeps an eye out for cook, we don't want any kitchen clatter to disturb our visitors.

Have they anyone outside?" "No, there is no car either. Presumably they planned to use your little van as your hearse."

Arthur's mood change had come unexpectedly when he remembered that the ageless bearded man of his dream and hallucination had told him to fight like a dragon.

He realised that meant he must fight with fire, and he knew how he could do it. He asked Maria to bring him four large balloon brandy glasses and two bottles of Strega.

Now that Mario was with her, she had complete control of her nerves. It took a minute or two, but she brought him a tray with the four large balloon shaped glasses and two bottles of Strega. Arthur looked at the bottles and smiled.

He then said, quietly to himself, "Oh you little beauties, Liquore Strega Superior, the Prince's special brew, sent to the Contessa for Christmas, yet all the better to burn them with."

He poured all the sticky yellow liquid, from both bottles, into a pan.

He switched on one of the rings of the eight-burner gas oven and heated the liqueur over a high heat, until at its edges there were tiny bubbles spurting blue flame as they burst. Mario was quick to spot Arthur's intention and heated the four balloon glasses and the tray over the other burners.

Mario was whispering, "The Carabinieri will be here in a few minutes, leave it to them for God's sake. The mafia hit men holding the Contessa are professional killers." But, Mario could do nothing to stop Arthur. It was though he had cast aside a cloak of old age.

He was young again, all disability put aside, with fear only acting as a spur. Arthur filled each hot glass about quarter full with the hot liqueur He poured the rest into the tray. "Quick Mario a lighter or a match," but it was Maria who passed him a lighter from out of a drawer under the table. She also understood what Arthur was going to do.

When Arthur tried the lighter, it lit a big flame at the first click. Arthur gave the gun he had taken from the dead man to Mario, before he said, "Right Mario, safety catch off, free to fire, but stay outside the door for now, but be ready to come in fast when the fun starts. You know what to do."

Holding the tray of drinks that was too hot for comfort with one hand, high in front of his face, his other hand behind his back, holding the lighter, he whispered "Mario the door." Standing back, Mario pushed open one side of the Blue Room doors.

Arthur walked in steadily, purposefully, trying to look every inch the English butler. "Contessa, before your guests take me away, I thought that you would like to offer them a little warming Strega on this miserable cold day."

He quickly moved between the two gunmen and Galiena placing the tray on the table, as near to the men as possible. "Gentlemen, Strega Superior" he sang out. At the same time, using the lighter, he lit the hot liqueur on the tray. It flamed up, with licking blue flames, as he knew it would, igniting the hot over proof Strega in the balloon glasses.

Without a second's hesitation, using the back of each hand, he knocked two of the flaming glasses, one each onto the laps of the gunmen. To make double sure, he then threw the flaming tray with the other two glasses straight at them. The draft, caused by the sudden movement fanned the flames that barked into a minor inferno. One of the gunmen did get a shot away, but as Arthur always said, with satisfaction, when retelling the tale, "It discharged harmlessly, through the assassin's groin."

Maria, who had followed her husband, quickly took the Contessa out of the room. Mario was covering the two men with the gun. To Arthur's amazement, Maria returned with a large old-fashioned enamel jug full of water that she carefully poured over a patch of smouldering carpet, ignoring the assassins who were still burning, and still screaming what Arthur took to be bad words and violent threats. The gardener followed, shouting angrily what Arthur thought might be obscenities of a higher order, while jabbing at the two prone bodies with the most frightening weapon of all, a two-pronged pitchfork.

Mario told Arthur that, amongst other things, he was telling him, "The bastards had me tied up in my shed with the cooks and Sophia, and that a recognisance party of the carabinieri had only just set them free."

Through the window, Arthur was relieved to see two armoured vehicles of the Carabinieri at the gate, with men deploying in military good order.

When he was satisfied that there was no further danger, he left the room on the way to the kitchen. Mario had taken possession of both obvious guns that the assassins had been pointing at the Contessa.

He had also searched the two villains, who he now had lying prone, face down on the floor. Mario's search produced one other very small handgun, and a flick-knife. The gunmen were both whimpering, obviously in much pain caused by their burns; one, suffering from his self-inflicted serious bullet wound.

A few moments later, Maria, who was crying, but now calmly, came to Arthur. She dipped a little old-fashioned curtsy before she said, "Signore Arthur Thomas, the Contessa is waiting for you in the music room." She then lost control, sobbing, "Oh sir, please, please, oh forgive me, go to her, but don't be so very bloody English. It is not right, it is cruel."

Before going to Galiena, Arthur held his wrist and the back of his hand under cold running water to cool the area where splashes of burning Strega had burnt through his skin into his flesh. He covered the burns, and deep cuts from the razor wire with a small hand towel soaked in cold water. Satisfied that it was the best he could do for now, he followed Maria slowly down the long hall to the music room.

Before leaving Rome, his job done, Arthur was still determined to say goodbye, without a fuss, and leave without explanation. He knew that he did not have the words to explain his fears for their future. Maria stood aside at the music room door. Arthur straightened up to his full height, pulled back his shoulders, and then with his usual habit when nervous, he smoothed his moustache with a quick sweep of his forefingers.

Thus prepared, after taking a deep breath, he knocked quietly on the great double door. After a brief pause, although there was no answer, he opened the door, and stepped just inside the room where he stopped, still unsure of what to say. He felt awkward holding the wet kitchen towel to his wrist, even though it eased the pain. Water, made pink with his blood, was dripping onto the polished parquet floor. Maria closed the doors behind him.

"Hello you" was all he managed to say. Galiena, who was standing in the middle of the large room, her body tense, her hands clenched tight, was crying quietly. "Oh Arthur, I have six names for you to choose from, also an ancient three word title. All that you can say, after all that has happened, is 'Hello you'. Is that all that you can say to a poor wretched woman, whose heart is breaking? Is that all you can say, a man who risked almost certain death by putting your own precious self between those horrid, cruel men with guns and my poor body? Why is this man afraid to use my name, afraid to touch me, afraid even to look at me? How is it that the man I know to be my brave chief of police is afraid to tell me that he loves me? Surely I cannot be wrong."

The gentle tears had turned to deep racking sobs. After an effort to stem the sobs and tears, she lifted her head to speak again. "I find that I must now be strong. I must speak for us both. I know that you love me, as I love you. If you do not take hold of me now, look at me as you once did in Andorra, after our coffee went cold, when we drank Strega together, then kiss me, and tell me that you love me, I shall have no reason to live. I shall die."

Arthur had withstood the traumas of killing a man, the assassin's threats, the gunfire, the burns, all with an apparent cool detachment, but her declaration of her love for him, with her added certainty that he loved her, broke both his determination and reason to leave.

Her passion exposed his emotions. Reason and logic did not have time to get in the way. For the first time since he fell in love with Galiena, Arthur Thomas got it right.

He crossed the room, to take hold of both of her hands in both of his. He looked straight into her eyes, willing her to believe. In a calm regulated voice, a tone lower than usual, he conjured fragments from romantic poetry, music, and prose that had inspired and comforted him during his long lonely watch since Jenny had died. He used them to compose the most important, the most assured speech of his life.

"Angelina Galiena Elizabetha Ruth Sophia, Vercente - Contessa Emilia-Romagna, I have loved you from that very first moment when I heard your spell binding voice behind me simply say, 'She is lovely isn't she'. That was even before I had turned my old grey haired head to look at you. What I saw then, I knew to be the most radiant, perfumed, elegant, exciting women I had ever seen, who in an instant, with sparkling deep brown eyes, teased out and took away my past. I was unprepared. I was therefore honest and true when I mumbled, really only to myself, but words I am glad that you heard, 'No it is you who are lovely'. I was enchanted. No, it was more than that. You are to me the reason for what I have been, and for what I am to be. The earth did not just move, the whole world stumbled and tumbled from its steady progress. The universe imploded. The forces induced in me obliterated my past, my present and any idea of what may be my future. That moment of new creation formed me into a new self, one whose total being is entirely, eternally yours. You have no cause to die. God and Merlin were with us this day. You must know that if I had died, but saved you, I would have been content at heaven's gate"

Then he took her in his arms, winced as his burns caught on his sleeve. He held her firm against his chest. He kissed her, but not on the lips, only on the top of her forehead. To kiss her on the lips would have meant pushing her away from him. He thought that unwise. Suddenly, Galiena felt his whole body give one great shuddering tremor, like a dog, after swimming, shakes off water. It was as though all the points in his body, stretched by events, suddenly broke free of their constraints.

Although he still held her firm against his chest, in solid contact, she now felt their bodies meld. The stresses broken by that great shudder were not those caused by his confrontation with assassins; they had gone when Mario had disarmed the gunmen.

The more severe remaining tensions, now shaken off, had been those caused by his self-imposed restraints, the attempt to deny his love for the woman he now held close, his conviction that he was not good enough for her, his fear of rejection.

He had broken all the taboos. He had looked into her eyes, he had declared his love, and he had called her by her many names and her title. He had embraced her, he had kissed her; simple acts of a simple man, made glorious when Galiena responded with insight, whispering, "Good; my true dearest love, all your imagined causes for separation have gone, we are already one. The formalities can follow in good time. Once, many years ago, a gypsy woman told me that I would marry one of her kind."

A loud double knock on the door failed to separate them. After a short pause, Mario came in carrying nothing more than a beaming smile. Maria, his wife, followed carrying a tray, complete with the silver tea set. Looking at the couple, still locked in their close embrace, Mario ignored protocol, "Well thank goodness for that; about time too. You two have been driving poor Maria silly, 'Will he, has he, has she, will she,' I think you both need a cup of tea after all the excitement."

Galiena spoke quietly, "Thank you both, but not for me, not just now." Turning to Maria, "Will you please take me to my dressing room where you must sort me out, I am a total wreck. I do not want my fiancée to see me like this."

Arthur who was delighted, said, "Well now, this time I am truly compromised, in front of two witnesses."

After Maria had taken the Contessa away, Mario poured and sweetened tea for them both. He told Arthur that ambulances had taken away the live assassins but the Carabinieri had put the corpse into a body bag that they had thrown into the boot of one of their cars.

However, he warned Arthur that they would come back later to take statements. He then said, "That was one hell of a stunt you pulled in there, with the Strega. I hope that you know of and believe the legend about the witches of Benevento. Couples, who drink Strega, while looking into each other's eyes, unite forever. Wherever did you dream up the fire bomb idea?" Mario asked this with so much admiration in both expression and voice, that it almost amounted to awe.

Arthur laughed, "Well I suppose it was from one of my favourite authors, Nevil Shute. It was in a book of his about French partisans going after German 'rambouts' with a flame-thrower. He said that the greatest fear that men have is of fire. I thought that if I could upgrade the Molotov to the Giuseppe Alberti Strega cocktail, we might have a chance. The witches' brew of Benevento is better than petrol or vodka, it is sticky, it clings; it burns deep."

Arthur never told anyone, not even Galiena, about the strange man with the wide brimmed hat, who first came to him on Halter Moor and later in a dream, even before he knew what was to be his quest; the stranger who had appeared to him again on that terrible day. It was all too real, too difficult to explain.

He was however convinced that hallucination, dream or manifestation, it was the magician Merlin, sent by King Arthur, to keep alive the spirit of Camelot.

271

Chapter 19

After Mario had cleaned up the razor wire cuts and burns on Arthur's hands and wrists, applied dressings, and made a neat job with sterile white bandages, he left him alone in the music room. This tactful withdrawal gave Arthur time to adjust, time to reflect.

He was now sure that all would be well between him and Galiena. She had made it possible with her declaration, 'My true dearest love, all the divisions and separation have gone; we are already one. The formalities can follow in good time'. He recited the words, over and again, determined to believe and commit them to perfect memory.

It was more than an hour before Galiena returned, but Arthur could see that she had spent the time well. She had obviously bathed and Maria had done her hair into a chignon. She was wearing a sheer silk Kimono style housecoat and very high stiletto heeled red shoes. Each shoe had a jewelled strap, crafted in the form of a snake, spiralling around the ankle and half way up her calf. Her ankles were as trim as were those of a teenage bobby-soxer.

She moved in a cloud of her perfume, the name of which Arthur still did not know, and would probably never know, but one that his memory would never forget. All signs of stress and tears had gone. Her eyes sparkled with mischief. "Just look at your shoes, look at the mud on my beautiful Tien Tsin Carpet. Not only are you content to burn holes in the Blue Room carpet you seem intent on turning my music room into a ploughed field. Now come here you big tall handsome man, bend a little, to give your fiancée a proper kiss, this time on the lips, please."

Then her mood changed; she became earnest. "Now, just for a few minutes, we must be serious. You must tell me why you erected so many barriers, why was it that you thought I might reject you, even though I gave you so many clues that any advance would be welcomed. Did you not recognise the tune I kept humming?"

Trying to look contrite Arthur stared at the floor, "Well no, not really, what was the tune?" Galiena went to an old-fashioned record player set on an occasional table. When she played the vinyl record, he immediately knew the tune. He sang along with the chorus he remembered from junior school. 'Da de diddle dum dee - diddle dum day-and she ran away with the gypsy oh'. They kissed again before Galiena pressed for an answer. "Come now, and be honest as I know you are; tell me."

Arthur took her hand to spin her around under his arm, as though they were dancing to an old-time valeta, "Well, look at you; a stylish city girl, with a title, well connected and clearly comfortably off. You have this wonderful house, loyal servants, and how many cars I don't know. Look at me; years older than you, with precious little to offer, a retired provincial policeman, living like a gypsy in a shed on wheels, 'Tootsie', my less than 'Winnebago'. My certain fear was that you, an Italian catholic, would not, could not, have a serious relationship with me, an irregular English protestant. Yesterday, I had convinced myself that these many differences would, inevitably lead to a great deal of unhappiness for me, perhaps even some slight regret for you. I had resolved to leave Rome. I had stocked Tootsie up with provisions for three days, sufficient to get me part way to Paris. Now I cannot go. If I did leave you, I would be desolate, I would founder."

Galiena took and kissed his bandaged hands before leading him to one of the deep cushioned window seats from where it was possible to look out over the ornamental garden. "Is that it, all of it?"

Galiena asked, tears back in her eyes. "I should not have been cruel. I should not have teased my prince of policeman, my shining silver haired knight. I should have understood. Please forgive your silly goose Galiena. Arthur, please remember that I will always want you to call me Galiena. It is my name, but you must always think of me as Ruth; my fourth baptised and confirmed Christian name. For between us there shall be no difference, no separation. Thy people shall be my people and thy God my God. Yes, I am a Roman and a catholic, but only because I was born here in Rome into a Roman family. You are an English protestant, but only because you were born in England of protestant parents. There is only one God, a forgiving loving God; he understands.

We shall be married in a civil ceremony. Later, I will ask yet another cousin to bless our union in some small church in the Vatican. To make sure that our vows will be acceptable and true, we will go to Yorkshire, where you must arrange for an Anglican bishop to give us his blessing. It must be a bishop, for parity, but we must persuade him to leave his cathedral to bless our marriage. I hope that it will be in a small church in a country village. We will live our lives together, part gypsy people, part Yorkshire folk; part Emilia Romagna of Italy's faded aristocracy. As gypsies, you will sell your paintings. I will tell fraudulent fortunes for small pieces of silver. In Yorkshire, we will eat roast beef with pudding, drink tea in cups and beer in jugs. In Italy, we will eat pasta with olives, drink espresso coffee in demitasse cups and wine from Piedmont, Tuscany and our own Zini Vini, in crystal glasses. Very good; that is the rest of our lives planned and assured."

She kissed him lightly on his forehead to seal the agreement in which Arthur was the silent but willing partner.

Arthur was still very serious, "Galiena, today, for the first time in my life I killed a man. I did it deliberately. I also intentionally seriously hurt two other men. The Carabinieri will soon come back to interview and almost certainly arrest me for unlawful killing and for failing to use reasonable force to detain the two men I prematurely tried to cremate. I don't know the law here in Italy, but had I done such terrible things in England, I would be in serious trouble."

The Contessa's expression was equally serious. "Yes, Maria told me that the man they called Carlo was dead. I do not think there will be too much fuss. If you had waited for the Carabinieri, they would have stopped you from taking part. It is almost certain that the men with guns who were holding me, to lure you in to their trap, would have killed me first, then Mario and Maria. They did not wear any masks, only dreadful hats. They would have died in a hail of Carabinieri bullets, but not before they had killed or wounded some of those sent to rescue us. Arthur, do not worry, all three were sinful men sent by wicked people to do an evil deed, in exchange for money."

There were several gentle knocks on the door before, after a nudge and a nod from the mistress of the house, Arthur took the hint to call out for the first time as master, "Come in." Maria opened the door to announce, all of a giggle, "Mr Peter Bainbridge is here sir." Galiena whispered, "Ask her to show him into the Blue Room, we will meet him there"

Arthur's reply was embarrassingly shy, "Oh, er, thank you Maria, please show Peter, sorry I mean Mr Bainbridge, into the er, Blue Room. Yes that's right." "Yes sir, that I have already done, he is waiting for you.

Once again, Maria dipped a curtsy to Arthur. Galiena was on her feet before Arthur had moved, "My! You have made an impression. I am surprised that she did not call you 'Mi-lord." The window seat was quite low, and without Arthur noticing, Galiena helped him to his feet.

Maria positively skipped down the corridor to open both doors to the Blue Room, announcing, as formally as a Guild Hall Toast Master, "Mr Arthur Thomas and the Contessa Emilia Romagna.

The two lovers, hand in hand, smiled at each other before going together through the wide double doors. Peter rose from his chair, started towards them with an outstretched hand, but then he paused, blinking, "Arthur, Contessa, what is going on? Before letting me in the armed carabinieri at the gate told me that there had been a rumpus, but have I missed something more important?"

Galiena, turning to Arthur on tiptoe whispered in his ear, "Give me a kiss." Arthur grinned, "Alright, but just a peck you wanton woman." A peck was all she got. Galiena whispered again, "I don't let strange men kiss me; you must tell him we are engaged to be married."

A blush showed though Arthur's ruddy complexion, "Oh yes, of course, wonderful, absolutely."

Arthur smoothed his moustache, as he always did when nervous. "Peter, my very old friend, I am pleased, no proud to announce, er, indeed er, in fact, to confirm, that Angelina Galiena Elizabetha Ruth Sophia Vercente - Contessa Emilia Romagna and I, er, well we are engaged to be married. I shall require your support when we have our Roman civil wedding blessed in Yorkshire."

Peter collapsed back into a deep leather chair. For quite some time he said not a word, sure that there was more to come. He was so shocked that he even forgot to congratulate them. All he could manage was the irrelevant question, "Who burnt the carpet?" Galiena was so excited when she told him what had happened that Peter began to believe that there were two incidents, not one, because Galiena exaggerated the part Arthur had played, while Arthur kept insisting, "It was nothing, really."

Telling the story jogged Arthur's memory, reminding him that that he had left 'Tootsie' parked behind the next-door insurance company office. Despite his injuries and Galiena suggesting that he should ask Mario to bring his Floozie back, he left Galiena with Peter while he went to recover what he now thought of as his motorised siege engine.

With Arthur out of the room, Galiena immediately took up her story. She took Peter's hand in hers, and spoke very seriously. "Peter, I think that you realised when we met at Castel Gandolfo that I hoped for more than friendship with your friend. In fact, I fell in love with him the moment I first saw him. You may never understand this, but today Arthur took on the mantle of a warrior king. His achievements when he faced almost certain death to save my life made him more than a king; to me he is a god. I shall live my life for him. Whatever happens, I will stay alive to be with my lord until death takes him away from me. He must never be alone again. When the dread day comes that I have to bury him, I will have nothing left to live for. I will honour his memory until I follow gently on, to where he will be waiting."

Peter was embarrassed at such powerful outward expressions of love, devotion and fealty. He was unsure how to respond. All that he did manage was a typical English understatement. "Just be happy together."

After a pause he said, "You must come to visit my home in England. My wife Anne will not rest until she has met you.

She recently tried to match Arthur with one of her glamorous lady friends, but Arthur fled the field as fast as a man chased by a raging bull would need to do. I thought he would remain unattached for the rest of his life. Today has been his double lucky day. He is lucky to be alive and lucky that the trauma broke down the barriers between you, but I am afraid that not all is good. "Peter continued, "I must warn you that Arthur is still in mortal danger, even though the horrible couple Servient-Higgins have left Rome. For as long as they believe him to be alive, they know that Doctor Edward Davenport has them stymied. They cannot sell the painting that we have duped them into believing is the original, nor will they be able to claim the reward money. By the un-natural mores of their world, they have no choice; they must kill Doctor Edward Davenport. What they do not know is that I shall have it done for them before they have time to re-organise. The TV and newspapers must carry the news of his murder worldwide. If the carabinieri and police arrange for it to have the hall mark of a contract killing, the mafia family Higgins employed to assassinate Arthur will assume that he must have hired a rival mafia low life mob, and that they had beaten them to the pay off."

Galiena brightened, realising she could be useful, "Well that should not be too difficult. If you mention my name to an old family friend of mine, Signore Silvio Mazzarella, he will help. He can publish the story in his newspapers. If you make the murder spectacular, I am sure that he will arrange for a little item on the television news."

Galiena's suggestion pleased Peter, "Excellent, you most fortunate well connected women. I am sure that to protect you the Carabinieri and the police will make sure the crime scene will be memorable. Thank you Contessa, I will ask your friend Signore Mazzarella to help. In return I will ask my old Interpol colleagues to suggest that your police and judiciary should interview Arthur here, not at their headquarters."

Galiena crossed to a table where she wrote down a telephone number and a password that she assured him would get him put through to her family friend, bypassing his officials and secretaries. Peter knew that the man controlled much of the country's media and was politically powerful throughout Italy.

Peter, who was still anxious for Arthur's safety, said, "Contessa, you must understand that Arthur cannot stay in Rome. The remaining members of the mafia family, who Arthur did not kill, or maim, will seek revenge. They now have a more urgent motive than a money-based contract to kill him. That is bad news, but I think that you are no longer a problem to Servient-Higgins or the mafia. Because he was able to steal back what he believes to be the original Ingres painting, three days after his wife saw you with Doctor Davenport in the casino, he will be content, but surprised, that the Doctor had not told you about the possibility that the Ingres in the casino was the original painting. If he had, Servient-Higgins's criminal mind would assure him that you would have told the Prince and that the Prince would have immediately removed it from the casino, pending proof. It is for Arthur's safety that we must provide". Peter continued, in haste, trying to finish his warning and outlining his ideas before Arthur returned. "The Prince's house at Castel Gandolfo is no longer a safe house. Arthur must go away from Rome until his alter ego Doctor Davenport is dead, the remains publicly cremated, and the ashes scattered over several of the roundabouts that confuse the stranger to Milton Keynes. Have you any ideas of how we can get him to agree to leave both you, and Rome, until it is safe for him to return?"

Galiena's eyes lit up, full of mischief. "He will never leave me, nor will I leave Arthur, but I have the ideal solution; a secret early honeymoon. A thousand Hail Marys will not be enough, it will probably warrant excommunication, but other than that my idea is perfect."

When Arthur returned, Galiena gave him no chance to say anything other than to report that Tootsie was safely back on home ground. "Now, Arthur," she said, coy as a teenager, "You have told me that you have made ready your gypsy caravan with provisions sufficient for a three day journey.

Well it would be a shame to waste all that expense. Peter says that we cannot stay in Rome. We will go south along the coast, looking for some spring sunshine. If you don't mind, I will ask Maria to put some of my things in the wardrobe and bathroom so we can go first thing tomorrow morning.

Peter must stay to get on with organizing the necessary detail of having you killed, cremated, and your ashes widely distributed, so that there will be no trace remaining of Doctor Edward Davenport, the too clever man who I thought I had left in Andorra."

Arthur was genuinely unsure of whether it was a good idea to go off together in his motorhome. "Are you sure Galiena? Tootsie is very small and what is all this about killing and cremating me. I can't die yet; I haven't enough coupons with the Co-op for a cardboard coffin or a half decent funeral tea, even with paper plates."

Peter urged them to leave Rome as soon as the investigating Magistrate gave his permission. "Use false names and do not stay more than one night in any one place. Such a plan will keep you safe. Keep in touch with Mario, but use public telephones or phones in bars, shops or restaurants. Do not answer the Swiss Mobius phone but keep it with you. If it rings three times then stops, then twice and stops, within a minute, ring me on a public phone".

That evening, a genial Chief Investigating Magistrate interviewed Arthur in the Blue Room, the scene of the dramatic finale to the horrible events of the day. He was content for Peter to be present.

The Magistrate had with him, senior officers from the Carabinieri, the Police, two advocates, and a clerk taking notes. Before the interview, Peter had arranged for a law officer from the British Embassy to be present. Both the law officer and Peter had cautioned Arthur to say as little as possible.

The Chief Investigating Magistrate said that he simply wanted statements of identity and fact, adding that he already had sworn statements from Mario, Maria and the gardener.

Arthur told his story, in English, as simply as possible. Other than establishing identity, the only question that the Magistrate asked Arthur was straight to the point. "Did you bring any weapon with you when you came to investigate your policeman's suspicion that something was wrong within the Contessa's home?" Arthur answered, "I was unarmed."

It was all that the Magistrate needed to sum up and close the proceedings. "Without any armament, how could you be accused of using unreasonable force to liberate the Contessa and her staff from three men who you knew to be armed with knives and guns? Sir, I shall direct that there will be no charges against you. As for the man with the broken neck, he must have been spineless, as all gangsters are when faced with a person who has true courage. I shall recommend that my country formally acknowledge your service in ridding us of an evil. Now, before we leave you to have your delayed dinner, I would like to shake the hand of a brave Englishman. Please give my special regards to the Contessa Emilia-Romagna, I do not need to see her, we have already talked on the phone."

Because it was late, Arthur and Galiena invited Peter to join them for a light supper.

Arthur tried, just once, to persuade Galiena that she would not be comfortable in his shed on wheels during the proposed holiday, but Galiena would not have the arrangements made any other way. "I will love the little gypsy caravan, but I would like you to make one change, can we please call her 'Less than Winnebago' as you did earlier today. Peter wanted you to go alone, what nonsense; I must come with you. You need me to look after you. You do not speak Italian, you would get lost without me." Arthur pretended to be hurt, at the same time as gallant, "I can read a map, I would not lose my way on the road, but what you say is true, I would be lost without you."

Early the following morning, Arthur and Galiena left Galiena's beautiful home to start their holiday and new life together. They waved goodbye to Mario and Maria, to the cooks, the housekeepers and maids assembled on the steps, and to the gardener at the gate, who was waiving his two-pronged pitchfork.

They drove south, seeking the sun, chattering like squirrels. They left those behind, with many thoughts, and much to do about many things. The three-day holiday planned stretched out to two weeks. Arthur was amazed how his fabulous lady coped in the travelling home, which she used to call 'Floozie', but which they now both called Less than Winnebago. Arthur was content with the change, and happy to let Tootsie go, because he only had room for one woman in his new life.

Galiena did cheat a little; every evening, from a shop or café, she rang Maria to tell her were they would stop for the night.

The following morning Mario set off early to bring out a case, packed by Maria, with new clothes for Galiena, and he took back clothes she had worn and Arthur's laundry. Three times, she left Arthur reading and listening to the World Service while she booked into a hotel to have a bath and have her hair done in the Hotel salon, but never for more than three hours.

Galiena also bought other clothes from little boutiques, and like an excited schoolgirl, even a very full brightly coloured glazed cotton skirt from a charity shop. However, she had more fun and spent more time, and more money, choosing new clothes for Arthur, until the wardrobe was full and she had to send Arthur's old clothes back with Mario.

Every morning, while they ate breakfast, they eagerly listened to the BBC Overseas Service. They cheered like football supporters when they heard, at the tail end of a news bulletin, that, in broad daylight on the steps of the Borghese Gallery in Rome, masked men had shot and killed Dr Edward Davenport, a research member of the UK's Open University film unit, before escaping in a black Fiat.

The report said that the Carabinieri had issued a statement that the killing was a mafia contract killing, connected to art thefts. Galiena went out to buy as many Italian and English language papers as possible, all of which delighted them. Although it had not made the headlines, the story had received wide coverage.

Two days later, when Arthur and Galiena returned to Rome Arthur moved into the house and Galiena arranged for their civil wedding and blessing. Her influence was such, that she was able to keep the news of their wedding out of the papers and the paparazzi magazines. "It was easy," laughed Galiena, "After all, I am supposed to be in Africa photographing wild beasts." Mario and Maria acted as witnesses at the short civil marriage.

The blessing of their civil wedding was also short, without witnesses, but very sincere. Galiena's cousin, Monsignor Borghese, using a small side chapel in one of the Vatican's many churches, blessed the wedding.

He spoke English well. Talking kindly to Arthur, he charged him, as befitted a man with the name of a great king, to honour his cousin with love and fealty until death. Arthur realised that the night before the blessing, when Galiena had left him to go alone to confession, she must have exaggerated the story of his overcoming the mafia assassins. He was tempted, but he did not ask the Monsignor, how many Hail Marys he had given her to absolve the sin of their early honeymoon.

After the catholic blessing of their civil wedding Arthur and Galiena treated themselves to a long lazy honeymoon, but when they returned to Rome Galiena was too active to be idle. When Arthur painted, Galiena sat just behind, but to one side of wherever he had set up his easel, so that she could see him work, while she occupied herself with her new lap top computer.

She would only admit to writing a novel, a novel in English, because the English language had a bigger market than her mother tongue. She told him that he had no need to be concerned, because he was not in it. She believed her little white lie would stop him worrying.

Between long weeks spent at their home in Rome, they spent several romantic gypsy trips touring the region close to Rome. However, in May, they cheated by arranging for a driver to ferry

Less than Winnebago to a Mercedes Garage on the outskirts of Paris where they picked her up after they had flown from Rome.

Arthur had earlier rung the Restaurant Bien-Découplé. When Madam Déclâre answered, he almost shouted, he was so pleased to hear her; "Madam, it is me, Arthur, the Englishman with the moustache and the motorhome. Please, can we come to stay for a couple of days, a week from today, to park in your courtyard? I have a surprise for you. I would like to book a table for three, for dinner, for each of the two nights, but preferably for four if you can join us. Oh! Please reserve your best room for a rather remarkable man, a friend of mine, Monsieur Alaine Cartet who will come from Vernon."

Madam was obviously pleased "A table for four it shall be, also the best room for your friend. When you reserved a table for four, you said 'We', is it possible that I can guess what the surprise will be?" Arthur had previously rung Alaine Cartet in Vernon and he had readily accepted Arthur's invitation to join him for two nights at Restaurant Bien-Découplé."

The visit to Paris was everything for which Arthur had hoped. The sun shone from a cloudless blue sky. His wife was an immediate hit with Madam Déclâre. They sent him off to the courtyard with his easel, folding chair, paints and brushes, as unwanted until dinner. Occasionally, when they brought him drinks, he caught scraps of their conversation, in French, that was at speeds only women can understand.

Just before six, when the light he needed for his painting was losing its warmth, he heard the familiar voice of Alaine Cartet. "Now what have you been up to. I have already met your lovely wife who, for some unfathomable reason, seems to think that you are a bit special. How did you manage to persuade such a petite, delicate, cosmopolitan beauty to come to Paris, roughing it with your bulky frame in your gorger vardo?"

Arthur greeted Alaine as an old friend, "Hello my French mentor; it really is good, very good, to see you. I have asked madam

Déclâre to reserve the best room for you as the guest of Galiena and me." Alaine said, with his arms extended and hands palm up, "What's this; have you suddenly come into money you old scrounger? Don't tell me, you have married an heiress."

Arthur put his index finger to his lips before saying, "You must keep this absolutely to yourself, it is almost a state secret. We found the object of my quest, the original Ingres painting, 'La Source'. The insurance company have paid the reward, two million pounds so far. There is also a chance that there may be more to come."

Both the evening dinners in the restaurant were special. Galiena did not stop talking to Madam Déclâre, sometime in French, sometimes in English, then she would look at Arthur, blush, and change to Italian. Arthur had to give Alaine, who questioned and probed at each juncture, a detailed, kilometre-by-kilometre, step-by-step, account of his quest.

After the first dinner, it was almost two in the morning when Galiena and Arthur finally got away, having had to resist Madam's plea that they must stay in one of the guest rooms.

They found it difficult to refuse her hospitality, but they preferred the privacy and content found in the little home of their own; a home that Galiena had made supremely comfortable with superb linen, new curtains, delicate lighting and pictures of castles and Romany caravans.

They spent the two days at leisure, with Arthur painting or reading art books, and Galiena admonishing her computer, as though it was a fractious child.

Arthur finally produced his picture. A meter long, sixty-six centimetre high painting on board, a study of a curve in the steps of the garden with a single tall cypress, rooted in an oak tub, set against the warm perimeter stonewall. Arthur thought it quite good, but Madam Déclâre would not accept it. Not aware of Galiena's wealth, or title, and unaware of Arthur's windfall, she insisted that he should sell it. "It will buy you many litres of Diesel and besides, I have your first picture set in pride of place in my sitting room.

Arthur and Galiena both became matchmakers because they were so happy with each other. They took to leaving Madam and Alaine together, as often as it could be tactfully arranged. Arthur thought there might be a spark between them; Galiena, with a woman's intuition, was sure of it.

At the end of May, the newlyweds arrived in England in time for Arthur to attend the reunion of the Grey Haired Knights. Again, they had cheated; Arthur had arranged for Less than Winnebago to be ferried to the long stay car park at Heathrow.

He had also allowed time to visit Peter and Anne at their home in Lurgashall. They also planned to go to Ascot, before driving up to Yorkshire, where Arthur, with the help of Galiena's cousin, Monsignor Borghese, had arranged for a blessing of their marriage by the Bishop of Bradford, in Burnsall's parish church of St. Wilfrid.

They picked up Less than Winnebago just before two in the afternoon. The trees and fields being at their English best, Arthur found the drive down to Lurgashall pleasant, but it took him most of the way to get used to driving on the left. He pulled over into the field gate he remembered, a mile or two short of Wicket Gate Cottage, where he set himself up in his folding chair. For more than an hour, he read one of his many illustrated books about art, while Galiena got herself ready, hair, makeup, nails, dress, jewellery, all given special care and attention.

"Goodness, I don't think I have ever known you to take more than ten minutes to get ready, not even for the opera," Arthur beamed at her. "I have told you not to worry, you will like Anne, she is normal." Galiena shook her head, "That is not the point, I want her to like me; please remember that my name is Ruth." Arthur smoothed his moustache; he then gave her a cuddle. "Come on, you look marvellous; let's go the last mile to beard them in their den." Galiena gave her conditional agreement, "Yes, I am ready now, but I will stand if it is only a mile; I don't want to crease my dress."

It took less than ten minutes before the two women sent the two men to the pub, charged to return at eight sharp, sober and ready for dinner. The two days of their stay went well with lots of laughter, but again they insisted that they preferred to retire to their gypsy bed, rather than accept the offered guest room.

Because the news was good, Peter was anxious to bring Arthur up to date on the ongoing affair of the recovery of the Ingres painting, and their hopes of finding DNA evidence to link Servient-Higgins to the murder of the museum guard.

Peter told Arthur, in confidence, that a man had already approached Swiss Mobius offering, in return for the reward, to recover 'La Source'. The man had also intimated that other deals might be possible. Arthur was excited at the news, "That is good, the sting is working. The clever clogs at Faux Art Works have not spotted the switch. Have forensic found anything to link Higgins to the murder?" "Not yet I am afraid," Peter replied, "But don't give up hope on that one; because of the usual French bureaucracy, the painting has only just gone to the laboratory. I am hoping to get a report before we meet again in Yorkshire."

The Anglican Bishop conducted the brief church blessing with dignity.

After the obligatory photographs, Arthur and Galiena took their four guests to a hotel near Bolton Abbey for a simple luncheon. Galiena had arranged for Mario and Maria to join them. Arthur had sent invitations to both Madam Déclâre and Alaine Cartet, including airline tickets to Leeds-Bradford return. He had also arranged for cars to bring them to the hotel, where he had booked and paid for their rooms.

After several toasts to the happy couple, to international relations, to Arthur's career as an artist, to Galiena's future as an author, the luncheon party began to break up, but the excitement was not over. Madam Déclâre and Alain Cartet came to him, hand in hand, looking a bit sheepish. "We want to thank you for the tickets, the reception, and the rooms; it was very kind of you, but we hope you will not mind, we have changed the arrangements you made for us, from two single rooms to a double room. You see we have been together almost from the first day that I came to the Restaurant Bien-Découplé. Love must be infectious; we think that we caught it from you and the Contessa."

Peter had further surprises for Arthur. He took him aside to give him his news, "Talk about 'muck to the midden', the sting worked. We have recovered the other two paintings; your reward has gone up another million.

Better new still; two days ago, the French Embassy rang to tell me that France's top forensic experts have examined the picture. When they took the painting off the stretches, they found congealed blood mixed with long hairs under one corner on the back of the painting. There was enough to identify that the blood was that of the murdered guard. You will remember that before he died of his wounds he told the police that a pony tailed skinny bloke shot him when he tried to stop them taking he painting. The hair caught in the blood was not that of the guard. We now have a positive identification of the person whose hair was caught in the blood."

Arthur's reaction was one of relief. "Oh that is good news. The French police will be able to re-arrest Higgins will they not, or will he be protected by the problem of double jeopardy." Peter shook his head, "Double jeopardy does not come in to it. We got it completely wrong. Higgins did not kill the guard. It was that mousy haired skinny wife of his, Greta Servient-Higgins. She is already under arrest on a French extradition warrant."

Although Peter had always been good friends with Arthur, and would remain so, he had been inclined to think he had been more successful than his friend who had stayed in Yorkshire to remain a copper. Because of this, when he was saying goodbye to Mario, although he did not mean to, he expressed himself badly.

"I do hope this marriage is going to work for them, Arthur is quite a bit older than the Contessa, still a bit of the uniformed beat copper in him, a bit set in his ways. She does seem to be making all the decisions."

There was a long pause before Mario replied. "You poor persistent pessimist, are you so dull that you cannot recognise romantic love? Their devotion is not the tawdry explicit lust of present fiction, but that of Romeo and Juliet, Ivanhoe and Rowena, Abelard and Héloïse, Robin and Marion, the Knights and Ladies of the Round Table. Do you not understand that each thought, every decision, and all actions that the Contessa takes are for his comfort, advantage and happiness alone? From the moment that she fell in love with your friend, and that was before he risked his life to rescue her life, she has never given her own condition any thought. She is utterly devoted to him, nothing else matters to her. Arthur is a lovely man who was well worthy of her love before that terrible day of fear, retribution and death."

Mario continued, "Peter, you must understand, when Arthur decided to investigate and come secretly to the house, his beat copper experience drove him, just the shadow of a hat. He knew that there was danger. Maria and I were captive and frightened. It was clear to me that if Arthur had not acted as he did, the assassins would have killed us all. The mafia do not like any living witness of their crimes. I was not only frightened, I was ashamed; I had failed in my duty to protect the Contessa. Arthur acted alone. He cast off the yoke of his three score years and ten. His instinct, initiative, skill, and courage overcame not only his fear, but also overwhelmed three armed assassins who Higgins had contracted to kill him. Arthur saved the Contessa's life, Maria's life and my life. His selfless actions gave him more than equality with her wealth and station. We who were under extreme duress believe that when he approached the house, sensing danger, something wonderful happened. Arthur had decided to leave Rome that day, convinced his love for the Contessa would be unrequited, because she was a Roman and catholic, he English and protestant, she a Contessa, he a gipsy. He did not believe in fairy tales. He was unarmed. He knew that he faced almost certain death if he tried to rescue the woman he loved, but intended to leave. He climbed a high wall covered in razor wire that no man of his age could possibly climb. With a weapon of base metal he drew from a stone he slew an evil man; a man armed with a gun. He overcame two armed sadistic killers with fire from his hands. That day, your friend Arthur wrote a new chapter in the golden book of chivalry."

Arthur left the party with his wife of three marriages, content that his quest was over, but on the steps of the hotel Peter touched his arm to ask, "What now Arthur?"

Arthur stood for a long time before he replied. "Today is Thursday, the summer solstice. At noon, in two days' time, I must return to Scagill for a reunion with my friends Tristan, Percival and Geraint. When we meet, we have vowed to tell true tales of how we measured up to our promise to go alone to seek adventure by following a worthwhile quest. Frankly, I am a bit concerned. Several times over the past year, I have thought that the vow was foolish. It turned what had been light-hearted idea of mine, inspired by the Arthurian legend, into a binding commitment. We even made silly bets on who would fare best. I have been lucky, but not all of Arthur's Knights survived the perils of their chosen quests. I just hope that God and Merlin have watched over my three friends who put aside age and infirmity, to go forth as Grey Haired Knights."

I here end my story of Arthur Thomas's quest. However, I must tell you that I have ready the stories of three other quests. How Merlin brought Tristan low to give him true wealth, how Percival found his grail and how Geraint destroyed a great evil.

www.ingramcontent.com/pod-product-compliance
Lightning Source LLC
Chambersburg PA
CBHW062133170626
46813CB00002B/682